JUSSI ADLER-OLSEN is Denmark's number one crime writer and a *New York Times* bestselling author. His books routinely top the bestseller lists in Europe. His many prestigious Nordic crime-writing awards include the Glass Key Award, also won by Henning Mankell, Jo Nesbø, Stieg Larsson, and Peter Høeg.

Praise for *The Marco Effect*

"Engrossing . . . a roller coaster ride through Copenhagen's seedy underbelly."
—*Publishers Weekly*

"This series goes from triumph to triumph. . . . This is the best book I've read in 2014 so far. Highly recommended."
—*Deadly Pleasures Mystery Magazine*

"*The Marco Effect* works, because Marco is a compelling hero, the villains are truly odious, and Mørck and his quirky, savvy subordinates ultimately carry the day."
—*Booklist*

"If you like the dark humor, wisecracking, and layered betrayals of Raymond Chandler, then read Adler-Olsen's Department Q series."
—*Men's Journal*

"A tense, pleasurable read."
—*USA Today*

"This Scandinavian crime series has enough twists and turns to keep readers enthralled in nail-biting suspense. The fast pace, intricate plot, and gritty style will appeal to fans of Michael Connelly's Harry Bosch mysteries."
—*Library Journal*

Praise for *The Purity of Vengeance*

"[A] sordid tale . . . inspired by actual events during a dark period of Danish history. Ah, but there is more, so much more in this frenzied thriller."
—*The New York Times Book Review*

"*The Purity of Vengeance* is an enjoyable and eye-opening way to learn about the real Scandinavia, a story so outrageous that not even the best mystery writer can make it up."

—*The Boston Globe*

"When your series relies on cold cases, it's not always easy to craft plots that have both historical interest and an air of urgency, but it's something Adler-Olsen is very good at."

—*Booklist*

"Adler-Olsen merges story lines . . . with ingenious aplomb, effortlessly mixing hilarities with horrors. . . . This crime fiction tour de force could only have been devised by an author who can even turn stomach flu into a belly laugh."

—*Publishers Weekly* (starred review)

"Another accomplished exercise in three-decker suspense."

—*Kirkus Reviews*

"Surprises, twists, and turns galore."

—Bookreporter.com

Praise for *A Conspiracy of Faith*

"A shattering parable of honest individuals caught up in the corruption of our times."

—*Publishers Weekly* (starred review)

"This series has enough twists to captivate contemporary mystery readers and enough substance and background to entertain readers with historical and literary tastes."

—*Library Journal* (starred review)

"Compelling . . . impossible to put down the book."

—Associated Press

"This mix of offbeat departmental politics, puzzling clues, and pulse-pounding pursuit delivers the goods."

—*Booklist*

ALSO BY JUSSI ADLER-OLSEN

The Keeper of Lost Causes
The Absent One
A Conspiracy of Faith
The Purity of Vengeance

THE
MARCO
EFFECT

A Department Q Novel

Jussi Adler-Olsen

Translated by Martin Aitken
Translation Consultant Steve Schein

A PLUME BOOK

PLUME
Published by the Penguin Group
Penguin Group (USA) LLC
375 Hudson Street
New York, New York 10014

USA | Canada | UK | Ireland | Australia | New Zealand | India | South Africa | China
penguin.com
A Penguin Random House Company

First published in the United States of America by Dutton,
a member of Penguin Group (USA) LLC, 2014
First Plume Printing 2015

THE LIBRARY OF CONGRESS HAS CATALOGED THE DUTTON EDITION AS FOLLOWS:
Adler-Olsen, Jussi.
[Marco Effekten. English]
The Marco Effect : a Department Q novel / Jussi Adler-Olsen ; translated by Martin Aitken ;
translation consultant, Steve Schein.
pages   cm
ISBN 978-0-525-95402-6 (hc.)
ISBN 978-0-14-751662-6 (pbk.)
1. Police—Denmark—Fiction.   2. Mystery fiction.   I. Aitken, Martin, translator.   II. Title.
PT8176.1.D54M3713   2014
839.81'38—dc23   2014014674

Printed in the United States of America
10   9   8   7   6   5   4   3

Set in Apollo MT Std
Original hardcover design by Alissa Theodor

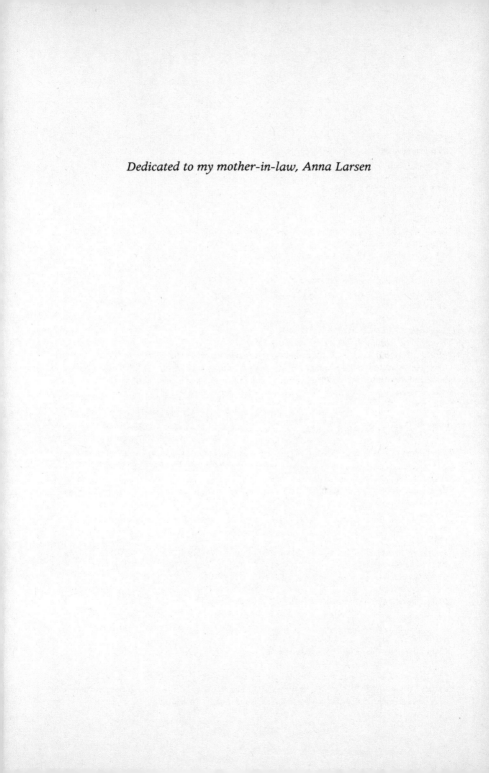

Dedicated to my mother-in-law, Anna Larsen

PROLOGUE

Autumn 2008

Louis Fon's last morning was as soft as a whisper.

He sat up on the cot with sleep in his eyes and his mind still a muddle, patted the little one who had stroked his cheek, wiped the snot from the tip of her brown nose, and stuck his feet into his flip-flops on the stamped clay of the floor.

He stretched, squinting at the light as the cackle of hens and the distant cries of boys as they cut bananas from the palms drifted into the sunbaked room.

How peaceful it seemed as he took in the sharp aromas of the village. Only the songs of the Baka people when they gathered around their fires on the other side of the river could delight him more. As always, it felt good to return to the Dja region, and to the remote Bantu village of Somolomo.

Behind the hut, children were at play, whirling up the dust from the red earth, shrill voices prompting congregations of weaver birds to burst from the surrounding treetops.

He got to his feet and went toward the light that flooded in from the window, placing his elbows on the sill and beaming a smile at the girl's mother who stood by the hut opposite and was about to sever the head of the day's chicken.

It was the last time Louis would ever smile.

Some two hundred meters away a sinewy man and his escort appeared from the path by the palm grove, an ominous sign right from the start. He recognized Mbomo's muscular frame from Yaoundé, but he had never seen the Caucasian with the chalk-white hair.

"Why is Mbomo here and who's that with him?" he called out to the girl's mother.

She gave a shrug. Tourists were not an unusual sight on the edge of the rain forest, so why should she be concerned? Four or five days' trekking with the Baka in the dense chaos of the Dja jungle, wasn't that what it was all about? At least for a European with plenty of money?

But Louis sensed something more. He could tell by the gravity of the two men and the attitude between them. Something wasn't right. The white man was no tourist, and Mbomo had no business here in the district without first having informed Louis. After all, Louis was in charge of the Danish development project and Mbomo was merely an errand boy for the government officials in Yaoundé. Such were the roles.

Were the two men up to something he wasn't to know about? The idea was by no means unlikely. Strange things went on all the time in the course of the project. Processes were slow, the flow of information had all but dried up, payments were continually delayed or else never transpired. Not exactly what he'd been promised when they hired him for the job.

Louis shook his head. He was a Bantu himself, from the opposite corner of Cameroon, hundreds of kilometers northwest of the village here in the borderland close to Congo. Where he came from, a suspicious nature was something you were born with and perhaps the single most important reason Louis had devoted his life to working for the gentle Baka, the pygmy people of the Dja jungle, whose origins traced back to the time when the forests were virgin. People in whose language malicious words such as "suspicion" did not even exist.

For Louis, these amiable souls were a human oasis of good feeling in an otherwise loathsome world. The close relationships he had established with the Baka and their homeland were Louis's elixir and solace. And yet this suspicion of malice was now upon him.

Could he never be truly free of it?

He found Mbomo's 4x4 parked behind the third row of huts, its driver fast asleep behind the wheel in a sweat-drenched soccer jersey.

"Is Mbomo looking for me, Silou?" he asked the stocky black man, who stretched his limbs and struggled to get his bearings.

The man shook his head. Apparently he had no idea what Louis was talking about.

"Who is the white man Mbomo has with him? Do you know him?" Louis persisted.

The driver yawned.

"Is he a Frenchman?"

"No," came the reply, Silou shrugging his shoulders. "He speaks some French, but I think he is from the north."

"OK." Louis felt the unease in his stomach. "Could he be a Dane?"

The driver pointed an index finger at him.

Bingo!

That was it. And Louis didn't like it one bit.

When Louis wasn't fighting for the future of the Baka, he was fighting for the animals of the forest. Every village surrounding the Baka's jungle fostered young Bantus armed with rifles, and every day scores of mandrill and antelope fell prey to their bullets.

Though relations were tense between Louis and the poachers, he remained pragmatic enough not to turn down a lift through the bush on the back of one of their motorcycles. Three kilometers along narrow paths to the Baka village in just six minutes. Who could say no when time was of the essence?

Even as the mud-built huts appeared in front of them Louis knew what had happened, for only the smallest of the children and hungry dogs came running out to greet him.

Louis found the village chief lying flat out on a bed of palm leaves, a cloud of alcohol fumes lingering in the air above. Strewn on the ground around the semiconscious Mulungo were empty whisky bottles like the ones they thrust into your face on the other side of the river. There was no doubt the binge had gone on through the night and, judging by the silence that prevailed, it seemed equally plain that just about all the villagers had taken part.

He poked his head inside the overpopulated huts of mud and bowed palm branches, finding only a few adults capable of acknowledging his presence with a sluggish nod in his direction.

This is how they make the natives toe the line and keep their mouths shut, he thought. Just give them alcohol and drugs and they'd be in the palm of your hand.

That was it exactly.

He went back to the musty hut and kicked the chief hard in the side, causing Mulungo's wiry body to give a start. A sheepish smile revealed a set of needle-sharp teeth, but Louis wasn't about to be appeased.

He gestured toward the litter of bottles.

"What did you do for the money, Mulungo?" he asked.

The Baka chief lifted his head and gave a shrug. "Reason" was a concept not much used in the bush.

"Mbomo gave you the money, didn't he? How much did he give you?"

"Ten thousand francs!" came the reply. Exact sums, especially of this order, were by contrast a matter in which the Baka took considerable interest.

Louis nodded. That bastard Mbomo. Why had he done it?

"Ten thousand," he said. "And how often does Mbomo do this?"

Mulungo shrugged again. Time was a relative concept.

"I see you people haven't planted the new crops as you were supposed to. Why not?"

"The money has not arrived, Louis. You know that, surely?"

"Not arrived, Mulungo? I've seen the transfer documents myself. The money was sent more than a month ago."

What had happened? This was the third time reality had failed to match up with the paperwork.

Louis raised his head. Beyond the sibilant song of the cicadas, an alien sound became audible. As far as he could make out, it was a small motorcycle.

Mbomo was already on his way, Louis would bet on it. Perhaps he came to offer a plausible explanation. Louis hoped so.

He looked around. Something was certainly not right here, to say the least, but that would soon change. For although Mbomo was a head taller than Louis and had arms as strong as a gorilla's, Louis was not afraid of him.

If the Baka were unable to answer his questions, the big man could do so himself: Why had he come? Where was the money? Why had they not begun to plant? And who was the white man Mbomo had been with?

That's what he wanted to know.

So he stood on the open ground in the middle of the village and waited as the cloud of dust that rose up above the steaming bush slowly approached.

Even before Mbomo dismounted, Louis would go to meet him, throw his arms wide and confront him. He would threaten him with brimstone and fire and exposure to the authorities. He would tell him to his face that if he had been embezzling funds intended to help secure the Baka's existence here in the forest, the next thing Mbomo would lay his itchy fingers on would be the bars of a cell in the Kondengui prison.

The mere mention of the place would frighten the wits out of anyone.

And then the cicadas' song was drowned out by the noise of the small engine.

As the motorcycle came out of the bush and entered the open ground, its tinny horn sounding, Louis noticed the heavy box on the Kawasaki's pannier rack, and then the village came alive. Sleepy heads popped out from door openings and the more alert of the men emerged as though the subdued sloshing that issued from the box were an omen from the gods of the coming of the deluge.

Mbomo first handed out whisky bags to the many outstretched hands, then stared threateningly at Louis.

Louis knew the score at once. The machete slung over Mbomo's shoulder was warning enough. If he didn't retreat, it would be used against him. And with the state the pygmies were in, he would be unable to count on their help.

"There's more where this comes from," Mbomo declared, dumping the rest of the alcohol bags from the box onto the ground and at the same moment turning to face Louis.

As Louis instinctively began to run he heard the excited cries of the Baka behind him. If Mbomo catches me I'm done for, he thought, his eyes seeking out openings in the bush or tools the Baka might have left on the ground. Anything at all that might be used against the man who now pursued him.

Louis was lithe, much more agile than Mbomo, who had lived all his life in Douala and Yaoundé and had not learned to be wary of the undergrowth's treacherous fabric of twisted roots, mounds, and hollows. For that reason he felt reassured as the sound of heavy footsteps behind him faded and the unfathomable network of tributary paths leading to the river opened out before him.

Now all he had to do was find one of the dugout canoes before Mbomo caught up with him. As soon as Louis crossed the river he would be safe. The people of Somolomo would protect him.

A pungent, damp smell wafted like a breeze through the green-brown bush, and an experienced guide such as Louis knew the signs. Another hundred meters and the river would be there, but the next second he was stumbling out into a swamp that sucked him down to his knees.

For a moment his arms flailed. If he didn't find a sturdy plant to grab hold of, the mud would swallow him up in no time. And if he was too slow to extract himself, Mbomo would be on top of him. Even now the sound of his tramping feet seemed too close for comfort.

He filled his lungs with air, pressed his mouth shut, and stretched his upper body as far as he could until his joints creaked. Thin branches came away in his hand, leaves fell into his wide-open eyes. It only took fifteen seconds for him to get a hold and pull himself up, but it was two seconds too many. There was a rustling in the undergrowth and then the sudden blow of the machete from behind, lodging itself deep into Louis's shoulder blade. The pain came swift and searing.

Instinctively Louis concentrated on remaining upright. And for that reason alone he was able to come free of the mire and get away, as Mbomo's curses sounded through the trees.

He too had fallen foul of the swamp.

Only when Louis reached the river did he become aware of the full intensity of the pain and feel how his shirt was clinging to his back.

Drained of all energy, he sank to his knees at the water's edge. And at that moment Louis Fon realized he was about to die.

As his body toppled forward and the fine gravel of the shore mingled with his hair, he managed to pull his phone from the side pocket of his pants and tap the Messages icon.

Every key press was accompanied by a frenzied beat of his heart as it pumped blood out of his body, and when the message was written and he tapped "Send," he faintly registered that there was no signal.

The last thing Louis Fon sensed was the pounding of heavy footsteps on the ground next to him. And then, finally, the phone being prized from his hand.

Mbomo Ziem was satisfied. The lunging of the 4x4 over the potholes of the dark red track through the jungle toward the junction and the main road to Yaoundé would soon cease and the man beside him had thankfully refrained from passing comment on events. Everything was as it should be. He had shoved Louis Fon's body into the river. The current and the crocodiles would take care of the rest.

All in all, things had gone well. The only person who could have posed a threat to their activities had been eliminated, and the future was once again bright.

Mission accomplished, as they said.

Mbomo looked down at the mobile phone he had snatched from the dying man's hand. A few francs spent on a new SIM card and his son's birthday present would be taken care of.

And as he pictured the gleeful smile on the boy's face, the display lit up in his hand to indicate the signal had returned.

Then a few seconds passed before a discreet little beep confirmed that a text message had been sent.

1

Autumn 2008

René E. Eriksen had never been a cautious man. It was perhaps why he had gone from success to failure and back again in an endless chain of unpredictable events, which in the greater perspective nonetheless gave rise to a certain degree of satisfaction with his life. At the end of the day he put it all down to some kind of innate luck.

Yet in spite of this, René was by nature a pensive soul. When faced by the big questions and confrontations of childhood, he had often sought refuge behind his mother's skirts. Accordingly, in adult life he instinctively made sure always to have a reasonably foolproof exit strategy on hand when casting himself into uncharted depths.

For that reason he had taken time to think things through when his good friend and former schoolmate Teis Snap, now managing director of Karrebæk Bank, had called him up that afternoon at his office in the ministry and put forward a proposal a man in René's elevated public position under normal circumstances would have considered highly inappropriate.

The bank crises had yet to begin wreaking havoc, but these were days in which the greed of speculators and the irresponsibility of government financial policy were becoming plain to anyone who earned a living lending money.

That was why Teis Snap called.

"I'm afraid to say that Karrebæk Bank will go bust within two months unless we can get our hands on extra capital," he'd said.

"What about my shares?" René blurted out with a frown, his heart already pounding at the thought of the first-class retirement under Mediterranean palms he had been promised now collapsing like a house of cards.

"What can I say? If we don't come up with something drastic right away, we're going to lose everything we own. That's the reality of the matter, I'm afraid," Snap replied.

The silence that ensued was a pause between friends. The kind of interlude that left no room for protest or more abstract comment.

René allowed his head to drop for a moment and inhaled so deeply it hurt. So this was the situation, and swift action was imperative. He felt his stomach knot, perspiration cold on his brow, but as head of office in the Evaluation Department for Development Assistance he was used to forcing his mind to think clearly under duress.

He exhaled. "Extra capital, you say? And what would that involve, more exactly?"

"Two hundred, perhaps two hundred and fifty million kroner over four to five years."

Sweat trickled down under René's collar. "For Christ's sake, Teis! That's fifty million a year!"

"I'm aware of that, and I find it most regrettable indeed. We've done everything in our power to draw up contingency plans these past four weeks, but our customer base just isn't stable enough. The last two years we've been far too eager to lend out money without sufficient security. We know that now, with the property market collapsing."

"Dammit! We need to do something quick. Haven't we got time to withdraw our personal assets?"

"I'm afraid it's already too late, René. The shares have plummeted this morning, and all trading's temporarily suspended."

"I see." René noted how cold his voice suddenly sounded. "And what do you expect me to do about it? I'm assuming you're not just calling to tell me you've squandered my savings, are you? I know you, Teis. How much did you salvage for yourself?"

His old friend sounded offended, but his voice was clear: "Nothing, René, not a penny, I swear. The accountants intervened. Not all accountancy firms are prepared to step in with creative solutions in a situation like this. The reason I'm calling is because I think I may have found a way out, one that might also be quite lucrative for you."

And thus the swindle was initiated. It had been running for several months now, and things had gone smoothly indeed until a minute ago when the department's most experienced staff member, William Stark, suddenly appeared, waving a sheet of paper in front of him.

"OK, Stark," said René. "So you've received some contorted text message from Louis Fon and haven't been able to get in touch with him since. But you know as well as I do that Cameroon is a long way from here and connections aren't reliable, even at the best of times, so don't you suppose that might be where the problem lies?"

Unfortunately Stark appeared less than convinced, and at that moment a warning of potential chaos in René's future seemed to materialize.

Stark pressed his already thin lips into a pencil line. "But how can we be sure?" He gazed pensively at the floor, his unruly red bangs drooping down in front of his eyes. "All I know is that this text message came in when you were on your way back from Cameroon. And nobody's seen Louis Fon since. No one."

"Hmm. But if he's still in the Dja region, mobile phone coverage is practically nonexistent." René reached across the desk. "Let me see that message, Stark."

René tried to keep his hand steady as Stark handed him the sheet of paper.

He read the message:

Cfqquptiondae(s+l)la(i+l)ddddddvdlogdmdntdja

He wiped the treacherous perspiration from his brow with the back of his hand. Thank God. It was gibberish.

"Well, it does seem rather odd, Stark, I'll grant you that. The question is, does it warrant further attention? It looks to me like the phone just went haywire in Louis Fon's pocket," he said, putting the paper down on the desk. "I'll have someone follow up on it, but I can tell you that Mbomo Ziem and I were in contact with Louis Fon the same day we drove to Yaoundé and we saw nothing out of the ordinary. He was packing for his next expedition. With some Germans, as far as I remember."

William Stark peered at him darkly and shook his head.

"You say it probably doesn't warrant further attention, but have a look at the message again. Do you think it's coincidental that it ends on the word "Dja"? I don't. I think Louis Fon was trying to tell me something and that something serious may have happened to him."

René pursed his lips. In all ministerial posts it was a question of never appearing dismissive of even the most ridiculous hypothesis. That much he had learned over the years.

Which is why he replied with, "Yes, it is a bit strange, isn't it?"

René reached for his Sony Ericsson that was lying on the windowsill behind him. "'Dja,' you say." He studied the phone's keypad and nodded. "Yes, it *could* be accidental. Look, D, J, and A are the first letters on their respective keys. Press three, five, and two and you've got 'dja.'" Not impossible while it's just lying in a person's pocket, though the odds would certainly seem slender. So, yes, it definitely is strange. I just reckon we should wait a few days and see if Louis turns up. In the meantime I'll get in touch with Mbomo."

He watched William Stark as he left the office, following his every movement until the door was shut. Again he wiped his brow. So it *was* Louis Fon's mobile Mbomo had been playing around with in the Land Rover on their way back to the capital.

Idiot!

He clenched his fists and shook his head. Mbomo being infantile enough to steal the mobile from Fon's body was one thing, quite another was that he had not come clean when René asked him about it. And how the hell could the big dope have been stupid enough not to check for unsent messages? If he'd stolen the phone from the body, why hadn't he removed the battery as a matter of course, or at least reset its memory? What kind of imbecile would steal a phone from the man he had just killed, anyway?

He shook his head again. Mbomo was a clown, but right now the problem wasn't Mbomo, it was William Stark. In fact, Stark had been a danger all along. Hadn't he said that from the start? Hadn't he told Teis Snap the same thing?

Bugger it! No one possessed an overview of the department's agree-

ments and budget frameworks comparable to Stark's. No one was anywhere near as meticulous as he in the evaluation of the ministry's
projects. So if anyone could uncover René's misuse of development funds,
it was William Stark.

René took a deep breath and considered his next move. The options
weren't exactly multiple.

"If ever you should run into problems in this matter," Teis Snap had
said, "then call us immediately."

That was what he now intended to do.

2

Autumn 2008

There weren't many people to whom William Stark could turn for a piece of professional advice.

In the gray world of the civil service, he was in charge of but a small island to which few wished to sail. If he felt unable to approach his head of office, the only other person available to him seemed to be the head of the department, but who would go to the head of the department with a suspicion of this nature—and, more particularly, of this magnitude—without first having secured tangible evidence? Not him, that was for sure.

To any superior in the upper echelons of the government services who happened to be reasonably kindly disposed, an underling who sounded the alarm on suspicion of abuse of office or other irregularities in the execution of government business was called a whistle-blower. Ostensibly this was laudable, like a siren warning of impending ambush, but if one were to press the point with these civil service officers, one would invariably find that such a person was considered to be a snitch, and snitches seldom fared well. In modern-day Denmark there were examples aplenty. One recent instance was that of an agent of the Danish military's intelligence service who was handed a prison sentence for having demonstrated that the country's prime minister had withheld vital information from parliament in order to lead his country into war in Iraq. Not exactly the kind of attitude that encourages candor.

Besides, William was not one hundred percent certain. Though the thought had played on his mind for some time, it was all still little more than an inkling.

After having briefed his head of office, René E. Eriksen, about Louis Fon's text message he had made at least ten calls to various individuals in Cameroon, people he knew the loyal Bantu activist was in regular contact with, and in each case he had encountered bewilderment at the fact that this untiring spirit should have been silent even for a few days.

Thus it was that just this morning William had finally gotten through to Fon's home in Sarki Mata and spoken to his wife, whom Fon had always made a point of keeping updated as to his whereabouts and how long he was planning to be away.

It was obvious his wife was anxious. The woman kept bursting into tears and was convinced her husband had fallen foul of poachers. What they might have done to him was something she could not yet bring herself to think about. The jungle was so vast and contained so many secrets. Louis had told her so on countless occasions. Things happened there, as she said. William, too, knew this to be true.

Of course, there could be any number of reasons for Fon not having been in touch. Temptations abounded in Cameroon and who could guess as to what a handsome man in the prime of his life might succumb to? The girls in that part of Africa were not exactly known to be timid or lacking in initiative, so the possibility that Fon was simply shagging his brains out in a grass hut and allowing the world to revolve as it saw fit was certainly not to be discounted. William almost found himself smiling at the idea.

But then he thought about what had happened before this situation arose, about how the first phase of the Baka project had proceeded. That fifty million kroner had been rushed through the ministry to ensure the continued existence of the pygmy population in such a far-flung corner as the Dja jungle was odd enough in itself. And why specifically the Baka, as opposed to any other people? Why such a generous sum?

Yes, William had wondered right from the start.

Two hundred and fifty million kroner over five years wasn't much in a total development budget of some fifteen billion a year, but still, when was the last time such a limited project had received such massive funding? Had they targeted the entire pygmy population of the Congo jungle, the second-largest primeval forest in the world, he might have been able to understand. But they hadn't.

And when the funding was approved, even an idiot with half an eye could have seen that normal procedure had been ignored on several issues. It was at this point that William's instincts had been activated. In essence, development aid in this case merely meant the transfer of funds to government officials in Yaoundé, leaving it up to the locals to take things from there. And this in a country generally considered to be one of the world's most corrupt.

For William Stark, a public servant in every sense of the word—and yet not without his own history of error—this was a worrisome situation. Therefore, in light of the turns the case had taken during the last few days, he now looked upon the role of his superior in these proceedings with new eyes.

When had René E. Eriksen ever taken such a personal interest before? When had he last flown out to oversee the commencement of a project? It had been years, surely.

Granted, that fact in itself might conceivably serve to guarantee that everything about the project was aboveboard and subject to the appropriate controls, but it *could* also indicate the opposite was true. God forbid. Eriksen of all people could foresee the consequences: years of the department's work being upended and scrutinized. It simply mustn't happen.

"Ruminating, eh, Stark?" came a voice, sneaking up from behind.

It had been months since he had heard that voice in his own office, and William looked up with surprise at his superior's unpleasant smile. The man's face looked all wrong beneath his chalk-white hair.

"I've just spoken to our contacts in Yaoundé and they feel the same as you," said Eriksen. "There *is* something wrong, they say, so your assumptions are probably right. According to them, Louis Fon may have done a bunk with some of the funding and now they want someone from the ministry to get down there and audit their payouts to the project from day one. Most likely they reckon it'll cover their asses in the event of anyone pointing a finger at them in the case of irregularities. If you should find any, that is."

"Me?" Was Eriksen intending to send *him* down there? William was confused. This was a development he hadn't seen coming and certainly one he didn't care for. "Do they know how much he might have ripped them off for?" he added.

Eriksen shook his head. "No one seems to have a clear idea as yet, but Fon has about two million euros at his disposal for the period. Maybe he's just out making purchases and is clean. Maybe he found out that the seeds and plants are cheaper or better quality somewhere other than where he usually buys. At any rate we need to pursue the matter. After all, it's what we're here for."

"True . . . ," said William. "But I'm afraid I'll have to pass on this one."

Eriksen's smile vanished. "I see. And on what grounds, if I might ask?"

"My partner's child is in the hospital at the moment."

"I see. Again? And what bearing does that have?"

"Well, I support them both as best I can. They live with me."

Eriksen nodded. "It's highly commendable of you to put them first, Stark, but we're talking two or three days at most. I'm sure you'll be able to work it out. We've already booked you on a flight to Brussels and onward. After all, it's part of your job, you know. There were no seats left to Yaoundé, I'm afraid, so you'll be flying to Douala instead. Mbomo will pick you up at the airport and drive you to the capital from there. It only takes about two hours."

William pictured his stepdaughter lying in her hospital bed. He wasn't pleased at this new prospect.

"Are you sending me because I was the one who received Louis Fon's text?" he asked.

"No, Stark. I'm sending you because you're our best man."

The word on Mbomo Ziem was that he was a man of action. This he demonstrated outside Douala International Airport, where half a dozen aggressive men squabbled over the rights to carry William's luggage.

"Your taxi is waiting, sir! This way, come on!" they implored, yanking at the suitcase wherever they could get a grip.

But Mbomo shoved them away, indicating with a brutal glare that he was not afraid to take on the whole pack of bearers to save his boss a couple of thousand francs.

He was a big man, this Mbomo. William had seen photos of him, but he had been standing next to diminutive Bakas, who made any non-pygmy look like a giant. Here in real life he realized that not only the Baka appeared small in Mbomo's presence, for the man towered like a cliff above the human landscape, and for that reason it seemed only natural that the word "security" should be applied to him amid this mad spectacle of frenzied men, each fighting for the privilege of lugging his suitcase and thereby perhaps earning the chance of a small meal.

"You'll be staying at the Aurelia Palace," Mbomo informed him as their taxi finally pulled away from the bearers and a couple of men hawking cheap jewelry who ran on behind, hopeful until the last second. "Your meeting at the ministry is tomorrow morning. I'll come by personally and pick you up. Unlike Douala here, Yaoundé is a fairly safe place, but you never know." He laughed, his whole upper body quaking, though no sound passed his lips.

William's gaze turned to the glowing sun as it sank beneath the treetops and to clusters of laborers idling along by the side of the road, machetes hanging limply from tired hands.

Apart from the packed minicabs, the speedy 4x4s, and the clattering pickups constantly passing them and putting everyone's lives at risk in the process, only battered, heavily laden trucks with broken headlights were on the road. It was no wonder that much of the wreckage that lined the dusty highway had a close resemblance to the vehicles upon it.

William was a long way from home.

Having carefully chosen his menu, William sat down in a corner of the lounge where there was a chair; a sofa with thick, patterned covers reminiscent of the seventies; and a timeworn coffee table on which a pair of dewy glasses of beer had already been placed.

"I always get two in at a time whenever I'm down here," said the corpulent man seated next to him, speaking in English. "The beer's so thin it trickles out of the pores again as quickly as you can get it inside you." He chuckled.

He pointed at the necklace that William was wearing, with the small masks hanging from it. "I can tell you've just arrived in Africa. You must have run into some of those jewelry bandits out at the airport."

"Yes and no." William fingered the necklace. "I've just got here, yes, but I've had this for a number of years. It *is* African, though. I found it once when I was inspecting a project in Kampala."

"Ah, Kampala. One of Uganda's more interesting cities." He raised his glass to William. Judging by the diplomatic-looking bag, he too was a civil servant.

William produced his portfolio from his leather briefcase and placed it on the table. To begin with there was the specific issue of fifty million kroner and how to channel it on to the Baka project. Then there were a number of documents to be skimmed and a series of questions to be prepared. He opened the manila folder and arranged its entire contents in three piles in front of him. One containing spreadsheets, a second comprising project descriptions, and a third of memos, e-mails, and other correspondence. Even the yellow Post-it note was there, with Louis Fon's text message jotted down on it.

"Do you mind if I sit and do some work here? There seems to be no desk in my room."

The man replied with a friendly nod.

"Danish?" the man asked, indicating the logo of the Ministry of Foreign Affairs at the head of the documents.

"Yes, and you?"

"Stockholm." The man extended his hand and switched to Swedish. "First time in Cameroon?"

William nodded.

"In that case, welcome," the man said, shoving his extra glass of beer across the table toward him. "Cameroon isn't a place a person ever gets completely used to, you know. *Skål*."

They raised their glasses, the Swede downing his in one gulp and then gesturing toward the waiter for a refill, all in one seamless movement. Alcoholic public officials like him were a regular feature in equatorial regions, as William well knew. He had seen a number of their own people return home firing on less than all cylinders after a stationing abroad.

"You might think I'm given to drink, but you'd be wrong," said the

Swede, as though having read William's thoughts. "Truth is, I just pretend to be."

He pointed discreetly toward a sofa arrangement at which were seated two black men in light-colored suits.

"They're from the company I'm negotiating with tomorrow. At the moment they're checking me out and in an hour or so they'll report back to their boss on what they've seen." He smiled. "No skin off my nose if they think I'll be turning up the worse for wear."

"You're in business, then?"

"You could say. I close contracts for Sweden. I'm a controller, and a good one at that." He nodded to the waiter who appeared with his next two beers and raised one to William. "*Skål*, then!"

William tried in vain to keep up with the Swede's liquid intake. A good thing he wasn't playing the same game. His stomach wasn't geared to it.

"I see you've got a coded message." The Swede indicated the yellow Post-it note in front of William.

"Well, I'm not sure, to be honest. It's a text message that came in from a partner of ours who disappeared down here a week ago."

"A text message?" The man laughed. "A beer says I can decode it in less than ten."

William frowned. Decode it? What did he mean?

The Swede took the note, placed a blank sheet of paper in front of him, pulled out his Nokia mobile from his pocket and put it down on the table.

"It's not likely to be a code, if that's what you think," William said. "That wouldn't really be how we operate in the ministry. Frankly, though, we've no idea what it's all about, or why it should look like that."

"OK. Written under difficult circumstances, perhaps?"

"Perhaps. We can't ask the man. Like I said, he's disappeared."

The Swede put pen to paper and began to write:

Cfqquptiondae(s+l)la(i+l)dddddddvdlogdmdntdja.

Beneath each letter he wrote another, all the while glancing at his mobile.

After a couple of minutes he looked up at William.

"Let's assume the message was indeed written under difficult circumstances, like I said. In the dark, maybe. I suppose you know that when the mobile's predictive text is turned off each key still represents several characters. Key number three, for instance, is D, E, and F. Press once and you've got D. Twice for E, three times for F. Then you can get other characters altogether. Add to that the eventuality of pressing the wrong key, usually the one just above or below the one you want, and all in all you've got any number of possible combinations. I've done this before, though, and it's fun. You can start my ten minutes now."

William frowned again and nodded for the sake of appearance. He couldn't care less how much time the Swede took. If he could solve the riddle, even partially, the drinks would be on him regardless.

It didn't look easy by any means, but when the first sequence, *Cfqquption*, turned out possibly to be a word beginning with "C," then a typo produced by incorrectly pressing key number three instead of six below it, then twice "Q," that should have been twice "R," followed by the correctly typed "uption," they suddenly had the word *Corruption*.

William sensed the furrows in his brow deepen.

Corruption. Not exactly a word with the most positive connotations.

After a quarter of an hour, and William having bought two more rounds, the Swede had solved the puzzle.

"Well, it seems plausible to me," he said, studying his notes.

He handed the sheet to William.

"Can you see what it says? *'Corruption dans l'aide de development Dja.'*" The Swede nodded to himself. "The French isn't entirely correct, but still. 'Swindle with development funds in Dja,' give or take. Simple as that."

William felt a chill run down his spine.

He glanced around. Was it him or the Swede that the black men in the corner were watching with such interest? Could there be others?

He looked again at the note in front of him, the Swede once more raising his hand in the direction of the waiter.

Corruption dans l'aide de development Dja was what Louis Fon had texted, and then he'd disappeared. Knowing this was not a pleasant feeling. Not pleasant at all.

William gazed out the window and tried to shield himself against the endless expanse of black beyond the pane.

The thought had occurred to him before, and now it returned.

He was truly a long way from home.

Far too long a way indeed.

"What is it you're saying, Mbomo?"

René E. Eriksen felt the perspiration gathering in his armpits as he tried to concentrate on the crackling voice.

"I'm telling you that William Stark was not at the hotel this morning when I went to pick him up, and now I have been told he has taken a plane home."

"For Christ's sake, Mbomo, how could that happen? He was your responsibility." René tried to gather his thoughts. The agreement had been that Mbomo or one of his gorillas would pick up Stark at the hotel that same morning and that would be the end of it. Where and how Stark disappeared didn't matter, as long as it couldn't be traced back to them. And now he was being told that Stark was on his way home to Denmark. What the hell was going on down there? Had Stark got a whiff of something that might incriminate them?

If he had, it was a disaster.

"What the hell could have happened since last night, Mbomo? Can you answer me that? I thought you had everything under control. Stark must have got wind of something."

"I don't know," Mbomo replied, oblivious to the fact that during the past couple of days René E. Eriksen had been through sheer hell at the thought of having sent a man to his death, and as things now stood was more than willing to go along with anything that might stop this juggernaut nightmare from developing any further.

To René's mind there was no doubt at all as to what should happen now. Not only must Mbomo Ziem be removed from the Baka project, he had to be removed permanently. No one who was involved in the project had anything to gain from having a man like him charging around and messing things up. A man who knew as much as he did and at the same time was so fucking inefficient and heavy-handed.

"I'll get back to you, Mbomo. In the meantime I want you to just take things easy. Go home, and stay there. Later today we'll send someone over who can brief you on what's going to happen next."

And then René hung up the phone.

Mbomo would be briefed all right. More than he could ever imagine.

The boardroom of Karrebæk Bank wasn't humble by any stretch of the imagination. Both the furnishings and the location suggested the head-quarters of one of the country's leading financial institutions, and nothing in the countenance of its managing director, Teis Snap, seemed to suggest otherwise. All that met the eye was extravagant: furniture, fittings, the works. Within these walls overspending had long been par for the course.

"Our chairman, Jens Brage-Schmidt, is listening in on this, René. As you know, he's in the same boat as us."

Snap turned toward a walnut speaker cabinet on the imposing desk.

"Can you hear us all right, Jens?" he said.

The answer was affirmative, the voice rather squeaky but still replete with authority.

"Then we'll begin the meeting." He faced René. "I'm sorry to have to be so frank, René," Snap said, "but following your conversation with Mbomo earlier today, Jens and I have come to the conclusion that the only solution to our problem is to do everything in our power to stop William Stark, and that in the future you personally are to make sure that no one with Stark's zeal ever comes anywhere near the Baka project."

"Stop William Stark?" René repeated the words softly. "And this is to happen in Denmark, is that what you mean?" he added after a pause. It was mostly here his reservations lay.

"In Denmark, yes. It has to be," Teis Snap went on. "We're disarming time bombs here, stopping Louis Fon, and soon Mbomo Ziem and William Stark, too. Once they're out of the way we'll be back on track. Officials at the ministry in Yaoundé will stay tight-lipped, of course, since they're in on this themselves. And if you continue to receive regular reports from some public servant in situ who is willing to call himself Louis Fon for a while and spread the word to your ministry about how

magnificently the project is running, then we shall have little to worry
about. It's the way of *all* African projects. A bit of encouraging news once
in a while, that's all anyone expects, dammit."

René heard Brage-Schmidt grunt over the speaker, and though he had
never met the man there seemed to be an underlying tone to his voice
that made René envisage a man who for all too many years had been used
to bossing people around in places far beyond the borders of his home
country. There was a harshness about the way he began a sentence, as if
everything he said was an order not to be disobeyed. The image of a British imperialist or shipping magnate with unfettered powers was easy to
conjure up. René had heard that every butler Brage-Schmidt had employed through the years he had addressed as "boy," and that if anyone
knew Africa, it was him: consul for a handful of southern African states
for as long as anyone cared to remember and successful businessman in
Central Africa even longer, though not always accompanied by the best
of reputations.

No, as far as René could make out there seemed little doubt that Brage-
Schmidt was the architect of the scam. Teis Snap had told him that after
some time as a successful importer of timber from equatorial Africa,
Brage-Schmidt had gathered all his assets in Karrebæk Bank and had in
the years that followed become the bank's largest shareholder by far. As
such it was hardly surprising that he had been elected chairman, or that
he should now guard his fortune so fiercely. René understood this completely, and yet besides their fraud they had now condemned three men
to death. So why did René not hear himself protesting?

He shook his head. The fact of the matter was that unfortunately he
understood this gray eminence a little too well.

What else could they do?

"Yes," said the chairman. "Taking such radical steps is certainly no
easy decision, but think of the jobs that will be lost, the small savers who
will lose their money if we fail to act in time. It is regrettable, of course,
that this William Stark should have to pay the price as well, but that's
how it goes sometimes. The few must be sacrificed for the many, as they
say, and in a few years everything will be good again. The bank will be
safeguarded and consolidated, society will go on as before, investments

will continue, jobs will be retained and shareholders will suffer no losses. And who in the meantime, Mr. Eriksen, do you think might bother to check up on how the pygmies of Dja are progressing in agricultural matters? Who would bother to investigate whether schools and health conditions have improved since the project was initiated? Who would even have the means to do so when those who launched the project to begin with are no longer of this world? I ask you."

Who, indeed, but me? René thought to himself, his eyes wandering to the tall casement windows of the room. Did that mean he, too, was in the danger zone?

But they weren't going to put one over on him, that much was for sure. He knew where he had them and thankfully could still look over his shoulder on the rare occasion he ventured out.

"I only hope you know what you're doing and keep it to yourselves, that's all. I don't want to know any more, are you with me?" he said after a moment. "And let's pray that William Stark hasn't left documentation in some bank box explaining how the fraud came about—as I've done."

He looked at Teis Snap and listened intently to the background noise from the speaker on the desk. Were they shocked? Suspicious?

Seemingly not.

"OK," he went on. "What you say is true. Maybe no one will notice that Louis Fon's reports are coming from someone else, but what about William Stark's disappearance? It'll be all over the news, surely?"

"That's right. And . . . ?" Brage-Schmidt's voice sounded deeper all of a sudden. "As long as nothing can be traced back to us, Stark going missing doesn't matter much, does it? As I see it, he goes to Africa, fails to turn up for his appointment, flies home without a word, and disappears. Wouldn't that indicate a certain degree of instability? Would one not be inclined to consider that his disappearance might be of his own volition? I would, certainly."

Snap and René exchanged glances. Karrebæk Bank's chairman of the board had chosen to ignore René's bank-box insurance scheme, so apparently their mutual trust remained intact, albeit perhaps a bit tarnished.

"Listen, Eriksen," Brage-Schmidt went on. "From here on, everything proceeds exactly according to our agreement. You will continue to ensure that fifty million per annum is dispatched to Cameroon. And once a year on the basis of Louis Fon's fabricated reports you will draw up a nice summary of how excellently things are progressing down there."

Then Snap picked up the thread. "Some weeks later, by way of a group of 'investors' in Curaçao"—Snap formed quotes in the air—"our friends in Yaoundé will as usual transfer the requisite funds to Karrebæk Bank. The rest we place in private equity in our custody account in Curaçao as a buffer against unexpected developments in the bank sector. In that way, Karrebæk Bank's equity portfolio gradually changes hands, all the while expanding, and yet in reality we maintain total control. Our portfolios grow larger by the year. Which means the three of us have every good reason to be cheerful. Am I right?"

"Indeed. We're 'all' happy." This time the air quotes were René's. "All of us, perhaps, apart from Louis Fon, Mbomo, and William . . ."

Teis Snap broke in. "Look, René, don't waste your time worrying about Mbomo and Fon. Once things have settled down a bit we'll donate some cash to their widows so they can get on. The authorities there are used to people disappearing all the time, so no one's going to make an issue of it. As for Stark, he has no family, does he?"

René shook his head. "No, but he does have a partner and a step-daughter who's ill." He stared intensely into Snap's eyes, as though expecting some display of sympathy, but they were cold as ice.

"Good," was Snap's brief response. "No family, then, just a couple of loosely associated individuals. They'll mourn a while, no doubt, and then life will go on. After all, he was hardly the sort you'd miss much, was he, René?"

René exhaled with a sigh. What was he supposed to say? Since they were already referring to the man in the past tense, what did it matter how interesting a person Stark had been?

But still . . .

The loudspeaker interrupted his thoughts. Brage-Schmidt didn't bother to comment on the last statement, but then why should he?

"As far as the two hundred and fifty million is concerned, we can with some justification claim it to be a form of camouflaged state subsidy from the Baka project to our continued banking activities. Is it not reasonable that the state be protective of Denmark's lucrative private companies, like Karrebæk Bank? Enterprises that create jobs, enhance the balance of payments and raise living standards. One way or another the wheels would grind to a halt if reputable banks such as ours were allowed to crash. Hardly what we or the government wish to see now, is it?"

René's thoughts were somewhere else entirely. If anything went wrong, Snap and Brage-Schmidt would distance themselves in no time at all, that much was certain. And he would be left behind alone, with both the responsibility and a prison sentence. He wasn't going to let it happen.

"I'll say it again: what you do from now on is without my knowledge, OK? I don't want to know. But if you *do* take such drastic measures, make sure I get Stark's laptop immediately. Who knows what he might have tucked away on it concerning our little project."

"Sure, of course you'll get it. And yes, we understand how difficult it is for you to take all this in, René. After all, I know you. You're an upstanding and decent man. But think of your family, OK?" Snap urged. "Just let Jens and me take care of this, and you stop worrying. We'll contact someone proficient at dealing with this sort of problem, who can arrange for Stark to be intercepted at the airport. In the meantime you can take pleasure in the thought of your stock rising by the day. The future remains bright, René."

3

Autumn 2010

The yellow van came and collected Marco in front of the scaffolding on Copenhagen's Rådhuspladsen at precisely five in the afternoon, as always. This time he had waited twenty minutes in the square outside the town hall to be on the safe side. If he wasn't there, ready when the van arrived, they would drive on without him. And if he had to join the city's commuters on the S-train and the bus instead, they would beat him. The very thought was enough, not to mention the possibility of sleeping a whole night in some damp basement passage, for the weather was far too cold.

So Marco was never late. He simply hadn't the guts.

He nodded to the others in the van who were sitting with their backs against the walls, but no one nodded back. He was used to that. They were all dead tired.

Tired of the days, of life, and of themselves.

Marco studied the group. One or two were still wet from the rain and sat shivering with cold. If he hadn't known better he might have taken several of them to be ill, skinny and consumptive as they looked. It was no cheerful sight, but then not much was, on a clammy November day in Denmark.

"How'd you do today?" asked Samuel, who was leaning against the wall behind the cab.

Marco counted in his head.

"I made four separate deliveries. The second time alone was over five hundred kroner. I think about thirteen or fourteen hundred in all, with the three hundred I've got in my pocket."

"I did about eight hundred," said Miryam, the eldest of them. She always drew a sympathetic response with her bad leg. That kind of thing was good at boosting turnover.

"I only got sixty," said Samuel, in such a quiet voice that everyone heard him. "No one wants to give me anything anymore."

Ten pairs of eyes looked at him with pity. He was in for a hard time once they got back to Zola.

"Then take this," Marco said, handing him two hundred-kroner notes. He was the only one to do so, for there was always a risk that one of them would snitch to Zola. As if he didn't know.

Marco knew what was wrong with Samuel. Begging became a dwindling option once a boy began to look more like a young man. Though Marco himself was fifteen, he still resembled a kid, so things were easier for him. He was small for his age, unusually so, with the wide eyes of a child, his hair fine, skin still smooth. Unlike Samuel, Pico, and Romeo, whose skin had become coarse, facial hair sprouting. And while the others had already indulged in their first adventures with girls, many still envied Marco for his slow development, not to mention the keenness of his wits.

As if he didn't know all this.

He may have been small for his age, but his eyes and ears were those of an experienced grown-up, and he was skilled at putting them to use. Very skilled indeed.

"Father, can't I go to school?" he had pleaded since he was seven, back when they lived in Italy. Marco loved his father, but on this issue, like so many others, the man was weak. He told him his brother, Marco's uncle Zola, insisted on the children working the streets. And so it became, for Zola was the undisputed and tyrannical head of the clan.

But Marco had a desire to learn, and in nearly all the small towns and villages of Umbria was a school where he could stand outside and absorb as though he were blotting paper. So when the sun began to warm the morning air he stood close up at the windows, listening intently, ears cocked for an hour or more before trudging off to scrape together the day's earnings.

Once in a while a teacher would come out and invite him inside, but

Marco would run away and not return. Taking up the offer would mean being beaten black and blue at home. In that respect, moving around the way they did was an advantage because the schools were always new.

Then came the day when one of the teachers nonetheless managed to get a firm grip on him. But instead of dragging him inside he handed him a canvas bag as heavy as the day was long.

"They're yours, put them to use," he said, releasing him again.

The bag contained fifteen textbooks, and wherever the clan settled Marco always found a secret hiding place where he could sit and study them without fear of discovery.

And so it was every evening and all the days when the grown-ups had other things to do than keep watch over the children. After two years he learned to do sums and to read both Italian and English, and as a result his curiosity was turned toward everything in the world he had yet to learn or understand.

During the three years they had now lived in Denmark, he was the only one among them who had learned to speak the language almost fluently. He was simply the only one inquisitive enough to bother.

All the rank-and-file members of the group knew that when Marco was out of sight he was sitting somewhere on his own, immersed in a book.

"Tell us, tell us," Miryam in particular would urge, she being the one he was closest to.

Zola and his associates would be rather less enthusiastic about his reading habits, if they ever found out.

That evening they lay in their bunks listening to the beating and Samuel's screams as they penetrated the wall of Zola's room, percolating down to Marco's like an echo of all the other injustices Zola had committed. Marco himself was unafraid of thrashings, for as a rule they were milder in his case, thanks to the influence of his father. And yet he clutched his blanket: Samuel was no Marco.

When once again silence descended and Samuel's punishment was over, Marco heard the front door open. It had to be one of Zola's gorillas, scanning the terrain before dragging the beaten and humiliated Samuel across to the house next door where his room was. The clan members were proficient at keeping up appearances and remaining friendly with the Danish families of the neighborhood. On the face of it, Zola was a somewhat reserved, rather elegant individual, and this was an image he definitely intended to maintain. He knew perfectly well that a present-able white man from the United States, speaking English—a language everyone understood—would in many ways be thought of as *one of our own*. One of those the Danes had no need to fear.

For that reason, punishment was always administered under cover of darkness behind soundproofed windows and drawn curtains. Similarly, it was imperative that all bruises and other signs of beating were never visible. The fact that Samuel would be aching all over the next morning as he dragged himself up and down Strøget, Copenhagen's pedestrian shopping street, was another matter entirely, but this, of course, went unnoticed by the masses. Besides, the boy's miserable appearance was good for business, and all experience showed that genuine displays of discomfort produced a better yield than false ones.

Marco got up in the dark, crept past the room shared by his cousins and knocked cautiously on the door of the living room. If the response was swift, then all was well. Hesitation, and one could never predict the mood Zola might be in.

This time almost a minute passed before he was called in. Marco braced himself.

Zola sat at the tea table like a king at his court, the television news blaring from the gigantic flat screen.

Maybe he brightened slightly when he realized it was Marco, but his hands had yet to stop trembling. Some of the group claimed that Zola liked to watch when they were being punished, but Marco's father said the opposite: that Zola loved his flock as Jesus loved his disciples.

Marco wasn't so sure.

For three days and nights, Detective Inspector Carl Mørck sat impris-oned here in this hermetically sealed room in the company of mummified corpses and had . . . said the voice on the screen.

"Turn that shit off, Chris," Zola barked, with a nod toward the re-mote. Within a second it was done.

He patted his new acquisition, a gangling, thin-legged hound no one else dared approach, then fixed his gaze on Marco's. "How brave of you to give Samuel money today, Marco. But do so again and you'll be punished in the same way, do you understand?"

Marco nodded.

Zola smiled. "You've earned well for us today, Marco. Sit down." He indicated the chair opposite. "What do you want, my boy? I suppose you've come to tell me Samuel didn't deserve it. Am I right?"

And then his expression changed. With a quick gesture he instructed his near-omnipotent henchman, Chris, to pour tea into a mug. When he had done so, Zola nudged it halfway across the table toward Marco.

"I'm sorry to disturb you here in the living room, Zola. But yes, I wanted to say something about Samuel."

Zola was impassive as the words were uttered, but Chris straightened up immediately and turned slowly to look at him. He was big and paler than most in the clan. His sallow presence was sufficient to make most in the flock retreat, yet Marco kept his eyes fixed on his uncle.

"I see. But Samuel is none of your concern, Marco. You understand that, I'm sure. Today he didn't come home with enough earnings because he didn't try hard enough. Unlike yourself." Zola shook his head and leaned back heavily against the sheepskin that lay draped over the back of the armchair. "You must learn not to poke your nose in where it doesn't belong, Marco. Listen to what your uncle tells you."

Marco studied him for a moment. In Zola's view, Samuel, unlike Marco, had not tried hard enough. Was he thereby saying it was indirectly his fault Samuel had been beaten? If so, that would be even worse.

Marco bowed his head and spoke his words as humbly as he was able.

"I know. But Samuel has become too old now to beg on Strøget. Most people ignore him completely, and those who don't seem afraid of him and keep their distance. In fact, the only ones who—"

Marco sensed Zola making a sign to Chris. He looked up at the same instant as Chris stepped forward and slapped his face hard, making his ear ring.

"I told you, it's not your business. Do you understand, Marco?"

"Yes, Zola, but—"

Another slap, and the message was received. It wasn't the kind of thing anyone who had been brought up in that environment made a fuss about.

He got to his feet unsteadily, nodded to Zola, and withdrew toward the door, forcing a smile as he went. Two slaps in the face and the audience was over. And still he mustered some courage as he stood in the doorway.

"It's OK to hit me," he said, lifting his head. "But it's not OK to beat Samuel. And if you make that bully hit me again, I'll run away from here."

He noted the inquiring look Chris sent his uncle, but Zola merely shook his head, indicating with a sweep of his hand that Marco was to get out of his sight. At once.

When he again lay under his blanket he tried as always to run through all the unuttered arguments in his mind. If only he had said this or that, things might have turned out for the better. As Marco lay there in the gloom, Zola often became more reasonable in these inner dialogues, on occasion even acquiescing.

Such thoughts gave solace of a kind.

"Samuel's a good boy at heart," he imagined having said to Zola. "He needs to learn, that's all. If you let him go to school, then maybe he could become a mechanic and look after the van. He'll never be a good pickpocket like me or Hector, he's far too clumsy, so why not give him a chance?"

And the words in his head made him feel better for a time. But as soon as he turned off the night lamp, the realities came tumbling down upon him.

The life he and his cousins led was a misery.

On the face of it they were decent people in yellow-brick houses, but the truth was they were criminals and delinquents with false passports, and in every sense they were in deep water. And as if that wasn't bad enough, there was more. The worst was that the clan was even more se-cretive internally and that few of the kids knew where they were from any longer, who their real parents were, or what the adults did when they themselves were out on the streets raking in money for Zola's empire. Marco knew the clan's past was nothing to brag about, but the little good there had been had gone to the wall with the advent of Zola's new style immediately before they left Italy. The only thing remaining from former times was the sum of their malicious crimes. Nothing had improved in any way. There were still only a couple among them who could read and write, though many would soon be grown up. But when they were out on the make they were full-blood professionals, albeit of the kind who saw no reason to boast of their peculiar areas of expertise: begging, pick-pocketing, burglary, colliding with old ladies so they dropped their handbags, from fast-moving bikes drive-by grabs of anything hanging from a shoulder or hand that seemed like it might be worth something. They were proficient to their fingertips, and Marco in particular demon-strated talent in every reprehensible domain. He could beg, eyes wide and imploring, with a smile that awoke compassion. He could wriggle through the smallest of windows in private homes without a sound, and out on the street among the busy throngs he was truly in his element. Nimble and adroit, he would relieve his victim of watch or wallet. Never a wrong movement or sound, often gesticulating excitedly to distract at-tention, always eliciting sympathy.

There was only one thing about Marco that was neither to his own nor the clan's benefit.

He hated his existence, and all that he did, to the depths of his being.

And so he lay in his bed listening to the other kids' breathing, trying to imagine the life he did not have. The life that other children had, the ones he saw outside. Children with mothers and fathers who went to work; children who went to school and perhaps received a hug or a small gift every now and then. Children who were given nice food every single day and who had friends and family who came to see them. Children who didn't always look afraid.

When he lay with these thoughts in his mind, Marco would curse Zola. Back in Italy they had at least formed a sort of community: play in the afternoons, songs in the evenings; summer nights around the fire, boastful stories of the day's exploits. The women played up to the men, and the men puffed themselves up, on occasion clashing and exchanging blows, much to everyone's amusement. That was when they still were Gypsies.

How Zola had managed to declare himself their indisputable guiding light was something Marco had difficulty grasping. Why did the other adults put up with it? The only things he did were to terrorize them, dominate their lives, and relieve them of everything they had struggled to scrape together. And when such thoughts troubled Marco's mind he felt shame on behalf of the grown-ups, and especially his father.

This evening he raised himself onto his elbows in bed, fully aware he had ventured onto thin ice. Zola had not really done him harm back there in the living room, but his eyes had warned of miseries to come. Of that he was certain.

He knew he must speak to his father about Samuel. He needed to speak to someone, at least. The question was whether it would help. For some time his father had seemed so distant. As though something had happened that had really affected him.

The first time Marco had noticed it was almost two years before, when his father had sat one morning with his brow furrowed in a frown, passively staring at the food put before him. Marco had thought he must be ill, but the following day he was more energetic than he had been for months. Some said he had begun to chew khat like a number of others, but regardless of what he was up to, the furrows in his brow had come to stay. For some time Marco kept his concerns to himself, but eventually he confided in Miryam and asked if she knew anything.

"You're dreaming, Marco. Your father's exactly the same as he's always been," she said, and tried to smile.

They spoke no more of it, and Marco endeavored to put it from his mind.

But then, six months ago, he had noticed once more the look on his father's face, though now a slightly different variant. There had been quite a bit of turbulence throughout the night, but after ten the kids were not allowed to leave their rooms, for which reason it couldn't have been caused by any of them.

Marco had been woken in the middle of a dream by the sound of tumult in the hallway. Judging by the nature of the groans he heard, hard punishment was being meted out. Punishment so harsh that knowledge of what had taken place seemed etched in his father's face the next morning as though branded there by hot iron. But Marco had no idea who had been on the receiving end, or for what reason. Certainly not a member of the clan, otherwise he would have known.

Since then, his father had slept in Lajla's room on the other side of the living room.

Now, hungry and unable to sleep, Marco threw off the bed covers and made his way down the hall toward the kitchen. As he passed the living-room door he heard his father's voice protesting vigorously behind it, then Zola's calming him down.

"If we don't put a stop to your son's rebellion, it will not only mean lost earnings, it will also mean he will be spreading his poison to the other kids. You have to expect he will betray us one day and destroy everything, don't you realize that?"

He heard his father protest again. This time with more desperation to his voice. It wasn't normal for him.

"Marco will never go to the police, Zola," he replied, urgency in his voice. "Once I've had a word with him he'll toe the line. He won't run away either. That's just something he says. You know how he is. A bright boy with too many ideas in his head. A little too bright sometimes, but never with the intention of doing us harm. Zola, surely you can see that? Won't you please leave him alone?"

"No," Zola replied curtly. It was his call. He had the power.

Marco glanced down the passageway. Any minute now Chris could appear with the absinthe Zola always demanded for his nightcap. And when he did, Marco mustn't be caught eavesdropping.

"You should know that Samuel has told me he's seen Marco hesitate when he's pickpocketing and stealing handbags," Zola went on. "If it's true, he can put us all in peril. You know that as well as I do. Those who hesitate will sooner or later be caught. And they're the kind who can't keep their mouths shut, either, when it really counts. You can't bank on him being loyal toward us or the clan when things go wrong. That's a fact."

Then Marco put his ear against the door, his breathing as quiet as a mouse so the dog inside would not begin to growl. Was that really how Samuel spoke of him? It wasn't true at all. When had he ever hesitated in his work? Never!

But Samuel had, on many occasions. And yet they had defended him. The fool.

"Marco's old enough now for the invalid scam, so there's no two ways about it. We know how great the benefits are. Look at Miryam."

"But can't you see there's a difference between him and Miryam?" It was his father's voice, imploring. "Her misfortune *was* an accident."

"You really believe that, don't you?" The words were followed by dry laughter. Marco felt a chill. What did he mean? That it wasn't an accident? Miryam had stumbled while she was running across the road, everyone knew that.

For a moment all was silent inside the room. He could clearly picture the shock on his father's face. But his father said nothing.

"Listen," Zola continued. "We must look after the youngsters, make sure they've a bright future, yes? That's why we can't afford to be soft and make mistakes, do you understand? Soon we'll have scraped enough money together to settle in the Philippines. I think you'd do well to remember that this has been our dream from the start. There's a place for Marco in that dream, too."

A minute passed before Marco's father replied. It was clear he was already coming to terms with defeat. "And that's why Marco must be maimed? Is that really what you want, Zola?"

Marco clenched his fists. Hit him, Father. Hit him, he urged in silence. You're Zola's elder brother. Tell him to leave me be.

"It's just a small sacrifice for the benefit of the clan, don't you agree? We sedate the boy and put his leg out into the traffic. It will be over in an instant. The Danish hospitals are good, they'll fix him up well enough. And if he won't go along voluntarily, we'll have to help him, yes? If you oppose me on this issue, I may select you instead, you realize that, don't you?"

Marco held his breath and saw Miryam's hobbling figure in his mind's eye. He fought back the tears. Was that how it happened? They had turned her into a cripple.

Say something, Father!, he urged again. But from behind the door came the sound of one voice only. The wrong one.

"Accident, disfigurement, insurance payout. So it will proceed," Zola continued. "And as a permanently beneficial side effect, we will have created for ourselves a thoroughbred beggar who is unable to run anywhere."

A faint draught in the passage made Marco turn, but too late. The kitchen door had opened and the figure that stepped out had seen him.

"What are you up to, boy?" Chris's voice slashed through the dimness.

In an instant Marco sprang free of the wall and made a dash as Chris leaped after him, and the door of the living room was flung open.

Many times before he had told himself that if ever such a situation should occur he would seek refuge in one of the neighbor's houses. But now everything around him seemed dead. The wind was whistling through the many trees between which the houses lay, quiet as mausoleums: dark, lifeless, deceased. All the windows around him were unlit. Only the faint glare of a single television screen was visible farther down the road.

And that was the house he ran toward, filled with dread.

"I won't make it," he kept telling himself as a cold rain began to wet his face. He would be caught before he ever roused the residents from their armchairs. He had to find another way.

Marco twisted round and glanced behind him as he ran, trying not to stumble over the curbs with his bare feet. Now he could see that two of his older cousins were on his heels, too, and they were fast. He hurled himself into the gravel on his stomach and squirmed through a hole in a hedge too small for the others to negotiate.

If he could cut through this garden and get to the main road, he might have a chance.

An automatic floodlight mounted on the house's gable end tripped, painting the garden bright white. He saw the people inside come to the picture window of the living room, but he was already on his way through the next hedge, from where he rolled down into the ditch at the side of the main road.

Behind him came shouts for him to stop, but Marco's attention was fixed on the passing cars and the thicket of trees halfway up the hill a few hundred meters beyond. That was where he needed to go. Any moment now they would have run down the residential street and emerge onto the road farther on. If he didn't get away now, he would be done for.

A blue beam of halogen headlights tipped over the ridge, revealing the rainy tarmac to be a glittering bridge to freedom. If he ran into the middle of the road and stopped the car it might save him. And if it refused to stop, he would throw himself into its path and put an end to his trials. Rather that than spend the rest of his life a crippled beggar like Miryam.

"Stop!" he cried out as the car came toward him, his arms waving. Then he made directly for the headlight beams, like a moth to a flame.

Over his shoulder he could see his pursuers coming round the houses and spilling out onto the road. From that distance he was unable to see who they were, but it had to be his cousins and some of the other kids because they were so quick. He would have only seconds to stop the car and convince the driver to help him before they caught up.

The car flashed its lights, but the driver did not slow down. For a moment he was certain it wouldn't stop and prepared to meet his fate when suddenly he heard the squeal of brakes and saw the vehicle begin to veer from side to side like a man inebriated.

Don't move, or else he'll just zoom on by, he told himself, trying to predict the direction in which the driver would next yank the wheel. He wasn't going to let him past.

For a split second Marco saw the front of the car loom toward him like an executioner's ax, and then with a whoosh of tires against the wet asphalt it came to a sudden halt, with Marco's knee against the front bumper, as an extremely agitated man hurled abuse at him from the other side of the thrashing wipers.

Marco sprang to the passenger side and flung open the door before the man could react.

"What the hell are you playing at, you little brat?" the driver yelled, his face white as chalk from the shock.

"You've got to take me with you or those men there are going to get me," Marco begged, pointing down into the dip in the road from where his pursuers were now approaching.

The man's expression changed from shock to rage in a second.

"What the fuck? Are you a Paki?" he screamed, leaning over to the passenger seat and without warning lashing a fist at Marco's head.

The punch caught him awkwardly, but hard enough to send him backward onto the road as the man slammed the door shut with a hail of invective to the effect that apes like him could damn well fend for themselves.

Marco felt the asphalt eating its way through his pajamas. It hurt but wasn't nearly as painful as lying flat in the middle of the road in darkness and seeing the car accelerate off with the beam of its headlights aimed straight at those who were after him.

"Stop the car!" one of them shouted. Then came the dull thud of gunshots, but the vehicle hurtled on, picking up speed and heading directly toward the flock, forcing them to leap for their lives. And then it was gone.

He heard the confusion among them as he rolled over into the ditch and crawled under a bush. They must have thought he'd managed to throw himself into the car before it sped away. He crawled on all fours deeper into the underbrush at the edge of the woods that bordered the road as he strained his ears to hear what his pursuers were up to.

Peering through the vegetation, he saw that some men had now joined his young pursuers. From their silhouettes he took them to be Zola, Chris, and his father.

The young ones pointed up the road to where Marco had stopped the car, then turned in the direction in which it had disappeared. Suddenly a fist flew through the air and a figure slumped to the ground. Punishment for failing to capture the fugitive came promptly. What else did they expect?

He heard a barked order to search the area, and the group consolidated and began jogging toward the place where he lay concealed. He needed to get into the woods or somewhere else they wouldn't look. He raised himself warily toward the dark, expansive landscape of tree trunks, shivering from the rapid cooling of his skin and the adrenaline pumping through his body. The rain had soaked his pajamas, making them feel like they were made of sponge as the icy cold bit through his skin and feet. He realized at the first step that he wouldn't get far without shoes, and now his pursuers were so close he could tell the voices apart.

It sounded like they were all there: Hector, Pico, Romeo, Zola, Samuel, his father, and the others. Even a pair of female voices vibrated above the trees.

Only then did Marco truly sense fear.

"I didn't see him in the car," Samuel shouted in Italian, another answering in English that they wouldn't have seen him even if he had been inside.

Again, Samuel had betrayed him.

And now Zola's fury rose up above this chaos of voices. Fury at their having allowed the boy to run, fury at their not having checked well enough to know for sure whether he'd been in the car, fury at shots having been fired. Now they would have to suspend all activities for a long time, he yelled at them, his voice trembling. It was going to cost them, and those who had fired the shots would be made to pay. The younger members of the clan would need to make themselves scarce in the days that followed, until the dust had settled. More than likely, the man in the car would go to the police, and when he did, the kids would have to be nowhere near the neighborhood if searches were carried out and questions asked.

"Comb the area and see if Marco's still here," Zola commanded. "And if he makes a run for it again, you've my permission to shoot. Just make sure you hit him, that's all. Marco has become a danger to all of us."

He was shocked. They were going to shoot him because he was dangerous. Yet he had done nothing but contradict Zola and run away. Was that all it took? What about the others who had deserted the flock from time to time? Had Zola had them shot, too?

Marco shuddered as he felt his way forward with his feet, twigs, pine cones, and thorns jabbing at his ankles and soles. A hundred meters into the woods, he was forced to lie down. Moving on was simply too painful and too slow.

They'd catch him if he didn't find cover, he told himself, the words pulsing in his mind as he prodded the ground and noted that the earth was cold as ice, hard as stone. The place offered no concealment.

He felt panic now, as he spread his arms out to his sides and wriggled a few meters forward on his stomach through the prickly undergrowth.

He pressed on, and after a minute he suddenly felt his knees sink. For a moment he thought he had ventured into bog, but the soil was dry and loose, as though it had been turned. It was perfect.

So he began to dig, and the farther down he got, the looser the earth became.

Before long the hole was big and deep enough for him to roll into it and draw the soil over his body, twigs and broken branches covering his face and arms.

They wouldn't see him now unless they stepped on him. Please don't let the dog be with them, he prayed, trying to control his breathing.

And then he heard the crackle of dry wood under many feet. They were coming.

They spread out in the underbrush, moving slowly toward the place he lay, the sweeping beams of two flashlights hovering between the tree trunks like gigantic fireflies.

"One of you stay by the road so he can't escape that way. The rest of you search closely, make sure he hasn't concealed himself underneath something," Zola shouted into the darkness. "Prod the ground with sticks, there's plenty of them."

A moment passed and Marco heard the snapping of branches all around, for Zola's word was law. Crunching footsteps vibrated through the earth, approaching where he lay as the sound of sticks jabbed against the cold ground made the sweat trickle from his brow in spite of the biting cold. Another minute and the flock was all around him. And then suddenly they were gone.

Stay where you are, he told himself, a stench of rot piercing his nostrils. Somewhere close by an animal lay dead, no doubt about it. He'd found them often when they'd lived in Italy. Dead, stinking corpses of all kinds: squirrels, hares, and birds.

When Zola called off the search they would return the same way through the woods. If they hadn't posted a man at the roadside he would have run back whence he came and then out across the fields. But just now he hadn't the courage, so what else could he do but remain as quiet as a mouse?

And after a long time—as long a time as it would take Marco to beg his way from Rådhuspladsen down to Kongens Nytorv—they came back and passed him by. He'd been lying in the ice-cold earth for nearly an hour now, as the rain poured through the canopy of fir.

He heard them one by one, frustrated by their unsuccessful manhunt, angry that Marco had betrayed them so. Some even expressed their fear of what his betrayal might lead to.

"He's in for it if we get our hands on him," said Sascha, one of the girls he'd liked best.

Bringing up the rear were his father and Zola, the sentiment in their voices equally unambiguous.

As was the whining of the dog.

Marco's heart stood still. He held his breath, knowing it would be no defense against the canine's sense of smell. And then the animal suddenly began to bark, as though the scent of Marco were the only thing in the world it was capable of focusing on.

Now he was doomed.

"This is about where we dug the hole," said Zola in a subdued voice, only meters from the place where Marco lay. "Listen to the dog, it's going crazy, so we must be getting close. Goddammit, you realize, don't you, that we've got an even bigger problem on our hands now? And *your* son is to blame." He swore again as he dragged the whining dog away. "We need to be real careful for a while. There's no telling what Marco might do. I think we should consider moving the body as well. It's a bit too close to home."

Marco slowly sucked in air through his teeth. With each breath he took, his hatred of Zola grew. The sound of his voice alone made Marco want to spring from his hiding place and cry out his contempt. But he did nothing.

When eventually the voices had left the underbrush, he began to shake away the soil. Later in the night or early the next morning Zola and

Chris were bound to return with the dog. It was something he couldn't risk.

He had to get away. Far away.

He pulled his frozen arms free with difficulty and arched his back so the soil that covered him could slide from his body.

Then he wriggled in the earth so as to gain purchase to draw himself upright, the sleeves of his pajamas catching as he swept sticks and twigs aside. Suddenly his hand struck a slimy mass covering something hard, and then came the stench, smothering him like death itself.

Instinctively he held his breath as he sat up and tried to see what it was his hands had found, which was barely possible by the dim light of the moon. So he tipped forward, his nostrils pinched, and then he saw it.

At that moment it was almost as if his heart had stopped. Before him lay a human hand. Helpless, crooked fingers with the skin peeled away, nails as brown as the earth itself.

Marco flung himself to one side. For a long time he sat on his haunches a short distance away, staring at the arm of the corpse as rain slowly revealed its decaying face and body.

"This is about where we dug the hole," Zola had said to his father. The hole in which he himself had been lying.

Together with a rotting corpse.

Marco got to his feet. It was not the first time he had seen a dead body, but he had never touched one before, and he never wished to again.

For a while he considered what to do next. On the one hand, his discovery had suddenly given him the opportunity to have Zola put behind bars and to finally free himself of the man. But on the other hand, his father had helped bury the body, and probably also more than that. That made all the difference.

As he stood pondering, slowly becoming used to the smell, he realized there was no way to get at Zola without incriminating his own father. And though his father was weak and in Zola's thrall, Marco loved him. What else could he do? His father was all he had. How, then, could he go to the authorities and ask for help? He couldn't.

Not now, not tomorrow . . . not ever.

Marco felt his icy skin turn even colder. Somehow the world had sud-

denly become too big for him. In this moment of pain he realized that
without his clan he had only the streets to fall back on. From now on
he was on his own. No yellow van would collect him again when the day
was over. No one would prepare his meals. No one in the world would
know who he was or where he came from.

He hardly knew himself.

He began to sob but then stopped. Neither pity nor self-pity were
emotions that were to be found in the world he'd been raised in.

He looked down at his night clothes. They were the first thing he had
to do something about. There were houses, of course, that he could break
into, but nocturnal burglaries were something he preferred to leave to
others. People never slept that heavily in Denmark. They often lounged
in front of their TV screens until the early hours, and in the darkness
ears had a habit of growing far too big.

He prodded the ground with a bare foot. Perhaps there was something
useful to be found in the grave with this dead man. He needed to check,
so he picked up a stick from the undergrowth and began to hollow out
the soil around the shoulders of the corpse, continuing until the torso
was completely exposed.

Despite the darkness and the dirt, the face was quite clear to him,
cheekbones high and chiseled, the nose long and straight. And the red-
dest hair Marco had seen in all his life. The age was impossible to assess,
for the skin of the face had almost liquefied. He sensed that, had it not
been so dark, the sight would have been as appalling as the smell.

There was nothing for him here, he decided, his eyes resting in a moment's distress on the tightened, decaying hand that seemed almost to be
trying to grab and hold on to life itself. To this man also, Zola had brought
calamity.

And then it was that Marco discovered the chain catch protruding
from underneath the corpse's withered thumb. A tiny, round fastener
with a lever. How many times had he opened one just like it as he stole
the necklace off some innocent individual's neck?

He took hold and pulled until the bones gave way and the chain
slipped from the hand. As easy as anything.

The trinket was heavy and foreign in appearance. Marco had never seen one like it. An intricate lattice of threads, with a few pieces of horn and small wooden masks dangling from it. It wasn't appealing, but it was unusual.

Unusual, perhaps, but hardly a piece that could be traded for money. Just something African.

4

Spring 2011

"**What the hell's going on?**" Carl wanted to know, as Tomas Laursen, the stocky former forensics officer and current manager of Copenhagen police headquarters' under-dimensioned cafeteria stuck his head out of the kitchen area. "What are all these horrible paper flags for? Is it my homecoming from Rotterdam you're celebrating? I was gone only a day."

Had it not been for the fact that he'd had to pick up that fantastic ring for Mona and because the jeweler's was so close to police HQ, not to mention his dying for a cup of coffee, he would have gone straight home from the airport.

Now he was feeling he should have done so anyway.

He stared around the room, shaking his head. What kind of shit was this? Had he walked in on some kid's birthday party, or had one of his colleagues got himself hitched for the third or fourth time in the vain hope that he was finally safe?

Laursen smiled. "Hi, Carl. No, I'm afraid not. It's because Lars Bjørn has come back. Lis has been putting up decorations, and Marcus has called the department in for coffee and a bite in half an hour."

Carl frowned. Lars Bjørn? Back from where? He hadn't even noticed the homicide department's deputy commissioner had been away.

"Uhh, *back*, you say? What, been to Legoland, has he?"

Laursen dumped a plate containing something green in front of the officer at Carl's side. It didn't look good. Carl felt sure his colleague was going to regret it.

"You haven't heard, then? Strange. Anyway, he's just got back from

Kabul." Laursen laughed. "If you can avoid it, I'd say you were best off not letting on you didn't know. He's been away for two months, Carl."

Carl glanced to his side. Was this poverty of common knowledge what was causing the hand of the man next to him to shake as he lifted his fork to his mouth? But who was the real laughingstock at the moment? Carl or Lars Bjørn, who apparently hadn't been missed?

Two whole months, according to Tomas. Gasp.

"Kabul, you say? A pretty dangerous neck of the woods. What the fuck's he been doing there?" It was hard to imagine a boarding-school wuss like Bjørn kitted out in battle dress. "Did they remember to check if he got back alive? You can never tell with a mummy like him," he added as the green substance slid off the jiggling fork of the man next to him.

"Bjørn was sent there to train the local police," said Laursen, wiping his hands on the tea towel that was wrapped around his ever-expanding waist. If he was intending to stay on in the cafeteria much longer he'd have to order some bigger tea cloths, thought Carl.

"You don't say? I reckon he should have stayed there, in that case."

Carl glanced around the room. The comment had drawn more than a couple of glares in his direction, but he didn't give a shit. As far as he was concerned they could *all* take up residence in the Afghan wilderness with its roadside bombs.

"Thanks very much, Carl," said a voice behind him. "Nice to know you hold my work in such high esteem."

Fifteen pairs of eyes converged on the space behind his shoulder. Suddenly a ripple of chuckles passed through the assembly—pure Schadenfreude. Carl turned calmly toward what he anticipated would be a face luminous in every conceivable shade of red.

But Lars Bjørn was looking annoyingly good and he knew it. It was as if a taut animal skin had been stretched over his slight frame and the sun had conspired to straighten his back and shoulders. Whatever it was, he suddenly seemed somewhat larger than usual. Maybe the colorful array of ribbons in four measured rows above his left breast pocket helped.

Carl gave a nod of acknowledgment. "Well, well, Bjørn. Gave you a purple heart, did they? Good for you. Play your cards right and the Cub Scouts will give you a merit badge next."

Carl felt Laursen's gentle tug on his sleeve, but he didn't care. What trouble could Bjørn land him in that he hadn't already?

"Anyone would think it was you who got hit on the head instead of Assad, Mørck. How he's getting on, anyway?"

"Such concern, Bjørn. Back on the job as head of personnel now, are we? But thanks, he's doing OK. We expect him to be firing on all cylinders again in a couple of weeks. Until then I've got Rose, and thank Christ for that."

He noticed wry smiles appearing at the mention of her name, but as long as that was all, he'd let it go. Otherwise he'd give them what for. What did he care? There wasn't a man here who could begin to match her.

"Assad's face is still a bit lopsided, though, isn't it?" Laursen interjected. He was probably the only one in the cafeteria to have noticed.

Carl nodded. "True, but then he's not the only one at HQ with his head off balance." He looked straight at Bjørn, who was over by the cashier, paying for his beverage. Oddly enough he ignored the slight.

"But you're right, Laursen," Carl went on. "The hemorrhage Assad suffered after the attack affected his facial muscles and his sense of balance, so he's been going for regular check-ups all this spring and is still taking a fair amount of medicine. The way things are going, I reckon he'll soon be completely recovered, which we're all very relieved about. He still has a bit of difficulty talking, but then he always did, didn't he?"

He laughed, though no one else joined in. And so what?

Bjørn stuffed his wallet into his back pocket and turned to face him, this time with the dark venomous look he had perfected over the years.

"I'm very happy for Assad that he's making such good progress, Carl. All we can hope is that the same will be true of you, down there in the depths. Perhaps we ought to accord you rather more attention in the future so we can keep a better eye on whether you need assistance, don't you think?"

He turned to Laursen. "Thanks for the reception, very nice indeed,

Tomas. Makes it a pleasure to be home. Wouldn't you say so, Mørck? Oh, and by the way, welcome home from the Netherlands."

Carl returned the snaky glare in kind as Bjørn marched past him and went off down the stairs. Apparently the cobra hadn't completely died of dehydration down there in the desert.

"Idiot," said a voice from behind. Carl didn't catch who it belonged to.

He felt Laursen tug at his shirt again. A brawl was the last thing he needed in his domain.

"What did those reports say from Holland, anyway?" Laursen asked, changing the subject. "Was there any link between the nail-gun killings in Schiedam and the ones here in Denmark?"

Carl snorted. "The reports said fuck all. Complete waste of time."

"And that's got you frustrated, I can see. Am I right?"

Carl studied Laursen's face. Not many people at HQ could be bothered to ask him such elementary questions, but on the other hand not many could expect an answer either, certainly none of the dickheads here now.

"Any unsolved case is always going to get a decent copper riled," he replied, his eyes scanning the faces, giving them something to think about. "Especially one in which a colleague is the victim."

"And Hardy?"

"Hardy's still living with me. I reckon it's going to stay that way until one of us kicks the bucket."

The man munching salad at his side nodded.

"You're a prick, Carl, but I'll give you credit for looking after the man. Not many people would have done that."

Carl frowned slightly. His lips may even have curled into a reluctant smile. At any rate, it was a strange feeling to hear such praise from a colleague. There was a first time for everything.

Downstairs in homicide it was all go. The number of paper flags seemed well over the top in the modest conference room, a bit like a cross between the queen's birthday and a convention of the Denmark Party.

"Hey, Lis. Looks like you've been on quite a rampage. Bulk offer on the flags, was there?"

Department A's absolutely most stimulating feature sent Mørck a side-long glance. "Bit cocky, aren't we, Carl? Do you want me to put them up again for *you* when you get back from Afghanistan?"

"Sure, whatever," he said, hungrily noting the slight curl of her mouth. It was pure sex, underplayed just the way he loved it. Not even Mona could smile like that, the way it hit home straight below the belt. "But unfortunately they'll all be covered in moss by then, won't they? Is Marcus in?"

She gestured toward the door.

The homicide department's head, Marcus Jacobsen, sat by the window staring out across the rooftops, his reading glasses pushed up onto his brow. Judging by the look on his face, his frame of mind was somewhere between chronic fatigue and a feeling of being eternally lost. It was not a pretty sight. But in view of the stacks of case folders mounted up on the desk around him, making the place look more like a paper warehouse, the oddest part was that he hadn't yet succumbed to sitting like that every single day.

He swiveled round on his chair to face Carl, studying him with the same sort of weariness as when kids in the backseat of the car began asking if they'd be in Italy soon, when they were only ten kilometers south of Copenhagen.

"What's up, Carl?" he asked, as though he'd prefer no answer. The man no doubt had a lot on his mind as it was.

"Party going on, I see," said Carl, jerking his thumb over his shoulder toward the front office. "When are the fireworks on?"

"God knows. How was the Netherlands? Are we any closer to tying up those nail-gun killings?"

Cark shook his head. "Closer? The only thing I got any closer to was the realization that we're not the only police force in Europe that can fuck things up. If that was what they call a draft of a coordinated report of all murders committed with a nail gun in our joint neck of the woods during the past couple of years, then I'm the Grand Mogul of Vesterbro. I couldn't come to any conclusion at all on the basis of the data they'd collected. In fact, the only decent job was Ploug's report on our own killings in Sorø and Amager. I'm afraid the Dutch did a shoddy piece of work indeed. Inadequate forensic analyses, incompetent investigation reports, too-slow reaction time. Effing infuriating, to put it mildly. We're not going to get any further pursuing that course unless they suddenly come up with something new entirely down there."

"I see. So I shouldn't be expecting one of your devastatingly detailed reports littered with the usual golden nuggets, is that it?"

Carl pondered for a moment on Jacobsen's sarcastic tone of voice. Something was definitely wrong here in the command bunker.

"That's not actually why I'm here."

"OK. To what do I owe the honor, then, Carl?"

"I've got a problem. Assad's still not up to scratch, so we're a bit adrift at the moment. I'm utilizing the time tidying up all my portfolios." He loved the word. No other was anywhere near as vacuous. "But it's hard going not actually being on a case, because Rose keeps interrupting me all the time. Maybe we ought to kill two birds with one stone and take the opportunity to upgrade her. Can't she tag along with a couple of your lads for a bit? She needs to be shown the ropes, learn how to knock on doors. I thought maybe she could team up with Terje Ploug or Bente Hansen's boys. From what I've heard, they're all moaning about how short-staffed they are."

His eyes narrowed as he peered in hope at his boss. While he'd been away, Rose had already amassed a pile of proposals as to what they ought to focus on. If he didn't get her supertanker of excess energy rerouted in the very near future he'd be up to his eyeballs in case folders in ten seconds.

"Manpower shortages, indeed. Nothing new under the sun, Carl." Marcus Jacobsen smiled drily and began to toy with the cigarette pack on his desk. "You'll have to make your own training program for Rose. None of my lot will want her getting in the way, that's for sure. She's not a fully trained police officer, Carl. She's no business out there on the streets, you tend to forget that."

"I forget nothing. Especially not the fact that since the beginning of the year we've successfully wrapped up two cases thanks to Rose, even though Assad's still on half days. In my book, Rose has completed her training to the full. Besides, we've got no investigation going on at the moment in Department Q. I'm sifting through cases in my own time and I don't want Rose getting bored. It's bad for the nerves."

Marcus Jacobsen sat up straight. "I'm afraid that now you mention it, I reckon I *do* have something she could help us with. But before you send her out onto the streets on her own to mess things up, I suggest you go with her for a couple of days, OK?"

He pulled out a folder ten centimeters down in a half-meter-high pile. If it was the right one, the man possessed a truly uncanny ability.

"Here," he said, handing it to Carl as though it was the most natural thing in the world. "Sverre Anweiler. Prime suspect in a case of arson involving a houseboat out in Sydhavnen. I've only skimmed the report, but it looks like insurance fraud gone wrong. Anweiler was listed as the owner and was nowhere to be found when it exploded and went down. Somewhat regrettable in view of the fact that his girlfriend, Minna Virklund, happened to be on board at the time and perished."

Perished. It had become a typical Marcus expression. A bit cynical, perhaps, even for police HQ.

"How do you mean, *perished*? Did she burn to death or drown or what?"

"Haven't a clue. All I know is that what used to be her body was found bobbing around the harbor, nothing more than charred lump among the wreckage."

"Sverre Anweiler, you say. Foreign?"

"Swedish. The bulletin we put out on him led us nowhere. It's like he just vanished off the map."

"Maybe he was a charred lump as well, at the bottom of the harbor?"

"No, they checked that thoroughly."

"So he's in Sweden, hiding out in some abandoned farmhouse in Norrbotten."

"A reasonable assumption, only now he's turned up in Denmark again, a year and a half after the event. Someone was going through CCTV footage and spotted him by chance on Østerbrogade last Tuesday. See for yourself."

Jacobsen handed Carl a surveillance disc labeled MAY 3, 2011 and a photo of the man. Anweiler's face was as blank as they came: high forehead; fair, wispy hair; dark blue eyes; eyelids seemingly bereft of lashes, almost like a delicate child's. It was the kind of face that could be transformed beyond recognition by simply adding a mole to a cheek.

"CCTV? Where from exactly?"

The chief gave a shrug. "There's more where that came from."

"It sure won't be easy, Marcus. But how in the world could anyone recognize someone so peculiar? He's like a waxwork; he could look like anyone, or no one at all."

"Have a look at the footage, then you'll know."

Carl shook his head. Marcus was clearly trying to put one over on him. "If this is the best you can give me, I'll go out with Rose, but only for a day, Marcus. Just so you know. This looks like it could end up taking all my time."

"Your needs, your decision, Carl. Do as you see fit."

Again, that rather defeatist tone, so unlike Marcus Jacobsen.

"Nice to have Lars Bjørn back, don't you think?" Carl ventured, in order to add some positivity to the general air of disgruntlement.

"Yes. And another thing, Carl. We've got a budget meeting tomorrow, and I want you to know that in the future there may be changes. Not immediately, but now that Bjørn's been pulled back home we're going to be redistributing responsibilities differently until things slot into place."

Carl didn't get it. "Bjørn was *pulled* back?"

"Yes, he was supposed to be in Kabul for another month and a half, but it was more practical this way."

"I'm not with you. 'Until things slot into place,' you say. 'More practical'? What's going on?"

"Oh, I'm forgetting you were away in the Netherlands yesterday, so you weren't at the executive meeting. Sorry, you won't have heard yet, then. Did I ask you how things went in Rotterdam yesterday, Carl?"

He gave a shrug. "Never mind that; tell me what's going on, Marcus."

"Oh, nothing much. It's just the wife and I have decided to retire before the government gets a chance to take our pensions off us."

"Pensions? Aren't you too young for that?"

"I'm afraid not. Friday's my last day." He gave a somewhat resigned smile. "Friday the thirteenth. It'll be all right."

Carl's eyes widened in disbelief: Friday was only three days away! It had to be some kind of fucking joke.

A plume of thundering invective came out of Carl's mouth as he descended the stairs. The homicide department without Marcus Jacobsen was inconceivable. What was more, Lars Bjørn was now in position to take over the reins. It was completely untenable. He would rather cycle through the forests of Norway while being consumed by mosquitoes. A devastating double whammy, and it was only Tuesday.

"What's up with you? You look like a pickled cucumber," said a dry voice from farther down the stairwell. It was Børge Bak, on his way up the stairs in his usual slothful fashion with stolen goods from the basement depot for some investigator who reckoned he'd had a good idea.

"That makes two of us, then," Carl riposted, more than ready to take two steps at a time to get rid of him.

"I hear your trip to Holland wasn't much of a success. That must have suited you."

Carl stopped abruptly. "What the fuck's that supposed to mean?"

"Well, that case was getting out of hand, wasn't it? You could have ended up in hot water."

"Hot water?"

"There's rumors going round."

Carl frowned. If this fat-assed fool didn't make himself scarce and take his ridiculous comb-over with him in the next two seconds, he was going to unbury the hatchet with ceremony, and nothing would please him more.

Bak could see where this was going.

"Anyway, best be getting off upstairs with this lot here. Be seeing you, Carl!"

He managed to lift his foot about three centimeters toward the next step before Carl's fist twisted his collar tight around his throat.

"What rumors, Bak?"

"Let go," Bak wheezed. "Otherwise I'll make sure those disciplinary proceedings you managed to avoid after the Amager incident are reinstated."

Disciplinary proceedings? What the hell was he going on about? Carl tightened his grip around Bak's double chins. "Let me tell you something, Bak. From now on . . ."

He paused at the sound of footsteps, releasing his clutch as one of HQ's new intake tried to squeeze past unnoticed, a sheepish grin on his face. Carl recognized him. The newcomer was a pain in the neck, and of all the possible names he could have been equipped with, his parents had chosen the highly un-Danish moniker "Gordon." A beanstalk of a lad with legs like ski poles, swinging arms more appropriate to a gibbon, the neatly parted hairstyle of an English public schoolboy, and not least of all a mouth on him that never knew when to shut up. Not exactly a boost for criminal investigation in Copenhagen.

Carl nodded reluctantly to the lanky lighthouse before returning his attention to the now gasping Børge Bak.

"I'm afraid I've no idea what you're talking about, Bak. But if you ever happen to find the courage to tell me what you're insinuating, you'll be more than welcome to come and see me in the basement and tell me to my face. Until then, I advise you to stay in your stolen-goods cage and save yourself the indignity of listening to any more unverified gossip. It makes you such a horrible little man."

And with that he shoved him aside and continued on down the stairs. Aside from the little silk pouch he had in his jacket pocket, Mona's reaction to which he could hardly wait for, his day had been crap. The flight home had almost made him throw up even before they had taken off from Schiphol, Marcus had decided to abandon ship, Lars Bjørn was already settling in on the throne, and now this. He should never have bothered coming in today.

Effing Børge Bak and his ilk. No matter what they all thought about the Amager shooting and his part in the investigation of that damned nail-gun killing, it was their fucking duty to respect a colleague's right to defend himself against all accusations, not least those left unsaid. He'd had it up to here with all their shit.

Amid the noise of builders on the job somewhere at the far end of the corridor and the dense fumes of incense sticks and tea made from candied fruit, he found Assad rolling up his prayer mat.

Apart from his lopsided face and an unusually pale version of his Middle Eastern complexion, the man was looking OK.

"Great to see you back, Assad," Carl said, doing his best not to glance at the time. Assad still had a couple of weeks of treatment left to go, so hauling him over the coals for being late would have to wait. "How are you doing?" he asked almost automatically.

"As a matter of fact I am doing splendidly."

Carl raised his head. He needed to hear it again.

"Did you say splendidly?"

Assad turned to face him with drooping eyelids. "Don't you worry, Carl. It will soon pass."

He leaned the prayer mat against the shelves and reached out for some of his caramel substance, keeping hold of the table for support. Who wouldn't need steadying, faced with the prospect of putting that sticky goo in their mouth?

Carl gave his assistant a pat on the back. He had made a marvelous recovery since the assault in December. The doctors had been in no doubt: without Assad's armor-plated skull and his iron constitution, the blow he had received to the back of his head would have turned him into a vegetable if it hadn't killed him outright. A few more burst capillaries in his brain and that would have been it. Apart from a tendency to depression, headaches, a rather crab-like gait and the slight sagging of the right side of his face, plus a host of other more minor things, the man was on his way to full recovery. It was close to a miracle, or whatever you wanted to call it.

"I have been thinking about Hardy, Carl. How is he doing now?"

Carl took a deep breath. It was a hard one to answer. Since Morten had started kissing and cuddling with his new physiotherapist friend, Mika, and since this Mika had begun to apply his considerable professional insights and equally firm muscle mass to Hardy's paralyzed limbs, things had been happening to Hardy that in many ways were unfathomable.

A couple of years ago the doctors at the spinal clinics had basically condemned Hardy to a lifetime of lying on his back in bed. But now Carl no longer felt quite so convinced that their conclusions were accurate.

"It's strange. Before, he used to have these kind of phantom pains, but now it's something else. I just don't know what."

Assad scratched his neck. "I wasn't thinking about if he can move now, Carl. I was thinking more about his frame of mind."

There were new posters on Assad's wall. Maybe it was because he'd been forced to take things easier and had more time on his hands, or perhaps the world situation had been having an influence. Whatever the reason, the exotic scenes bordered with fluttering Arabic letters had now made way for a small poster of Einstein sticking out his tongue and a slightly larger one showing a slim young man with an electric guitar whose name Carl was unable to pronounce. MAHMOUD RADAIDEH AND KAZAMADA PERFORM IN BEIRUT, it read.

"New decorations," said Carl, with a nod to the posters. It was a comment that should have been followed by a polite inquiry as to its subject matter, but somehow he never got that far.

It was as if Assad wasn't really all there. His usual keen and expressive face seemed extinguished, and his shoulders sagged pathetically under his checked shirt. But he was like that sometimes.

"I've got a CD. Would you like to listen?" Assad asked absently, without waiting for Carl's deliberations. He pressed a button on his CD player and before Carl had time to react, the microscopic office space was subjected to an auditory blitzkrieg.

"My God," Carl spluttered, his eyes darting longingly in the direction of the door.

Talk about a wall of sound.

"This is Kazamada. They play with all sorts of musicians from the Arab world," Assad shouted back.

Carl nodded. He didn't doubt the man. The only thing was, it sounded like Kazamada were playing with all of them at once.

He cautiously pressed the stop button.

"You asked about Hardy's frame of mind," Carl said in the earsplitting silence that ensued. "Mika gets him to laugh a lot, but I don't think he's doing that well. He says his thoughts are all over the place. All the things he's missing out on in life. The things he was planning to do when the time came. He's helpless now, Assad. Sometimes we'll hear him crying in the night, but he won't share his pain with any of us. It can be pretty agonizing to listen to."

"'The things he was planning to do when the time came,'" Assad repeated with a pensive nod. "I think I understand. Perhaps better than most."

Carl's eyes traced the fine lines of anguish that crisscrossed Assad's face. "OK, you may be a bit depressed, Assad, but it's hardly surprising after what happened to you. In my own case I, too, have—"

"No, Carl. I am not thinking of the assault now. It is something else. Something else entirely."

And with that his mind turned inward again.

If that was the mood he was in, Carl might just as well throw in his hand grenade now. "I'm afraid I've got some bad news, Assad. Marcus Jacobsen's quitting."

Assad turned his head slowly. "Quitting?"

"Yeah, on Friday."

"This Friday?"

Carl nodded. Had the man gone into slo-mo or had a couple of chips in his cerebral cortex lost a component or two?

Come back, Assad, wherever you are, he thought as he related his conversation with Marcus. "So unfortunately it looks like we're saddled with Lars Bjørn."

"How odd," Assad replied, staring emptily into space.

It was hardly the reaction Carl would have expected.

"How do you mean, *odd*? Disastrous, yes. Horrifying, certainly. But odd? What are you getting at?"

For a moment Assad sat chewing on his lip, seemingly once more on another planet. "Odd because he did not tell me," he said eventually.

Carl frowned. "And why should he do that, Assad?"

"I've just been looking after his house while he and his wife were away, so I was there when they came back last night."

Carl reeled. He *what*?

Assad's head jolted suddenly and he gasped as though he had just nodded off and a reflex had snapped him back to reality. His eyes were wide-open, the expression on his face inscrutable. He appeared startled, his mouth half agape.

"You've been looking after Lars Bjørn's house for two months? How come? And why wasn't I informed? Why would he think he knows you well enough to ask you a favor like that? And what was his wife doing in Kabul? Is she a nurse or something?"

Assad pressed his lips together, his gaze dancing across the floor as though he were trying to cook up a plausible answer. What the hell was going on?

Then his nostrils flared, a sharp intake of breath, and he straightened up in his chair. "I had no place to live and Bjørn helped me. We know each other from the Middle East, that's all. Nothing special. And yes, his wife is a nurse."

Nothing special. Who the hell did he think he was he kidding?

"You know each other from the Middle East?"

"Yes. We met by chance, before I came to Denmark. I think he was the one who advised me to seek asylum here."

Carl nodded. It was quite understandable for Assad to have his secrets, and considering the state he was in, inadvertently expose his vulnerabilities. But it hurt, dammit, that Assad could use words like "by chance" and reckon that Carl's professional interest and curiosity would thereby be eliminated.

And just as Carl was about to let rip with all his least appealing personality traits, his furious eyes suddenly met Assad's.

Seldom had he seen his assistant look so attentive, his gaze so piercing and intense. All of a sudden, after months of being apart, the two of them now sat divided by mistrust and all that remained unuttered between them. A moment's silence where all discussion and evaluation took place without words.

Will you please leave me in peace, Carl? I am back on the job now, Assad's eyes seemed to plead.

Carl gave him a pat on his thigh and got to his feet. "It'll work itself out, you old bugger, you'll see."

"'Bugger'?" came the despondent reply.

"Yes, well. For once, Assad, I'll pass on that one."

The poor sod needs cheering up, Carl mused, as he headed for Rose's office. A dose of her unorthodox personality could usually get Assad laughing.

Though her door was half-shut and the builders had just launched a pneumatic assault on a wall somewhere in the vicinity of the stolen-goods depot, it was hard not to overhear the exchange of voices from within.

"Knock it off, Gordon. There's nothing doing, OK?"

"All I'm trying to say is . . ."

Carl shook his head. The place was almost falling down around them, and yet here was this young fettuccine trying to get it on with Carl's next-most trusty colleague, and on his turf to boot.

He reached out and was about to fling open the door with a roar of outrage, only to pause abruptly as Rose's philanderer upped the ante.

"I'll do anything for you, Rose, absolutely anything. Just tell me and I'll do it."

"In that case, you can go and sit down in the middle of the motorway, or donate your services as a pontoon bridge over Lake Titicaca."

Nice one, Rose! He could picture her exactly, no messing about. Department Q in your face, mate!

A brief silence ensued, the testicle brain seemingly awestruck.

Then he cleared his throat, trying to sound as macho as he could. "OK, then. But no matter what you say, Rose, you're still so divinely ravishing that you make me tingly inside."

Carl didn't know whether to feel incensed or crack up laughing. What was it he said? *Divinely ravishing*? *Tingly inside*?

Had police headquarters gone entirely round the bend, or was it just him?

5

Autumn 2010

As the night progressed, Marco realized the necessity of finding somewhere to sleep, a pair of shoes, and some dry clothes. The people who were after him had called off the search, so the question now was whether they still had a man posted at the edge of the woods or somewhere else.

On the opposite side of the road, away from the trees, it was a good way up to the closest smallholdings and farms, but how was he to cross the road without being seen if someone was keeping watch? It would be just like Zola to make sure.

Marco knew the next few hours would be decisive. If he failed to get far enough away from Zola and the rest of the clan, they would track him down. Walking through the woods on bare and battered feet was out of the question, so there was no alternative: he had to cross the road.

In Italy the children's favorite game had been a version of hide-and-seek. The objective was to run from one's hiding place back to base unseen and kick over a tin can. Marco had always been best, so he tried to imagine himself back in Umbria on a carefree sun-drenched day, lying in the bushes, waiting for his chance to kick the can.

He imagined that the base was across the fields, behind the farms whose lights he could see in the distance. All he had to do now was stay low, emerge at the top of the ridge, and then leg it like a ferret after its prey.

Think of it as a game, Marco, then it will work, he told himself.

He waited until the beam of an approaching car's headlights swept across the landscape, allowing him to see whether the coast was clear. He saw the silhouette of a figure some fifty meters farther down the hill.

Marco couldn't tell who it was, but the way he stood huddled it was obvious the sentry was struggling to keep warm, just like him.

This wasn't good.

He'd have to crawl flat across the road. If he got to his feet and ran, he would be discovered.

He lifted his head and peered into the darkness across the fields. Not only would he have to crawl over the tarmac in pajamas as luminous as a magnesium bomb, but afterward he would need to continue in the same way at least two hundred meters across the black furrows of the field. And what then? Who could tell what awaited him if he made it to one of the dwellings? Perhaps Zola had someone over there, too?

He hesitated, waiting until the moon slid behind denser clouds. If he was lucky, he would need ten seconds at most, and then he would be over in the opposite ditch.

He wormed his way forward, easily at first, but farther out the wet road surface glistened in the moonlight, drawing everything into relief, so he turned his head toward the figure and studied its movements before pulling himself up. He would have to be ready to run if he was discovered.

The two of them heard the heavy vehicle at the same time, coming toward them from the other side of the hill. The figure drew back instinctively, turning in the direction of the sound, directly toward the place where Marco lay.

Marco lay still as a mouse in the middle of the road. The hard tarmac felt like ice, his heart pumping like a threshing machine inside his chest.

In a moment, headlights would bathe the road surface in light and he would be exposed. Seconds later the vehicle would be upon him, crushing him flat if he didn't move, but the man keeping watch still stood with his eyes turned in Marco's direction.

He felt the road tremble beneath him. It was as if the gates of hell were slowly being opened with the sole purpose of dragging him down into the depths.

And maybe that was what was about to happen.

Marco closed his eyes. It would all be over in an instant. Perhaps the world after this one would be better.

The rumble of the approaching diesel motor gathered intensity and as Marco submitted to his fate, he filled his last seconds with thoughts of his mother, of where she might be now and how things might have been if they had fled together when they'd had the chance. Then he thought of how he was about to be killed and the next morning, when birds would peck at what was left of him.

In these final moments of life he felt for the first time that he had never really meant anything to anyone. And thus he lay, consumed by sorrow and loneliness, as the blinding headlight beams appeared over the ridge and descended toward him with alarming speed.

At that moment, a dog began to bark at the bottom of the hill.

Marco was in no doubt: it was Zola's hound.

Instinctively he opened his eyes, realizing at once, as the headlights lit up the night, that the figure had reacted to the barking and turned toward the sound.

As though by reflex he sprang to his feet as the truck and its driver, whose attention was on the mobile phone at his ear, bore down on him without noticing his presence.

He leaped for his life with an eruption of sudden strength. The edge of the front bumper grazed his back, the blast wave sending him flying into the ditch.

Pain seared through his body, and yet as he lay half submerged in drainage water with his lungs wheezing and the adrenaline pumping, his abdomen cramped up with suppressed laughter. Maybe in a minute or two the dog would pick up his scent, the hunt thereby coming to an end. But right now the moment was his.

He had crossed the road in one piece.

And as he skulked through the landscape like a fox, his head down and his body bent, he continued to laugh as the shouts behind him grew fainter and fainter.

The door of the woodshed on the outer edge of the yard was fastened only by a stick through the hasp. It was an open invitation, a gift in the cold, black night that warned of approaching winter.

Marco looked up at the house, his teeth chattering. The windows were dark and only the wind made a sound. He sighed with relief. He would bed down here for the night, and in the smell of cat piss, woodchips, and pine resin he settled with his legs drawn up to his chest and a pair of old sacks covering his feet and lower body. Now it was just a matter of waiting until morning and then hoping the family inside the house had errands to run during the course of the day.

Even before the sun rose he was woken by laughter and voices from within. People at ease, seeking each other's company. So different from the harsh commands to which he had become accustomed in his life. He felt the sorrow and yearning of the night return to him. For a moment it was superseded by hatred and anger, though he couldn't say toward whom it was directed. Was the family here at fault for loving each other? And could he be certain that his father, or even Zola, had not at some point loved him?

How will I ever know? he wondered, again feeling overcome by solitude. What use were such thoughts, anyway?

He dried his eyes. He promised himself that one day he would make a family of his own and he would be certain what they felt for him.

With this solace he waited four more hours until the family drove away. Perhaps to do the weekend's shopping or to take the children to some leisure activity. The kind of thing of which he had only ever dreamed.

He crept up to the house and made sure no one was inside before picking up a stone that seemed heavy enough.

It took only a single blow against the pane of the back door and he was inside, a comforting landscape of material wealth of the kind all Danes took completely for granted. He stood for a while, taking in the blending of smells he'd had to do without for so long. The sweet variety of scents of the bathroom, a mother's perfume, yesterday's cooking, and the sharp aromas of new purchases. Furniture, wood, cleaning agents.

He had watched the father, mother, daughter, and son through a gap in the boards of the shed as they got into the car. An aura of security surrounded them that made them appear loving and kind. For that reason, perhaps, he stole only what he needed: clothes and food.

As well as a book that lay on the living-room table.

He found the garbage can to the right of the shed, lifted the uppermost bags of rubbish and tossed his ruined pajamas and underclothes onto the pile underneath, ridding himself of all that might remind him of his past.

An old bike in the outhouse tempted him sorely, and yet he hesitated. More than ever, he knew he had to keep away from public places: main roads, bus stations, railways—anywhere that might provide a swift escape route from those who would be looking for him. It was in such places they would search for him first, and for that reason he left the bike behind.

He stole away wearing a thick sweater and shoes that were a size too big, with the book placed in the waistband of his trousers and pockets bulging with cured meat and bread.

During the next four days small towns and villages appeared on his way with names he'd never hear of, like Strø, Lystrup, and Bastrup, potential pantries on his zigzag passage escape along hedgerows and woods toward Copenhagen. And when his supplies from the break-in ran out, the rubbish bins became his best friends. Only seldom was the abundance of household rubbish in these outlying areas lacking, and Marco wasn't too choosy to turn his nose up at leftover food and stale bread. At least not at the moment.

His timing was good and he reached Rådhuspladsen late enough in the day not to risk running into Zola's troops on their way home with the day's haul.

Before him lay the city's familiar streets and getaway routes, but this territory also belonged to others besides himself. An unguarded moment, the briefest lapse in concentration, and they would be upon him if he should dare to venture forth. And that would be the end.

From the building site of the House of Industry he craned his neck to peer over the fencing toward the ongoing metro extension and beyond to the Palace Hotel and the offices of the *Politiken* newspaper. Construction projects wherever he looked. Roads dug up, stacks of portable huts, mountains of concrete rubble, and truckloads of building materials, steel and concrete modules in every direction.

It was pandemonium.

Marco found his new life in the Østerbro district. The reasons were several.

On this cold November day he stood amid the roar of traffic on Østerbro's Trianglen, a hub that bound together the city's various neighborhoods. It was a place he had never been before. He looked down at himself and at the throngs of people going by, and he wondered where he was going to sleep at night and how he would find food. For who would help a filthy kid who wasn't one of their own?

The busy crowds were a temptation for Marco. An invitation almost. He was hungry, he had no money and no idea what to do when the night came. He looked around as thoughts reflexively crowded his mind regardless of his reluctance to acknowledge them. For the women's bags were slung so casually over their shoulders at the bus stops, and the men so carelessly placed their briefcases on the ground at their feet while they paid for their things at the kiosk.

Here he could earn enough to keep him happy a whole day in just half an hour, simply by stealing from people, that much was plain to him. But was that what he wanted? And even if it wasn't, would he be able to say no if he wished to survive?

He thought for a second about sitting down on the pavement by the telephone kiosk, holding out his hand, and begging. And then a snowflake settled on the back of his hand. First one, then another. Within a moment, people turned their faces skyward as the snow began to fall, spattering the facades of the buildings. Some smiled, others pulled up their collars, and when the air became a swirl of white the women clutched their bags and the men lifted their briefcases from the ground. The weather was against him.

If he sat down to beg now he would soon be even wetter and colder, and if he huddled beneath the meager shelter of the kiosk roof he knew he would quickly be shooed away. He was more acquainted with the psychology of begging than almost anyone, and a beggar at too close quarters was unwelcome. Besides, people were now heading off in all directions, winter having arrived without warning, their clothing suddenly inappropriate, Marco's included.

What now?

He surveyed the new scene. Buses with sweeping wipers, cyclists dismounting to step through the slush onto the pavements. Flagstones now slippery, once-empty windows now teeming with life as people settled in the cafés to enjoy hot, steamy beverages. But Marco remained standing outside.

It was no good.

He pressed his freezing lips together and picked out his target coming toward him from Blegdamsvej. He could tell she was going to veer off any minute to wait at the pedestrian crossing, for he had seen how her eyes appeared to be fixed on the 7-Eleven on the other side of Østerbrogade.

A schoolteacher, he reckoned. There was that kind of authority about her, as though she were used to maintaining discipline. Her bulging, well-worn shoulder bag was half-open. It wasn't the cheapest of bags, but certainly no flashy accessory either, bought to be used and to last. Marco's hands had been inside so many like it. He knew the wallet nearly always lay outermost. If there was a pocket, it would be there.

He walked past the buses to the crossing and waited.

It took only a second from her coming to a halt until he found the fold into which the wallet had been placed. He stood motionless until she stepped out onto the crossing. His hand slipped out as she moved away. She might feel a slight bump against her hip as the bag fell back into place, but her attention would be elsewhere.

Marco remained standing with a strange feeling inside him, the wallet now concealed up his sleeve. Usually his eyes would be darting to make sure he had not been seen by pedestrians coming from behind, and he would be away from the scene in an instant.

But this time, shame immobilized him.

Zola had warned them all against such emotion: "You realize, of course, that no one expects anything but the worst of us. The Roma will forever be branded untrustworthy. So feel no shame. It's the ones you're stealing from who ought to feel shame for their distrust. Their loss is our compensation and reward."

It was pure rubbish, for the feeling was there regardless. Zola had never worked the streets himself, so he knew nothing about it.

Marco shook his head. He saw the woman inside the 7-Eleven now, already with the items in her hand that she wanted to buy. In a moment she would be at the counter.

This was the first time he had ever really seen the vulnerability in one of his victims. Normally he would have been far away by now and the possessions he had stolen already passed on to one of the other clan members. The victim would be out of sight and mind, and Marco would already be targeting the next.

Was there anything in the wallet, the wallet he now felt burning his skin, that the woman would be truly sorry to lose? Did it contain anything but money and credit cards? He didn't want to know, nor did he want to be tormented by this feeling of shame. As of this moment, the days of Zola ruling Marco and his life were over.

He brushed the wet snow from his face and hurried over the crossing when the signal again turned to green. To anyone else, this would have seemed easy enough, yet for Marco these were the longest twenty-five meters of his life.

The woman was already rummaging through her bag in a panic by the time he reached the glass door. The assistant behind the counter was trying to appear patient, but it was obvious he felt she was wasting her time.

Marco took a deep breath, hardly aware of what he was doing as the door slid open and he went inside.

"Excuse me," he said, reaching the wallet toward her. "Were you the one who dropped this outside?"

The woman stiffened, her facial expression blurring like a strip of film caught in the projector, melting. Worry turned to dark suspicion, then to the kind of relief a person might feel when an object hurtling toward them misses by a centimeter. It was strange, watching her reactions. Marco braced himself, unsure what to expect.

If her movements were too fast he would drop the wallet and leg it. He had no desire to feel the tight grip of her hand on his wrist.

Marco watched her intently as she finally thanked him and reached to take the wallet.

He bowed almost imperceptibly and turned quickly toward the door, already on his way.

"Stop!" The woman's voice cut through the air. It seemed obvious to Marco that her life had been defined by issuing commands.

He glanced warily over his shoulder as the doorway was blocked by two incoming customers. Why did he have to go and hand back the wallet? They had seen through him, of course they had. Anyone could tell what sort of an urchin he was.

"Here, take this," the woman said. Her voice was so soft now that everyone heard it. "Not many people would be as honest as you."

He turned slowly to face her, staring at the hand extended in front of him. In it was a one-hundred-kroner note.

Marco reached out and accepted it.

Half an hour later he tried the trick with the wallet again, this time without success, as the woman he had picked out became so upset by her carelessness and loss that she clutched at her breast, unable to staunch the shock wave of sobbing that Marco had precipitated.

So he withdrew without his reward, but with the resolve that this had been the very last time.

The hundred kroner would simply have to last.

6

Early 2007 to late 2010

Marco received the shock of his life the day Zola gathered the flock and without warning revealed that from now on they would no longer live as Gypsies and had never belonged to that tribe, anyway.

It was the day Marco reached the age of eleven, and at that moment his respect for Zola ceased.

He expected his uncle to explain what he meant, but Zola merely gave a wry smile when he saw how the children reacted. Then he told them of the nights he had lain with a raging fever, his mind suddenly becoming clear, his thoughts collecting to focus on whole new pathways in life.

Marco turned and stared at the grown-ups who stood in a ring behind the children. They looked so odd with sheepish smiles creasing their otherwise stern faces, as though at once both glad and apprehensive. It was obvious something momentous was in the offing.

"I have awoken from my delusions," Zola went on, this being the way he spoke to them when they were gathered. They were used to it.

"As from today, you are blessed with a spiritual leader, a man who not only serves to unite the family in common endeavors, but who will also steer you on toward new and greater goals. Do you know what I mean, children?"

Most shook their heads, but Marco sat quite still, absorbed by the intensity of the man's piercing gaze.

"No, I am sure you do not. But though we have lived as Gypsies for many years, Roma we are not. Now you know." His words were as simple as that.

Marco frowned as his window on the world disintegrated. It was as though all life had suddenly been sucked out of him.

"And even though we feel tied together by the flesh as a family, this is not the case for all of us. But fear not, for we are all of us brought together by God."

Everyone sat as though hypnotized, but not Marco. He stared at the ground and tried to focus his gaze on a blade of grass. Zola said they were not all family. What then?

Zola spread his arms as though to embrace them all. "Yesterday it came to me that Almighty God created one singular day on which nothing whatsoever occurred in the world. A day when everything stood still. Yes, yesterday I read about this one unique day on which no plane fell from the sky, no wars raged, no event of significance found its way to the front page of any newspaper. On this day, not one notable personage died or was born. The wheels of history ceased to turn, if only for a day, for God desired that this day should be the purest, least eventful day on earth. And it was surely on a day such as this that the Lord Jesus was born." He nodded pensively. "And why did God create such a day? I shall tell you. He did so to perfectly frame one, single momentous event that took place on exactly the day in question." He closed his eyes tight. "And do you know what day that was, children?"

Once more, the majority shook their heads, even many of the adults could not refrain.

"The day was April 11, 1954, the least eventful day of our time. And several of us present here know why he chose that very day, and why the silence of sudden peace in the world descended in veneration of one special occurrence that was to outshine all others. And now I shall reveal to you all what it was." His face lit up in a smile wide enough to expose his gums. It had been a long time since he had smiled so much.

"The reason God did so was because this was the day on which I was born."

Nearly all the adults broke into applause, but most of the children merely stared blankly at Zola as though having failed to truly grasp the momentous nature of that fantastic day. Marco was among them.

For he believed it to be a lie.

Zola lifted his head and gestured for them all to be quiet. And then he told them of how as a young man in Little Rock he had fled the draft that would have sent him to the war in Vietnam, and of how later in Italy he saw the flowers of peace and love bloom among like-minded peers in the Damanhur movement.

The garb of the hippies became his uniform and during those first months he became enthralled by northern Italy, soon joining up with the other flower children who would become his family. And on one particularly enchanting night when the stars were out in their multitudes they vowed to establish their own community on the plains of Umbria, where they would live together like the Roma in solidarity with the fate and circumstances of that martyred people.

There were many difficult words, but Marco understood what they meant. The grown-ups had lied to him and the other children. They were not Roma at all, and from that moment, being Marco would be so much harder, no matter what Zola said. It was like having your skin removed and replaced by another.

Marco looked around at the other children. They were silent and motionless. He didn't like it at all.

Behind him stood two of the adults with somber faces. Once, Marco had heard them whisper that Zola had been expelled by the Damanhur movement for stealing. The other adults seemed not to have paid attention to this seditious comment, for they stood like an arcade of statues, as entranced as the children.

Zola raised his arms above them. "Just as with the Jews, God sentenced the Roma to wander the earth until they made themselves deserving of his grace. A curse lay upon them, as it had upon Job, so they were compelled to beg, steal, and rob their way through life. Yet this was but one example of the trials imposed by God, as when Abraham was instructed to sacrifice his own son. But friends, I say to you: we no longer need to bear the chalice of the Roma, for I have received a message from God and will show you how from this moment forth we can live as ourselves."

At this point Marco stopped listening. What could he ever believe in now? Were the clothes they wore not like those of the Roma? Had the spittle with which the local inhabitants so often had humiliated them been hawked for no reason at all? Had he listened to their oaths and been shoved aside daily on account of something he was not?

In the course of those few minutes Marco was stripped of everything. And he was shaken, even though he had hated his life almost every day he had lived.

He got to his feet and looked around. He was aware that he had a better head on him than most, but he had not known how painful this could be.

So who were they all now? Was Zola, who called himself his uncle, perhaps not even his father's brother? And were his cousins just some random children?

And if so, where was his real family? Who was he?

Therefore, Marco considered the day that one newspaper had referred to as the dullest in history as the day that had fostered the worst that could ever befall him: the birth of Zola. The one who beat and tormented them and forced them to beg and steal. The one who forbade them to go to school and denied them the chance to live their lives like everyone else. Zola, who with God's help now had more power over them than ever before.

The eleventh of April 1954, he'd said.

It was a day Marco truly loathed.

Some four years had now passed since Zola had made that speech and elevated himself by the grace of God to clan leader. It had been four years of terror and angst like never before.

The night following his address they decamped, leaving behind everything that belonged to their nomadic existence: tents, Primus stoves, cooking utensils, and many of the primitive tools they employed in their break-ins. The group numbered twenty adults and as many children, all dressed in their finest clothes that they had stolen from the outfitters of Perugia.

As they journeyed through northern Italy, Austria, and Germany during the days that followed, they broke into a total of ten shiny luxury cars with leather interiors, equipping them with false number plates and then heading in a convoy for the border of Germany and Poland at Świecko and on toward Poznań No one mentioned how they got rid of the vehicles and how much money they brought in, but one night the whole group found itself traveling northward by train through the Polish night. Some said Zola had summoned two of the men to his compartment to guard the money, and Marco mused that if the job required the services of two, then the sum must be large indeed.

In the ensuing months, Zola demonstrated to them unambiguously what he meant when he had told them new times lay ahead. In any case, these new times were in no way synonymous with good times, and so it was that several members of the clan disappeared without a word. Marco knew why. They had grown sick of beatings, being forced to work, and a life of need.

Everyone in the group knew Zola was a wealthy man and that he loved his money. He always had. The problem was that he kept it all for himself, coercing the others by means of threats into earning more each day. The begging and the stealing on which the clan had survived all through Marco's life was destined to continue as before.

When winter came they settled in Denmark, renting two adjoining single-story homes on a residential street within comfortable striking distance of Copenhagen. By then their numbers had fallen to only twenty-five in all, and had it not been for Marco's father's weak character, he and Marco would probably have disappeared along with the other apostates and the woman Marco had called his mother, and who no longer was mentioned by anyone.

Zola gathered the group together at regular intervals and equipped them with new, presentable clothing. He told them it made a better impression out on the streets. The women and young girls were given long skirts and tight, colorful tops; the men received dark suits and black shoes. Marco found it both wrong and impractical to sit on the pavement begging in his fine clothes, but it was another matter when picking pockets, snatching bags, or breaking and entering. In such cases, the suit was a help, making him a less conspicuous culprit.

In this way three and a half years had passed.

———

After battling the snow and strong winds, Zola, his brother, and their helper, Chris, eventually found the place in the woods where they had buried the body. The dog was with them, though in the circumstances it had been of little help. Frost and wind had banished all scent from the landscape, the ice-blue glare and glittering crystals of snow conspiring to conflate all visual impressions. It was sheer hell to be out in such weather.

"Goddammit, why didn't we do this before the weather turned? Now the ground's as hard as stone, we'll have to hack the corpse free," Zola's brother cursed, but Zola was not dissatisfied. Traces of a decomposed body were almost impossible to remove from the ground under normal conditions. A frozen one was that much better.

The most important thing, however, was that they had found it.

But Zola's spirits sank a moment later when Chris brushed away loose dirt from the body and its red hair lit up like a torch against the white background. Why was it not covered in earth?

"Do you think some animal's been at work here?" Marco's father wondered.

It was a naive question. What animal of decent size and strength would not have gnawed on the meat? None of which Zola was aware. The hound at his side, at least, could hardly contain itself, even though the corpse was frozen solid.

"I thought I told you to keep the beast in check, Chris," he hissed. "Tie it to the tree and start digging the body out."

Zola turned to his brother. "Unless he was still alive when we chucked him in the hole, someone else has been here."

"He *was* dead," his brother replied.

Zola nodded. Of course he had been dead, but who had removed the earth around the body and yet not raised the alarm? There were even finger marks where the soil had been scraped away.

His eyes scanned the scene in detail, stopping at the thin branch of a fir tree that reached out over the hole. It was covered in snow, but at its tip something was visible that obviously did not belong.

Zola nudged the branch with his boot, sending a powdery cloud of snow over the corpse and prompting him to shield his eyes.

"Do you recognize this piece of material?" he asked, pointing to the little shred caught on the point of the branch.

The way the color disappeared from his brother's face was answer enough.

Zola considered the situation. "Disastrous" was probably the best way to describe it.

"So now we know why we didn't find Marco that night. He was lying in this hole while we were out searching for him. He may even have heard what I said to you."

Zola's brother's eyes were dark and troubled as he stared disconsolately back at his leader. Desperation had set in, and that was the difference between them. Zola never grew desperate. That was why his younger brother had been appointed bloodhound.

"I can see from your expression that you realize I need to think about this. Only now there is no way back, do you understand me?"

His brother nodded almost imperceptibly, more a tremble than a nod. It was all he could muster.

"But that's how things stand now, and you need to grasp the fact. Marco must be eliminated. Completely eliminated."

Money aside, to a man such as Zola only two things really mattered: awe and respect from those around him. Without them, he would be unable to manage the clan. Without the aura of divine light in which he always took care to be reflected, there would be limits to what he could demand of his subjects. The absence of these limits was crucial.

The years in Denmark had been good to them. The Schengen Agreement, the police reforms that had increased bureaucracy and reduced the numbers of police on the street, the cutbacks in public services, all had been beneficial to Zola's setting up a network that took on all manner of shady activity. Here in Kregme, they could live without risk of being checked by the authorities, unless they were reported by neighbors. From Denmark, stolen goods could be transported across the borders without control. And within Denmark it was easy to recruit any number of Balts, Russians, and Africans, already resident in the country with the purpose of milking its hubristic abundance in every conceivable and inconceivable way. As long as he could keep the Eastern Europeans in check and his own clan in reverential esteem all was in order. But Zola was wary of the downside. The moment he showed signs of weakness, there were those in the group who would gladly and unscrupulously attempt to topple him from the throne.

Thus Zola maintained his grip as undisputed leader by acts of vengeance and other demonstrations of power, and no one withdrew from his circle without knowing they would be wise to stick to the unwritten laws and above all keep their mouths shut. But now he had encountered a problem that compelled him to submit to the decisions and motives of others, and here he wanted no witnesses. Not even Chris. For that reason, Zola locked himself in his bedroom at the appointed time and waited for the phone to ring.

"We have a renegade," was the first thing he said when his contact called.

His words were followed by an uncomfortable silence.

Although the man at the other end hired Zola's people to do his dirty work, he was more than capable of doing it himself if the need should arise, as Zola knew from several of his informants. The deal had been unequivocal from the start. If anything went wrong it would be Zola's responsibility and his alone. And if Zola proved unable to fulfil his responsibility it was he who would have to suffer the consequences.

"Our relationship exists within a web," the man had said when they entered into agreement. "It is a web of unanimity, silence, and loyalty from which we cannot and must not withdraw. And if in spite of this you should be tempted to try, the threads of this web will run with blood. That is the condition, and I shall assume we are in agreement."

There were no ifs, ands, or buts. Zola realized the man was capable of anything.

"A renegade," said the voice. "Would you be so kind as to explain to me how this occurred?"

Zola considered his reply. There was no other way than to tell it like it was. "One of the boys in the clan has run away. By chance, during his flight he hid himself in the grave we dug for William Star—"

"Careful what you say," warned the voice immediately. "Where is the boy now?"

"We don't know. I'm organizing a search."

"How well do you know him?"

"He's my nephew."

"Is that a problem for you?"

"Not at all. He will be treated like anyone else."

"Description?"

"Fifteen years old but looks younger. Approximately five foot five but still growing. Black curly hair, green-brown eyes, rather dark skin. No distinguishing marks, I'm afraid. He ran off in his pajamas, but we can assume he's managed to change since then." Zola laughed nervously with no response. "We know he took a necklace from the body. African origin. We might hope he decides to wear it himself."

"A necklace? You left a necklace on the body? Are you stark raving mad?"

"We meant to retrieve it, but we never got round to it."

"Idiocy!"

Zola clenched his teeth. It had been years since he had been spoken to like this. Had the man been a member of the clan it would have cost him dearly.

"And the boy's name?"

"Marco. Marco Jameson."

"Jameson, right. Does he speak Danish?"

"That and several other languages besides. He's clever. A bit too clever."

"Track him down and bring him back in. Where is he likely to have gone?"

Zola rubbed his brow. If only he knew. What the hell was he supposed to say? That Marco could be just about anywhere by now? That he had learned well and could be as inconspicuous as a chameleon in a rain forest?

"No need to worry," Zola replied, as convincingly as he was able. "Our network covers the whole of Sjælland. We'll take Copenhagen district by district, street by street, day and night. We'll keep at it until we have him."

"Are you up to it? Who's on the job?"

"Absolutely everyone. Everyone in the clan, the Romanians, the boys from Malmö, my Ukrainian fence. His organization is especially widespread."

"OK. I don't need to know everything." A brief silence ensued. "I'll be following this closely, do you understand?"

And then he put the phone down.

Yes, Zola definitely understood.

Marco mustn't have a chance.

It was imperative.

7

Spring 2011

The shadows were long and heavy when Carl finally pulled into a space in Rønneholtparken's parking lot. Normally the sight of the light from the exhaust hood over the steaming pots and casseroles would have given him a sense of comfort at having returned to the nest, but not today. Crap days at work always had their price.

He lifted a hand in acknowledgment as Morten, his lodger, waved to him at the window. But for once he wished the house had been empty, devoid of all life.

"Hey, Carl, welcome home. Fancy a glass of wine?" were the first words of greeting, as he dumped his jacket onto the nearest chair.

One glass? This was one of those evenings he could drink a whole bottle, no bother.

"Your dear ex-wife, Vigga, called," was Morten's second offering. Carl groaned. "She says you owe her mother a visit."

Carl glanced at the bottle. Unfortunately it was already half empty.

Morten handed him a glass and was about to pour. "You're looking a bit peaky, Carl. Didn't the trip go well? Is it one of those nasty cases again?"

Carl shook his head, took hold of his lodger's wrist, and carefully removed the bottle from his grasp. He'd pour the stuff himself.

"Oh, like that, is it?" Morten wasn't always the brightest of souls when it came to gauging Carl's moods, but today seemed to be an exception. He turned and went back to his cooking. "Dinner's in ten minutes."

"Where's Jesper?" Carl asked, downing the first glass in one gulp with scant attention to bouquet, oak-wood aging, or vintage.

"You might well ask. God knows." Morten spread his fingers in the air and shook his head. "He said he was off to do some homework," he tittered.

Carl found this rather less funny, his stepson's final exam being only a month away. If he didn't pass it would be a new Danish record for uncompleted preparatory exams and what would a lad of twenty-one do then, the way the world was shaping up these days? No, there was damn little to laugh about.

"Aloha, Carl," came a voice from the bed in the middle of the living room, indicating that Hardy was awake.

Carl switched off the perennial drivel emanating from the flat-screen TV and went over to sit at Hardy's bedside.

It had been a few days since he'd studied his friend's ashen face so closely. Was that a little sparkle in the paralyzed man's eyes? Certainly there was something there he hadn't noticed before. It almost reminded him of someone whose love life was suddenly looking up, or perhaps a promise that had just been fulfilled.

But besides that, Hardy was equipped with a built-in prism that served to filter the moods of his surroundings and that most probably had evolved through years of experience in the questioning of criminals. It was as if he possessed the particular ability to draw all the colors from a person's aura that represented his state of mind and emotions. It was through this filter he now looked at Carl.

"What's up, mate? Things not go well in Rotterdam?" he asked.

"Can't say they did, no. I'm afraid we're no closer to clearing up the case, Hardy. Their reports were like a bad movie script. No substance, poor groundwork, and very little reflection in any of it."

Hardy nodded. It obviously wasn't what he'd been hoping for, yet strangely enough he didn't seem bothered. What's more, he'd called him *mate*. When had he last done that?

"Anyway, I was going to ask you the same thing, Hardy. What's up with you? Something's happened, I can tell."

Hardy smiled. "OK. Well, in that case maybe you can also make a swift assessment and tell me what you reckon, Mr. Detective, though it may not be that obvious at the moment. Let's just call it a party game, shall we?"

Carl took a sip of his wine and scrutinized Hardy's long frame. Six feet, nine and half inches of ill fate under a duvet cover as white as only a home-health-care nurse could procure. The shape of his immobile size 14½ feet and bony legs that had once been so muscular. A torso that in days gone by could press anyone resisting arrest into submission. Arms as thin as spaghetti that were once more than a match for the flailing haymakers of weekend drunks. Yes, this was but the shadow of a whole person lying before him. The lines of his face, etched by endless days and nights of grief and worry, were ample evidence.

"Have you had your hair cut?" he asked idiotically. He couldn't see anything at all out of the ordinary.

A cry of hilarity went up from the kitchen. Morten never missed a thing.

"Mika!" shouted Morten. "Come upstairs a minute and give our detective here a clue, would you?"

Ten seconds later and Mika was up the stairs from the basement.

He was decently dressed this evening. There were days, even when the frost lay thick on the bike shed outside, when Morten's muscle-bound physiotherapist had no qualms about going around in outfits more appropriate to a gay beach in San Francisco. Unlike Morten, he had the body for ridiculously tight trousers and T-shirts, but still. If any of Carl's colleagues or his soon-to-be boss, Lars Bjørn, happened to stop by unannounced they'd never be able to look Carl in the eye again.

Mika nodded briefly to Carl. "OK, Hardy. Let's show Carl how far we've gotten."

He pushed Carl gently aside, then pressed a pair of fingers into Hardy's shoulder muscle. "Concentrate now, Hardy. Concentrate on the pressure I'm exerting and focus. Come on!"

Hardy's lips curled, his gaze seemed to turn inward, as though he were in pain. His nostrils flared. And thus he lay for a minute, perhaps two, before a smile appeared.

"It's coming now," he said, his voice stifled.

Carl's eyes darted over the figure of his friend. What the hell was he supposed to be seeing?

"Blind as a bat," said Morten.

"Who? Me?"

And then he realized what they were talking about.

It was as if a light breeze ruffled the cover of the bed, about halfway down. Carl looked back over his shoulder, but the patio door and the kitchen window were both shut, so it couldn't be a draught. He reached out and pulled the cover aside and understood immediately what it was they were all so eager to show him.

Inevitably, his astonishment was accompanied by a mournful flight back in time to the moment when Anker was killed and Hardy was hit by the bullet that paralyzed him. The moment when he felt Hardy's towering frame come tumbling down on top of him. Then to the days of Hardy begging to be liberated from the torment his life had become. And finally back to the present, where Hardy's left thumb was moving, if only slightly. Four years of Carl's despair and shame tossed away by the flutter of a couple of finger joints.

If he had not felt so oppressed and annoyed by the day's events he could have burst into tears of joy. Instead, he merely sat there as though turned to stone, trying to comprehend the significance of these almost imperceptible body movements. They were like beeps from a display measuring a heart rate. Tiny movements that represented the difference between life and death.

"Look, Carl," said Hardy softly, accompanying each movement with a sound.

"Dit, dit, dit, dah, dah, dah, dit, dit, dit," he said.

Fucking hell, this was amazing. Carl pressed his lips tight. If he didn't hold back he was going to start crying like mad. But he simply didn't have the energy at the moment. He swallowed a couple of times until the lump in his throat receded.

The two men looked at each other for a while, both clearly emotional. Neither of them had ever believed things would progress this far.

Carl collected himself.

"Hardy, for Chrissake. You Morsed the SOS signal with your finger. You did, didn't you? You Morsed, you big daft bugger!"

Hardy nodded, his chin colliding with his chest, exalted as a boy who had just overcome his reluctance and yanked out a loose baby tooth.

"It's the only Morse code I know, Carl. If I could . . ." He pressed his lips together and stared up at the ceiling. This was a momentous occasion for him. ". . . I would have Morsed a great . . . hurrah!"

Carl reached out and ran his hand gently over his friend's forehead. "This is the best news of the day. Of the year, for that matter," he said. "You've got your thumb back, Hardy. Just what you wanted."

Mika gave a grunt of satisfaction. "There'll be more fingers yet, just you wait and see, Carl. Hardy's so good to work with, there's none better."

With that he planted a kiss on Morten's lips and disappeared off to the bathroom.

"What happened, actually?" Carl asked.

"I can feel things if I try hard enough." Hardy closed his eyes. There was so much he had to think about now. "Mika has made me able to sense that my body isn't completely dead, Carl. If I work at it hard enough, I might learn to use a computer again. Maybe move a joystick with my finger. Perhaps even operate an electric wheelchair without needing helpers around me."

Carl smiled cautiously. It all sounded so promising and yet a little too improbable.

"What's this on the floor?" came Morten's inquisitive voice from the kitchen. "A silk pouch! Is this yours, Carl?"

He turned to his boyfriend, who was nonchalantly doing up his trousers. "Have you seen this, Mika? I do believe romance is in the air in our humble abode." They gazed lovingly at each other and hugged with less inhibition than was warranted.

"Can we have a look?" they asked in unison, looking like they weren't going to wait for an answer.

Carl got to his feet and prized the pouch carefully from his lodger's peach-soft hand.

"You lot keep your mouths shut about this if Mona calls, yeah?" he said.

"Oooh, a surprise! A super-lovely romantic surprise! And you're quite sure she hasn't caught on?"

Morten had become ecstatic. Inside, he was most likely already thinking about the get-up he could wear that would best match the bride.

"Absolutely positively not." Carl smiled. Their enthusiasm was catching.

"Hey-ay, Mona! Ooo-ooo, Mona! Tell you, Mona, what I wanna do . . . !" they inevitably began singing. In falsetto.

They didn't need to be *that* enthusiastic.

Dinnertime was all about Hardy. Only a single sour note served to dampen the euphoria.

As if it were the most natural thing in the world, Morten, his face a perspiring moon lit up by smiles, announced that from now on he and Mika would be pooling their resources. Morten's Playmobil collection had been packed away for online auction and, as everyone could see, Mika had already moved in. Carl considered wearily that by rights such vital matters might be discussed beforehand, but what good would it do to mention it now? Aside from the fact that Jesper now preferred crashing at his girlfriend's to sleeping at home, the domestic population had thereby gone up by twenty-five percent. And now Mika was sorting out his and Morten's wardrobes in the basement, so their acute shortage of space could be ameliorated by donations to the town's Red Cross shops.

No doubt he'd be keeping his pink sweater.

Rose was in a phase of hers that involved dressing from head to toe in black, albeit with the exception of an off-yellow scarf. For a time, the department would be treated to knee-length, black laced boots, tight cut-off pants, angular black eyebrows, and more metal stuck in her ears than there was in a medium-sized office stapler. It might have been all right for a punk gig back in the seventies, but it wasn't exactly the most appropriate outfit when knocking on doors in a murder investigation.

Carl gave a sigh, staring at her ears and explosive hair. If nothing else, she was keeping the hair-gel manufacturers in business. "Haven't you got a cap or something, Rose? We're going out on a little job."

She looked at him as if he'd just come home from Siberia.

"It's the eleventh of May and sixty-eight degrees out there, so what would I want with a cap? Sounds like you need to adjust your inner thermostat, if you ask me."

He sighed again. Clearly, there was nothing he could do. Staples in her ears or no.

On their way to the car, Gordon "just happened" to come charging over from the direction of the duty desk with more than one indication that he had been sitting in the window on the third floor, keeping an eye out for a situation like this to arise.

"Well, I never! Are you on your way out, too? How riotous! Where are you off to?"

He failed to notice the venom in Rose's eyes. It had been there since Carl told her what the day's job involved. As if he didn't know she preferred to choose her own assignments.

Rose's gaze descended the length of Gordon's spindly legs. "I'd say it was more relevant to ask you how far into town you're thinking of going without any shoes on your feet. Dickhead!"

The man stared down self-consciously at a loose pair of size 13 socks that already appeared in dire need of a wash. Then, looking like a turkey trying to jab its head in all directions at once, he endeavored in vain to conceal his reaction. "Humiliation" was too tame a word for it.

"Oops. Must have had my thoughts elsewhere," he proffered lamely.

Rose pinned him like an insect with her kohl-black eyes. "Moron," was all she said. And it stung.

Though Carl could hardly refrain from passing comment on her less-than-desirable young suitor, he stuck professionally to the job at hand and filled her in on the details as they drove toward Østerbro.

"So this Sverre Anweiler's never been arrested?" she asked, staring at the man's photo in her hand.

"Yes, he most certainly has," Carl replied. "He's been done for loads of things before this, but only minor offenses. Passing off false checks, renting out apartments that didn't belong to him. Deported from Denmark for five years at one point."

"Charming bloke. How could anyone ever point a finger at such a nice guy, I wonder."

"The victim who burned to death on the boat was a woman who had left her husband a note only hours before, telling him she'd found someone else. There's a statement to that effect from a witness."

Rose looked again at the photo of the man as Carl parked the car at the curbside.

"Was she right in the head? I mean, leaving her bloke for *this*? I can hardly imagine anyone less attractive."

Carl was about to suggest Gordon but kept it to himself.

"Yeah, well. As things turned out it was a bit of an unfortunate swap she made," he said.

"You said he'd been seen on CCTV. Anything else show up there?"

"There's footage from three cameras, all covering the pavement outside storefronts on this side of the street, so the angle's not that good on any of it. We'll be lucky if we can see anything at all on the other side, I reckon. The first camera's got a bit of the area outside the Park Café, though."

He pointed across Østerbrogade in the direction of the combined café and nightclub.

"He was hanging around outside the supermarket over there, keeping an eye on women going into the café, it looks like."

"And?"

"Well, then he disappears over to this side of the street. There's a theory he popped over to the grill there for a bratwurst. Then, on the second tape he's seen a few hours later outside the café with a woman on his arm, a woman quite a bit taller than him. I've printed a still photo, it's in the folder there somewhere."

Rose flicked through the papers and pulled out the cloudy image.

"It's the same man, all right, I can see that, but the woman's image is really blurred. How tall do you reckon she is?"

"According to Sverre Anweiler's record he's five foot nine in his shoes. I'd say she must be about six-two, wouldn't you?"

Rose held the photo up close and squinted. "I can't tell if she's wearing high heels, so how tall could she be, actually? Have you seen the stilts women wear these days, Carl?"

He declined to comment. When the mood took her, there wasn't a woman in a five-kilometer radius of police HQ who owned heels as high as Rose. Maybe it was why that flagpole Gordon had got himself worked up.

"The technicians had a good look at the tapes and she's wearing flats. Dead certain, they were."

"What about the third tape?"

"Yeah, well, that's why we're here now, Rose. As you can see from the time, it's only a minute and a half later and the two of them are no longer in the area here."

He pointed to the map.

"In that case they must have gone off through Brumleby."

"Yeah, they'll have cut through along there by that building where it says Rambow, but they can't have gone all the way through the rows of houses because they never show up on the fourth tape that's positioned on Øster Allé."

Carl nodded to himself. Brumleby, the oasis of Østerbro. Originally built by the Danish Medical Association to house workers in the mid-nineteenth century. Now the tidy rows comprised two hundred and forty desirable dwellings. It would be a hell of a job and most likely impossible to go through them all. In any case, it had been the first time the police had gone knocking on doors there.

"And the investigators never found out who the woman was?"

"Apparently not. Maybe the technicians were wrong about her wearing flat shoes. Maybe she wasn't nearly as tall as they thought."

"Did they put the photo up around Brumleby? If she lived there it'd be bound to turn up a result. People round here must know one another, don't you think?"

"The problem is, they couldn't really do that because the surveillance wasn't entirely kosher, if you know what I mean. The cameras were put up for the May Day celebrations in Fælledparken the previous Sunday, only they were slow to take them down again. That didn't happen until Thursday. The investigators were told by Police Intelligence that the material could not be used in the way you're suggesting. There are plenty of enterprising people in this city with the expertise and resources to make life hard for PI if their operational procedures become too widely known."

Rose looked at him as if he'd gone off his rocker. "But we're allowed to show the photo to people when we knock on their doors, aren't we?"

Carl nodded. She was right. It was pure shit. Bureaucracy and the surveillance society at their worst.

One after another, they took the narrow streets between the yellow and white two-story houses that had been converted into apartments, down one street and up the next. It was a Wednesday morning of mind-numbing routine. If only everyone had been in so they could be crossed off the list, but many of them weren't.

By the time they got to the hundred and tenth house, Carl was more than ready to step into the role of Rose's boss and let her get on with it on her own.

"OK, this is going to be the last one," he said, his eyes following a figure pottering about behind the panes of the front window. "You can do the apartment upstairs, then carry on with the next streets."

"OK." It was one of those two-syllable words that could be used in all sorts of contexts with a variety of meanings. In this instance it was intended to convey anything but appreciation, approval, or agreement. At best it was an invitation for him to provide an explanation, but Carl couldn't be bothered to argue.

"Marcus Jacobsen's packing in his job as chief of homicide on Friday. I need to get back," he said abruptly. She could ponder on it, if the information even sank in. But then she hardly knew the man.

"Not exactly the coolest way of showing someone the ropes, if you ask me," she muttered, then pressed the doorbell.

Carl listened. It sounded like the person he'd seen through the window was pacing up and down behind the door before eventually opening up.

"Yes?" inquired a heavily powdered version of his former mother-in-law. She was at least twenty years older than anyone else they had interviewed so far.

"Just a minute," she added, removing a pair of rubber gloves of the same sort Assad used when he cleaned their basement once in a blue moon.

"Just a minute," she repeated, dipping a hand into the pocket of her apron and stepping out into the sunlight of the entrance. She produced a pack of smokes, lighting up and inhaling with such contentment that her shoulders quivered. Carl nearly salivated.

"Right," she said. "I'm ready now. What do you want?"

Carl produced his ID.

"No need for that," she said. "You can put that piece of plastic away. We all know who you are and what you're going around asking about. Don't you think people talk?"

Their jungle drums must have been in damn good working order. They hadn't been here three hours yet.

"Are you trying to bother us, or help us?" she asked, a defiant look in her eye behind drooping eyelids.

Carl studied the list of Brumleby's residents. "As far as I can see, no woman your age is registered at this address. There's a Birthe Enevoldsen, aged forty-one, so who might *you* be then? Let's get that cleared up first, shall we?"

"What do you mean, *my* age?" the woman snorted. "You think I'm old enough to be your mother, I shouldn't wonder."

Carl shook his head accommodatingly, but the truth was another story. Going by the layers of wrinkles, he'd have said she could have been his granny if anyone asked him straight-out.

"I do the housecleaning," she said. "What does it look like I'm doing in there? Creating haute couture in a pair of rubber gloves?"

Carl smiled awkwardly. The sarcasm and use of French had disturbed his overall impression.

"We're investigating a case of arson in which a person was killed," Rose explained, making her first mistake. "In that connection we're looking for this woman here," she added, making her second. She held the photo up in front of the woman's face.

With that, all their cards were already on the table. If this woman did know the woman they were looking for, she'd be keeping her mouth shut now.

"Oh, my goodness. Arson, you say? And a person killed? What would this lady here have to do with it?"

"I'm sorry," Carl interrupted. "Obviously, the case isn't quite as clear-cut as that. The woman we're looking for isn't under suspicion, we'd simply like to speak—"

"Do you mind not interrupting just because a lady's doing the talking? You pipe down, mister, I prefer to deal with your punk rocker here. It might teach you not to be such a male chauvinist worm in the future," the woman responded amid a cloud of cigarette smoke.

Carl avoided Rose's gaze. If there was a grin on her face, the war between them that was always lurking latently would break out with an almighty explosion.

"Do you know her?" Rose went on impassively. People could call her a punk rocker or whatever they liked, she didn't care. Carl wouldn't have either, if he possessed her inclination to change identity.

"Know her? I wouldn't go that far. But perhaps I *do* recognize her. As far as I recall, she's in here on the desk."

She didn't ask them in, but there was little doubt she expected them to follow her, so they did.

"She's over here," she said, as they stepped into the living room.

She picked up a framed photograph showing a small group of women standing with their arms around one another and handed it to Rose. "Yes, I thought so; that's her on the far right. Nothing wrong with my memory, if I say so myself. Probably one of Birthe's friends from the conservatory."

Carl and Rose bent forward at once, squinting their eyes at the photo. It certainly looked like it could be her.

"She doesn't seem that tall in this photo," Rose noted.

"Which one's Birthe Enevoldsen, the woman you work for?" Carl asked.

She pointed to the girl in the middle. A smiling blonde-haired woman who also seemed to be in most of the other photos on the desk.

"I'm assuming Birthe actually lives here?" said Carl.

The cleaning woman glared at him, then turned to Rose.

"I started working for her just after she moved in, when Carlo was still alive. So it must be ten years ago now."

"Carlo was her husband?" inquired Carl.

"Good God, no. Carlo was my dog. A Small Münsterländer, lovely brown color he had."

Yeah, and the same to you, lady.

Carl frowned. "How tall is Birthe Enevoldsen, would you say?"

"Good God again. You'll be wanting her shoe size next."

"I'm sorry, please excuse my assistant," Rose broke in. "But is she taller than me, for instance?"

The woman hesitated for a moment, cigarette in hand, giving Rose the once-over. Then she turned triumphantly to Carl, who just stood there, wide-eyed and speechless.

Had Rose just called him her assistant?

"I'd say Birthe's about the same height as your boss here, Mr. Plod."

Carl ignored the smirk on Rose's face as they got back in the car. "Two things, Rose. One: never again refer to me as your assistant. I have a sense of humor, but it stops right about there, OK? And two: try running those half-baked thoughts of yours through a filter before you spout them out like that. You were lucky today, but if you're just as careless another time, you'll have people shutting up on you like clams."

"Yeah, yeah, Carl, I'm with you. But let me ask you this: which of us has got a hundred percent success rate and which of us hasn't? Besides, I'm quite partial to clams, so try again."

Carl took a deep breath. "For the moment, things are going fine, and that's good. We know the woman they were looking for last week isn't as tall as six-two, more like five-nine, if we compare the height of those women in the photo. So there must be an error in Sverre Anweiler's height as stated in the police report. I wouldn't be surprised if he was standing on tiptoes the first time he got hauled in and measured. But if we look at the still we got off the CCTV footage and compare the girl-friend's height with Anweiler's, he comes out more like five-five than five-nine in his shoes. A fairly short guy, in other words."

"Quite a guy all round, if you ask me." Rose snapped the folder shut. "If what the cleaning lady says is right, Birthe lends her apartment out to friends and other people she knows whenever she's away. If this girl-friend of hers needed a place to crash for only a couple of days, then it's hardly surprising if no one in Brumleby noticed her."

Carl started the car. "OK, so far so good. Now you can get out again, Rose, and stay here until Birthe Enevoldsen gets home. We don't want her slipping away from us, now, do we? Chin up, and get yourself a brat-wurst over on Sankt Jakobs Plads if you're feeling peckish. I'll entertain Gordon while you're away."

He watched her black-plastered face in the mirror as he pulled out of the parking space.

That mascara would come to a boil if she didn't watch out.

8

Winter 2010 and Spring 2011

"How much time will it take?" asked Marco, pointing down at his clothes. The elderly man in the dry cleaners threw up his hands and shook his head. What was the boy thinking? he seemed to say.

"How long to get this clean?" Marco repeated, and began to take off his sweater.

"Now hang on a minute, lad." The man threw his head back as though he'd just caught a whiff of smelling salts. "We don't clean clothes while you wait. You can't sit here in the shop in the buff, you can understand that, surely?"

"But I haven't got any other clothes."

There was a rustle from behind the racks of clothes packed in plastic, and a row of coats was pushed aside.

The man now peering out at him wasn't quite as effeminate as the first, but nearly. Marco could spot old gay couples at a glance. On the streets they went about with their little handbags strapped to their wrists and tucked tight under their arms. Always genuine leather clutched in soft, well-manicured hands and often with contents of considerable interest for an experienced pickpocket. But these gays tended to be more careful than most, which was the downside with this kind of prey. Perhaps years of hostile looks had taught them to be wary and take care. Perhaps they were just more fussy about their belongings than most. Marco had never really sussed them out.

"He's probably quite lovely, otherwise, Kaj," said the man behind the racks to his partner. "Shouldn't we give it a go? Look, he's even got a book with him, so he can't be that bad." He flashed a friendly smile at

Marco, revealing a pair of rather protruding canines. "But what about paying? Have you any money at all, young man?"

Marco produced his hundred-kroner note. He had no idea if it was enough.

"A hundred kroner?" The man smiled. "Well, let's see if we can find something else for you back here for the meantime. People these days are so busy that they systematically forget to collect their things. Or maybe they just can't be bothered. That's why we always want payment up front. Pretty slipshod, if you ask me."

Marco was given clean clothes from the back room and allowed to keep his money. If he came back in a couple of days, his gear would be ready, even if, as the men said, it was the dirtiest pile of laundry they'd ever had to deal with. And he could keep the clothes they gave him since they'd been hanging in the back room for over a year.

He saw the two men nudge each other and giggle as he went out the door. Perhaps he had made their day.

They had certainly made his.

Living on the streets was hard, especially to begin with. Marco was hungry round the clock. But he learned to maneuver without breaking the law, taking every little job that came his way. He started the first one at five in the morning when he offered to clean the windows of a bakery. In return they gave him an enormous bag of bread rolls. He wandered over to a coffee bar and traded the rolls for a cheese sandwich, a warm drink, and the chance to wash all the floors. And all of a sudden he was fifty kroner better off.

Soon his hustling between shops became a network of employers who would give him odd jobs to do. He ran errands, carried heavy shopping bags for people from the supermarket to waiting cars, split cardboard boxes apart and threw them in the trash, even though his lips turned blue and his hands trembled from the bitter cold that gripped the country like a vise that winter.

For weeks he slogged away in the snow and slush. From shop to shop and up one stairway after another. Often the jobs were difficult and laborious, and the customers demanding, like the madwoman whose week's supply of groceries had to be lugged up to the fourth floor in a cardboard box. She never opened the door but shoved the money out through a malodorous letter slot. One time he lingered farther up the stairs until she opened the door to take in her groceries, half-naked, her skin pitted with filth.

"What are you staring at, you little freak?" she yelled, jabbing a crooked black fingernail at him.

It was a side of Denmark he had never seen before.

Marco balked at nothing and did his work well enough that the majority of those he helped out didn't trick him. After a while he was raking it in, as Miryam would have said.

And all the money was his and his alone.

Work from eight in the morning until ten at night except on Sundays. Sixty kroner an hour for errands from the shops, seventy for putting up posters on the streets. It all added up. More than fifteen thousand a month, and he had neither rent to pay nor expenses for food and clothing. For the time being he wore what he'd been given by a woman who ran a pizzeria and thought he needed something less ill-fitting.

"You're a proper Latino, sweetie," she told him. "Don't hide it. Put this on, it belonged to Mario. We sent him packing back to Naples last month." And everyone behind the counter burst out laughing. As if any of them had ever been near Italy.

At night he bedded down on the street. This was nothing new to him. And yet he knew it couldn't last long, for it wasn't only the cold that was dangerous. Though most of his money was stashed elsewhere, there were still lunatics aplenty on the streets who would work him over for a lot less. His family, for example.

It was the gay couple from the dry cleaners who helped him away from such perilous sleeping arrangements. Perhaps they had seen him huddled in a corner of Nordhavn station, or maybe they had heard of his plight through others they knew. In any case, their faces were full of concern when they stopped him on the street one day in late January.

"You can do deliveries for us," one of them said. "And in return you can stay with us until we find you something else."

Marco recoiled instinctively, almost stumbling into a pile of snow. What they had in mind was definitely not on his agenda.

"Listen, young man. If we trust you not to do things to us that *we* don't like, then *you* can trust us in the same way, don't you think? You can't stay out here in the cold at night, it's asking for trouble."

The one who did the talking was called Eivind. It was he who would later come to regret their arrangement the most.

Out here on the upmarket side of the City Lakes that curved through the western margin of Copenhagen's center, Marco learned to view street life with new eyes. Whereas he had previously observed only objects ripe for theft, he now saw people of flesh and blood with jobs to do, errands to run and families to provide for, as well as plenty of people in whose lives all this was absent. Here he saw all facets of the city and its citizenry and realized that in most respects these people were no different from those he had seen walking the streets of other large cities. It was the empty, expressionless faces he noticed most. Unless their attention happened to be diverted by the display in a shop window, most people's eyes were fixed far enough ahead to avoid dealing with anything close at hand. Positive distractions, however, like the sudden appearance of a friend or acquaintance, prompted folk to stop abruptly and immediately flash smiles at each other that neither the situation nor their frame of mind a moment before would have inspired.

When this happened, Marco stopped, too, and started his inner stopwatch. As a rule it took less than half a minute for him to predict when they would say their good-byes and part company with convincing excuses about how busy they happened to be just now. And when his predictions proved accurate to the second, he would laugh and shake his head, rather impressed with himself. But if these people with their distant gaze were distracted by something less positive, their reaction was often less than amiable. The homeless who sold their own newspaper made people automatically veer away, just as they did from the junkies, the winos, the crazies, the confused, unkempt, or outrageously dressed, or the man with the accordion outside the Netto supermarket whose music could make the paving stones sing and gave the street scene a splash of color.

The Dane was at his kindest and most attentive when he was in familiar surroundings with people of the same ilk, that much was obvious.

And this counted Marco out entirely.

The first time someone hurled abuse at him, telling him to piss off back to where he came from, he withdrew to an alleyway and felt confused, small, and alone.

"Fuck off back to wogland, you stink like hell!"

"What's up, you fucking monkey, can't find your tree?"

That kind of thing.

On days like that, it could be hard to get out of Marco why he was so quiet at the dinner table. But after a while Kaj and Eivind coaxed him into opening up, and they taught him some potent phrases in colloquial Danish with which to retaliate: "What are you doing here on the street, haven't you got a home to go to?" "It takes one to know one." "Find yourself a job to do, like the rest of us!"

It cheered him up a bit.

Respect was something you had to earn. The street taught him that. He only wished it didn't have to be that way.

Weeks and months passed like this as Marco distanced himself from his past, and in spite of everything began to find faith in life and a future that consisted of more than just one aimless day after another. During these months in Kaj and Eivind's tidy little ground-floor apartment he learned to look forward and make himself ready to lead a normal life. He accepted everything they suggested to him. He honed his pronunciation, extended his vocabulary, and learned elementary Danish grammar. And if he misunderstood a word or his accent was too thick, they jokingly called him Eliza, singing, "The rain in Spain stays mainly in the plain."

"All of us live with a certain number of words inside us," Kaj told him, time and again. And in Marco's case the number of words was growing all the time.

In this small apartment on one of the humbler streets, Marco not only learned to trust people, he also realized that daily routines could make life easier instead of being the constant humiliation he had witnessed at home with the clan. Time became more amenable when his days were organized. And the desire to be part of a family grew stronger by the day in this apartment with its heavy brocaded curtains and porcelain displayed in every niche and cranny.

There could be boisterous evenings playing cards, with laughter that never ceased, but there could be more serious evenings, too.

"We've been thinking, Marco," said Eivind, one such evening. "You're here in this country illegally, and we're concerned about your future. Without the proper papers the day will inevitably arrive when all this will come to an abrupt end."

Marco knew this. Of course he did. He thought about it every night when he turned out the light. So that evening he made a solemn promise and defined his goal. He wanted to be the same as everyone else in the country as soon as possible. To that end he needed a residence permit, and there was no way the authorities were going to give him one. He, too, read the papers and knew the lay of the land.

He would therefore have to find himself another identity and the papers to go with it. This was imperative if he were ever to nurture hopes of leading a normal life with an education, a job, and a family. He needed this at any price. He'd have to find someone to get him the necessary documents.

Surely it was just a question of money.

The best paid job Marco found was putting up posters. To start with, the freezing cold made it hard work scraping the old ones off the poster columns and slapping on the thick paste, but once the leaves appeared on the trees and the warmth of spring set in, going round the city pasting up these colorful proclamations of coming events became Marco's favorite activity.

He was out in all kinds of weather and did his job well. He donned his cap and didn't cut corners by tossing half his posters in the nearest waste basket or pasting them all up on the nearest wall or billboard. Marco put his posters up in the designated areas, conscientiously scraping off the previous layers so the new ones would be less inclined to succumb to gravity. Few of the other poster boys could be bothered, so he had most of Østerbro and a good stretch up toward Hellerup to himself.

He found it fun, too. It was like scraping away layers of time. Often he found himself thinking how much he would have liked to have been part of all the events that had taken place. To have been in the audience at concerts, to have attended openings of art exhibitions, to have joined in the Workers' Day celebrations. But such amusement was denied him, for no matter where he went, he ran the risk of being confronted by those who were searching for him. When Marco was out in the open he was always on the lookout, never able to simply relax and enjoy life like normal people. It was just the way it was, at least for the time being.

Perhaps a day would come when he'd be able to live like these people, for Marco had his plans. A day when he was more grown up and had perhaps changed his appearance. A day when the clan would no longer be driven by its thirst for vengeance. A day when they acknowledged he didn't present a threat to them. But all this would take time.

For now, he would do all he could to secure his false identity papers. Hopefully it would be his final criminal act. Afterward he would earn his money aboveboard and begin to study. That, more than anything, drove him. It was the studying he was preparing himself for in his limited spare time.

At the libraries Marco found peace, for Zola's people would never set foot in such places. He knew that for sure. And Eivind and Kaj had told him that as long as he just sat and read in the reading rooms without borrowing anything, he would never need to show an ID to anyone. It was perfect.

Every day, Marco skimmed the headlines in all the newspapers. Every day, he paged through a new book. Those around him took note of his presence, he sensed it clearly. They saw that he was unlike the other dark-skinned boys who were always making a disturbance and hanging out at the computers to play games on the Internet. When Marco visited the library, it was to read, and if he used the computer terminals, it was to search for answers.

In just over two years he would be eighteen and would apply for enrollment at the Frederiksberg Preparatory College, and from there he would go on to university, no matter what. He had read a study somewhere that found women had to make an extra effort on the job market in order to secure the right job, something the study had been highly critical of. Marco thought they should have mentioned it was even more difficult for boys with an extra dash of pigment in their skin. Especially those who had not been able to afford proper schooling.

But Marco was determined. If he took care of his money he would be able to study without a student grant. And he wanted to study medicine; he wanted to get ahead in the world and be somebody. Not like his family, but rather the opposite.

Marco wasn't naive. He knew that all this at the very least required that he avoid the long arm of the law. Therefore, he needed to stay away from the kind of people who always paid under the counter, who more often than not turned out to be careless and ended up in court. It was what Marco was most afraid of: being turned in by those he knew and had trusted. For that reason, he was always cautious when dealing with any potential new employer.

Marco was ever wary.

At the same time, he kept a watchful eye on those who made a living from street crime. He saw them everywhere, like black shadows in the crowds. Suddenly they would step forward and pounce. Most often, their victims failed to notice, but Marco did. He knew the game from the inside.

Out here in Østerbro he never saw anyone from the clan. It didn't surprise him much. Zola's people operated in the city center, where the pickings were best, the crowds denser, so Marco stayed away. He also had to remember that Zola had many shady friends and business connections, not all of whom Marco would recognize by sight. He knew Zola's net was expansive and fine-meshed. Zola could trawl the streets for allies and anyone whose work might boost his earnings with no questions asked. Most were from Eastern Europe, but thankfully they weren't too difficult to spot. Criminal Poles, Balts, and Russians had a style all their own.

In no time at all the cityscape changed as warm, piercing sunshine brought Østerbro to life like a garden. Girls with bare arms, frisky children hopping and skipping. Only occasionally had days in Italy given Marco the same feeling of gladness. All of a sudden his aluminum ladder, his bucket of paste, and all his posters seemed so light upon his shoulder.

He waved across Østerbrogade to the kiosk owner who was leaning against the wall, taking in the sun as though he were home in Karachi. Then he deposited his gear behind the statue of the man who had given name to the square. It was out of the way there and would bother no one.

The poster column here was one of the city's best, at least on Marco's route. Squat and expansive, not too tall. Someone had told him the city had once been dotted with others just like it, but it must have been a long time ago.

It was a good spot, too. Gunnar Nu Hansens Plads. Bistros and coffee shops, the stadium, café tables in the middle of the square, cinemas just down the street, and throngs of well-to-do young people who were the target group for the events Marco's posters advertised. Which was why the column had grown a two-centimeter-thick layer of notices, advertisements, and event posters whose collective weight now threatened to remove the entire mass from its mooring. It was just the job for Marco. He took out his scraper and set to work.

When he was down to the next-to-last layer, he noticed a "missing person" notice. He had seen many that were similar, taped to telephone poles around the district, only they were for pets, not people. *Help! My cat has run away*, or *Has anyone seen my dog?*

But this one was different.

MISSING, it read. IF YOU'VE SEEN MY STEPDAD, WILLIAM STARK, PLEASE CALL THIS NUMBER, ran the text above a photo of a man, and then a phone number and a date underneath.

Marco stared at the image. It was as if the man's eyes and his shock of hair had suddenly become electric. At once, every fiber in Marco's body suddenly tensed and began to tremble, for it seemed that all the crimes of his past lay embedded in these sorrowful and yet so accusing eyes.

Marco took a deep breath and felt shock and nausea kick in, for now he knew he had stared into this face before. He began to shake, unable to resume his work. It was a sight that would remain etched in his memory forever: the face, the red hair, the African necklace.

The necklace Marco was now wearing beneath his shirt.

At once he felt hot. He loosened some buttons and tossed his cap onto the ground, studying the poster once again with bated breath.

He looked at the date. The man had disappeared three years ago. It all fit. This was the man Marco had seen in the shallow grave in the woods. The man whose decomposed body he had touched with his own hands. The man he had at first sensed to be a dead animal. The man his father and Zola had buried in the underbrush close to Kregme.

WILLIAM STARK, the notice read.

Now he had a name.

Marco stood as if paralyzed. *Have you seen my stepdad?*

And he had.

In that brief moment as he stared at the notice, with despair and bewilderment pumping through his body, his concentration lapsed. Normally his eyes were darting around, always on guard. But not at just this moment.

Like a hand brushing against his coat, he sensed a shadow come from the side. A figure silhouetted by the sun taking a swift, seamless movement over the flagstones toward him. Marco turned abruptly to face the man who was about to strike. So lithe and silent was the attacker that it could be only one person: Hector, his cousin. (Perhaps he was even Marco's half brother. Zola had never been choosy about his sleeping partners and neither had Marco's mother.) Hector had more beard and seemed coarser now than the last time Marco had seen him, but there was no doubt it was him. Yet even the brief moment it took Marco to recognize him and react was too long.

Hector made a grab for the African necklace, but Marco turned and Hector latched on to his jacket sleeve instead. Instinctively Marco let himself topple off his ladder, knocking his cousin to the ground and wriggling out of his jacket as he fell.

And with that he'd broken free.

He knew every corner of this part of the city. Over on the other side of Østerbrogade lay his escape route, a lattice of possibilities, a cobblestoned web of streets. He heard his own pounding feet against the cobbles as he ran through Ålborggade, across Bopa Plads and down Krausesvej without looking back. There was always an open door somewhere, or a backyard that led to other backyards. In this rabbit warren Hector didn't have a chance in hell of finding him if only he could gain a half-street lead.

It wasn't until he reached Svaneknoppen and the gentle rhythm of Svanemølle Harbor, where people were readying their yachts for the summer season, that he dared glance back over his shoulder.

This was his turf. Here he would always be able to disappear among the boats. Hundreds of masts had already sprouted forth in the spirit of springtime, auguring renewed life in a landscape of container terminals that lined the old harbor front.

He stopped to get his breath back and assess the situation.

What had just occurred was the worst thing that could have happened. They had his jacket and his tools. They had everything. Without his tools he had no income. And what was worse: in his jacket pocket was his mobile with the numbers of many of the people he worked for. And worst of all, they now had Eivind and Kaj's numbers, too. How could he be so careless? Why had he typed in *Dry cleaners* and *Home* in his list of contacts?

Marco drew his fist up to his lips. What was he to do now? He knew the ways of Zola's pack. Soon they would be on the scent, they would find out where he lived, of that he was in no doubt. Hector would not hesitate a second in reporting back to his leader.

Now it had happened.

He'd been found.

9

Spring 2011

"**All right, Rose, have** you found our perp? What did Birthe from Brumleby have to say for herself?"

Carl pictured his funereally clad and almost certainly thoroughly pissed-off assistant as he held the mobile to his ear and Assad's face popped up in the doorway. He waved him in with a wry smile and turned on the mobile's speaker. No doubt Rose had waited in vain for the woman most of the afternoon, and he didn't want Assad to miss out on the tantrum he felt sure was coming. It ought to cheer him up a bit. Rose at full throttle was always the high point of the day. Carl chuckled to himself. He wouldn't be surprised if the cleaning woman with the bad attitude had given them the runaround and her employer had never showed.

Oddly enough, Rose was as dry as a slice of toast. "Sverre Anweiler was staying in the apartment for a couple of days last week," she began, much to Carl's surprise. "He'd lost his own key to the place, but the woman he was with on the CCTV footage, a Louise Kristiansen, was staying in the apartment at the same time and she had one. So Anweiler arranged for them to meet up so they could go back together. Anything else you'd like to know, my little assistant?"

Carl's smile wilted a little as he did his best to ignore Assad's mirth. "OK, Rose, I'd say that joke's wearing a bit thin now, wouldn't you? Anyway, interesting information, but run it by me one more time, eh? Are you telling me this girl, Birthe, had invited the wanker to stay in her place?"

"Yeah, and this girl, Birthe, as you call her, is sitting right here next to me, so you can speak to her yourself if you like."

Good Lord, how indiscreet of him, but judging by the knowing grin now spreading across Assad's face, he found it funny, at least.

"I'm sure you can manage on your own, but thanks anyway. How come Anweiler was staying with her? Were all three of them there at once, or what?"

"No, Birthe's playing flute in the Malmö Symphony Orchestra at the moment, so they just swapped apartments for a couple of days while she's over for rehearsals. It's a very demanding concert, apparently."

"Whoooaa, just hold on a minute, will you, Rose? This is going too fast for me. Have you told Birthe there's a warrant out on Anweiler?"

"Yeah, and she didn't know. Neither does Anweiler, she says."

"She must be damn naive if she believes that."

"Do you want me to tell her? Like I said, she's sitting—"

"No, thanks, I'd rather you didn't. Just tell her we'd very much like to get in contact with the man."

"I've got his phone number."

Jesus! This was almost too much.

"Full report as soon as you get back, OK? And we'll keep an eye on this Birthe. She'll have to inform us of her whereabouts the next few days."

"I've already told her."

Assad emitted a suppressed grunt. It wasn't helping Carl's mood.

"One more thing, Carl," Rose continued. "We're sitting here at a table outside the Park Café, and next to us there's this ladder leaned up against a poster column. It looks kind of strange. Like whoever was up it suddenly did a bunk. Left his scraper stuck there and everything."

"No, you don't say. Man leaves job. Do you want me to phone it in to the Work Authority?"

Carl let out a sigh. What the hell was she doing, sitting at a café instead of back at Birthe Enevoldsen's apartment? If she thought he was going to get her latte refunded, she had another thing coming.

"Just listen, Carl. I'm about to get to the point. Just where his scraper's stuck in the layers of posters there's a notice about a missing person, a man. I'm pretty sure it's one of our cases, so I've taken it down to bring back with me. Just so you're warned."

Christ! No sooner had he let Rose loose than she was digging up more work for Department Q. If she reckoned every missing persons case in Denmark was best off on his desk, he might just as well book his bypass operation now.

He concluded the conversation, expecting to see a glimmer of irony in Assad's crumpled face, but the man's thoughts seemed to be buried in the folder he'd placed on the other side of the desk.

"I've been reading the Anweiler report, Carl," he said. "There are many things I do not really understand, especially now that Rose tells us this about the man."

What the hell? Had Assad started on a new case off his own bat? Was he picking up Rose's bad habits? What a fucking pair they were! Under normal circumstances Carl would have sent up a couple of blimps to ward them off, but right now he could hardly conceal his delight. Not in regards to the Anweiler case, which as far as he was concerned they could chuck into the Mariana Trench, but because Assad appeared to have mobilized an interest in something. What a welcome miracle.

Since yesterday's blunder about his relationship with Lars Bjørn, it was as if Assad had suddenly woken up, and Carl, for one, definitely didn't want him spacing out again.

"What exactly don't you understand, Assad?"

"The houseboat had no motor."

"No engine. Really? And so what?"

"It was quite a big boat, Carl, with lots of rooms and everything, almost like a little house. A living room with furniture, a kitchen, and two bedrooms. Cheap rugs and bookcases. Reproductions on the walls."

Carl shook his head. This was brilliant. If Assad kept going on like this he'd probably end up confiding that he used to be an interior designer.

"There was even a stereo they found among the wreckage."

Oh, boy, more details. Next thing, Assad would be telling him what sort of music they left in the CD player.

"And there was a Whitney Houston CD in the CD player."

There it was. Of course. Carl nodded and gave him a look that said, *Get to the point, Assad*.

"There are so many things that do not fit in with this fire on the houseboat, Carl. Especially the insurance."

Carl frowned. He knew what it meant when Assad's round eyes suddenly transformed into fathomless pools. It looked like this was going to take more time than he'd bargained for.

"The policy had been canceled. Yeah, I know that. And you think that's odd?"

"Yes, because only a week before, the boat was fully covered. Home contents, third-party liability, hull coverage, everything. Sverre Anweiler must have liked that boat and all the things inside it very much, don't you think, Carl?"

"Yes, maybe. Insurance fraud was my first thought, too, until I started reading up. If you read closely, the police report faults him exactly on that count, Assad, for the insurance having been canceled. The theory is that the woman's death was planned and the lack of any insurance payout would make sure no one suspected him of anything. The policy would have given him a hundred and fifty thousand for the boat and a hundred thousand for the contents if it hadn't been canceled. Not exactly a fortune, but a tidy little sum. Since Anweiler's got a record for fraud, linking the death with another insurance fiddle would have been the first thing to spring to mind if the barge had been insured. Some reckon he might have canceled the policy to give himself an alibi, and that the woman was killed for reasons other than economic."

Assad nodded. "Yes, I know this, Carl. But what is then the motive behind the killing? And the music in the CD player, what about that? I don't think a man like this Anweiler would listen to Whitney Houston, so most likely he did not put it there himself."

"Maybe. But what are you getting at? And what on earth makes you think a man like him wouldn't listen to Whitney Houston? Because he looks like a skinhead? You don't have to have hair to listen to pop, surely?"

Assad gave a shrug. "Have a look at this police photo."

He pulled it out of the folder and handed it over the desk to Carl. Anweiler was definitely an unappealing, anemic sort by the looks of him. Indeed, it was hard to imagine why anyone would want to have anything to do with this withered creature.

Assad jabbed a finger at the man's open-necked shirt. "There's a tattoo visible here. You can read about it in the reports on the other cases Anweiler was involved in. He had it done during his first stretch in prison."

"I'm guessing it doesn't read 'Whitney Houston.'"

"No, it reads 'Aria' in Russian letters. Look: A, and then a P that is an R, an upside-down N that is an I, and a back-to-front R, which in this case is an A."

"OK, easy as pie, I can see. I didn't know you knew Cyrillic script. 'Aria,' you say. Opera buff, is he?"

Assad's lip twitched. "Ha, ha, not exactly. One can hear you're a little stuck in the mud, Carl. Aria is a heavy metal band from Russia. Quite well-known."

A heavy metal band! Jesper had most probably given him a barrage of their decibels at some point.

Carl nodded. He could see that Assad's reasoning made some kind of sense. A devoted heavy metal freak was hardly likely to go soppy over Whitney Houston's cuddly vibrato.

"OK, so you think it was the victim, Minna Virklund, who put the CD in the player. But so what? There must have been loads of time between her arriving and the explosion that killed her. Why shouldn't she have put some music on? You probably reckon that if she'd just done a bunk from her husband, Whitney Houston probably wasn't the first thing she made sure to bring with her. Is that it?"

"Do you know what, Carl? I don't believe at all that story about Anweiler and her. And if it is true, why should Anweiler want to kill her then? What would be his motive? The report calls it a probable crime of passion. But on what do they base this? Cries had been heard coming from the boat, but nothing has been said about whose cries they were. I don't think this tells us anything. Perhaps she was trying to sing along to Whitney Houston. Have you ever been to a market and heard the camels bellowing all at once, Carl?"

Carl gave a sigh. What a fucking case. After all, he'd never asked for it. Not like this, anyway. What were they supposed to do now?

Assad rested his stubbly chin in his palm. "When you look at the crimes Anweiler was doing a few years back, you can hardly call him stupid, can you, Carl? They were quite complicated ones, were they not?"

"The last one was, at least. The online fraud. Still got done for it, didn't he?"

"Even so, Carl. This man is not without brains. But don't you think it would be dumb of him to return to Copenhagen of his own accord only eighteen months after killing a person in that way? And then on top of that, give his address in Malmö to an acquaintance? No, Carl. As we say: a single camel at the trough cannot yield a calf."

Carl raised his eyebrows. His assistant was beginning to sound like his old self again. Thank Christ for that. Was there anything Assad couldn't work his damned camels into?

Assad studied him charitably. "I can see you are not quite with me, Carl. But this is what we say when something is missing from the whole."

Carl nodded. "OK, so what you're saying for the moment is that Anweiler might be innocent. Is that it?"

"Right, Carl. Unless another camel suddenly comes trudging along."

Her face was as red as a lobster's as she dashed along the basement corridor. Together with the black mascara, billowing black hair, and yellow scarf around her neck, she looked just like the German flag in a stiff breeze.

"Looks like you've been doing some serious sunbathing, Rose," said Carl, gesturing toward a chair next to Assad. It was a scorching that was going to hurt like hell in the morning. The sun in May could be deviously malicious when, like Rose, your skin was as white as chalk. He assumed she must have discovered that by now.

"I know," she replied, putting her hands to her blazing cheeks. "We couldn't stay at Birthe Enevoldsen's. That cleaning lady was impossible, wouldn't leave us in peace. Used to sing opera, she says. You don't hear a vibrato warble like that every day, I'm telling you." She pulled a crumpled sheet of paper and a couple of postcards from her pocket and deposited them on Carl's desk.

"According to Birthe Enevoldsen, Anweiler sold his houseboat at the beginning of the month prior to the fire. He told Birthe he got a hundred and fifty grand for it with contents and all, but she didn't know who bought it off him, or that the boat caught on fire and sank a few days later. My impression was that she wasn't the type who bothers to keep up with the news or listens to gossip. Bit of a nerd, really. Know what I mean?"

Assad nodded eagerly, always glad of a good cliché.

"At any rate, she was dead certain Anweiler wasn't in Denmark when the woman died in the fire. She reckoned he was at his mother's in Kaliningrad. I can follow her on that. Have a look at this."

She shoved the first postcard across the desk. It looked like it had been made at home with an inkjet printer. The motif was utterly charmless.

"That puts everything in a new light, wouldn't you say, Carl?"

The picture on the card showed a smiling Sverre Anweiler with his arms round a woman in uniform. The two of them were standing in front of stacks of shipping containers in some concrete dockland.

A speech bubble had been drawn coming from Anweiler's mouth. *Best wishes from me and my mum!*, it read in Swedish.

"Apart from the gender, the son is the spittle image of the mother," Assad commented with a snort.

"The *spitting* image, Assad."

He was right, though. Ignoring Anweiler's tattoo and his mother's ample bosom, they were dead ringers: poor skin, pallid complexion, narrow lips, and drooping eyes. Two faces revealing that neither the inherited DNA nor life itself had been optimal.

Carl turned the card over. It was postmarked Kaliningrad, the day before the houseboat burned out. "Can either of you read these squiggles?" he asked.

"A very funny expression, Carl. 'Squiggles,' I understand this." Assad nodded enthusiastically, practically straightening out his partially paralyzed face.

Rose picked up the card again and began to read aloud: "'The trip from Karlshamn to Klaipeda took fourteen hours. The onward journey by bus nearly the same due to three flat tires.' It's in Swedish, of course."

Carl's eyes narrowed. Getting away from Copenhagen was certainly easy enough. The journey to Karlshamn required only a ticket available at any railway ticket office, no ID needed. In merely a few hours Anweiler could be at the ferry terminal, two hundred and fifty kilometers away in southern Sweden.

He picked the card up off the desk again and studied it more closely.

"OK, Rose. I'll admit it looks convincing, but the card could have been made a long time before it was postmarked. I mean, it's homemade, isn't it? What would stop him from getting his mother to send it on at some agreed point in time? The postmark only indicates where it was sent from and when. It doesn't tell us a thing about whether he actually dropped it in the mailbox himself."

Rose fidgeted with the end of her scarf. It seemed she wasn't buying Carl's take at all.

"But since you're giving it so much importance, I suppose we'd better take it seriously," Carl went on. "Check the registration numbers of those Maersk containers stacked up behind Anweiler and his mother, OK, Rose? One verified piece of information to the effect that they were stacked there after the fire and we go to Marcus with this." He nodded in acknowledgment: "Nice work, anyway, Rose. What else have you got for me?"

She let go of the scarf. "Birthe Enevoldsen's known Anweiler for years. She said he'd often gone on about visiting his mother in Kaliningrad, and afterward he was going to buy himself a motorbike and cross Russia from west to east following the Arctic Ocean, the Bering Strait, and the Pacific to Vladivostok, then back again from east to west through the border regions in the south. Maybe this card here suggests he actually did it."

Carl leaned across the desk. The next postcard was obviously a bought one. A little map of Russia on which a line had been traced with a blue felt-tip pen from Saint Petersburg through Arkhangelsk, Magadan, Khabarovsk, Vladivostok, and Irkutsk, where a ring had been drawn around Lake Baikal. From there, the onward route was marked by a dotted line going through Novosibirsk, Volgograd, Novgorod, and Moscow.

"On the back he writes that this was his route to Baikal, where he stayed the next four months. After that he ran out of money and worked for a while before heading on. The dotted line is the way he was planning on going."

Assad took the card and cast a glance at the postmark. "Look, Carl. The date is six months after the fire."

They sat for a moment as if trying to guess one another's thoughts, before Assad spoke.

"So Sverre Anweiler had a Russian mother and probably a Swedish father. And now I seem to remember that both Sweden and Russia allow dual citizenship. Am I right?"

Carl wondered how the hell he was supposed to know when he was neither one nor the other. Too bad.

"Then Anweiler could travel freely in both countries," Rose interjected. "I don't know the visa restrictions between Lithuania and this Russian enclave, Kaliningrad, but I'm sure he could have flown from Kaliningrad to Saint Petersburg without any bother."

"And the motorbike?"

"I reckon he probably bought some Russian job for a handful of coppers, don't you?" She gave him a dozy look. Was he thick or what?

Carl chose to ignore it and turned to Assad.

"So Interpol's warrant on Anweiler wasn't put out until he'd already swanned off across the tundra, is that what you're both thinking?"

His two assistants shrugged. It was by no means unlikely, they all knew that.

"What about after he got home, Rose?"

"He sublet a apartment in Malmö and became a roadie for Daggers and Swords."

Carl frowned, but she was ahead of him.

"A death metal band from Skåne, Carl. Anweiler's just been in Copenhagen with them, they played a gig at Pumpehuset last week. That's why he was here."

He nodded. "OK, it's taking shape. In theory, then, he was in Russia from a few days before the fire broke out until just a short time ago. In the intervening period there's been a warrant out on him from Interpol, but most likely he hasn't been in contact with the Russian authorities, and Swedish-Danish border control on the bridge over the sound isn't

exactly likely to put anyone off. But if we're right about this, then Anweiler never knew about the fire and just carried on with his life like
nothing ever happened. The apartment in Malmö was only a sublet, so
the police won't necessarily have much to go on in respect of his movements." Carl nodded to himself. It all sounded plausible, though he wasn't
convinced.

"And this Birthe woman borrowed his pad in Malmö while he was
over here, is that right?"

"Yeah, the place is practically next door to the opera house, so it's
very convenient for her," Rose replied.

Assad stretched back in his chair. "A rather odd friendship, I would
say then. How did Birthe Enevoldsen and Anweiler get to know each
other in the first place, Rose?"

"Through Louise Kristiansen. The woman on the CCTV footage who
he met up with outside the Park Café. She was trained as a percussionist
at the conservatory and played in a few bands Sverre Anweiler roadied
for. She was playing in Copenhagen last week, too."

Carl looked at the time. He was meeting Mona in half an hour. At a
posh café, for once. Not exactly her style, but for him the choice of venue
was excellent, for otherwise he risked the bonus of having to deal with
her unmanageable, eternally snot-nosed grandson.

"OK," he said in a suitably subdued tone of voice that signaled the
meeting was over. "There is a lot that points in Anweiler's favor, I can
see that. And a lot that would have been nice to find in our colleagues'
reports. Things that might have shed a better light on his circumstances,
such as his income source the last couple of years and his dual citizenship,
not to mention the Kaliningrad connection. Whoever was responsible
was most likely up to his ears in work while the investigation was in
progress, so it's hardly surprising if those ears turn red."

He smiled at the cleverness of his wit, but his assistants were non-
plussed. Then he slapped his palms down on the desk. "Let's adjourn,
then, shall we? I've got things to do, so maybe you can check up on those
containers in the meantime, Rose. And Assad, you can go upstairs to
Department A and fill them in. I think we should spare Marcus, seeing
as it's his last few days. But tell Lars Bjørn there's been a development in

an old case that'll probably give rise to some criticism being leveled. And then I don't want to have any more to do with that case."

He was about to get to his feet when Rose held the crumpled notice up in front of him. The edges were frayed and there was a rip through the middle, but the message came across clearly enough:

MISSING, it read.

What the hell did he care, only a quarter of an hour from the day's most interesting meeting?

He clenched the silk pouch in his pocket and felt immediately buoyant as the song began to play in his mind.

Hey-ay, Mona! Ooo-ooo, Mona . . . !

10

Marco was shaken up. He was just as unnerved as the people around him who pottered about in the sunshine on the walkways between the boats were relaxed.

The clan had found him. His secure day-to-day life had been abruptly torn away from him. Moreover, he was now marked by a dead man's stare.

The dilemma he found himself in was crushing. What was he supposed to do now, when all his instincts were screaming at him to get out of the city for good if he valued his life, and at the same time he knew he could not?

He had to protect his friends from Zola's brutal methods, and he had to protect himself. But in which order was he to proceed?

He looked out across the masts and tried to calm himself. The first thing he needed to do was to call Eivind and Kaj and warn them. Then he would have to pick up his things from the apartment. Without them he would be set back months, unable to pursue his goals.

And he would also need to do the rounds and collect the money he was owed. Altogether, it was a fairly large sum.

Marco buried his face in his hands. The case of the man with the red hair was sickening. He needed to go back and see if the notice was still there. All he could do was hope it was, for then he would take it with him and do some investigating. Perhaps then he would be able to understand why his father . . .

He shook his head. If only Hector hadn't got his jacket and his mobile, all these worries would be superfluous.

Now, instead, he had to be more alert than ever: he needed the eyes of the deaf and the ears of the blind.

He stood at the pay phone at Svanemølle station, eyes closed, trying to remember the number of Kaj and Eivind's dry cleaners. What were the last three digits? 386 or 368? Or maybe something else entirely? If only he had his mobile, a press of a button and he'd be connected. But now . . .

At his fifth try, the ringing tone sounding in his ear, he felt reasonably sure. And then he got through to voice mail.

"You've called Kajvind's Cleaners," came the sound of Eivind's soft voice. "I'm afraid we're not here at the moment. Our normal opening hours are . . ."

Marco hung up. He was worried now. Why couldn't they come to the phone? Had Zola's people been round? He prayed they hadn't. Maybe they'd just called it a day and gone home? No, that couldn't be it, not this early. What, then? How was he to warn them when he was too scared to venture anywhere near where they lived, at least for the time being?

And then he realized why the shop was closed. Today was Wednesday. For months, Kaj had complained about his bladder playing up, and he wasn't the type who went to the doctor on his own. Eivind had promised to go with him to the hospital, Marco remembered now. The CLOSED sign was already in the window when he'd passed by the place a couple of hours before. How could he have forgotten?

He turned away from the yachts down in the harbor, knowing this would be the last occasion in a very long time when the cries of the gulls and the salty breeze would be able to elicit happy thoughts about a future life.

Some time later he approached Østerbrogade from Strandboulevarden. He gauged the distance to Gunnar Nu Hansens Plads, about six hundred meters, and noted nothing untoward on the pavements or the street. Still Marco preferred the cover of the trees and bushes, now in leaf. They would offer him protection against being spotted from a distance, so he chose the longer route by way of Jagtvej and Fælledparken.

It took him twenty minutes, but he was leaving nothing to chance.

All around him, people lay on the grass, relaxing in the sunshine, but who were they? Were Zola's spies among them? Removing your shirt and pretending to be taking in the sun would be effective camouflage here. Hector would certainly think so, but then modesty had never characterized Zola's world.

Marco scanned the square minutely as he approached from the park. Again, there were too many people, too many dabs of color. Which one would leap out from the palette and accost him? Who among the café guests would suddenly turn in his direction, revealing an all too familiar face? It was impossible to keep an eye on them all. The café tables were all occupied, and everywhere young people sat cross-legged in clusters on the paving stones with bottles in hand, spirits high.

As far as Marco could see, his ladder was still where he'd left it. And behind the statue, his bucket with all his gear.

He found it odd that his things should have remained untouched. Had Zola instructed Hector to leave them where they were? Were they the bait?

Marco put his hands behind his head and stretched his back. He realized the cramp in his stomach was the result of nervous tension. Trepidation was the worst thing he knew. Rather the disaster itself rearing up before him than the knowledge that it was about to happen.

Would Hector leap forth the moment he stepped out into the open? Were there other clan members in the area? Should he cry for help if they caught him?

Would anyone even react if he did?

The doubt was real, for Danes preferred to stay in the shade when things heated up. He had seen it so often before. How many times had anyone tried to stop Marco or any of the other clan members in their crimes, even to the cries of *Stop, thief*? Formerly this passivity would make him feel secure. Now it served only to increase his feelings of unease.

He proceeded cautiously, step by step, across the square toward the poster column. And when eventually he got there he realized the missing persons notice was gone and his scraper lay on the paving stones.

Why was the notice gone? Had Hector seen him studying it?

He nodded. Perhaps that was precisely why Hector had removed it, so he could take it back to Zola and they could try to figure out what it meant to them and why Marco was so interested in it.

But although it made sense, Marco just couldn't understand why Hector would have taken it. It was unlikely that Hector knew about the dead man, and besides, he was as thick as a plank and hardly likely to give it a thought, even if he *had* noticed Marco's interest.

Marco stared at the space where the notice had been. Shit. Now the information he needed was gone.

"Hey," said a voice all of a sudden.

Marco gave a start. Were they behind him? If so, he would drop everything and leg it toward the stadium. It was not a voice he recognized, but then he didn't know everyone Zola had on his payroll.

"Take it easy, mate. I swiped one of the posters you took down. Is that OK? If not, you can have it back. It's just that my sister was at the gig, so I thought she might like . . ."

Marco heaved an enormous sigh of relief. The young guy sitting on the ground laughed as he held up a crumpled poster for a Sade concert the day before, and the girls around him giggled accordingly.

Marco nodded curtly and picked up his ladder. He needed to get away and quick. He'd already been there too long.

It was awkward, hurrying along with all the tools of his trade dangling, but Marco could see no other option.

If he was quick, he could trace back along the route and see if the notice was on any of the other columns.

Later, when the sun had faded and there weren't as many people about, he would check into the depot, get his money, and then do the rounds of the businesses on his turf. He would ask them to keep their mouths shut about knowing him if Zola's people happened to show up.

After that, I'll check out the man on the notice, he thought. Maybe there'll be something on the Internet.

And though, knowing Zola, he anticipated having to abandon the idea, he resolved nonetheless to see if he could get near Kaj and Eivind's apartment when the day drew to a close.

He would have to be extremely cautious, for who could tell what

Zola's next move might be? When it all boiled down, it was more than likely he'd already sent his people out to ransack the place.

Thank God they weren't at home just now.

He glanced around, breathed in deeply, closed his eyes, and folded his hands. "Dear God," he whispered. "If they come, please don't let them harm Kaj and Eivind. And please don't let them find my money."

He stood for a second, then repeated the prayer for emphasis, just as his mother had taught him God would appreciate. When he opened his eyes, he struggled to find peace in this new alliance, but it wasn't easy. The thought of them finding his savings behind the baseboard made his blood run cold.

The money was his only security, his only way forward.

A couple of hours later, when Marco had almost given up hope, he found what he was looking for, a good way out along Strandvejen. By that time, he had scraped four columns to the base without result, but on the fifth were two of the missing persons notices.

He removed them carefully, folding them up and concealing them under his shirt. Now he had the information he wanted. It felt good and bad at the same time. It struck him rather overwhelmingly that he had taken on the responsibility of finding out who this William Stark was and, if possible, the circumstances that had surrounded his disappearance.

What on earth had this man had to do with Zola and Marco's father? So many things seemed to depend on the answer to that question.

The best thing would be if he could get Zola behind bars without his father getting into trouble, too. But if that couldn't happen, he would have to consider the possibility of them both being brought to justice.

Marco folded his arms in front of his chest. The very thought was painful to him. He loved his father, and yet he hated him for standing in Zola's shadow and being so weak. It was the kind of weakness that only led to malice and betrayal. How often had he wished for a father who might provide him and his mother with a life that did not include Zola's daily doses of poison? No, Marco had had enough.

Something had to happen.

He had thought of visiting the library like he usually did, but his courage failed him. Instead, he decided to go to Kasim's Internet Café, in the most inferior of locations on Nordre Frihavnsgade, but close enough to Nord-havn station for Marco to be able to get away through Kasim's backyard in an emergency and jump on a commuter train within a minute. Thus, he sat now in the dim light at the farthest whirring computer and typed in William Stark's name.

To his surprise, he got thousands of hits. He refined his search to in-clude only Danish results, but there were still thousands.

Most were copies of each other, but the general message was plain enough. William Stark was not some down-and-out who'd had enough of sleeping in cardboard boxes on the street, or staggered about the city in an alcoholic daze, or shouted dementedly at the crowds. No, William Stark was apparently an ordinary man with a respectable job whose function Marco didn't quite grasp and would therefore have to look up afterward. What he did understand was that Stark had worked for a government minister and at the time of his disappearance had just re-turned home from an assignment in Cameroon. That much was clear.

Marco looked up at the net café's peeling walls with an odd feeling in his stomach. Why would they want William Stark out of the way? Nothing he could find online seemed to provide even the slightest hint of an explanation. On the other hand, he could see how old Stark had been when he went missing, and where he had lived. And he knew now that Stark could not be declared dead until five years after his disappear-ance, and that he had left a girlfriend and her daughter behind.

Marco found the phone directory on the net and typed in the number given on the notice, but without result. Disappointed, he typed the same number into Google's search bar, though with little expectation of a hit. Mobile numbers tended to be changed very quickly, especially those of young people. But an old Web page about a girl suffering from some pain-ful illness mentioned this mobile number as one that other girls in the same situation might call if they needed someone to talk to.

Marco carefully highlighted the number on the screen. So the girl who had put up the notice was apparently sick, her name was Tilde Kristoffersen, and her stepfather had gone missing. Gone missing because Marco's own father . . .

It was so dreadful he couldn't pursue the thought to its conclusion.

A gleam of light from the entrance door at the other end of the room filled him with a sudden rush of adrenaline, prompting him to look up from the screen. A man wearing long robes came in, and Kasim, the café's owner, greeted him warmly. It was a false alarm, thank God.

Marco stood up and approached the two men. "Kasim, would you have a mobile phone I could buy?" he asked. "I've lost mine."

The elderly Indian said nothing, indicating to his friend with a gesture that he would be back in a moment.

Kasim led Marco into a back room that in many ways seemed atypical for an Indian: bright walls, rather than white; IKEA furniture, rather than massive, dark-stained wood; a green office chair with yellow flecking, and a radio playing classical music. No cold light emanating from hand-chased brass lamps or a flickering TV screen with old Bollywood movies.

"Take one of these," Kasim said, pulling out a drawer. "I've a couple of old ones you can have for nothing, but you'll have to pay for the SIM cards. If you want a scratch card for foreign calls you can buy one of them, too."

"Maybe just a SIM card and a two-hundred-kroner pay-as-you-go card." Marco put his hand in his pocket and produced a note. "I've only got fifty for the moment, but you know you can trust me, don't you?"

The sun-seasoned man studied him with a look that all too clearly showed how these were words that had proven to be empty on far too many occasions.

"Of course," he said, after a few seconds of thought. "All in all, with the Internet time, you owe me three hundred and fifty kroner."

"Thanks. Is it OK if I go back to the computer again? I need to look up the phone numbers of some people I know. I can't remember them offhand."

"I'd already figured that one out," Kasim replied.

The calls he made were dispiriting. The greengrocer, the shopkeeper, and the guy who supplied him with posters were furious. What was he up to that prompted such suspect individuals to be looking for him? Was he some kind of criminal?

Their disappointment was worded most succinctly by the man from the bicycle shop: they were sure as hell having nothing more to do with a boy involved in crime. Was he a member of the mafia, or what?

All of them had been threatened with having their businesses burned to the ground if they refused to spit out what they knew about Marco, so they did. The mini-mart's counter had been smashed and the manager punched in the face.

Marco was on his own again.

He picked up the piece of paper on which he had written down the number of the girl, smoothed it out on the desk, and dialed.

After a few seconds there was a jingle, then a woman's voice at the other end. "The number you have called is unobtainable. Please try again."

In other words, the number no longer existed.

The doorway across the street from Eivind and Kaj's ground-floor apartment was one preferred by the youngsters of the area when they needed a place to hang around smoking, making out, or just messing around. Bicycles no one knew who owned were abandoned for no apparent reason against the wall, and the ground was littered with enough cigarette ends to make any bum more than happy. Marco now stood there as well, hugging the wall, his face turned toward the darkened windows.

He had been there an hour and would stay another hour or more, if necessary. As long as the lights didn't go on in the living room and he couldn't see the figures of Eivind or Kaj, he dared not step into the street.

Amorous youngsters kept hassling him, telling him to get lost when they realized he wasn't going of his own accord. But Marco didn't care. His only thoughts were for Eivind and Kaj and his belongings inside the apartment, and how to get in touch with the girl named Tilde, whose phone number was no longer in use. He wanted to know more before he went to the police with the posters he'd stuck inside his shirt.

Perhaps the girl or her mother could help him establish some connection between William Stark and Zola and his father. And if he couldn't get hold of the girl, at least he knew where they used to live. He had the address. Maybe there was someone at Stark's house he could talk to, someone who might know something.

He heard the drag of footsteps before he saw the figure coming along the street, outlined against the sinking sun. The man had a slight limp, as though his knee were unable to bear his full weight, and at this sedate tempo he crossed the side streets that knitted the district together. In his hand were two plastic bags from the dry cleaners. He used them for receipts and invoices when the books needed doing. So Eivind had gone to the shop after they had been to the hospital. But why wasn't Kaj with him? Was he so ill they'd kept him in? Was that why Eivind's gait seemed heavier than usual, or was he just tired?

Marco frowned. It was good that Eivind was coming now, but there was something about it he didn't like. Maybe Zola's people were inside the apartment. So he decided to step forward into the light of the street lamps.

The smile that lit up Eivind's face when he saw Marco was worthy of any father. But his expression changed to perplexity when he realized something was afoot.

"What are you doing standing here, Marco?" He looked up toward the apartment. "And why isn't there anyone in?" he wanted to know, as the unlit windows and Marco's silence made his smile wither.

"Why isn't Kaj with you, Eivind?" Marco replied.

"Isn't he home?" Eivind's smile vanished completely.

"I don't know. I've haven't been in yet. I thought the two of you were together."

"Good Lord!" Any second now, Eivind was going to go charging into the apartment, driven by apprehension. Suddenly the feelings for the man he loved had been converted to anxiety at the prospect of unexpected loss. Marco could feel it, too.

"Wait!" Marco blurted. "You can't go in. There might be someone waiting in there. Someone who's after me, Eivind. Someone you don't want to meet."

Eivind stared at him as though of all the disappointments life could inflict, he was standing face-to-face with the greatest. And then, in spite of Marco's warning, he let go of his bags, rushed across the street, and entered the apartment building. Seconds passed and a light went on in the window, accompanied by Eivind's wails of distress.

Marco hugged the wall. At the slightest sound of a scuffle inside he would have to make himself scarce. It was cowardly, but if the front door was flung open he would have to disappear in a flash. These were his thoughts as his heart pounded in his chest, aware that Zola's evil had now spread to these two people's lives through him. And then he thought of his savings, hidden away behind the baseboard, realizing shamefully that they were foremost in his mind.

"MARCO!" Eivind shouted from inside. It wasn't a cry for help. This was rage of the kind Marco had so often seen followed by violence in Zola's world. He had never heard Eivind yell like this before.

His eyes scanned the street. All was quiet.

So he crossed over and stepped through the front door, which was still open. Even from a distance Eivind's indecipherable ranting could be heard from within.

As in all the gay homes he had broken into, the hall was an overture to the dwelling's contents and character. This narrow passageway provided clues enough to identify the passions of those who lived there. In Eivind and Kaj's case it was actors, and especially actresses, of old, all presented in the most exclusive of mahogany and silver frames, adorning the walls like icons in the churches of northern Italy where Marco had once tried to find solace. Now these idols lay strewn across the floor amid shards of glass and broken frames. And beyond the alarming disarray, two feet in familiar slippers protruded from the doorway. Marco's heart almost stopped.

He glanced warily into the rooms he passed before stepping into the living room.

The sight that met him was a shock, but unfortunately not unexpected.

Eivind was kneeling beside Kaj, holding his head in his hands. Thankfully, he was alive and his eyes were open, but the blood that covered his face and the floor around him was a sign that everything might easily have ended differently.

"What have you done, Marco?" Eivind's voice was shrill with emotion. "Who were those people? Are you in trouble, you little bugger? How dare you bring this into our home! Tell me who did it! I know you know!"

Marco shook his head. Not because he didn't want to answer, or because he couldn't. He shook his head because it was the way his shame came to expression.

"Call an ambulance, Marco. NOW! And then leave. Get out and don't come back! Do you hear me? Get out!"

He made the call as Eivind, with stifled sobs, tried to console his life's companion on the floor. And when Marco went to his room to get his things, noting in a moment of relief that the baseboard was still intact, Eivind came charging in after him.

White in the face and convulsed with all the emotions that accompany complete and all-consuming rage, he took a swing at Marco and yelled: "Give me your key and get out of my sight, you fucking Gyppo runt. Right this minute!"

Marco protested and asked for permission to take his belongings with him, but in desperation Eivind tried to hit him again, then thrust his hand into Marco's pocket and poked around until he retrieved the key to the apartment.

He wanted to make sure the boy wouldn't be coming back.

The last Marco saw of Eivind was when he threw open the window and unloaded Marco's earthly possessions onto the pavement below.

Everything but his duvet and what lay concealed behind the baseboard.

Forced to leave behind the most important thing of all.

The couple in the doorway just sniggered.

11

That evening, Carl lingered outside his house waiting until the light was turned off in the kitchen, having no desire to deal with Morten's monkish compassion or Mika's gestalt-therapeutic manipulations. All he wanted was to get upstairs into bed and lick his wounds. In fact, he was planning to stay there until he went moldy.

Mona had given him the boot, and he was at a total loss. He hadn't a clue why, especially just now; nor could he understand why he hadn't charmed the panties off her before she demolished all his hopes with just a couple of sentences. He didn't get it at all, and the way he was feeling now he suspected he never had. At least not where women were concerned. What made them act so outlandishly, with such predictable unpredictability? Soft and fluffy on the outside; jagged and prickly underneath.

When would he ever learn?

He crept up the stairs, his spirits in free fall, and threw himself down on the bed with all his clothes on, trying desperately to understand what had happened and what the consequences might be. Usually he would reach for his mobile and consult Mona when such a Gordian-knotted noose tightened around his neck. But what about now? What the fuck was he supposed to do?

Café Bohème had not been Carl's choice, but when he finally looked around this exclusive restaurant and gazed out the windows along the Esplanade, he realized it wasn't the worst place in which to declare his undying love. He had been waiting for an opportunity like this for a long time, but it wasn't until a couple of days before, when he'd stumbled upon the shop of a Russian silversmith who created jewelry worthy of the gods, that he realized the time had come.

Carl had the ring with him, expectations sky-high, his fingers already clamped around the silk pouch in his pocket, when she looked him straight in the eye.

"Carl, I want to talk to you today because we've been together long enough now to ask ourselves what we really mean to each other."

Carl smiled to himself. It was perfect. No one could wish for a better prelude to what he was going to do next.

He felt the warm silk against his palm and prepared to place his gift on the table the moment she declared it was time for their relationship to be consolidated. A joint household, a marriage certificate at city hall—whatever she wanted, he was willing. There would be an outcry back home, of course, but it would all work out. As long as Hardy continued to provide the household with a regular income for Morten's assistance and Mika chipped in, 73 Magnolievangen wouldn't need to change ownership.

"What do we want with each other, Carl? Have you thought about it?" she asked.

He smiled. "As a matter of fact, I have. I was . . ."

She looked at him with such benevolence that he felt quite moved and paused for a moment. He had an incredible desire to smooth his hand against her cheek, to feel her downy skin, kiss her soft lips. And he noticed how her breathing had become sharper and more resolute, recognizing it as a reflex that usually signaled major deliberations and final decisions. But she was taking her time, and that was OK. Navigating through occasions as momentous as this couldn't be hurried.

"Carl, I'm so very fond of you," she said. "You're a lovely man, but are we actually going anywhere? I've thought about it so many times. Would it make any difference if we were closer together? If we lived together and woke up beside each other in the mornings?" She took his hand in hers and squeezed it harder than he'd anticipated. She seemed to be having difficulty getting it said. Perhaps she preferred he take charge. But

Carl merely smiled. He would allow her to answer her question herself, and *then* he would produce the ring.

The answer came without passion or enthusiasm. "I can't see it would change much, to be honest. I think we'd soon run short of things to talk about. And the good sex we have once in a while would happen less and less, don't you agree? Lately you've grown distant from us, Carl, and from yourself. Maybe it's best that this should happen now. You forget when we're supposed to see each other, and often you're miles away when you're with my daughter and grandchild. You don't see me as you used to see me, and you're unable to confront your own situation. You've stopped your therapy sessions in spite of what we agreed. I'm looking for development here, Carl, and have been doing so for a very long time. Long enough, if truth be told. Which is why I think we should stop now."

Carl turned cold as ice. He had wanted to say something epochal and decisive, but now he was reeling. Was that really the way she felt about him? He shook his head and felt dazed, unable to collect his thoughts. Words stalled in his throat, but Mona seemed clearheaded and determined. In any other situation he would have loved her for it.

"I don't know why it's taken so long for us to have this discussion. It's my profession, after all," she went on. "But now it's high time we did. I mean, neither of us is getting any younger, are we, Carl?"

He gestured for her to stop, and in the minutes that followed he tried anxiously to reassure her that things had been going fine until now, in spite of everything, but that of course he'd been having thoughts of his own as well. He mobilized his self-defense and charm offensive into a kind of symbiosis that safeguarded every word, every intonation. Where any pause too long might signal indifference, any pause too brief could make him appear panicked.

Christ, he was careful with those pauses.

Eventually she seemed softened and more compliant. As though the whole sorry situation had been caused by some kind of midlife crisis and all she had needed was to hear him talk. And so in this hour of reckoning he ventured to smile, making sure by way of conclusion to leave her the opening that all dealings between adults of equal standing required.

"So I'm one hundred percent open to any suggestions you might want to make, Mona." And for one tiny moment he had the delicious feeling of being back in business. Any second now she would take it all back and climb down, and then he would be ready with the reward: a small, but very expensive ring.

She gave him a rather odd smile in return and nodded. But instead of meeting him halfway where they promised to do their utmost for the good of their relationship and allow each other space for spontaneity, she seized her chance and turned his words against him.

"Thanks, Carl. In that case, my suggestion is that from now on we concentrate on leading our own separate lives."

Her words slammed into his stomach like a battering ram. His self-image, his sense of reality, were in tatters. He simply no longer knew the woman sitting across from him.

And the ring remained in its silk pouch.

It was too late.

It was one of those mornings when it took ages to become Carl again. How on earth he managed to make his way into the city he had no idea. The rear lights of cars in front and the recollection of Mona's eyes as she swept him out of her life were the only things he was aware of.

He made room among the piles of folders on his desk so he could put his feet up and resume the night's failed attempts at sleep. His body and soul needed it more than anything. But Rose appeared in front of him in full gear the moment he sat down, squawking something about the missing persons notice she'd shown him the day before.

As if he wanted to think about anything that had to do with yesterday.

He tried to shake some life into his cerebrum. He was supposed to be at work, after all, but his thoughts refused to get out of the rut that kept circling around Mona. A mere three hours of sleep was all the shock had allowed him. Even Hardy's remarkable progress that he had witnessed on Tuesday had completely receded into the background.

"Here, Carl." A dark hand shoved a pair of cups the size of thimbles over the desk toward him and Rose, and the stench of something decidedly other than coffee rose up from the clay-colored substance.

"I'm not so sure," he said, peering into the cup while Assad assured him that as far as he knew no one had ever died from drinking chicory coffee, and that its beneficial effects were well documented. It was something he remembered his grandmother telling him.

Chicory coffee? Wasn't that what they'd tricked innocent citizens with during the war? Had this affront to centuries of careful refinement of the noble bean really survived such a definitive, universal holocaust? What horrible injustice.

"It's like I say: weeds and cockroaches will be the only things left when we finally press the button," he said with a sigh.

They stared at him as if he'd suffered an acute brain hemorrhage. He was able to sense it, but so what if he *had* skipped a couple of steps in making his deduction?

He let it be and studied Rose's sunburned nose instead. She looked almost human all of a sudden. "Why is that notice so important to you, Rose? We've still got the Anweiler case, you know."

"The Anweiler case needs a name change if you ask me. Hopefully we agree that the man's innocent, don't we? I've written Lars Bjørn a report giving the department's investigation a good kick in the nuts. Assad and I have reached the conclusion that either the bloke the dead woman ran out on is worth having a chat with, or else maybe we should try and find out if she was technologically illiterate."

" 'Technologically illiterate'? Don't know the expression. What the devil does it mean?"

"Someone dysfunctional in matters electronic. A person who's unable to operate devices that have more than one handle or button. Thick as a half-wit when it comes to understanding a manual, switching from a dial telephone to a mobile or from sink to dishwasher. You know the type?"

Assad nodded attentively. No doubt it was he who'd coined the expression in the first place.

"You don't say. So you reckon the fire on the houseboat could have been an accident, is that it? And all the experts who've been involved are no more than a bunch of superficial chuckleheads who never bothered to let that possibility sink in and pursue it?"

Assad raised a finger in the air. Carl stared at it, fascinated. Where did all those hairs on it come from? Chicory coffee?

"That was good, Carl. Letting the possibility *sink* in. Just like the boat, yes? Very clever."

Carl closed his eyes and gave a sigh. Had his two most trusted and only colleagues been downing soda all night in a kindergarten, or what? Christ on a bike. If only they'd leave him in peace.

He turned to Assad. "What do the fire investigation boys have to say about this accident?"

"It seems they do not believe there was anything on the boat to cause such a very big explosion. Neither the gas bottle, nor—"

Rose interrupted. "When you're a lamebrain all sorts of accidents can happen. The right combination of hair spray on the kitchen counter, the stove leaking gas because she forgot to light it. Lamp oil to get the heating stove going, nail polish remover on the shelf. And how did Anweiler make his living? Think about it. He was a roadie and lighting man, wasn't he? Don't they have all sorts of things that get dead hot when they're in use? A spotlight, maybe, that he'd left behind, and the woman turned it on by mistake, and then it falls on to the sofa where she's left a couple of bottles of household spirits. There are so many possibilities, we just don't know. And basically I don't care, because it's not our case, is it? I was just told to ring doorbells, right? That lot on the third floor can work out all the answers."

Carl took a deep breath. With an imagination like that, Rose had no need to worry about her future. A new Agatha Christie was born.

"And Carl, you'd do well to think back on yesterday. Wasn't there something you couldn't be arsed about with this Anweiler case?"

Carl straightened up in his chair and donned his mental work clothes. It was high time he quelled his emotional hangover and reminded this cheeky shrew whose door had a shiny brass plate on it and whose didn't.

"I dunno, was there? Anyway, I know perfectly well where you're heading with this, and the answer is that today I can't be arsed with dealing with missing persons, so you might just as well get it into your head. You don't kick off a new case until you finish the one you're on, especially when not all its aspects have been investigated thoroughly, right? Besides, we've got any amount of cold cases as it is."

Assad gave a shudder of delight. Like when you realize your backside is freezing off because it's sticking out from your duvet on an ice-cold winter's night, and then you draw it back it again. His eyes sparkled in anticipation of Rose's reaction.

"So tell me, why would we need another case on our hands?" Carl went on. "Or have you forgotten the ones still up on the board out there in the corridor? All those cases joined up with Assad's red and blue strings? How many have we got at the moment, Assad?"

"What? Strings?"

"No, cases!"

Rose's mascara glare rumbled in his direction. "Sixty-two cases in all, don't you think I keep count? But this one's—"

"Listen, Rose. They may have done a shoddy piece of work upstairs on the Anweiler case, but so will we if we don't get our act together and tie up the loose ends we've uncovered."

Assad nodded zealously in agreement. Obviously some element of syntax had gone over his head.

"We need to take into account that the fire investigation was severely inhibited by the boat being totally burned out and having sunk to the bottom. On top of which weather conditions were bad and the current in the harbor was relatively strong. For Christ's sake, Rose, these technicians know what they're doing, they're experts."

She gave him a surly look.

"And don't sulk either, because it happens to be true. I've been in this job since you were a snotty-nosed kid, remember? And if you don't acknowledge the fact, then that's what you are still."

Assad rasped his hand across the stubble of his chin. It almost drowned out Rose's sigh.

"OK," he finally said. "We must speak to Anweiler. We need to know what condition the boat was in. Was it good or bad? Who was the victim? We must investigate her profile."

"My thoughts exactly, Assad. You might even bring Mona Ibsen in on that one. I think she might need something to get her teeth into." He smiled to himself. If she thought she could get rid of him just like that, she'd have to relocate to northern Greenland.

"Assad's right," he continued. "We need to get *all* that sorted before we can even think about letting go of the case, and you know that as well as I do, Rose."

She said nothing but looked like she was counting to ten inside her head. One never knew when the latent explosion she carried inside her was about to detonate.

Carl smiled wryly. He quite fancied trying.

"And yet here you come with another case that tickles your fancy." He gestured toward her missing persons notice. "What was it that caught your attention? The bloke's carrot top? Or maybe his bedraggled smile? Something about his eyes, perhaps, that awakens your motherly instinct? Whatever it is, I'll be buggered if I can see it."

She nodded, releasing the safety catch on the icy incendiary she was about to discharge. "OK, Carl. But you probably never had the kind of loving relationship to your father as the girl who made this notice had to hers, am I right?"

"Did *you*, Rose?"

Assad's eyebrows shot up as though released by a spring.

Of all the things Carl could have said to her, this obviously shouldn't have been one of them.

Before he even realized his gaffe, Rose had turned on her heel, leaving her coat and bag on the floor, and was gone, a departing "Bye" hanging in the air like an icicle.

"Oops," ventured Assad quietly.

Carl knew what he was thinking. Rather a boil on the ass than Rose on the warpath. Still, fuck her. Fuck her and the Anweiler case. Fuck Marcus for running out on them, and fuck Bjørn, too. Fuck Vigga and Mona and everything else to boot. Basically, he didn't give a toss about any of them, as long as they left him in peace.

And then he felt a trembling in his abdomen that spread to his sides. Not exactly uncomfortable, but still pretty spooky. It was as if all the veins and arteries of his torso and limbs contracted at once, then expanded again, and had decided to keep it up.

Then came a tingling sensation that ran along his shoulder blades and under his armpits. He began to sweat, then felt a chill. He didn't know if he was too hot or too cold.

Was this the prelude to an anxiety attack? He'd had them before.

Or maybe it was just Mona, coming back to haunt him?

With trembling fingers he grabbed Rose's coffee cup and downed the tepid contents in one gulp.

All his facial muscles twitched as if he'd just bitten into an unripe lemon. The rancid taste of chicory clutched at his throat. For a moment he was gasping for air, and then the sensation left his body.

Embarrassed and bewildered, he sat for a while staring up at the ceiling.

And then he let out a deep sigh.

Assad broke the silence. "I've already been upstairs to see Lars Bjørn like you said I should. He said they were completely on top of the Anweiler case and that Rose's criticism was a mile wide."

Carl cleared his throat, otherwise he would have been unable to say a word. "Did Bjørn really say that? Well, he would, wouldn't he?"

"Yes, he said the case was still on his desk, and they would make sure to nail Anweiler. He had everything under control, Carl."

Their eyes met for a moment, then Assad expelled a snort from the depths of his respiratory system like the snore of a man with sleep apnoea.

"Just kidding, Carl. The man doesn't know his ass from his tip."

Carl smiled. "His *tit*, Assad. He doesn't know his ass from his *tit*. Anyway, I reckon I'll just pop up and have a word with Marcus Jacobsen. In the meantime, perhaps you wouldn't mind calling the deceased woman's ex-husband and ask him to come in as soon as possible? Tell him he can choose between a taxi or a patrol car."

12

There was an odd mood about the homicide chief's office. Opening the door of this confetti-strewn hell was like entering a chaotic crime scene. Shredded or torn-up documents, technical reports, photos that ordinary citizens would be unlikely to forget in a hurry, the contents of drawers littered across the desk. Carl could see Marcus was clearing out, but it looked more like the mementos of centuries of discord and strife.

"Who tossed the hand grenade, Marcus?" he ventured, trying to pick out a surface that could be sat upon. He couldn't find any.

"Lis'll be here soon with some trash bags. Can't it wait half an hour, Carl?"

"I just wanted to say that Department Q will be taking on the Anweiler case. We've had a breakthrough."

Jacobsen paused, his hand inserted in a drawer among a mishmash of old erasers, broken pencils, empty pens, and the kind of crud that accumulates in such places by the kilo in the course of a number of years.

"No, Department Q is not, Carl. That case belongs up here. It wasn't a freebie, just something to give Rose some practice, remember? You must have learned by now that your cases are the ones we formally send down to you. You can't pick and choose, only decide what order you want to take them in."

"Now you're oriented, Marcus. Think of it as a farewell present. Before you know it the case will be solved and you can give yourself another merit badge. You deserve a nice little success story to wrap up your final days. How are you doing, anyway? All right?"

Marcus looked up with a jolt, as if all the nerve endings under his professional exterior had suddenly been exposed. If this was what his retirement was doing to him already, what would he be like in a month or a year? Why the hell was he going through with it? And how old was he, anyway? Sixty?

"I have to warn you, Carl. I know how you feel about Lars Bjørn, but he's a good man, so there's no need to get on the wrong side of him."

"Thanks for the warning. But if he can't take it, he can give me the boot, I couldn't care less. And then he can have a little think about what he's going to do with Department Q. He's not going to run the risk of saying good-bye to all the funding our department brings in for you lot to siphon off, is he? Besides, he hasn't got a clue what that case is about, believe me."

The homicide boss leaned his head back and closed his eyes. Perhaps he had a headache. Carl had never seen him so distracted.

"Maybe, maybe not," he said, sounding fatigued. "But Bjørn could quite easily hand your department over to someone else if that's what you want, Carl. You built Department Q up, but it was Bjørn who was the architect, not me. So I'd keep a low profile if I were you."

"The husband of the woman who died on the boat is upstairs at the duty desk, Carl," said Assad, popping his head round the door of Carl's office. "He's an oil worker on one of the rigs, so we were lucky he was at home."

Carl nodded. "Oil worker" sounded not half bad. Men like them were used to gritting their teeth in a gale and taking things in their stride. Which was why their secrets weren't the most difficult to uncover either.

He'd expected a man with fists like a vise and shoulders as broad as the Storebælt Bridge, but he was mistaken. The man actually looked a lot like Sverre Anweiler. The type of man their victim apparently had a hard time saying no to.

He looked small beside Assad, almost like a person transformed by some inner vacuum. Chest concave, shoulders meager as a child's. Only his eyes revealed mettle, the will to do what was required. A man with the right stuff.

"What kind of hole's this you've dragged me into? Looks like an effing dungeon." He expelled a hollow laugh. "I hope you realize torture's not allowed in Denmark." He extended a hand. In spite of its inferior size his handshake was strong. "Ralf Virklund, Minna's husband. What did you want to see me about?"

Carl asked him to take a seat. "My assistant and I have taken over the case of the fire in which your wife died. We've been going through the details and there seem to be a number of issues outstanding."

The man nodded. He seemed cooperative enough. If he was nervous he was keeping it well hidden.

"According to the files, your wife left you immediately prior to the fatal event. She wrote you a letter informing you she'd found something better. Would you like to comment on that?"

Virklund nodded and looked at the floor. Obviously, this wasn't something he was proud of. "Can't say I blame her. How would you like sharing a bed with someone who was only home once in a blue moon?"

Touché! What the hell was he supposed to say to that? Once in a blue moon with Mona would have been a world record. Why did he have to start thinking about that now?

"That's not so unusual, many people live like that," Assad replied on his behalf with an exaggerated smile. OK, so this was a good cop/bad cop interrogation, and now it was Carl's turn to be the bastard. The way he was feeling, he didn't mind one bit.

He leaned across the desk. "Listen, Ralf, you can forget the shit, OK? You can't really believe it makes sense for her to swap you for someone else who was hardly ever home either."

Virklund stared at him, perplexed. "I thought we'd sorted that one out. Dammit, I've already told the police several times that Minna didn't even know the man. She bought his houseboat off him, that's all. End of story!"

Carl looked at Assad. Like some pensive nomad asked about where best to find shade in the desert, he sat nodding wisely and rather absentmindedly. What was he up to?

"Listen here, Mr. Virklund. What you're telling us now isn't anywhere in the report," said Carl. "And since any statement like that would *have* to be included, I don't believe you ever really told them."

"And I know for a fact I did. What's more, I explained to them I had no idea there'd been a fire on the houseboat and that Minna was dead before the cops told me. It was a shock, and I hope that effing report says so. I also told them Minna had nothing to do with the bloke besides buying his boat off him. Otherwise I want to see that report. I'm assuming I can?"

Carl gave Assad a look that said, *Your turn, friend.* After all, unlike Carl, Assad had read the report in detail. But what was the man doing? Nothing, apart from sitting there under his palm tree with a daft grin on his face.

It was enough to get on your nerves. His frustration needed an outlet.

"I reckon you did your wife in because she was being unfaithful, and you started that fire—"

"Erm, Ralf," Assad interrupted. "How much crude oil does one of those rigs pump out of the sea bed on a good day?"

The man gawped quizzically. He wasn't the only one.

"You see, I'm asking because then we can work out how much gas and other shit comes up with it. Like the crap you just fed us, yeah?"

A furrow appeared on Virklund's brow.

"I called your employers," Assad went on, still smiling inscrutably. "They are very happy with you, Ralf. This was my impression."

Virklund nodded and grunted an acknowledgment. The look on his face said he was curious as to what was coming next.

"However, since I was asking, they also felt obliged to tell me you have a bit of a temper. And that you like to show people you aren't afraid of anything. Am I right?"

The man gave a shrug. The interview was taking a turn in the wrong direction and he clearly sensed as much. "OK, that's true, but I've never been violent with Minna, if that's what you're implying. There might have been the odd fight in a bar now and again, but I've never been done for violence, as I'm sure you well know."

"I'm thinking now that the inspector and I will go round to the building you and Minna lived in and have a chat with some of your neighbors about this. What do you think about that?"

Virklund snorted. "Do what you fucking well like. They were never any friends of mine anyway. Muslims and country bumpkins from Jutland and other forms of dross."

Country bumpkins from Jutland? Was this his way of picking a fight? Pretty ingenious.

Assad got to his feet, still smiling broadly, and punched the bloke in the face.

An action as astonishing as it was wrong and mean, especially here on HQ turf.

But Assad stilled Carl's protests with a nod of his head. He leaned calmly over the man, with his hands planted firmly on his knees, and peered into Virklund's nose-bleeding face.

Less than ten centimeters separated their eyes.

What the hell was happening? Any second now, Virklund would be on his feet and going berserk. His rage was unmistakable. Was Assad planning on throwing him in the slammer for assaulting a police officer? Were they going to have to lie about who threw the first punch?

Then, to Carl's utter surprise, both men burst out laughing. Assad straightened up and gave the man a pat on the shoulder, reached into his pocket and handed him a handkerchief.

"He has a sense of humor, Carl, did you see it?" Assad grinned.

Virklund nodded. His nose was throbbing, but he seemed pleased they'd got *that* sorted, at least.

"As long as you don't do it again," he said.

"As long as you don't say I'm from Jutland," Assad replied.

And then they broke out laughing again. Christ on a bike.

Carl had been completely sidelined, but that wasn't what bothered him. It was like a wedge had been driven through his impression of Assad. On the one hand, the resolute nature of Assad's intervention made him feel oddly enlivened, for it was a sign that his assistant was getting back to his old self again. But on the other hand it raised the issue of what there might be about Assad's nature, or perhaps his past, that made him capable of using violence in such a controlled manner. In any case, it definitely wasn't something one saw every day.

"One more question before we throw you out," said Assad.

What was he doing? Virklund wasn't going to get off that lightly, surely? They'd only just started.

"Your wife was, how do you say, all thumbs, yes?"

Virklund jerked his head back as if another jab from Assad's calloused fist was on its way.

"How the hell do you know that?" he asked, astonished.

"She was, then?"

"Minna was so damn clumsy, my mother didn't want us coming round. You've never seen as much broken china as the first time she was there." Virklund nodded. "Yeah, it didn't take much to get her into a right dither."

Assad looked at Carl inquiringly.

"To get into a dither means to become flustered or confused, Assad," he explained.

It didn't seem to clear matters up.

"So what you're saying is she was no good with electronic gadgets and machines, and stuff like that?" Assad went on.

Virklund suppressed a chuckle. "I'll put it this way: if she used a toaster it was the toaster that got burned, not the bread. But—"

He stopped in mid-sentence.

They all looked at one another.

"I need to say to you, Assad, that I can't condone your beating people up in my office," Carl said, after the man had gone. "I hope you realize that one more incident like that and you'll be out on your ass. Explain yourself."

"Come on now, Carl, you saw how it lightened up the mood. You know, when a camel farts there can be two reasons."

Oh God, not those effing camels again.

"Either they have eaten too much grass or else it's just to hear some music beneath the desert sun."

"For Pete's sake, Assad. Is that supposed to justify your punching the man?"

"I am only trying to say that being out on an oil rig so much of the time must be a little dull."

"I'm sure it is. So you were demonstrating that brawls are just a form of entertainment for the man, is that it?"

"Yes, he fights for the fun of it, Carl. You saw what happened. He knew he was insulting us and I showed him how one deals with it and that afterward there need be no hard feelings. I punched him and we were even. He understood this."

"So like the camel he lets go of his inhibitions for the sake of bringing a bit of music into his life, and that's why he's always getting into fights. But why shouldn't he let loose on his wife for the same reason?"

"Because beating up your wife is not half as much fun as beating up your friends, that's why."

"I'd say that was a very wobbly basis on which to write him off as a killer, Assad."

"I am not writing him off. But, Carl, he who prods the camel's ass may find himself with a hoof in the balls. This is how it is."

Christ!

"So this time the camel's female, or what? And your point is that there's no fun in punching someone if the other party doesn't think it's fun as well. Is that it?"

Assad smiled. "You understand it then. Well done, Carl."

Back when Carl was a young officer, reports could be written in twenty minutes with two fingers on a typewriter. Nowadays it required ten fingers and fifteenth-generation word-processing software and took two and a half hours if you were lucky. Reports were no longer conclusions but more like conclusions of the conclusions' conclusions.

Under normal circumstances, Carl detested the bureaucracy of it, but today it suited him fine to hole up in front of the computer, even though he had difficulty focusing his thoughts.

He heard Rose's and Gordon's voices in the corridor.

As far as he could make out, she was bragging about how close she was to solving the Anweiler case for Department Q, and it was impossible to overlook Gordon's consuming adoration. If there was anything down in the archive he needed to check, his strategy appeared to involve getting into Rose's panties first.

Carl tried to ignore them. Who wanted to listen to that, the way he was feeling?

"All right, Gordon," he called out as they passed his door. "Got the buggy into the shed yet?"

Rose gave him an icy glare and slammed the door in his face.

Carl frowned. Had that lanky bugger, who'd hardly been weaned off his baby food, actually succeeded in turning Rose's head?

He turned back to his flickering screen and began his summary of the Rotterdam debacle. It was no easy job. If truth were told, the investigators who had gone through the nail-gun killings in Schiedam had a surprisingly poor command of the English language compared to other Dutch people he'd met.

Two pages was all it came to. Probably not enough. Again, he was having difficulty concentrating. Maybe it would help once he received the supplementary material from the meeting in Rotterdam. There had to be someone at HQ who could translate that bristly language.

He shook his head.

Help? Like hell it would.

The only way he was going to get any peace of mind was to raise the curtain on the second act of his Mona drama. And it had better be more constructive than the first.

He dialed her work number. Predictably, someone else answered. In a fit of innovation Mona had moved her practice a couple of months earlier into a shared clinic, the only snag being that callers always had to go through the secretary, a young woman who apparently considered herself as competent a psychologist as those who conducted their therapy in the rooms behind her desk.

"I'm afraid Mona Ibsen isn't available at the moment, she's with a client. Well, maybe he's not a client, but the fact is, the sign on her door says she's in a session."

He'd give her some facts next time he stood leaning against her counter.

The fact is! He had hardly put down the phone before the ugly inappropriate feeling came over him that Mona might have had a hidde agenda in giving him his marching orders.

Could she have been running around with other men while he'd been trawling the streets in search of a wedding ring? Had he missed the signals?

No, Mona wasn't like that. If she'd met someone else she would have told him.

Nevertheless, a nasty sense of betrayal crept over him. It was a feeling he hadn't known since he was twelve. Not since that blistering summer day when he had caught sight of his one and only childhood flame, Lise, posing at the water's edge at the outdoor swimming baths. All of a sudden, there she was in a low-cut bathing suit with taut, suntanned thighs, and light-years away from him. They had grown up together, been blushing almost-sweethearts, and suddenly her beckoning smile was turned in the direction of others. And when finally she noticed him, her smile changed. In one second she had become a woman and he had been left behind, humiliated, still imprisoned within the body of a boy.

It had taken him at least ten years to rid himself of that feeling of desolation in which she had left him, and now here he was again, sidelined, left on his own. It wasn't jealousy but something deeper, more painful.

"For Christ's sake, man," he said to himself. "You can't do without her. And when did *that* happen?"

13

They heard the stamp of Rose's approaching footsteps and braced them-selves. Time to face the music for yesterday's blunder. How could he have said that about her father? He knew it was a touchy subject.

"Take it easy, Carl. I had a nice chat with Allah this morning. This will be a fine day," Assad assured him.

Amazing, how well connected the man was.

"Right, come on, you two," were Rose's first words. Her eyes were sparkling and she seemed her old self. "I've got a little surprise for you."

It was clear she was expecting protest, so she turned on her heel and marched off again in a manner that defied disobedience.

Apart from her nose peeling after her tour of Brumleby, the lass was on the top of her form. Assad still had his injuries to contend with, and Carl's lack of sleep and tar-clogged lungs served likewise to slow their tempo. Both were already gasping for breath as they reeled past the duty desk out into HQ's courtyard in time to see Rose striding over Hambros-gade toward the parking spaces across the street.

No tour van could have been better suited to the name scrawled across its sides in barbed-wire lettering. The sight of this spray-painted wreck must have been a joy for death metal fans, with its fiery red flames lick-ing from bumper to bumper.

Daggers & Swords from Malmö had definitely gone all out.

Rose pulled the sliding door open with a clonk and indicated for them to get in.

Hard to believe, but there sat Sverre Anweiler, his pasty face nodding darkly in their direction. He gestured toward the bench opposite his own and produced three cans of beer that he shoved over to them without a word.

"I'll run through this quickly," said Rose. "Sverre has to be getting on. He's off to Århus in ten minutes, got a ferry to catch."

Carl sat down, shifting a guitar case against the wall and pulling Assad down next to him. Here was the man Interpol had been yearning to find for more than a year. From the heap of a vehicle in which they now sat there were only a hundred meters to the headquarters of the Danish National Police, and next door to it Copenhagen's police HQ with Lars Bjørn and his rapid response unit. What made him think he was going to be allowed to drive off to Århus, just like that?

"I actually figured Anweiler was probably in Malmö, so I was going to take the train over there this morning. But then I checked Daggers and Swords's tour schedule and found out they played up in Hørsholm last night," Rose explained, sounding rather pleased with herself. "So I called the promoters and asked them if they knew where the band was now. And wouldn't you know it, they were still having breakfast at Hotel Zleep in Ballerup. They'd had a bit of a late night, apparently, so they were running late."

"I thought she was a groupie when she called," the Swede added, in something that apparently was supposed to resemble Danish.

"I did sound a bit eager, didn't I?" Rose sniggered.

Carl responded with a frown. When they were done here they would have to have a word with her about the inappropriateness of calling up murder suspects wanted by Interpol and making appointments to meet. There was only one procedure in a situation like this, and that was to go out and arrest the bloke.

"Rose filled me in on the situation, and to be honest I was appalled. I didn't even know about it," the human leftover went on. "Tragic thing to happen, but I can assure you I had absolutely nothing to do with it."

Quite articulate for a Swede.

"I wouldn't expect you to say anything different," replied Carl.

"I know, but I've been off traveling all this time, so I had no idea. I haven't been in Sydhavnen since I sold the houseboat, but I was actually thinking of stopping by the new owner to see if everything was all right once I got the time."

"I can confirm we've seen evidence to suggest you've been away, but how do we know for sure?" asked Carl.

"Well, I've got all kinds of stuff I brought back with me. Receipts, photos and all sorts of things. It's all in the apartment in Malmö. All you had to do was ask."

Carl nodded. "OK, if what you're saying here is really true, then it makes you a little less of a suspect. So far so good. But perhaps you can tell me what might have been on that houseboat that could have caused such a huge explosion? A bit hard to account for, isn't it?"

Anweiler turned something in his hand. It looked like some tubes from an old radio, or maybe something that belonged to one of the amplifiers in the back of the van. It was the morning after the night before, and the Swede's dull eyes were underscored by heavy shadows. There was something melancholic about the expression on his face and the hard-boiled accessories he'd decorated himself with, the pierced ears, the tattoos crawling up his neck, his shaved head.

"I don't think it is, actually," he replied matter-of-factly.

A peculiar feeling of relief and clarification spread through the van and its clutter of studded black leather and polished boots.

"I did the boat up ready for her. Varnished the floors a few times, treated all the woodwork. There was a bit of leftover varnish and teak oil down below in the old engine room. I told her I still needed a day to put everything in order, but she said she'd be sure to do it herself and remember to air the place out, too. It suited me fine."

"So what you're saying is that she forgot and all that stuff ignited itself? But if that was really what happened, the fire investigation would have reached the same conclusion. Plus they'd have found remnants of the containers at the bottom of the harbor."

"No, because the varnish and wood oil were in plastic buckets." He looked distressed about it. "It was probably a combination of that and something else. I should have thought about it when I was showing her around the boat. She did seem a bit preoccupied. Just kept saying yeah to everything I was explaining, without looking like any of it was really sinking in."

"What about the gas stove?"

"No," he said, with a sad look. "I was thinking more about the generator."

"Down in the engine room, was it?"

Anweiler nodded slowly.

"Tell you what, Anweiler, why don't you and I pop over the road and explain to my boss what you've just told us?"

He gave a shrug, reminding them he'd already said he was in a hurry and had to catch a ferry.

But Carl knew better. The unwillingness to cooperate that he saw was an ex-con's implicit mistrust, the ingrained doubt that he would be listened to with an open mind.

They hadn't been born yesterday.

It was a heavy trudge to the third floor, and the Chivas Regal in Carl's hand felt anything but sufficient.

Farewell reception, read a note on the door of the cafeteria. They might just as well have written *Department A's demise* or *Dangerous criminals' victory celebration*.

Nothing would ever be the same as it had been under Marcus Jacobsen. Why the flaming hell did he have to go and retire now? Couldn't he at least have waited until Carl threw in the towel, too?

Ms. Sørensen, the formidable Department A secretary, had risen to the occasion and baked cakes of such leaden substance that only those truly ravaged by hunger would dare set their teeth into them. Lis had inserted little Danish flags into the icing. And underneath all the disposable tumblers with hardly anything to fill them up with—it was during working hours, after all—someone had gone to the trouble of using his best handwriting to decorate the tablecloth with the sorely inappropriate words: "Enjoy your retirement, boss. Thanks and farewell. Long live Department A."

The commissioner's speech was brief and avoided all the pitfalls her long and often acrimonious association with the homicide chief might otherwise have caused her to stumble into. For that reason, too, it was surprisingly devoid of content. Lars Bjørn, on the other hand, spoke almost exclusively of what he was planning to carry over from Marcus's leadership, and, more to the point, what he wasn't.

When he had finished, only Gordon went up and shook the idiot by the hand. In return, Bjørn beamed at him and slapped him on the back, an unexpectedly accommodating gesture.

They put their heads together and exchanged some words. The rookie and the homicide chief to-be. What on earth did they have to talk about in such confidence? Wasn't Gordon just an annoying law student who'd been given the chance to get a whiff of what life was like at the sharp end of the legal system?

Or was he simply Bjørn's man?

If he was, then maybe he was more than just a horny idiot with a penchant for loopy women with kohl around their eyes.

"I'm watching you, you lanky bugger," he said under his breath, turning to send his boss of many years a comforting smile. If Marcus Jacobsen were to change his mind now, Carl hoped he would kick Bjørn's ass back to Afghanistan, from where it had just returned.

"You deserved a better send-off than the speeches you got there, Marcus. I'm really sorry," Carl proffered, self-consciously handing him the whisky bottle in its crappy cardboard box. "No one could ever wish for a better or more competent boss than you've been," he said in a clear, resounding voice, so not a single person present, including the commissioner and Lars Bjørn, could be in any doubt.

For a moment Marcus Jacobsen stared blankly at Carl, then, mustering a smile, he put the gift down on the table and gave Carl an exceedingly warm embrace.

No doubt it would be the only one all day.

Thus came twenty years of service at police HQ to an end. There was no big fuss. One day they were here, the next they were gone. It all went a little too smoothly.

Carl for one wasn't expecting fanfares when his turn came. It suited him fine.

———

With a heavy heart Carl issued a couple of directives to Rose and Assad before slumping down at his desk to wrap up the Anweiler case with the obligatory report.

Their conclusion was that the fire was an accident and that the worst that could happen to Sverre Anweiler was a minor fine for having neglected to properly dispose of inflammable materials before handing on the boat to the new owner.

It was a sad and not particularly exciting or prestigious case for Bjørn to present to the press, but a good one for Marcus Jacobsen to bow out on. Last case solved, thank you and good night. There were no doubt other investigations during his long career that had been far from successfully concluded, which he would look back on without satisfaction. Like any other investigator in the homicide division he would just have to live with it.

An unconcluded murder case would keep gnawing away until death itself intervened.

Carl printed out his report and wrote *CONCLUDED* across the front page in block letters.

He stared at the word and began involuntarily to think of Mona again. Would it ever stop?

Carl and Assad stood in front of the array of cases covering the notice boards on their basement's corridor wall. Though some had been cleared away during the last few months, more had unfortunately taken their place. In the latter period, under Marcus Jacobsen, Department A's success rate had touched ninety percent, but in the rest of the country the picture was rather less flattering, a fact amply illustrated by the seeming disorder at which they now stared. Moreover, the past ten years had left its mark in other ways equally tragic. Inexplicable disappearances and deaths, most likely genuine suicides, also added to the clutter of documents on the boards, crisscrossed by Assad's system of red and blue strings.

The blue strings joined cases that may have been related, however tenuously. The red strings joined those that seemed more obviously connected.

A colorful spiderweb of death and disaster. And then all the cases that were hanging there on their own.

"Plenty to get started on, Assad," said Carl.

"My words exactly, Carl. Like minds think greatly."

"It's the opposite, Assad. Great minds think alike, OK? But, yeah, I reckon we're thinking the same thing: Can we really be bothered with yet another dubious case? A missing person from ages ago?"

"But still, Carl. I think Rose deserves it. She has just cleared up a case on her own."

"Yeah, but that one never even made it up on the wall here, remember?"

"Nevertheless, then, I think we should put this one up, Carl." He smiled wearily but roguishly, just like the Assad of old. A bit more peppermint-tea soup, a touch more bone-penetrating Middle Eastern caterwauling on the CD player, a few more twinkles in his eye and daily doses of linguistic befuddlement, and the man would be back in business.

"You reckon so, do you?" Carl gave a deep sigh. This wasn't a day where his defenses were fully functioning, Mona being at the end of his every train of thought. "In that case, you can give her the news yourself, OK?" The overpowering manner in which Rose sometimes responded to such gestures made him heedful. She wasn't necessarily the one he needed a close encounter with just now.

He tumbled onto his chair and tried to pull himself together. A couple of deep hits on his first ciggie of the day.

Why couldn't he stop thinking about Mona? Goddamn it!

In no time at all his cigarette became ash, and uneasiness seemed to take a firmer hold with every drag. And then, out of nowhere, Rose was standing in front of him, coughing and wafting away the smoke with the missing persons notice in hand.

"Thanks, Carl," was all she said, pointing at her little poster. No exuberant gush of elation that would knock him off his feet. Just a simple "thanks." Coming from Rose, it spoke volumes.

She ignored his pained expression and sat down on one of the horrendous chairs she had once managed to sneak into his office.

"I've been looking into what might have happened to our missing person here, but that won't surprise you, I'm sure." She jabbed a finger at the photo of the red-haired William Stark. "The phone number on the notice is no longer in operation, of course, but I've found a new one, so we can get in touch with the girl who put it out."

"OK. What is it exactly that's got you so turned on about this case?" he asked.

"Assad, come in here a minute, will you?" she hollered.

A moment later he shuffled in, hungry for something new to sink his teeth into, ready for action with his hand-chased metal tray and three tiny cups of steaming, sticky goo. "I think this calls for some Turkish delight," he announced, with a nod toward the colored blobs of sugar on the tray as if they were the contents of the Holy Grail.

"Assad's done a background check, and I've been researching the situation as it stands now," Rose explained, as if this were just a matter of course.

Carl shook his head. The two of them together were like a herd of stampeding gnu on the plains of Africa. Heads down and full steam ahead, and if he wasn't going to join in, he'd better get out of the way.

Assad deposited his saccharine shock on the table and sat down next to Rose, notepad at the ready.

"A clever guy, this William Stark. Top of his year at law school. Very strange, in fact, that he then did not rise higher in the hierarchy before he disappeared." Assad laid some papers in front of him. "Forty-two years old and fifteen years as a ministerial civil servant. Before that, a legal clerk and consultant for a number of lobby groups. Unmarried, but has been living six years with a Malene Kristoffersen and her daughter, Tilde. Malene is forty-seven now, Tilde is sixteen, and they live out in Valby."

"What about Stark's personal finances?"

Assad nodded. "Twenty years of careful saving up. Mortgage paid off and more than eight million kroner in securities. Mostly inherited from his mother, who died just before he went missing. He was an only child, and there were no other close family members."

"Eight million? Wow!" Carl whistled. If he had that kind of money he'd buy two tickets to Cuba and force Mona into coming with him. A month under the palm trees and a bit of rumba to loosen the loins and ruffle the sheets, and she was bound to soften up.

He shook the thought out of his head. "OK, have we got any statements from people who knew him? Anything that might give us a hint as to why he disappeared?"

Rose took over. "No, nothing. His colleagues at work describe him as the quiet type, but at ease with himself. The report says that nothing at work or on the domestic front gave cause to suspect he was depressed or anything like that."

Lucky bastard.

"But again, Rose, why are you so interested in this case? Other than feeling sorry for the young girl, which I completely understand. What else is there?"

"The circumstances, Carl. I can understand going to Africa and disappearing there. Of course it could have been against his will, with all the dangers there must be in a place like that, but intentionally vanishing in a region with no rule of law could be a possibility, too. It could have been a lust for adventure, or he might have just been sick and tired of the daily routine back home. Sick and tired of his work and his colleagues. Fed up with the cold and dark of winter and the political climate in Denmark. Or maybe he needed more sex. Maybe he had a preference for young, dark-skinned girls. He wouldn't be the first, would he?" She paused to give weight to what followed. "Or young, dark-skinned boys, for that matter. He might have had secrets. We all have them, you know."

Carl nodded. If anyone would know, she would.

He turned to Assad. He, too, nodded, though rather more hesitantly. Like a seasoned criminal, realizing his story had to be as close to the truth as possible, and yet holding back on just the right details.

It was a very odd kind of nod.

"Did Stark have secrets, do you think?"

Rose shrugged. "Who knows? The fact is, he *didn't* disappear in Africa, and that's what's so damn puzzling. He comes back to Denmark, Carl, right? He's been in Cameroon only a few hours before canceling his return flight and booking another. And he lands here at Kastrup just like he's supposed to. We've got the passenger list from the airline as well as some CCTV footage of him trundling his suitcase along. And then all of a sudden he's gone. Maybe for good."

Carl tried to picture the situation. "Perhaps he was clever. Our eyes are on Denmark because this is where he disappeared. But he might have driven straight over the bridge to Sweden, just like Sverre Anweiler, and wandered off in some forest. Or maybe he turned round and went back to Africa with false papers, or went somewhere else entirely."

"Rose and I have talked about this, Carl," said Assad. "Did Stark have enemies? Did he like gambling? Had he embezzled funds? Was there a pickup of some money? Had he forgotten something in Denmark, something he had to come back for? Could there have been another woman who was supposed to come along? We have talked about it all, and yet none of it seems very plausible."

Carl thrust out his lower lip. The two of them were certainly getting involved in the case, but it didn't look like they'd got much of a handle.

"Not a lot to go on, really, is there? What does the report say? Is there anything else at all that might point in some specific direction the earlier investigation could have missed?"

They both shook their heads.

"So where does that leave us? Have we anything at all?" If it were up to him, it would be a short investigation.

"William Stark has never been declared dead," Rose said, bowing her head with a dark look in her eyes.

"No, of course he hasn't, Rose. It's not been five years yet."

"And his house is still pretty much the way it was when he went missing," Rose continued. "What's even better is that I got hold of a set of keys from Bellahøj station. They had sealed the place off."

Carl frowned. The bloodhound wags its tail when it picks up the scent and with a single sentence, Rose had got him going.

Dammit.

"OK," he said, reaching behind his chair for his jacket. "Let's go and have a look."

14

It wasn't a good day for Marco. Shadows made him jump and even the slightest sounds were fatiguing.

He was back in Østerbro, for Zola had always told them never to go back to the same place if they were ever discovered. So Østerbro was probably the only part of town where they wouldn't be looking for him.

It was well past midnight when he finally bedded down at the bottom of a Dumpster, hoping for a couple of hours' respite from his fears of what the new day might bring.

It was no longer a question of them making him an invalid if they found him. Now that Zola probably knew Marco had seen the missing persons notice and could link it to the dead man in the woods, his life was at stake.

He woke up abruptly when a wino opened the lid and almost dropped dead from fright when Marco leaped out.

It couldn't have been much more than half past six, but sunlight already glared down between the buildings that towered over the narrow street. Marco could hear the first faint rumble of traffic from the main thoroughfares. The city was awakening.

He gathered his things in a black trash bag and headed purposefully for the library on Dag Hammarskjölds Allé, taking care not to walk too quickly and draw attention to himself. The library had everything he needed. Toilets where he could wash, computers so he could print out maps of places he would go later in the day. And there was a place to stash his gear, a shelf above the electricity meter in a cupboard where no one ever came. He had previously made note of the place should he ever have need.

Here in the embassy quarter there were plainclothes security guards everywhere. Russians keeping an eye on Americans, and vice versa. And in the midst of it all was an impressive building that he had been told once belonged to the Red Cross, reminding him that there were children in this world worse off than himself. Not that it made him feel any better. The children who skipped past him now on their way to school certainly had no need for charity.

When finally the library opened and he had taken care of his errands, he crossed over Sortedamssøen, carrying on along Ryesgade, and then heading north, eyes peeled for any untoward movement in the landscape.

Good thing he had his map.

He reached Stark's house at a time of day when the suburbs seemed all but deserted. Friday midday was probably the easiest time of all to commit burglary in a tidy and peaceful residential neighborhood anywhere in Denmark. It was a country where both parents worked, decent living standards more often than not requiring two incomes. In a ghetto of affluence such as this, everything went by the book. What glued the place together were not the kind economic constraints with which Marco was familiar, but the exact opposite, and any child growing up here knew that to achieve the same status as their parents, they had to stay in school. For that reason nearly every house was empty. What he needed to watch out for were dogs, pensioners, and the occasional housewife. But Marco was used to being careful, so he mobilized everything he had learned, the trained thief ambling impassively along a street in which he did not belong. A far cry from the asphalt cowboys from the Baltic countries or Russia, who could be spotted a mile away in their grubby, ill-fitting faded jeans or tracksuits that had gone out of fashion ten years ago. They might as well have been wearing a sign that read THIEF. Shambling and unkempt, always in pairs, with tattered backpacks or a couple of bulging plastic bags too many. It was just the wrong way to look.

Marco, by contrast, was inconspicuous, his eyes seemingly fixed on some point farther down the street, but in fact intensely scanning every home he passed.

It was a pretty neighborhood, definitely the sort of place where he planned to live one day. Swings and seesaws, playhouses with little verandas. Beautiful, tall trees lined one side of the street, their branches reaching out over the lake and marshlands, while fine, spacious homes occupied the sloping grounds on the other.

And in the midst of this well-to-do idyllic setting, his thoughts turned toward the dead man. So strange to think that the corpse with which he had shared a hole in the ground had once walked these streets, as large as life.

Now he was gone from this world. No more than a face on a poster.

Approaching the address, he saw a woman on her knees before a flower bed next door to the garden that must have been William Stark's. She was engrossed in her gardening and Marco counted the plants in her planting box. Ten left, perhaps fifteen? The way she was working it would be a while before she was done. Until then, no one could walk up the path to Stark's house without her noticing. He would have to be patient, carry on down the street and come back later.

As he came to Stark's home he noticed a dark blue Peugeot 607 parked a little way up the drive. A serious setback.

He reasoned that if he could see a girl inside as he walked past, then she was likely to be the one who had put up the notice, and he resolved in that case to ring the bell. He slowed down. The woman next door would just have to wonder.

Behind the pane of the bungalow's front window he saw shadows moving against the walls. Holding his breath, he heard the faint sound of voices. Perhaps the house had been sold, although it was still only William Stark's name that popped up on a Google search.

He shook his head. Of course there could be possibilities he hadn't considered. The place could have been let. If so, he might just as well give up straightaway, for there would be nothing for him to find.

Marco noticed the man in the window before the man saw him. He seemed to be pondering, in no hurry with whatever he was doing. Not a young man, but seemingly alert, with eyebrows raised, head turning this way and that. He was examining the room methodically, almost like a carpenter or painter appraising a job. But he wasn't, Marco's experience told him so. He knew better than anyone what policemen looked like and the kind of movements they made. He remembered how he and Samuel sometimes played a game when they were working the streets, where they'd see who would be the first to spot cops in the crowd. The mere way they checked out people around them was usually enough.

Marco took another look at the dark blue car. There, on the dashboard, was the blue lamp. He would have to make himself scarce.

But just as he was asking himself why they might be there, the policeman turned his face directly toward him. Only the briefest of seconds, and yet Marco had never before felt himself so sized up.

Those eyes have already seen enough of me, he thought, and began to run.

Not until he reached Husum Torv, his lungs wheezing and mouth parched, did he stop and consider what had happened.

The police were at Stark's house. The case had not been closed. And the knowledge made his next move unavoidable.

He had to go back and get into that house.

The house, a small yellow bungalow from the thirties, lay on sloping ground with a spectacular view across the Utterslev marsh, the monumental ugliness of the Høje Gladsaxe ghetto beyond. In this area of Copenhagen, history was thus laid bare, a grim manifestation of why humanity was the worst thing that could happen to this green planet.

Carl shook his head. Welfare-state concrete slapped down in a landscape of beauty, a pillar of shame in Danish architecture. What a flagrant lack of foresight.

"A nice mast, don't you think, Carl?" said Assad, pointing through the trees toward the Gladsaxe TV transmitter's Babylonian lattice against the sky.

As far as Carl was concerned, the whole structure could collapse and he wouldn't bat an eyelid.

"There was a break-in, you say. When was that?" he asked.

Rose produced a key and opened the front door.

"Shortly after William Stark disappeared. His girlfriend and step-daughter hadn't moved out yet, so we've got a fairly clear picture of what went missing."

"The usual stuff?"

"You could say. The thing is, they really made a mess of the place. Slashed mattresses, paintings torn down off the walls. It wasn't vandalism, more like they were looking for something."

Carl nodded. Neither a typical disappearance nor a typical break-in. He could understand Rose's curiosity.

Inside, there was a musty smell about the place, the kind that came when life ground to a halt and no one cared. This was the place where Stark had lived, and most likely he would never live here again.

Carl stepped into the neat front room and stared out of the panorama window across the garden toward the delights of Brønshøj. The lawn had been mown, red currant and black currant bushes pruned and ready for the next harvest.

"Who looks after the place?" he asked.

"His partner still comes, I think. Doesn't it say in the report, Assad?"

He nodded.

Carl looked around. The whole setup seemed to indicate Stark had made do with less than might be expected of a man in his position. Maybe he just wasn't interested, judging by the cheap wooden ceiling boards and shoddy DIY extension. But cozy, nevertheless. Not at all the sort of place that gave immediate rise to thoughts of suicide or the urge to vanish.

A few photos on a pinewood shelf told the tale of togetherness and the pleasure of one another's company. Stark, his partner, and her daughter standing close, a warm huddle. It was easy to see from the way they were laughing that Stark had pressed the shutter timer and had just got back in position in time. The sort of photos that never won prizes.

Malene Kristoffersen was a roundish, pleasant-looking woman with dimples in her cheeks and healthy in appearance, in contrast to her daughter, who seemed exceptionally thin and disheveled in the way of a weak fledgling whose sibling would instinctively push it from the nest.

Stark seemed happy in all the pictures, his arms around his family's shoulders, bending to put his head between theirs. A man whose most daring fashion exploit would be to wear a purple tie or perhaps even a green-checkered shirt with short sleeves. It was plain to see on this basis alone why his excellent education had failed to elevate him into the upper echelons. The man had been too quiet, too tentative, and probably, in many ways, too honest. He simply radiated this, and Carl was fascinated. If irregularities suddenly intruded upon the life of an upstanding guy like Stark, they usually left traces.

"Tell me about the break-in, Assad," he said.

Assad opened his folder and pulled out the copy of the report.

"It was a professional job. No fingerprints, no DNA. Some neighbors said they saw a couple of guys arrive in a yellow van wearing blue overalls and black caps, and they waved to the people next door. Very ordinary-looking men, though perhaps rather tanned for the time of year." Assad smiled. It was an expression he wouldn't hesitate to use on himself.

"But you can't really tell with skin color these days, can you? Everyone's traveling all year-round. Ski trips, vacations at the beach. Soon everyone will look like me, only not quite as handsome." He raised his eyebrows ingratiatingly. If he was expecting a compliment he'd have a long wait.

He gave a shrug. "In any case they came in through the front door, probably using a lock gun so no one had any idea something was going on. A woman tending her garden next door kept an eye out to see if they came out again with their arms full, but they had nothing. All in all, they were inside for about an hour and then they left again with a wave."

"Did Malene Kristoffersen report the break-in herself?"

"Yes, and it was the reason they moved. They were uneasy about the place after that, especially with Stark being gone."

"And the house is still as it was?"

"Yes."

"How can that be? Who's paying the mortgage?"

"It's all paid off, Carl. All other expenses are taken care of by the returns on his assets."

"Hmm." Carl scanned the room again. "I wonder what they were looking for since they didn't make off with the hi-fi over there? Cash, securities, jewelry? Are we sure his money wasn't from something illegal? Have you checked out the validity of that inheritance? Have you seen the documents from the probate court?"

Assad stared at him in disappointment. Of course he had.

"It all looks innocent enough," Carl went on, "but that could be a mistaken assumption. Maybe it has something to do with narcotics. Maybe he's got property or other assets abroad that he hasn't declared to the Danish authorities. Something he got by way of some criminal activity. Maybe he came back from Cameroon so quickly because something had gone totally wrong and there was a welcoming committee waiting at Kastrup Airport to get rid of him. Is there any CCTV footage showing how he carried on from there?"

"Yes, he took the metro."

"And then what?"

"You see him on the platform and then that's it."

"Is that footage still available?"

Assad shrugged. On that point he had to pass.

"Have a look over here," said Rose, over by the double doors.

She pointed across the hall to a small office with a safe up against the wall. Fair-sized, massive, and with a handle in the middle.

"Was it open before the break-in, too?" she asked Assad.

He nodded. "Malene Kristoffersen said it was never locked. William Stark never used it. He had a safe-deposit box with Danske Bank, but it was canceled a few months before he disappeared."

"Did she have any idea what that deposit box might have contained?" Carl took over. "There must have been *something* of value in it, or there'd be no point in having it, would there?"

"Malene said he had some floppy disks and CD-ROMs, and his parents' wedding rings. But he took all of it home, went through the disks on his computer and wiped the disks clean."

"Do we know what was on them?"

"His doctoral thesis," Assad replied.

"Doctoral thesis? Are you saying he has a PhD?"

"He never got that far. He hadn't even tried to get it approved."

"Sounds daft, if you ask me. Why would he delete all his work?"

"The same reason you didn't want to be a chief inspector, I suppose."

Carl stared at Assad. What the hell was he on about?

"And why didn't I want to do that, Assad?"

"Because then you would have had to do a different job, Carl." He smiled. "You don't want to end up a commissioner in northern Jutland, do you?"

Assad was right. God forbid that ever happening.

"So you reckon he was afraid of being booted upstairs if he got his PhD. Did Malene Kristoffersen tell you that?"

"She said he was happy where he was and that he was not the kind to bloast."

"I think you mean *boast*, Assad. But then why the hell did he go to all the bother of writing that thesis?"

"Malene Kristoffersen said his mother wanted him to, because his father had a PhD. But when she died, he changed his mind."

Carl nodded. His picture of William Stark was slowly taking shape. He found himself liking the man more and more.

"And do we know what this thesis was about?"

Assad flicked through the pages. Malene Kristoffersen couldn't remember exactly, but something about setting up foundations in international contexts."

"Sounds like a barrel of laughs."

He got down on his haunches and peered into the safe. Like they said, it was empty.

Then they went downstairs into the basement, finding nothing of immediate interest.

As they were getting ready to leave, Carl scanned the ceilings and walls for anything irregular, but everything seemed nice and orderly. Almost too nice for his taste.

"Anything in the loft?" he asked, as Rose's backside appeared in the hatch at the top of the ladder.

She brushed her hands across her face, then shook her head. "Nothing but a load of cobwebs. I *hate* cobwebs."

Carl nodded. Getting to the substance of a case was never easy such a long time after the event. Maybe Malene Kristoffersen had been too thorough with her cleaning. Maybe something important had gone into the trash, or into the pockets of a pair of thieves. There may once have been traces of evidence that time had now erased.

"OK, I'd say we are done here. Not that it's told us much. But let's go next door and ask about these jokers who did the break-in. She's out in the front garden now, I see."

He looked out at the woman on her knees with her box of plants at her side, and as he did so he noticed the boy standing on the opposite pavement looking up toward the window. It wasn't so much the appearance of him that made Carl frown, though he seemed both sad and neglected. Rather, it was the way he looked at him in the split second their eyes met. Like a defendant meeting the judge. The kind of look that sometimes appeared in a person's eyes when they realized they had just encountered an enemy.

The boy quickly looked down and turned his head away, making off faster than Carl could manage to step closer to the window.

Clearly, he didn't want to be discovered. It was all very strange.

"Did you see that lad there?" Carl asked. Both Assad and Rose shook their heads.

"Whoever he was, he didn't look pleased to see us here, that's for sure."

15

Marco waited an hour before cautiously sneaking back to find both the woman in the garden and the police car gone.

He walked calmly up the drive, his eyes fixed on the front door. As far as he could see, there was no sticker saying the place had an alarm, so he carried on round to the back of the house, where he discovered a basement window without hasps, thirty centimeters high at most, the frame screwed tight to the jamb from inside.

Marco smiled now. He was on familiar ground. He placed his elbow against the center of the pane, applying pressure to the glass, then striking his clenched fist sharply with his free hand, turning the bone of his elbow into a chisel. The sound as the pane splintered into a star was almost imperceptible, and Marco began to pick away the shards one by one, leaning them neatly up against the wall.

The opening of the window was a black hole into the dark basement. He lay down on his back, arms tight against his sides, then wriggled forward, legs first. Even a much smaller window would have provided space enough for a guy like him.

The basement was no more than a single room, about two-thirds the width of the house. Lime-washed walls and a fusty smell of damp and washing powder. A combined laundry, workshop, and storeroom for pickled cucumbers, obviously unused for some time. There was a carton of Tide on top of the washing machine. Marco upturned it, noting with satisfaction that the contents had long since congealed. He was certain now. No one came down here anymore.

His eyes passed quickly over tins of old paint and neglected tools as he stepped toward the door into the passage, unlocking it and opening it wide, his first emergency exit now secured.

Then he went up the stairs to the ground floor, found the patio door and opened it, too. Second exit secured. He paused and scanned the room for sensors, listening for the faintest hum, anything that might reveal the presence of a more sophisticated alarm system, a hook-up to a mobile phone or a neighbor's landline.

Finding nothing, he set to work systematically. His eyes ate their way through room after room. During a normal burglary they would have routinely skipped anything that might make him think of those who lived there. Sympathy for the people from whom he stole was the worst of all evils, Zola always said. "Pretend all the possessions belong to you, and the people you see in the picture frames there are insignificant strangers. The toys you see belong to your own small brothers and sisters and have nothing to do with the children of the house. Remember this."

The last part was especially hard to think about.

But Marco was a thief no longer. He wasn't here to steal these people's possessions but to take in their history, the tiny indications of who they might be and why.

So he started with the drawers and their contents of personal papers.

It was clear William Stark was a man who set store by order. Marco determined this immediately as he pored through cabinets and cupboards in the living room and dining room. Most people's drawers were a mess: a Ronson lighter from days gone by, discarded mobiles, toothpicks in plastic containers, half-empty packets of tissues. Tablecloths here, birthday decorations there. Marco had rifled through the like at least a hundred times, but here it was different. William Stark didn't keep such things. Even the walls and the shelves were devoid of anything reminiscent of times past. No photo of the young William standing between proud parents at his confirmation, a grinning face beneath a graduation cap; no Christmas cards saved in a box. Nothing in the way of nostalgia. Instead, Marco found handwritten tax reports and insurance documents in separate folders, a bowl of foreign coins in small plastic bags, receipts, boarding passes in bundles, travel brochures, and handwritten descriptions of hotels at various destinations, arranged in alphabetical order and held together by rotting elastic bands.

He nodded pensively. He had never met a man such as this in real life.

He found girls' things in the adjoining rooms. The scent was different there. The objects that had been left in the daughter's small, yellow-painted bedroom were most likely ones in which she had lost interest. The aquarium was dry, the birdcage empty, the drawing paraphernalia laid aside, the boy bands on the wall presumably superseded by new idols. By contrast, the mother's room seemed more up-to-date, more representative of the person she had been and almost certainly still was. An array of books on shelves, a pile of handbags and summer hats stacked on top of the wardrobe. Boots of all kinds arranged neatly on the floor, and colorful scarves hanging from a hook next to the mirror.

Marco frowned and began to wonder. It almost seemed like the woman still lived here. But why the musty smell of absence? Why the congealed laundry detergent? Why the empty fridge, its door ajar?

And if the two of them really lived elsewhere, as was likely the case, why had the girl's mother not taken her things with her? Didn't she want them anymore? Or was she planning on moving in again? Marco had no idea, but then he had never been close to any female. Not even his mother.

Perhaps the woman believed William Stark was still alive and would show up someday. Perhaps all these things were just waiting to be put into use again. Perhaps life with Stark was simply on stand-by.

Marco stood quite still. It pained him to stand in that room knowing none of it would ever happen, that Stark was irrevocably dead. Maybe that was why he went back into the living room and began to study the few private photos there were. Right away he recognized the one the girl had used for her notice. Stark between the girl and her mother, smiling. She'd cropped it and blown it up, but it was the same image.

It was a family situation that would never be replicated.

Marco turned round, noticing for the first time the sharp incisions in the sofa and all its scatter cushions.

He stepped forward, sensing the desperate action to which the room had been witness. How else could he describe it? What did this act of vandalism indicate if not desperation? Was it Stark, who'd lost his mind? Was that why the woman's boots and all her things were still in her room? Had she and her daughter simply taken to their heels? Was that it? Maybe they'd been really afraid of him. Marco knew the feeling.

He shook his head, unable to get a handle on the situation. Why would his stepdaughter then want Stark back? It didn't make sense. There had to be some other explanation.

He began to poke at the slits in the cushions. They were dusty, suggesting it had been a while since it had happened. Clean, decisive incisions, probably made with a Stanley knife. Marco shook his head. He felt certain a man of Stark's orderliness would never have done such a thing unless he'd simply lost his marbles.

Was it jealousy? Had the woman done something she oughtn't? Had this man, whose life was arranged so neatly, gone berserk because his partner had been unfaithful? Had such a devastating event made him wrench away, from himself and those around him?

Or was it something else altogether?

Again, Marco studied the photo the girl had used. Here was William Stark wearing his African necklace—the one Marco himself now wore— beaming at the camera, the garden in the background in full bloom. So carefree they seemed, so happy. Even the girl, despite her sickly appearance, with dark shadows under her eyes and pale sunken cheeks.

No, Marco had never quite been able to grasp the fluctuations of ordinary people's lives, and this instance was no exception. The slits in the sofa and the cushions, Stark's disappearance, the woman's clothes in her room. He didn't get it.

Normally, he wouldn't have cared, but this time was different. He needed to understand, it was why he was here. It was imperative for him to find out why Stark had to disappear, why his and Zola's paths had crossed. Perhaps the answer lay somewhere here.

Looking around once more, it struck him that the cuts in the sofa could be Zola's work. Had Stark possessed something Zola was looking for? Had he found it?

Marco turned to the largest of the chest of drawers, automatically doing what thieves do. Feeling all the surfaces, searching for anything that might be concealed, inserted in a secret place, affixed with tape some-where inaccessible to view. Then he looked behind all the paintings, lifted the rugs and then the tattered mattresses on the beds. As though searching for wads of banknotes or precious jewelry, he worked his way systematically through the house, room by room, nook by nook, but found nothing.

He wondered about the open safe in the little office with the teakwood bookcases next to the front door. It was empty, but since all else had proved fruitless he got down on his knees and ran the nail of an index finger along all its joints. This too was without result, much as he had anticipated. It wasn't the kind of safe with secret compartments and min-ute locking systems. It was the regular, old-fashioned sort, tall as a table, with one single interior and a dial lock on the front.

And yet, to make sure, he stuck his head completely inside the safe, examining for cracks, turning his gaze this way and that. Nothing. Not a thing. Until he twisted onto his back and lay outstretched on the carpet in front of the safe. Only then did he see the sequence of black letters and figures written in felt-tip on the red metal wall above the upper frame of the door. They read: *A4C4C6F67*.

He repeated the sequence out loud four or five times until he felt sure he could remember. It had to be significant. Why else would a person write such a thing there? The question now was when it was written, why it was written, and more specifically: what did it mean?

He pulled himself out of the safe and got to his feet. He took one of the folders marked TAX from the desk drawer, flicking through its con-tents at random, searching for the numbers four and seven. They weren't hard to find, for the pages were covered in them, sums done by hand, and Marco saw it immediately: the same curling fours, the same angular sev-ens as those in the safe. If William Stark had written these figures in his tax files, then his was the hand that had written them in the safe.

Marco sat down on a chair and buried his face in his hands. *A4C4C6F67*. What could it mean?

The sequence was progressive, figures and letters alike. No leaping back and forth. Only ACCF and 44667, mixed together. But why wasn't there a letter between the last 6 and 7? Was it because the two last figures were actually one: 67? Or was the correct interpretation rather F6 and F7? What was the system?

The Internet abounded with tests and puzzles claiming to yield a person's IQ. Marco found exercises like these easy to solve, but this was harder. It could be a system for archiving data. It could be a code that might be rearranged in numerous combinations and deal with countless subjects. It could be a computer password, or something to do with secret societies. In fact, it could be anything at all, and to compound the problem the sequence might even be incomplete, written in random order, or perhaps simply in reverse.

Marco's most immediate and logical thought was that it was a password, or the combination of some other safe in some other location. The question was whether the series of letters and numbers were still relevant. It could, of course, be old and outdated.

He stood up, went over to an old Hewlett-Packard computer and switched it on. The hard drive whirred and groaned for a minute or so until a gray-green image appeared on the bulky screen. No password. Nothing but old games for kids. He turned it off again.

Finding no other computers in the house, he tried to put the thought from his mind, descending again into the basement in the hope of uncovering clues that might give him something to go on.

He was deeply absorbed, eyes once more scanning the room, when he heard voices outside in the garden.

He froze and held his breath.

It was two dark voices. Voices he knew all too well. A mix of English and Italian as only Pico and Romeo were capable of.

"Someone got here before us," Pico whispered from outside. They had already noticed the broken window. This wasn't good.

"Look at the glass, the way it's all leaned up neat against the wall. And look, the door's ajar, and the patio door's wide-open."

"Goddammit, you're right, Pico." It was Romeo now. How many times had the three of them done break-ins together? It made the next sentence inevitable:

"Marco's been here."

Marco retreated a single step up the stairs toward the ground floor. If they discovered he was still here, he would be trapped like a spider in its own web. Knowing Pico and Romeo, one of them would be slipping in through the basement door any second now, the other keeping watch by the patio door in the garden. And it seemed just as certain that a third clan member would be posted outside in the street. No doubt he was standing there now, leaning against a willow, pretending to look out over the marsh and lake. But he wasn't positioned there to enjoy the scenery. The instant anything untoward occurred, a bird cry would go out, louder and shriller than the residents here were used to. And Pico and Romeo would be gone before anyone knew. They were fast, those two. Surely the only ones in the clan who could catch up with Marco. And in a moment, the hunt would be on.

Marco held his arms tight to his chest, breathing deeply to calm his pulse.

His only way out was through the front door, and he would have to run like the wind.

Silently, he backed up the stairs, conscious that they would know Marco's preferred escape route was always a door that opened onto a garden, and therefore Pico would come from below while Romeo would be waiting at the door to the veranda. Had there been a second floor he would have sought refuge there immediately. A roof had on occasion likewise proved to be a good solution for a thief disturbed during a break-in, but there *was* no second floor and the roof was as flat as a pancake with no place to hide.

Maybe he could cry for help? Fling open the window facing the neighbor's house and scream at the top of his lungs, as heartrendingly as he was able while clinging to the window frame, in the hope someone would appear and frighten the hell out of Pico, Romeo, and their man in the road.

He rocked on his heels for a moment, his brain churning in search of a solution.

It wouldn't work. They would be inside any minute and find something hard to hit him on the head with. Pico wasn't afraid to use violence, and if they knocked him unconscious he would never wake up again, or else wake up without legs.

What do they want here? he asked himself. The image of the slashed sofa and the tattered mattresses suddenly made more sense. They had been here before. They were the ones responsible, and now they were back. But why? What were they looking for?

They couldn't have known beforehand that he was here now because they'd sounded surprised when they found the glass splinters. All they knew was that he had been here at some point. Which meant *they* had to be here for some other reason.

What could it be?

Come on, Marco, think! he urged himself.

He looked around him. The basement offered no hiding place, he knew that, and the ground floor contained no built-in wardrobe or cubbyhole. Just some shelves in the bedroom with a curtain in front.

If they had been here before, as he felt certain they had, then they had come for something they had failed to find last time, or else something they now needed on account of the situation Marco had imposed upon them.

A creaking noise came from the basement. Marco held his breath and listened. Someone was already inside. It was difficult to hear what was going on because the sounds were drowned out by Romeo's voice from the back garden ordering the man in front of the house to keep a good eye on the main door.

Another exit strategy foiled.

Mind Romeo doesn't see you through the window, Marco admonished himself, scuttling to the wall underneath the windows of the living room. There was nowhere to conceal himself here, no place they would fail to look. The dining room was the same. Only the bedrooms remained. Marco darted into the hall and stared into the small rooms one by one. It was hopeless. Beds and shelves, that was it. Nothing in which to vanish.

And then his eyes fixed on the safe in the little office, its door ajar.

It was his only chance, because if Zola's crew were sure of anything, it was that the safe was empty, having undoubtedly checked it the first time they were here.

They'll look everywhere but there, he tried to convince himself, crawling inside and pulling the door closer.

His eyes narrowed as he assessed the situation and its three possible outcomes. They might find him and beat the daylights out of him, or he might remain undiscovered and get away. But there was a third terrifying possibility: that they would find him and lock him inside the safe.

He noticed he'd begun breathing more deeply. If they shut the door on him he would suffocate and never be found until the house was again inhabited.

Marco pressed his lips together. And when that time came they would find him because of the smell. His smell.

They would find a dead boy no one knew. Suffocated and decomposed. A boy with no distinguishing marks and no identity papers.

His heart was beating so fast that his breathing could hardly keep up in his upright fetal position and he began to sweat. Even his fingers perspired, and the tenuous hold they kept on the thin edge of the safe door became increasingly hard to maintain.

Now came the sound of Romeo's voice from the patio door by the living room, and the man at the front door responded. Only Pico was silent. Marco knew he was checking the basement.

The floorboards creaked as Pico climbed the stairs from the basement to the living room, and Marco felt the house to be alive, an organism whose rooms were thick bundles of nerve endings. A foot placed randomly on a floor sent electric impulses shooting into all corners of the house and into the safe where Marco strained to remain silent, though everything inside him screamed for help. The pounding of his heart, the explosive activity of his brain, the clothes on his skin, the tangle of his limbs, his fear, the enclosed space, all combined to thrust up his body temperature, his pores opening accordingly. And as Pico made the whole house tremble even by the very lightness of his step, sweat poured from Marco's skin. Most perceptibly from his wrist to the index finger that kept hold on the door. And it was through this little digit, slippery with moisture, that he registered how close Pico was to finding him.

I'm not here, he repeated over and over in his mind, willing the words into Pico's sensory apparatus. Marco's not here, he left a while ago. Do whatever it is you're here for, Pico, but do it quickly. The neighbors will soon suspect something's wrong when they see your man at the front door. He squeezed his eyes tight shut as cupboards slammed and furniture was shoved aside.

Pico was nothing if not thorough. Which was why Marco was so petrified.

"Have you found anyone?" Romeo whispered from the patio door.

"Not here," Pico replied, without bothering to speak softly. "There's no one in the dining room either."

And then he came closer, flinging back the doors of the bedrooms. Marco heard him kick at the beds and get down on his knees to peer underneath, then get up again to tear back the curtains.

"No one here either. The kitchen's clear, too," Pico practically shouted.

"Look in the shower, it would be just like him," Romeo instructed.

Marco felt the tremble of the floor beneath him. Pico paused at the bathroom door in the hall, only three meters away. It was as if his gaze was drilling its way into the office toward Marco's hiding place. As though the steel that enveloped Marco's being only barely resisted Pico's X-ray vision.

He knows I'm here! The thought hammered in Marco's brain. And his finger responded to his anxiety by secreting more moisture so he could no longer keep his grip and the door slipped gently away from him, white light slicing through the crack like the blade of a knife.

Through the tiny aperture that ensued, he saw Pico's feet disappear into the bathroom. Adidas running shoes, new and soundless. Pico in a nutshell.

Marco feverishly pushed open the door of the safe, realizing now that he had to get out and find a place Pico had already looked. But in the same instant, Pico shouted out his frustration from the bathroom: the little bastard wasn't there either. So Marco withdrew his hand immediately, wiping his finger on his shirt, hooking it onto the inner edge of the steel door and pulling it to again.

He got just a glimpse of the toe of a running shoe as it crossed the doorsill from the bathroom before the door of the safe swung almost shut again.

Pico was in the room now, looking around, and the whole house creaked in the silence. Every tiny breath Marco took sounded like the pumping of a leaky bellows, his body on the brink of exploding. All his dreams of freedom and a life of his own rained down on him like molten metal. Reality was about to take over.

The feet on the floor took another step forward, and again Marco sensed this piercing X-ray vision burning up the room.

Pico was in the office now, so close to the safe that Marco could almost touch the fabric of his trousers through the crack. It sounded like he was rifling through the shelves above the safe. Pico wasn't one to leave a stone unturned.

He muttered something to himself, shoving books and ring binders aside. Then a book fell to the floor with a bang, landing directly in front of Marco's hiding place. Marco gasped, adrenaline hurtling through his body. If Pico couldn't hear his heart thumping now, he had to be deaf.

He saw Pico's dexterous arm reach down to pick up the book, brushing the door of the safe so that Marco lost his grip. The crack of light gradually widened as Pico stooped. Any second now he would be on his knees, peering inside.

At the very moment Marco was considering giving himself up voluntarily so he wouldn't be beaten to a pulp, a sudden infernal bird-squawk split the air, causing Pico to stop in his tracks.

"Pico, quick! Grab the photo and get out!" Romeo shouted from outside.

Pico's response was an athletic sprint through the hall and living room, followed by the sound of breaking glass and finally the patio door slamming against the outside wall.

And then all was quiet. The man at the front door had called the whole thing off with his alarm. Apparently someone had got too close to the house.

Marco tumbled out onto the floor of the office like a lump of compressed metal that would never regain its shape. All his limbs were numb, even though he rubbed them vigorously. If he didn't get his circulation going so he could get out of there, he risked being cornered if someone came barging in.

Then he forced himself onto his feet. His only chance was to take the patio door out into the open, through the back garden and hedges to the houses next door and beyond. And he would have to pray to God he didn't run into Pico and the others.

The last thing he saw as he left the house were the shards of an over-turned picture frame in the living room. That, and the empty space where the photo of William Stark had been, the one his stepdaughter had used in her poster appeal.

16

Zola sat for a moment and reviewed the situation. Any minute now, his contact would be calling routinely to hear his report on how the Marco case was developing. The timing was hardly appropriate.

He had sent the others out of the room, which was how it had to be. Only the dog remained behind. What had happened had happened and there were undoubtedly going to be repercussions the clan members definitely didn't need to hear. It was imperative his near-divine status within the family remain uncompromised, for Zola's dominance relied solely on maintaining his authority. No, this was a phone call of the utmost privacy.

When it came, he tried to begin without humility, declaring boldly that the whole sorry business was merely the fault of a silly young boy and that, as usual, he had the situation under control.

A frigid voice turned this arrogant sword of Damocles against him.

"We should never have chosen you people for the job," came the curt reply. "If this boy is allowed to wander the streets, the consequences could be enormous for everyone, not least for yourselves. I take it you're aware of that?"

"I know what I'm doing."

"So you've said before. How long has the boy been on the loose?"

"Listen! Marco's been spotted in Østerbro. All the men operating out there have been alerted."

"And what good is that when you've just told me he committed a break-in somewhere else in town entirely? He could be anywhere."

Zola clenched his teeth. The man was right. It wasn't good.

"Listen to me. All my own boys are out in Brønshøj right now. We're dragging a net from there toward the city. Besides that, we've got three cars cruising the whole area up to Gladsaxe and out toward Husum."

The voice at the other end didn't sound satisfied. "I hope for your sake it's sufficient. Apart from having his personal description, we know now that he's actually wearing Stark's necklace. Make sure the photo of it that you've procured gets out to everyone who's searching. Next time you see him, just be absolutely certain you catch him, otherwise it's better that you let him go. Do you understand? If he doesn't realize we're looking for him, it probably won't be that long before we get another chance. OK?"

Zola nodded, though he resented the tone. The job had already been too costly by half. His brother had protested at the time, saying they should let it go, but the three hundred thousand they took in for taking care of Stark's disappearance had been too tempting. The consequence of that decision had meant half the clan had been preoccupied since the end of November when Marco disappeared, and especially the last couple of days, which was extremely bad for business. With begging and thieving activities brought to a minimum, twenty-five thousand kroner were being lost every single day. The three hundred grand they'd got for kidnapping and murdering William Stark had long since been swallowed up.

A curse on that Marco! He should have clipped the boy's wings the first day he realized how smart he was.

"We'll be careful, don't worry," he assured his contact. "He won't give us the slip again."

"What was he doing out in Stark's house?"

"We don't know. We don't know how he found it either. We'll try to sort it out, OK?"

"We've talked about this before: Do you think the kid will go to the police?"

Zola paused to think. Anything he said in response would be a shot in the dark. Of course there was a chance he would turn them in. But the boy had been lying in that shallow grave when Zola and his father had discussed the body, so he knew his father was an accomplice. Maybe that would be enough to prevent him. On the other hand, it was true that he had broken into Stark's house, and why had he done that? Blackmail was the first thing that came to mind. The little parasite would likely turn all his criminal tendencies back upon those who had fostered him. The more Zola thought about it, the more probable it sounded. Under no circumstances could Marco be given the chance.

"Go to the police? Yes, I'm afraid there might be a risk of that," he therefore replied. "The boy must be stopped, whatever the price."

"Excellent." A long silence ensued, a clear sign that his employer found it anything but. "You must understand that I am compelled to mobilize my own network now, Zola," he went on. "And by the way, don't count on us contacting you the next time a similar job arises."

Bank manager Teis Snap was so stunned, he had to steady himself against his desk. Seconds before, his chairman of the board, Brage-Schmidt, had informed him that his men in the field had conceded that the boy they were looking for had broken into Stark's home. And before the full gravity of the information had kicked in, Brage-Schmidt had demanded half a million kroner in cash, to be paid into what he called the *seek and neutralize the kid* account.

"Murdering a child, here in Denmark?" Snap protested quietly. "Do you really want Karrebæk Bank's shareholders to finance that? Murder carries a life sentence, and who's going to be the fall guy if we're found out?"

"No one," came the curt reply.

"No one? I don't follow you. What do you mean?"

"It needn't come to that. But if it does, I suggest we make René E. Eriksen accountable."

Teis Snap stared at the photograph of himself and René on the desk in front of him. Two young students with beaming smiles and an ocean of broken ideals since.

"You're out of your mind," he said as calmly as he could. "René would never accept that under any circumstances. Why on earth would he?"

"*If* it becomes necessary, we shan't be asking him. He'll confess of his own accord."

"How?"

"In a suicide note."

Teis Snap pulled his Strand & Hvass office chair from the desk and sat down heavily on its soft leather. *Suicide, if it became necessary*, Brage-Schmidt had said. He hoped to God it wouldn't.

"To be on the safe side, and to make sure we don't suddenly run out of time, we have to formulate that note right away," Brage-Schmidt went on. "First of all we need to cover up any links between Eriksen and our middlemen among the Cameroon officials. I want you to instruct him to do that himself. He's the best choice in that respect. Is everything under control with our stocks in Curaçao?"

"Yes, they're all still in the safe-deposit box at Maduro and Curiel's Bank there."

"And we've got the keys?"

"Yes, René and I have both got our own, but I'll need his power of attorney."

"OK, sort it this afternoon. After that, you fly down there and gather all the stock certificates, then cancel his safe-deposit box agreement with MCB. We have to get those certificates out while he's still alive. If something goes wrong and we need to beat a fast retreat, then we'll have them as well as our own. Are you with me?"

"I suppose, yes." Teis Snap was sweating profusely as he struggled to assess the consequences. "If worst does come to worst, how do we explain his suicide?" he ventured, the final word petering into a whisper.

"Sexual abuse of a young boy, of course. That René E. Eriksen, along with his subordinate, William Stark, regularly had sex with this Marco, and the shame of it had long ago prompted Stark to choose the ultimate way out by committing suicide."

Teis Snap may have been shaken, yet he felt his heart rate steady somewhat. The advantages of such an explanation seemed plain. Even William Stark's disappearance would be accounted for.

"But this of course presupposes that we get our hands on the boy.

After all, we can't have him denying the story. And what then, if we find him? Once he's out of the way, who's going to point the finger at Stark and Eriksen for abusing him?"

"They'll accuse themselves in Eriksen's suicide note. We will include details of precisely where he got rid of the boy's body before doing away with himself."

Snap frowned. So many disagreeable decisions with equally disagreeable consequences had originated behind that same brow in the course of time. But fake suicides and kids' corpses were not obvious fixtures in his world. He had known René from their schooldays, on top of which he had children of his own, albeit older than the boy they were searching for.

"I understand. A truly frightening perspective, I must say, and yet logical. But we still need to find the boy."

"Exactly. Which is why I want you to immediately release the half million for our search operation. My contact has bloodhounds who are used to sniffing people out. All we need is to get them flown in. Transfer the funds and we're in business."

Snap smoothed his hand over the desktop. The money was no issue. The quicker it was done, the better, no question about it.

"I'll organize the transfer right away. But woe betide us if the authorities ever catch on. That's *your* department, OK? Make sure it never happens." The emphasis on "your" was pronounced. "I don't want to know what you do or where and when you do it, understand? René is an old friend of mine, after all."

"They'll do their best, I'll make sure of it."

"Who are these people you'll be flying in, anyway?"

"I don't think you should worry about that, Teis, do you?"

René E. Eriksen had been sitting in his office, routinely running through the presentation his minister was scheduled to make in the parliamentary debate the following day. Over the years, he had learned to steer his superiors through the roughest of gales, and no matter who happened to form the opposition, their attacks invariably came to naught, for René E. Eriksen had mastered the art of saying nothing of importance. When debates were most heated, the crux of the matter always remained untouched, because it was known only to him, his closest officials, and the minister himself. Eriksen was therefore revered among his peers in the steep pyramid of government officialdom, and the ministry's permanent secretary could safely turn his attention to other matters.

This was one of those good, average days when René E. Eriksen felt he was on top of things. At least until a thrumming noise from a desk drawer informed him of someone wanting to speak to him on the rarely used prepaid mobile.

It meant Teis Snap had some important news.

This time his briefing was short and steeped in detail, a far cry from Snap's usual style. It was almost as if his old school chum had learned every word by heart. But whether this was the case or not, the information he imparted was alarming indeed.

A boy who could reveal the murder of William Stark was on the loose. And to prevent the otherwise unavoidable avalanche of scandal, he had to be done away with. The search was already on.

A boy!

"For that reason we need to wipe out our tracks. I want you to get rid of anything that might link you to us and to your lackeys among the officials in Yaoundé. For our part we're erasing all traces of our connections to the folks distributing the funds and removing as much evidence as we can that links us with Cameroon, OK? Moreover, I want you to call the relevant authorities down there and tell them the project's on the back burner for a while. Tell your staff it's a routine investigation of administrative irregularities in Yaoundé, but make sure those damn pygmies get some of what's coming to them until the storm has blown over. Get hold of Louis Fon's replacement and instruct him to buy lots of banana plants as quickly as possible. Get it sorted now, not tomorrow. Are you with me, René? You're the only man we have who can do this easily, without fuss and without a trace."

"Hold on a minute, Teis. I thought I'd made it perfectly clear I didn't want to know what you were up to behind the scenes."

"You did. But the way things are at the moment, there is correspondence and records we need to get removed from the system. I'm telling you this so you'll understand the gravity of the situation. Just as you made sure to secure Stark's laptop and prevent anything compromising leaking from that source, we now need to get hold of this boy, because if we don't, the whole shebang could come tumbling down around us, especially if we're not prepared. But we *will* be prepared, won't we, René?"

René nodded to himself. He could follow the logic, yet at the same time a devil was prodding his subconscious with its fork. Teis Snap and Jens Brage-Schmidt might benefit from his carrying out these orders, but what about him? Would he, in reality, be worse off? Would he then risk being left alone in the firing line if the scam was uncovered? Or was there something more to this nagging doubt?

"One other thing, René. We're a bit worried about our stock in Curaçao. If things go wrong here in Denmark, Brage-Schmidt reckons the stocks can be traced back to us, in which case there's a risk of it all being confiscated. But now we've found someone willing to give us ten percent below the day's quotation, so I need a signature from you to the bank in Curaçao, a power of attorney so I can get into the safe-deposit box and retrieve all the certificates."

"I see. And what if I want to keep my share? Why should I hand over ten percent of fifteen million to some stranger when I can get the full rate on the market? I'm not with you."

"You know as well as I do that we need to stick together on all our decisions, René, and on this one you're in the minority."

René felt his neck muscles tense. It was as if the executioner's hatchet hung in the air above his neck. All alarms were going off at once. It wasn't only Snap's instructions but also the circumstances in which they were issued. Calling him about something as important as this without prior warning. It was most irregular. It required a personal meeting at the very least, where they could make the appropriate decisions in consensus.

Were they going to make off with all the proceeds and disappear? How could he be certain they respected his interests and that his share wouldn't suddenly vanish into thin air?

He mobilized all his instincts and experience. This eruption of chaos was not going to be at his expense. That much he knew.

"I want guarantees, Teis. Written guarantees, so I know where I stand. You can buy my shares in Karrebæk Bank at the going rate. Transfer the sum to an account in Danske Bank. Until you do, there'll be no power of attorney. Once you've sold the stocks, you're to send all documents of transfer and registration by courier to my office here in the ministry, along with your written declaration. I'll be waiting here until it's done, Teis."

Snap sounded calm, but René knew better. Teis Snap was furious.

"You know I can't do that, René, so stop all that. We haven't the funds to purchase your stocks at market price, and if *we* can't, then you'll be forcing us into the hands of third-party shareholders who we can't control. They'd be able to demand seats on the board and gain too much insight. It's not on; I can't allow it. Not for the moment!"

"OK. So what if my response to that is to go against your killing the boy?"

He counted the seconds. In their student days, Teis Snap had never possessed the sharpest mind, and little had changed in that respect. Despite his financial acumen, Snap would never be the source of any groundbreaking ideas. Experience told René that the longer Snap's pause, the greater the dilemma he felt himself to be in.

This time, however, the interlude was surprisingly brief, and Snap's reply likewise.

"But you won't, René."

And then he hung up.

During the next half hour, René E. Eriksen was not to be disturbed. He closed his door, signaling to his subordinates that he'd gone into hibernation.

Since the fraud had been initiated, René's shares in Karrebæk Bank had risen by two hundred and fifty percent. His stock was now worth precisely 14.7 million kroner, a sum that, if managed wisely, could be converted to twenty-five years of relative affluence somewhere on the other side of the world. However, after all these years his wife was still influenced by the ideals that an office girl from the provinces during the course of a long life sees, reduced to residential bliss in the suburbs of Copenhagen and two weeks twice a year somewhere in the sun. Attempting to separate her from her mail-order catalogs and the occasional looking-after of grandchildren too full of snot to go to kindergarten would be tilting at windmills.

But regardless of whether his wife could be persuaded or not, here in this dusty office, whose dark panels and reams of bureaucracy-driven paper comprised his horizon, grew the increasingly incontestable notion that this was how it had to be. And since Teis Snap was refusing to help him, pummeled as he was by impending catastrophe and unpalatable decision making, René opened the drawer and took out the calling card that had been pressed into his reluctant hand a couple of years before by a zealous young man who apparently thought it was OK to recruit financial clients at kids' birthday parties.

It was this thin-haired upstart of a backstreet banker whom he now called, and within two minutes had cheerfully agreed to sell René's shares in Karrebæk Bank for half the usual six percent commission. For 441,000 kroner he could head off to Karrebæk Bank's headquarters and collect the registered shares out of the deposit box. Just like the transfer, the transaction itself was a mere formality.

René was content. There was a risk that the unregistered stocks in the custody account in Willemstad in Curaçao would be lost, though he would not give them up without a fight. But without being willing to make that sacrifice if the situation so demanded, he would be unable to free himself of Snap and Brage-Schmidt. And this was imperative.

He got up and pulled a folder from the shelf. In it were fifteen sheets of paper, tantamount to a life-insurance policy.

The first pages were copies of the personnel department's dossier on William Stark: personal data, terms of employment, curriculum vitae, and all kinds of facts relevant to his position. The rest of the pages were manipulations of files he had found on Stark's computer, and, finally, a single sheet left in his desk drawer pertaining to his stepdaughter's latest treatment.

The idea for these manipulations had come about when the police had questioned him about Stark in regards to his disappearance. At the time the interview had been quick and painless, the questions simple and superficial, his answers likewise. But what if they should come back with more questions? And what if Teis Snap and Brage-Schmidt pulled the plug on him?

In case that happened he needed to construct a story, one that could hold water. Therefore he had removed the little lithium battery that powered the clock and put it in Stark's laptop and had begun to modify information in the files concerning the Baka project.

This he had done one evening at home, long after Lily had gone to bed. Beneath the light of the architect lamp on his desk he delved into Stark's virtual universe with bated breath, noting immediately the presence of two login identities, MINISTRY and PRIVATE, of which only the latter required a password.

Within a few minutes René realized the wisdom of their having done away with William Stark. All too many of Stark's entries concerned irregularities and anomalous procedures relating to the Baka project. While these entries uncovered nothing specifically illegal, they sowed suspicion that there could be something that warranted further investigation. The fact that Stark hadn't gone that far was their good fortune. Now, in any case, he no longer had that option.

After he had finished, René sat up most of the night trying to establish the password Stark used to access PRIVATE. When eventually he was forced to give up, he went downstairs into the basement, opened the trapdoor to the crawl space under the floor and hid the laptop. There it could remain undisturbed until he needed it again.

And now, a couple of years on, he was sitting with the modified documents based on Stark's notes. Notations that had once cast doubt upon René's management of the project but which, thanks to his manipulations, now pointed the finger at Teis Snap and William Stark himself.

Next it was only logical that he took out the rearmost sheet from the folder and in the corner, using William Stark's characteristic handwriting, wrote:

Transfer to Maduro & Curiel's Bank, followed by Teis Snap's mobile phone number.

17

For yet another entire night he had slept outdoors like one of the homeless as the gray tones of the street began permeating his clothes and countenance.

Marco was not afraid, yet he felt insecure and had every reason to be.

Kasim, who owned the Internet café, had already warned him as he drove down Randersgade in his shiny BMW and caught sight of Marco rummaging through the local supermarket's Dumpsters in search of discarded fruit and bread. He was there by chance, though Dumpster diving was a lot more productive there than behind the big supermarkets like Netto or Brugsen, where there was competition from young Danes living in communes who were unwilling to share. Class warfare existed, even on that level.

"Every piece of scum on the street is out looking for you," Kasim called out to him. "Best to stay away from here, Marco. Find somewhere safe."

So the hunt was still on.

But Marco couldn't just vanish. He didn't really believe they would be looking for him in Østerbro, and he still had thousands of kroner stashed in Eivind and Kaj's apartment. The money was his, and until it was in his possession again he would remain in the neighborhood.

Several times he had walked by and seen their windows lit up in the evening. He had also noted the sign was still hanging on the door of the dry cleaners, saying they were closed due to illness.

Apparently Kaj had yet to recover.

But when he did, and they began going to work again, he would force entry into the apartment in some way. The important thing now was to keep an eye out for Zola's people. In a week's time they would probably believe he'd disappeared and he would hopefully be able to move more freely.

For that reason he kept away from the crowds, wary of any sudden shadow, anything unexpected or untoward. He observed where the cars with foreign plates and tinted windows parked, and thus knew when all-too-alert, foreign-looking men were in the vicinity.

This Saturday morning everything seemed normal. Østerbro had awoken to a lazy summerlike weekend. It was the kind of day where the Danes mingled and meandered along the pavements, benevolent smiles of spring on their faces.

Marco had made his daily reconnaissance of the dry cleaners, hugging the wall on the other side of the street and noting that his wait would continue.

He wondered if Kaj was more badly injured than he had thought, since Eivind was apparently still unable to look after the shop.

He stood in the basement well of a disused corner shop on Willemoesgade and pondered for the thousandth time the series of events that had led him here. If Kaj and Eivind had helped him instead of throwing him out, he would have felt more guilty about what had happened to Kaj. He understood how scared they were and how reluctant to have him stay on with them after what had happened. But it wasn't *he* who had assaulted them. He hadn't volunteered to live the life of a slave in Zola's service either, or chosen a father who was prepared to sacrifice the health and life of his own son in order to please his younger brother. And had he, Marco, ever killed a person?

He raised his head and straightened his shoulders. No, he had no reason to feel guilty or ashamed. Perhaps he was beginning to smell a bit rancid and his pockets were empty, but the important thing was he had broken free. He no longer stole, and he'd begun deciding for himself who he was and what he wanted to become. For the time being he was a gypsy, and when all this was over with he would just be himself.

Staring at the facades of the buildings across the street, he saw a pale face withdraw quickly from a curtain in a ground-floor apartment. Something's wrong, he told himself instinctively, and in the same instant a van he knew all too well tore round the corner from Fiskedamsgade against the traffic and bore down on him.

Immediately he realized a second vehicle was headed toward him from the opposite end of the street and any second now he would be trapped.

When he recognized Hector behind the wheel of the van, his pulse raced wildly as he made a dash along the cobbles of Lipkesgade.

Where to, where to? he thought feverishly, as tires squealed behind him. Classensgade was too open and too wide, so he would make for Kastelsvej and see if he could find a bolt hole.

It was simply the worst possible place to be discovered. Here, of all places, where the traffic was so light and where he had felt safe. How could he have known they also had spies inside these apartment buildings?

He heard them shout from the windows for him to stop, that they meant him no harm.

Now the British Embassy loomed before him on Kastelsvej with all its labyrinths of gates and security sluices. A car parked outside the complex had attracted attention, drawing a swarm of security guards out onto the street where they now stood blocking the path that led down in the direction of Garnison's Kirkegård cemetery. A security guard was exchanging words with the driver, who seemed ill at ease with the situation. Any irregularity in this particular neighborhood was a matter of utmost concern, and the last guard to arrive turned his stern authoritative face toward the oncoming vehicles bearing down on Marco, thereby prompting them to slow down.

Marco glanced toward Østerbrogade. The distance to the cemetery, where he knew of several hiding places, was too far.

A couple of men in bulletproof vests approached him, telling him in no uncertain terms to get lost.

Realizing he could expect no help from the guards, he ran on. Within seconds his pursuers had abandoned their car and had likewise been waved on by security, and now Marco had no choice but to turn down a street lined by lush trees and homes whose residents could never imagine the calamity that was about to befall him.

He heard the van brake behind him and the door being flung open. Their mission was almost complete.

Marco ran for his life, tearing to the bottom of the cul-de-sac where, thankfully, a path running between an apartment house and a fenced-in asphalt soccer pitch appeared before him.

A group of boisterous immigrant kids were running around after a ball on the pitch while their more indolent companions hung out on the other side of the fence, smoking and making comments about the match.

"Help me, the biker pigs are after me," he pleaded, as he sprinted past.

For once his ethnic appearance stood him in good stead. Cigarettes were dashed to the ground, and the soccer game was abandoned so abruptly that the ball was still in the air as every dark face turned to confront Marco's pursuers.

As he veered off toward side streets leading down to the marina, he glanced back and saw Hector and the others come to an abrupt halt, hands raised defensively before the immigrant kids jumped them.

He didn't dare contemplate the results of such a one-sided match, but it was hardly going to make things easier for him next time he ran into Hector and company.

He had to make sure it didn't happen.

He waited on Randersgade until the headlights of Kasim's blue BMW appeared beyond the rows of parked cars.

He seemed tired, and yet somehow surprised, when Marco stepped out and held up his hand to stop him.

"Are you still here, Marco? I thought I told you to vanish."

"I've got no money." He bowed his head. "I know I already owe you. I haven't forgotten."

"Can't you go to the police?"

Marco shook his head. "I know a place I can stay. Maybe you could drive me there. You live out of town, don't you?"

"I live in Gladsaxe."

"Can you give me a lift to the Utterslev marsh?"

Kasim leaned across the passenger seat and swept a pair of paper bags onto the floor. "Keep your head down until we're out of the city, OK?"

It was a rather silent drive, Kasim clearly not wanting to know too much if anyone should ask.

"The neighborhood shopkeepers are frightened, they don't want you contacting them again," was about the only thing he said before dropping him off.

And what more was to say, really? Marco knew the trouble he had caused, and he wasn't proud of it.

The walk from the log cabin at the beginning of the motorway along the lake to Stark's house became a journey through the layers of Marco's conscience. He did not wish to steal, but in Stark's wardrobe were clothes he could use, and in the basement was a washing machine as well as jars of pickled vegetables, even though he wasn't crazy about the taste. And there were beds with sheets and duvets. All of which could help him get back on his feet.

Thus he woke up on the Sunday morning with a fraudulent feeling of having entered a new period in his life. Even the curtains and the sunlight that edged its way into the bedroom where he lay seemed completely unfamiliar. To lie all alone in a nice, well-equipped bedroom was not only a luxury for him, it was practically a picture of the future he sought.

He stretched his limbs under the duvet and tried to push the thought from his mind. Of course there was no way he could stay here, it was too risky by half. They had almost caught him yesterday, and last time he'd been here had been a close call as well. If he was to avoid something like this happening again, he'd have to turn the tables on them, make it so he observed them rather than the other way round. He needed to be one step ahead at all times.

Looking around him as he chewed on a pickled gherkin in the kitchen, he found it hard to imagine anyone but the man in the shallow grave had lived in this house. In earlier times, if he had broken in to a house like this one in the same kind of neighborhood he would at least have expected to find a couple of good kitchen appliances and a set of easily flogged knives by Solingen, Masahiro, Raadvad, or Zwilling. But this place was different. No aprons or knickknacks or anything to suggest a woman had lived here either.

Presumably they had taken all the kitchen items with them when they moved.

Only one thing stuck out. A glossy magazine left by the side of the stove. An ordinary women's weekly with the usual model on the front, the tantalizing captions about health and fashion. Nothing special, and yet it stuck out.

Marco got to his feet and picked it up. *Thursday, April 7, 2011*, read the date on the cover. Hardly a month old.

He frowned. How had it got there? Who had been in this house? The place seemed cleaner than might be expected. Did Tilde and her mother still come here? Had this magazine been in Tilde's hands? Had they stood here waiting for the kettle to boil, flicking through the pages before enjoying a cup of tea together? Perhaps they had forgotten to take it with them again and hadn't been here since.

He sniffed at the paper, but it smelled of nothing. He was disappointed.

He skimmed a few more pages before tossing the magazine back onto the counter. It was then that he noticed a small wad of what looked like crumpled plastic on the floor at the foot of the stove.

He went over and kicked it across the linoleum. Something about it made him curious, so he picked it up and flattened it out. It was some sort of foil bag with a label on it saying *Malene Kristoffersen* and her address on Strindbergsvej in Valby.

Kristoffersen! The same surname as Tilde's. Maybe it was her mother.

Marco nodded to himself. Of course, it had to be.

So now he knew where she lived.

The house was bigger than he had expected. Yellow, with an odd, almost vertical section of roof where a normal one would come to an end. It was the kind of neighborhood the clan steered well clear of when out making their break-ins. Though there were gardens all round and no shortage of places in which to hide or routes by which to steal away, the houses were so close together that the neighbors could see most of what went on behind the windows next door. Accordingly he proceeded with caution as he sneaked through the parting in the hedge and up to the names on the two mailboxes hanging next to the red-painted door.

It meant two families shared the place. On the uppermost box was a weather-worn label, which read TILDE & MALENE KRISTOFFERSEN.

Marco took a deep breath and stared at the windows above. So this was where she lived, and since it was Sunday she might even be home.

Did he have the courage to ring the bell? What would he say to them?

He stood for a moment, a trembling finger raised toward the bell, when he heard two female voices and the rustle of shopping bags coming from the street.

Someone was coming, he realized, ducking reflexively behind a bush. Then he heard laughter and two figures appeared, walking their bikes through the opening in the hedge.

He couldn't see their faces in his awkward position, but his eyes followed them as they went round the side of the house, where it sounded like they were parking their bikes.

Tilde's mother was the first to appear again. Dark-haired and rather good-looking, with a bulging shopping bag under her arm.

"Have you got your key, Tilde? Mine's underneath all this flea-market junk we hadn't the sense to ignore."

There was more laughter. It made Marco feel warm inside.

And when at last he set eyes on Tilde, he couldn't help smiling from behind the foliage of his hiding place. She was so lovely. A bit thin and gangly with big feet, yet she seemed almost to glide across the flagstones like a ballerina, dangling her key in the air in front of her.

"You're a treasure," said her mother as Tilde opened the door.

"Takes one to know one," she riposted. And then they were gone.

Marco froze the image in his mind. He wanted to remember her features. He wanted to remember them for having just made him feel so warm inside. Even the sound of her voice moved him.

Don't forget your father killed her stepfather, he told himself. How would he ever be able to approach her, especially now, after he'd seen what she was like? Now, when that inexpressible tenderness he had previously felt for her on account of William Stark and her appeal to find him had materialized in flesh and blood, with light and luminous laughter to boot?

How could he approach her with the feelings he had, knowing he had done nothing in spite of what he knew?

Marco extracted himself from the bushes and wandered farther up the road, past gaudily painted homes that only made him feel dirtier inside.

He had to do something. Even though it would hurt her a lot to learn the truth, she needed to know. He felt he owed it to her. Which was why it had become necessary to go to the police, even if it meant sacrificing his father.

The next morning he rummaged through the wardrobe of women's clothes and found a checkered shirt better than the one he had, and more or less his size. He took a Windbreaker from the hall and went down into the basement, where he pulled his clean underwear and socks out of the drier.

He considered himself in the bathroom mirror and nodded. He looked so decent all of a sudden, certainly tidy enough for what he had to do. All he needed now was a little cash, and that was the hard part.

If only he could sell off the clothes that Stark would definitely no longer be needing, his financial problems would be somewhat alleviated. But he knew no one who bought secondhand clothes or everyday china and furniture. No one wanted analog TV sets anymore, or computer towers or hi-fi systems, and nobody would ever buy the other knickknacks. So while it may have resembled a perfectly average Danish home, it contained absolutely nothing that could be sold for money. Danes simply adored spending money, so anything that was more than a few years old quickly became worthless.

Maybe it was better this way. The only things he had stolen in a long time were a few clothes and half a jar of pickled gherkins, and he wanted it to stay that way.

He walked round the house for five minutes in his bare feet just to savor the soft, ticklish feeling of plush carpets and imagine what it would be like to have a home of his own, surrounded by things he owned and was fond of.

When he came to the safe, the uneasiness rose up inside him again. He got down on his knees and peered inside to see if he could still remember the code.

He could. *A4C4C6F67*.

The enigma of it made him smile briefly, and then he suddenly realized the letters and the figures were not all written in the same way, but in different pairs of black and gray. The way the morning light slanted into the room made it obvious now. *A4* was bold and black. *C4* was lighter and rather more fuzzy, as though the pen had almost run out. Looking closer, he could see that *C6* and *F6* and *7* had apparently also been added at different times. So the code had gradually been extended. He sat down on the floor, leaning against the safe as he pondered the problem. Behind the sequence lay perhaps a series of separate actions rather than just one.

He let himself out through the back door, standing for a moment on the patio to take stock.

If there wasn't a bike he could borrow in the shed, he would have to walk the whole way.

But there was.

His first stop was a library in Brønshøj, the closest to his route. He sat there reading for some time, close to the counter where he could keep an eye on who came in. Some went straight to the adults' or children's section, others first returning books they had borrowed. The latter were the ones he was waiting for because part of the process of returning books entailed scanning their national identity cards.

He picked out a boy his own age. Like most other young Danes, he lacked respect for the value of material things and was careless with his possessions. Marco watched as the boy slipped his ID back into his wallet, which he then casually stuffed into the open front pocket of his shoulder bag. Before long, the bag was lying on the floor at his feet while he surfed the Internet on one of the computers.

Marco approached slowly, and when the adjoining computer was vacated he sat down, silent as a cat, and typed in a Web address off the top of his head.

An hour later he parked the bike a couple of streets from his destination. Strictly speaking it was stolen, even though he was intending to return it.

Bellahøj police station on Borups Allé was rather bigger than he had anticipated, monumentally menacing and loathsome to the eye. Gray concrete surfaces, people endlessly coming and going. Marco couldn't help feeling defenseless as he went inside.

Considering he had spent his entire life in the shadow of criminal activity, it felt more than a little strange that the first time he ever entered a police station, or even came in contact with the law, was something he was doing voluntarily. No one so much as looked at him as the automatic doors opened, and he walked in almost sideways in order not to expose his face to the cameras above the entrance. He gazed around the place in wonder. The duty desk was a study in streamline procedure and surprisingly devoid of drama. Neat sky-blue shirts and black ties all round, and most of the officers he saw were young.

Apart from Marco, only two women sat on the benches, waiting for their turn. As far as he could make out, one of them had had her bag snatched while the two were cycling together. Its contents had obviously been important to her, since she was sobbing and seemed to be in a state of shock.

It didn't make Marco feel any better as he sat on the edge of the bench, trying to memorize what he was going to say when his turn came.

When eventually he was called forward, he placed Stark's African necklace on the counter together with one of his missing persons notices.

The duty officer stared at them, slightly disoriented.

"The necklace belonged to the man in the picture," Marco began, keeping an eye on the two officers who sat farther back behind the counter, typing away at their computers.

At this point he'd intended to say he had been given the necklace by a friend of his, and that this friend knew the man was dead and where he was buried. That this friend had told him who might have killed him and disposed of the body. And then he was going to say that his friend was too afraid to come in person, whereupon he would hand the officer the ID he had stolen from the boy at the library to "prove" that his friend existed. The boy would of course be unable to help the police if they contacted him, but at least they would have this to go on. And Marco they would never see again.

Only things turned out differently.

"Do you have any ID, son?" the officer asked.

It was a development Marco had not anticipated. Had he known, he would have stolen *two* cards, not one.

"You understand what I'm asking you for, don't you?" the officer added.

Marco nodded and placed the ID on the counter.

The officer studied it for a moment.

"Thank you, Søren," he said. "The way things work here, we're going to have to speak to your parents because legally you're what's called a minor. So if you give me their mobile number, I'll give them a quick call before we do anything else. Then they can be present while you tell us about it, all right?"

Marco's brain went into overdrive. "I'm sorry," he said, clutching at straws. "I can't remember their phone numbers 'cause they're always changing them. My mobile has their numbers, but it's being repaired."

The officer smiled. "That's OK, Søren, I know what you mean. I'll just look them up from your address here." He indicated the ID card and rolled his chair over to a computer.

A second later he raised a finger in the air. He'd found them.

Marco backed away toward the entrance as the cop picked up the phone. It was all going wrong.

And as the duty officer waited for the reply, he looked up at Marco again and immediately sensed something was amiss.

"Hey, where you going, kid?" he asked, raising his voice.

At that moment Marco heard footsteps from the corridor behind the duty desk and a plainclothes policeman appeared, greeting a uniformed colleague and sending a shiver down Marco's spine. It was the policeman he had seen through the window of Stark's house only three days before, and this time their eyes met.

"All right, Carl, good to see you, too," the officer said in return.

This was when Marco made a run for it, through the glass doors and away.

A cry went up behind him, commanding him to stop, and as he legged it past the parking lot two officers stopped in their tracks and stared open-mouthed. Before they had a chance to realize what was happening he was over the fence that ran alongside the building, tearing across a lawn and over another fence. A hundred meters farther on by the next road, Stark's bike was parked outside a kindergarten, and seconds later he was pedaling hell for leather toward the city, choosing the narrowest, most inaccessible side streets he could find.

It had all gone wrong. He hadn't been able to tell them where Stark's body was buried or who had killed him. Almost even worse: he had been seen by the policeman who had spotted him outside Stark's home.

Marco swore in as many languages as he knew.

Knowing the police as he did, they would not stop there. Before he realized it, they, too, would be after him. He only hoped that for all his caution he had not been caught on their CCTV.

Now you've got to find a place in the city to hide out where they won't find you, and where you can keep an eye on them all, he told himself. Once he had found the place he would have to wait and see what happened before trying to retrieve his money from Kaj and Eivind.

Reaching the junction of Jagtvej and Åboulevard, he paused to consider his options, none of which were without peril. The issue was where he could best keep an eye on them in relative safety. Østerbro or the city center?

He stood for a moment straddling the bike and then made his decision. At four o'clock Miryam and the others would be picked up by the van at Rådhuspladsen. If he kept his distance he would be able to see who had been sent out to steal and who'd been sent out searching for him.

At Rådhuspladsen he looked around the square for a place to leave the unlocked bike without the risk of someone taking off with it. It was a tall order, considering this was perhaps the busiest place in all of Denmark.

And then, right next to the Tivoli Gardens, an enormous renovation project loomed up in front of him. He had seen it countless times before without ever properly having registered what it was.

Not until now.

His housing problem was solved.

18

Carl had been feeling lousy all weekend. Mika and Morten had thrown a party Saturday evening, partly to celebrate their publicly confirmed cohabitation, partly to blow a portion of the outrageous sum of money Morten's Playmobil collection had fetched on eBay.

"He got sixty-two grand!" Jesper had exclaimed at least a dozen times, while they busied themselves putting little umbrellas into cocktail glasses. He was already wondering if he could make an earner out of his retired Action Men in the attic.

Sixty-two grand. Christ on a bike!

It was for this reason that the wine and beer, not to mention the contents of a large number of glitzy-looking bottles of spirits, flowed more copiously than Carl could remember ever having occurred at his end of Rønneholtparken. By ten o'clock the neighbors from number 56 were definitively down for the count, and the only ones besides Carl who kept afloat until after midnight were Morten and Mika and a pair of their rat-arsed, dance-crazed gay friends.

Finally, when Carl was dragged to his feet to dance for the umpteenth time by a forty-year-old bloke in tight trousers and a leather hat coquettishly angled on his head, he staggered resolutely past a ruddy-faced, heavily sleeping Hardy and made for his bed.

The host couple were engaged in a slow and intimate dance at the foot of the stairs.

"Damn shame about Mona," Mika slurred, giving him a pat on the shoulder.

"Yeah," Morten added. "We're gonna miss her."

How many times had he ever even seen her? Twice?

Were they expecting him to thank them for cheering him up?

He awoke on Sunday with a taste in his mouth like dead rodent. His head was ablaze with both a hangover and qualms of conscience, but worse than that was a more than latent feeling of being at odds with himself.

"Goddammit, you're not going to lie here feeling sorry for yourself, Carl Mørck," he growled to himself, though to little avail. The more his head pounded, the more certain he became that people such as Lars Bjørn and especially Mona Ibsen had to be direct descendants of Tycho Brahe or others who always brought only bad luck.

A couple of hours passed during which he lay packed inside his duvet, shivering and sweating in turn, now full of wrath, now meek as a mouse.

You're not going to get over this until you speak to her, he told himself over and over again. But his mobile remained untouched as those downstairs began to stir, then spill outdoors into the blessings of the month of May.

And then he fell asleep again, staying in his bed until another Monday morning threatened.

"Assad," he yelled. "Get in here a minute, will you?"

No reaction.

Was he splayed out on that prayer mat again with his head turned to Mecca? Carl looked at his watch. No, he couldn't be, not yet.

"ASSAD!" he tried again, at full volume.

"He's not come back yet. Don't you listen to anything, or has that hangover of yours made you deaf?"

Carl looked up at Rose, who stood in the doorway scratching the last of the peeling skin off her nose. "Back? From where?"

"Stark's bank."

"What the hell's he doing there?"

"He's been in touch with the probate court, too, and the tax authorities."

Why the hell couldn't she ever just answer a question? Was it a rule now that he had to drag every little piece of information out of her?

"What are you two up to this time? You're hiding something from me, Rose, I can tell."

She gave a shrug. "I've been on the phone with Malene Kristoffersen. As luck would have it, she and her daughter just got home from a vacation in Turkey a couple of days ago."

"OK. Can you get her in here, do you think?"

"I reckon so. Sometime tomorrow, maybe."

Carl shook his head. "Hallelujah. Not exactly keen, then, or what?"

"Sure she is. She could have been here in a couple of hours, but Tilde's at the hospital all day for a check-up, so I thought we should give them a bit of breathing space till tomorrow."

"All right, then. But what's it got to do with what you and Assad are up to?"

"You'll find out when he gets back."

He turned up five minutes later, his hair looking like an explosion in a mattress factory, a sure indicator of his level of activity.

"Carl," he began, breathlessly. "After Rose and I spoke to Stark's girlfriend, she and I both felt something was not quite right."

Really? Why wasn't Carl surprised?

"Rose said Stark had helped her daughter, Tilde, with some very expensive treatment over the course of about five years before he disappeared. In fact, he spent a lot more money on it than he had."

"But there was Stark's inheritance, remember?"

"Yes, Carl. But that was not until 2008, the year he went missing. This was a hundred years before, as far back as 2003. At the bank we could see he spent nearly two million kroner more than he had saved up. At first I thought he must have borrowed the money and paid back the loan with the money he inherited, but not so."

His curly-haired assistant's eyes narrowed the way they did only when a new meaty case tickled his fancy. Carl gave a sigh. What a way to start the week.

"OK, so tell me about Tilde's treatment and this money, Rose."

She unfurled her tightly folded arms, the prelude to what was bound to be a longer briefing than necessary.

"Tilde suffers from a nasty inflammatory disease of the bowel called Crohn's disease. It means her intestines are in a chronic state of infection. Malene explained to me that William Stark took an enormous interest in her illness and spent loads of money on alternative treatment when the usual methods like surgical removal of infected sections of the bowel or cortisone treatments didn't have the intended effect."

"Thanks, but you're avoiding the question, Rose. Where does the two million enter into it, and how? It's a lot of money, I'd say, even for medical treatment."

"Malene told me Stark was obsessed with finding the ultimate treatment for the disease, even though it can't be cured. Tilde's been treated at private clinics in Copenhagen and in Jacksonville, Florida. On top of that she's had homeopathy in Germany and acupuncture in China. He even paid to have her infected by living parasites from the intestines of pigs. Everything imaginable to the tune of two million kroner, according to Malene's estimate, over the five or six years they were together before Stark went missing."

"Two million. If she's telling the truth, which we don't know."

"Oh, yes, Carl." Assad dropped a pile of transaction slips onto the desk in front of him. "It's all there. Stark had his bank transfer the amounts from his account."

"OK. So what am I supposed to deduce from this?"

Rose smiled. "That Stark was a wizard at poker, or got exceptionally lucky at the casino. What else?"

Carl frowned. "I detect some sarcasm, Rose. But can you actually prove he *didn't* get the money like that?"

"Let's just say that Stark raised a lot of capital that he channeled on without accounting for where he got it," Rose replied.

Carl turned to Assad. "What about the tax authorities? Rose says you've been in touch with them. They must have known about all this income."

Assad shook his head. "Negative, Carl. They had nothing registered in the way of increased income during the period in question, and Stark was never called to explain. So it seems they knew nothing about these transactions because the deposits were only in his account for a few days before the exact amount was paid out again. The balance at the end of the year was never higher than at the end of the year before."

"And because he was a regular wage earner he was never picked out for a routine spot check, I imagine. Am I right?"

Assad nodded. "There was something else that bothered me, too. The safe-deposit box he rented. I began to wonder why he canceled it. Malene Kristoffersen told me he took home some jewelry from it, his parents' wedding rings and some other items. But then Rose asked her what had become of these things."

"Yeah, I asked her if she had them in her possession. But she said she'd never actually seen them, and I believe her. That was why the items were never reported stolen when they had the break-in. She was simply unable to describe them. She wasn't sure they even existed, let alone had been stolen."

"Stark could have rented a safe-deposit box in another bank and stored them there."

Assad shook his head deliberately. "I think not, Carl. Malene believed that the jewelry existed, and if it wasn't stolen, he must have found a really good spot to hide it in the house. She said she was still hoping he would come back and retrieve them."

Carl noted the first wrinkle of a frown being born between Assad's eyebrows. His assistant had never been one for blind optimism.

"Can you see what we're getting at, Carl?" said Rose. "The whole thing stinks!"

Was she gloating, or was it commitment that made her face light up like that? Carl had never quite been able to tell the difference.

"This case is like a spiderweb," she went on. "Malene loved William Stark, and he certainly loved her and her daughter. He'd have done any-thing for them. Then all of a sudden he disappears just like that, and Malene says he hadn't the slightest reason for doing so."

"Then what makes her think he might come back? If he really had no reason to vanish, then most probably he's dead, in which case he's hardly likely to come back, is he?" said Carl. "Maybe she's got a screw loose, or else the opposite. Maybe she's the one who made him disappear. We don't know for certain if he actually made it all the way home the day he came back from Africa. Are we quite sure of her movements leading up to his disappearance?"

Assad sat fidgeting and looked like he was miles away, so it was Rose who answered.

"Forensics went through the house with a fine-toothed comb. Dog units were out and everything. The garden hadn't been dug up for ages and there was no sign of recent home improvements or DIY jobs. So if his body was there, or still is, it means something must have really gone wrong for them two and a half years back."

"Y'know what?" said Assad suddenly. "Unless he had ten million lying around in a cardboard box and Malene nicked it all, he'd be worth more to her alive. As far as I can see, this is about something else entirely. This is about a man who should have been in Africa for several days, but then he changes his plane ticket and flies back to Denmark ahead of time. Why did he do this? Did he have something to sell? Did his money come from illegal diamond trafficking and he was supposed to meet someone here in Denmark who then did away with him? Or was it an accident? Did he take ill and fall in the marsh? This I do not believe, because it was trawled thoroughly." He shook his head. "There are too many possibilities here, I think. Another thing is that he was afraid of water, it says so in the report, so he wouldn't have ventured too close under any circumstances. So what happened after he left the airport? If only we could find out where he went."

Carl nodded. "Rose, next time you speak to Malene I want to be there, OK? Until then I want you to check out her background. Talk to her colleagues. Ask around at the hospital where Tilde was being treated when Stark went missing. What were these people's impression of Malene? Stark, too, for that matter."

He turned to Assad. "And, Assad, I want you to go through those bank slips and check if the dates when Danske Bank transferred large sums for Stark can be connected with any criminal activities that occurred just before the withdrawals, that can't otherwise be linked to Stark. I'm talking about all kinds of things: narcotics, robberies, smuggling, whatever.

"Any other piffling, little jobs we can assist you with?" asked Rose. "How about we sort out Kennedy's assassination or maybe square the circle while we're at it?"

Assad smiled and dug his elbow into Rose's side. Pair of effing comedians.

"There is actually one more thing I'd like to say before I ride out to Bellahøj and have a chat with the lads who investigated the break-in at Stark's place."

Rose gave Carl a look of resignation. What now?

"Dear friends. This is a festering boil of a case you've got your teeth into. Well done, both of you."

One could have heard a pin drop.

"Rattlesnake" was what they called Deputy Chief Inspector Hansen. He received Carl with a pair of piercing, slanting eyes and a characteristic whistle of air issuing from between his front teeth. Totally without enthusiasm. They had patrolled together for two weeks back in the days of yore and it was two weeks too many.

Now Hansen was the man they sent out when ten cars had had their paint jobs scratched on some quiet residential street, or at best when someone had done a couple of decent break-ins in the district. "Decent" was hardly the word to describe the job that was done on Stark's place, but since the house had been sealed at the time in connection with an ongoing investigation, Hansen had been instructed to be meticulous so any indications of the burglary and Stark's disappearance being linked could be properly uncovered.

"Why didn't you just use the phone?" Hansen asked, without taking his eyes off the report he was reading.

"If I'd known it was you who was working this case, I'd have sent a telegram."

A smile of microscopic dimensions creased Hansen's lips. "My name's on the damn report, or haven't you read it?"

"There are a whole lot of nice people who are called Hansen. Who could have suspected it was you?"

Hansen looked up. "Still the charmer, eh, Carl?"

"Joking aside, Hansen, I've got the report here from the first search of the house after Stark's disappearance. Comparing it to yours, it strikes me there apparently wasn't so much as a butter knife taken in the later break-in. But that can't be right, can it? Straight up, just how thorough were you when you went through the place after that break-in? Are you sure there was nothing missing? A shoebox, a sheet of paper off a notice board, a basket from the shed?"

"As you can see in the report, I brought along William Stark's lady friend and one of the lads from HQ who'd been there the first time. We went through the place together, yes, quite thoroughly I'd call it. The attic, all the drawers, the basement, the garden, all over. There wasn't a thing missing. They could have nicked a decent pair of speakers and some silver cutlery and the lawnmower, too, but it was all left untouched."

"What about fingerprints?"

"There weren't any."

"Professional job, then?"

"So we reckon. Like I said, it's all in the report," Hansen replied drily. "The neighbor's description of the perpetrators wasn't worth much, I'm afraid. It was anything but precise. One of them was a bit darker than the other, she said, but not as dark as Africans or Pakistanis, and not like Turks or Arabs either. So basically, it could have been anyone."

OK. That was what the neighbor had said to Hansen. The question now was whether Carl could get anything more precise out of the woman.

"And what exactly does this report of yours conclude regarding the nature of the break-in and its motivation? As far as I can see, it doesn't say a thing."

"I only write facts, Carl. We can't all go around telling fairy tales like you."

"Right now you're not writing anything, you're talking to me, so give it a try. What's your conclusion, Hansen? I need the opinion of a burglary expert."

Hansen sat up a bit straighter in his chair and stuffed his sky-blue shirt into his trousers. Clearly, he wasn't a man used to dealing with compliments.

"Could just have been someone who read about the case in the papers and saw an easy job in an empty house. Pretty common these days. Funeral notices in newspapers are a case in point. Might as well just tell people there's no one in. Then you've got all the morons who post their vacation plans on Facebook and other places. When the cat's away the mice will play, as the saying goes."

"Any other ideas?"

"The alternative is someone looking for something in particular. To be honest, I think that's your best bet."

"Why would that be?"

"Because the thieves concentrated only on certain places in the house even though they were there more than an hour. It was as if they'd been there before."

"What makes you think that?"

"Because otherwise, dear Carl, everything in the drawers would have been scattered all over the place. Instead, they immediately started slashing mattresses and sofa cushions and pulling the furniture out from the walls to see if there was anything behind. Makes one think they were already familiar with the place, as though for example they'd been there before."

This was just what Carl wanted to hear. He thanked Hansen and headed for the duty desk. Next stop would be Stark's neighbor. He wanted a description of the thieves from the horse's mouth.

But then something happened instead.

The moment he stepped into the desk area, exchanging brief hellos with a former colleague, he saw a boy standing by the entrance.

Carl realized it wasn't the first time he'd looked into those eyes.

What the . . . was all he managed to think before the lad made a break for it, through the entrance doors and away, the duty officer calling out after him.

Carl began running, too, and just managed to see him disappear over the perimeter fence and head off toward Hulgårdsvej.

His cries to stop were in vain.

"Who was he?" he asked the duty officer.

The policeman gave a shrug and handed him an ID card.

"Søren Smith." Carl tilted his head. "Hmm, he didn't look much like a Søren to me."

"No, he didn't. Trace of an accent, too, I'd say. He could have been a late adoption, of course. I'm about to give his folks a call. Maybe they know what was bothering him. Oh, and he just managed to dump these things on the counter. Not sure they're his, though. Might belong to someone who did something he wanted to report to the police."

He pointed toward a necklace and a poster of some kind.

Carl felt his jaw drop.

"Well, fuck me," he almost whispered.

He put a hand on the duty officer's shoulder. "No need to make that call. I'll get over to the family straightaway. And I'll take these with me, OK?"

The house was unusually neat compared to most others in Copenhagen's Nordvest district. Who would have thought that behind the rose hedge in this industrial-looking area with its urban planner's nightmare of heterogeneous blocks of apartments and anarchistic lattice of plots of land would be found such an idyllic little thatched cottage?

The woman who opened the door, however, looked rather less idyllic and was certainly not used to strangers ringing her doorbell.

"Yes?" she inquired hesitantly, eyes scanning Carl as if he were carrying bubonic plague.

He pulled his badge out of his back pocket. As could be expected, the effect it had wasn't comforting.

"It's about Søren. Is he in?" he asked, knowing full well he probably wasn't, seeing as he'd only just left the police station.

"He is, yes," the woman replied anxiously. "What's this about?"

Jesus! The lad must have had a bike parked nearby, otherwise there was no way he could have gotten home so fast. "It's nothing serious. I'd just like to have a word with him, if you don't mind."

She ushered him inside into the front room, wringing her hands and calling for the boy a couple of times before eventually darting up to his room and dragging him away from his computer and downstairs again under vociferous protest. Separating a teenager from his favorite toy wasn't easy, Carl knew the problem all too well from back home.

A run-of-the-mill Danish youngster with hair the color of liver paste wriggled free of her grip. It was not the boy he was looking for, not by a long shot.

"I think you lost something," Carl said, handing him his national identity card.

The boy took it reluctantly. "Yeah, I did. Where'd you find it?"

"I'd rather ask you why you don't have it yourself. Did you lend it to someone?"

He shook his head.

"And you're sure about that? There was a lad at Bellahøj police station half an hour ago using it for ID, saying he wanted to report something on behalf of a friend. That wouldn't be you by any chance?"

"No way. The card was in my wallet that got nicked out of my bag at the library in Brønshøj. And I'm pretty sure who took it. Have you got my wallet as well? There was twenty-five kroner in it."

"I'm afraid not. What were you doing there, anyway? Aren't you supposed to be in school at that time of day?"

The boy looked affronted. "We're doing a project, if you know what that is."

Carl looked at his mother, whose shoulders had gradually relaxed. He wondered if she took an interest in his school project.

"What did this thief look like, Søren? Can you describe him to me?"

"He had on a checkered shirt and didn't look Danish. Not black, more brownish, like he came from southern Europe. I've been to Portugal and he looked like a lot of the people there."

Carl was certain. It was the same boy he'd seen at the police station and outside Stark's house a couple of days before. So far, so good.

"How old do you reckon he was?"

"I dunno. I didn't really look at him. He was just sitting at the computer next to me. Fourteen or fifteen, maybe."

It wasn't the first time Carl had been inside the building that housed the public library on Brønshøj Square. He recalled the time his patrol car was sent out there to detain a drunk who had been playing Frisbee with the library's LP collection. And though it had been some years ago and the building had since been freshened up a bit, it still looked like the old Bella cinema that, like so many others around Copenhagen, had given up the ghost and been superseded by supermarkets and, in this case, a bank and local library.

"I think you'll need to ask Lisbeth. She stands in for our section leader sometimes," said the librarian at the counter. "She was on duty at the time you mention."

Ten minutes passed before she arrived, but it was worth the wait.

Lisbeth sent sparks tingling down his spine. The kind of woman who recharged a man's batteries at a glance. Mature and self-aware, with an astonishing forthright gaze. If Mona's silly capriciousness turned out to be serious—and he most definitely hoped it wasn't, even though the way he felt about her at the moment she could kiss a certain part of his anatomy—he knew it would not be the last time he paid a visit to this library.

"We're a bit short-staffed at the moment due to illness, so we're all taking turns to lend a hand. I've only been assisting here for a month, so you want to show your colleagues you're not afraid to give it a go."

He was in no doubt she was able.

"Yes, I do remember the boy you mention. In fact, I know him better than you might think. It's actually quite odd to see him all the way out here in Brønshøj."

"You mean you'd seen him before, somewhere else?"

"Yes. Normally I'm deputy head of the Østerbro branch on Dag Ham-marskjölds Allé. He's been coming there every single day for months."

Carl smiled, partly because of what he'd just been told and partly because of Lisbeth herself, in equal portions. "Excellent. Perhaps you also remember what his name is."

She shook her head. "He always came at different times each day and immediately sat down in one of the chairs to read, or else he'd go over to the computers. He never borrowed anything, so we never needed to see his ID."

Carl stood completely still for a moment, trying to gauge what lay behind those candid blue eyes. Was she flirting with him or just surprised by the singularity of the coincidence?

"He seems to be quite a fantastic boy. All of us at the Østerbro branch agreed we'd never seen someone his age so eager to learn. It became a kind of a sport for one of my colleagues to check what he'd been reading after he put the books back on the shelves."

OK, so it must have been the boy she fancied.

"What was he doing here in Brønshøj, then?"

"He just turned up one day. Sat over there reading magazines, technical stuff, then he went over to the computers. I don't know how long he was there, because I swapped duties with one of the other librarians."

"Did things go missing from people's bags a lot when you were at Østerbro?"

She baulked at the question. "Why do you ask? Do you suspect him of stealing? I'd have a hard time believing it, I can tell you."

It was all Carl needed to know. If she couldn't believe it, he certainly wasn't going to destroy her image of the lad.

He shook his head. "This colleague at the Østerbro branch who was curious about what the boy was reading, I'd like to speak to her. Do you know where I can get in touch with her? Would she be at work now, do you think?"

"Liselotte's on maternity leave. But I can check and see where she lives if you want to call her. Just a minute."

His eyes followed the gentle sway of her hips in her tight skirt all the

way to the office. Christ, if only Mona would call tonight and tell him
how sorry she was.

Liselotte Brix was most certainly pregnant. In fact, she was so pregnant
he would have been unable to describe her body's proportions without
making a chauvinistic reference to her condition.

She received him with arms extended over her midriff, looking clearly
dismayed in a home already fully equipped for the baby's arrival. Packs
of disposable diapers lined the shelf. The cradle, complete with canopy
and battery-driven mobile, ready and waiting in the corner. Apparently
she wasn't superstitious.

"I do hope the boy hasn't got himself into trouble. He was just *so*
cute." She patted her distended navel. "If I knew what he was called I'd
name this little terror here after him!"

Carl smiled. "No, we're looking for him because we think he may have
some important information in connection with a missing persons case."

"God, how exciting."

"Your colleague, Lisbeth, told me you used to check up on what he'd
been reading."

"Yes, it was because he seemed to devour almost anything. And also
because he never noticed how fascinated we were by him. It was really
funny."

"Can you give me a couple of examples of things he read?"

"Like I said, it was everything, really. At one point he was heavily
into career choices and forms of education. Everything from 'What Do I
Want to be When I Grow Up?' pamphlets to university admissions cri-
teria or brochures on preparatory courses. All pretty advanced for a boy
his age. Other times he'd be reading about Denmark and Danish society.
Sociology, domestic politics, contemporary Danish history. Books on the
Danish language, dictionaries. I remember once he spent time studying a
handbook on Danish opera. There were books on Gypsies, on the legal
system, biology, and math. There were really no limits to his curiosity.
He read novels, too, even the old Danish classics. And yet he never once
borrowed anything to take home with him. Strange, don't you think?"

"What was the reason for that, do you reckon?"

"I have no idea. But he was different, you see. A bit like an immigrant, but not like the other immigrant boys. I thought he might be a Gypsy, in which case his being so bookish was probably frowned upon at home."

"A Gypsy?"

"Yeah, you know. That lovely brown skin color, and all those black curls. But he could also have been Spanish or Greek. His accent was different, though, more American sounding, but he definitely wasn't mulatto."

"OK."

"The odd thing was, his accent seemed to dwindle away. His Danish kept improving by the week and his vocabulary expanded all the time. It seemed totally autistic, the way he just soaked everything up."

"If I understand you right, there were never any adults with him. Was there anything else that might indicate where he belonged?"

"Not really, no." Liselotte's eyebrows gave a slight twitch. Most likely due to a kick from her baby. "He was just so *cute*, that's all."

"Do you know if he still uses the branch on Dag Hammarskjölds Allé?"

"Yes, he does. I talk every day with one of the girls who works there. Just this past week he hasn't been coming much, but I suppose you can ask them yourself."

19

"That's correct, Bjørn. I took those effects with me from Bellahøj and now we've taken on the William Stark case."

Marcus Jacobsen's acting replacement nodded, though it seemed clear to Carl he would have preferred to have shaken his head instead. Again, it was Bjørn in a nutshell, never the one to let a person know what he was really thinking. But Carl had him sussed.

"Good," Bjørn replied, again meaning something else. "Hansen out in Bellahøj says you swiped those items straight off their counter without their consent. I presume you know you're out of order there, Carl, seeing as how the effects are connected with a break-in on their turf."

"Yeah, yeah, Hansen says a lot of things when he ought to keep his mouth shut. This is about a missing person, which is not exactly Rattle-snake's specialty. But if he thinks he'd enjoy having a gawp at the neck-lace and that poster, he can drop by and I'll show them to him. The bottom line is that I've taken over the case."

"Taken over? Pretty big words, coming from you, Carl." Bjørn smiled, mouth half-open. It didn't suit him, though no doubt he thought it did. "You say you saw this boy outside Stark's house and then again at Bella-høj station, and both times he got away? Yes, Carl, that's definitely what I'd call taking over."

"Listen here, Bjørn! I'll get hold of him, don't you worry. You're not talking to one of your own dickheads now. It's only a matter of time."

Bjørn straightened up in his chair behind Marcus Jacobsen's desk. Wrong man, wrong desk. It couldn't have been more obvious.

"Temper, temper, Carl. Just a little misstep, I'm sure, but let's move on. It is my impression the time has come to make a few changes in Department Q. You will remain as leader of the department, of course, but during the last couple of years our work seems to have overlapped somewhat, which both Marcus and I have found disruptive."

Carl shifted forward in his chair.

What the fuck was this?

Carl's hands still trembled with rage as he accepted Assad's intricately decorated little cup of pungent spiced tea. He stared dejectedly into the slimy substance. It looked poisonous, but that was nothing compared to its smell.

"Take it easy, Carl," said his assistant. "We just carry on as normal. No one is going up to the third floor, and I will not work for Bjørn. That I will take care of."

Carl raised his head. "And you reckon you've the clout for that, do you? May I ask what makes you think that? Was it part of the deal for looking after his house?"

Assad's eyes wavered for a second like those of a criminal who stops himself from confessing at the last moment, or those of a boy loath to reveal his true feelings for a girl.

"I don't know what this 'clout' means, but I will take care of it, Carl. Lars Bjørn will listen to me." He tried to smile his way out of his predicament, well knowing the issue was still open.

But then his face lit up with a sly look. This was going to be about camels, Carl could tell.

"Just remember the story about the camel who thought he was an ostrich but got sand in his eyes when he was frightened and stuck his head into the dunes."

Carl shook his head wearily. If he added up how many camels Assad had driveled on about, the Sahara wouldn't have room for them all.

"What the hell's that supposed to mean, Assad?"

"You see, Carl, if only we stick to our true nature we will never get sand in our eyes."

"Thanks for the advice. The fact of the matter, however, is that I am *not* a camel. Remember that, Assad. Besides, I haven't a clue as to that animal's intellectual capacity, but I can tell you that to me it looks like you're the one sticking his head into the sand. Don't you reckon it's about time you came clean and told me how come Bjørn suddenly out of nowhere, and despite your apparent inexperience, places you down here with me, whereupon you begin to demonstrate skills and abilities normally associated with years of policing experience? If I want an answer to that, do I go to you or Bjørn?"

Assad frowned, and deep in his trouser pockets Carl sensed a pair of clenched fists.

"What's going on here?" came Rose's blowtorch voice from the doorway. "There's enough sparks flying around in here to light a bonfire."

Carl turned his head reluctantly toward her. "That arsehole Lars Bjørn has decreed that Assad is going to be working for him and that you and me, Rose, are being moved up to the third floor. And now Assad claims he can talk him out of it. Naturally I asked him what the hell made him think he had the clout."

Rose nodded pensively. "And what did you say to that, Assad?"

The bulges in Assad's pockets smoothed out. The sparkle in his dark eyes returned. He'd extracted himself from Carl's web. Shit!

"Bjørn and I go back some time and he owes me a favor. We know each other from some work in the Middle East. I cannot tell you more. I'm bound hand and foot."

"Can't, or won't, Assad?"

"Yes" was all he said.

Fifteen minutes later Carl's phone rang and Lis informed him that Assad was now sitting in Bjørn's office and if it wasn't too much to ask, might the esteemed Detective Inspector Mørck care to join them immediately and bring Rose with him?

"I'm not keen on Assad and Bjørn chumming up like this, Carl," said Rose, as they trudged up the stairs. "What's your feeling about it? Any idea what's going on with those two?"

Carl raised an eyebrow. Had she really just asked him for his opinion? There was a first time for everything.

"I—" was all he managed to say before she cut him off. Back to normal. "Personally, I don't like it one bit."

And that was all she had to say on the matter.

Bjørn's office had undergone a transformation during the last two hours. Lis and an army of workers had raided the shelves and cupboards, leaving them all but empty, and now a service technician was busy screwing an enormous whiteboard on to the wall just where Marcus Jacobsen used to have photos from crime scenes.

Assad was seated in a chair that had doubtless been removed from the commissioner's office. Hopefully without her consent, Carl thought, imagining the repercussions with glee.

"Assad and I have been discussing matters a bit," said Bjørn. "It seems he's declining the offer I've made him."

Assad nodded emphatically. Couldn't have been much of an offer, Carl mused, feeling increasingly like for the time being he couldn't be bothered with anything or anyone on top of the hangover he was still nursing after the weekend's exploits.

"Far be it from me to spoil his plans, or your routines, for that matter. I just want the three of you to know that the administration of Department Q belongs under me, for which reason it is imperative I maintain the necessary control over what's going on down there."

Carl looked over at Rose. She was already about to blow.

"I'm sure you know that all private businesses of a certain size use so-called controllers whose job it is to keep an eye on the viability of the organization's various operational sections. In our case we can say that viability is determined on the basis of two main factors. One factor is our success rate in clearing up individual cases, and in this respect your department scores reasonably well, thank God."

Fucking prick, I'm going to get him for this, Carl promised himself. He deserved to be skewered on a stick and toasted in boiling oil, he did. Reasonably well! Was understatement the new leadership strategy?

But Rose beat him to it. "Now you listen to me, Mister So-called Boss

of Department A. I'd give my right arm to head up Department Q's investigations and do it half as well as Carl." Then she turned to Assad and
bellowed into his face: "And you, Assad! What's the matter with you?
Have you gone soft in the head, since you can't give up your seat for a
lady when she's standing up?"

The shock almost launched his eyebrows into orbit.

"Right," she continued, having sat down in the vacated chair. "Now
we're at eye-level, Bjørn. Get used to it."

"On the other hand," Bjørn went on, unmoved, "your level of expenditure is unsatisfactory. In terms of man-hours against budget, Department Q is nearly twice as costly as Department A. That needs to be
rectified. For that reason, I've taken on a new man to keep an eye on
costs. I believe you've already met Gordon Taylor."

Carl was gobsmacked. Gordon? Bjørn had hired *Gordon* to control
Department Q?

"No *way* am I having that gangly scaffold snooping around in *my*
basement. He's still wet behind the ears, for Chrissake! Is he even out of
secondary school yet?"

"He's in his final year of law school and getting top marks to boot.
He'll be joining us full-time before long."

"Like hell he will!" Carl threw up his hands as though in self-protection
and made ready to back out of Bjørn's office. "You can send him back where
he came from, we simply haven't the time to waste on him."

Then the situation took a turn that Carl never, in his wildest imagination, could have predicted.

"We can give it a try, can't we, Carl?" said Assad.

"C'mon, he's not *that* bad," Rose pitched in.

Checkmate. Thanks for nothing.

Carl watched the fizz in his glass and tried to remember how many headache tablets he'd actually taken since their meeting with Bjørn.

Soluble relief in large amounts invariably wrecked your stomach, he
knew that, but on the other hand it got his brain working again and

now he felt sufficiently speedy to make sure Rose and Assad both got his message.

"Not a word about Bjørn or Gordon, do you understand? It's got me on a short fuse and we've got other things to do, OK? You start, Rose. Please make it brief and to the point."

Rose nodded. She looked completely unfazed by the morning's pandemonium.

"OK, this is the CCTV footage, Carl. You can see the boy going into the police station, but he's got his face partially covered, so it's hard to see him properly." Rose paused the video, freezing a gray image of a glass door and a figure seen from above.

Assad and Carl stepped closer to the screen.

"He doesn't look like an Arab, Carl. His ears are set rather high on his head, so most likely he is not from the Balkans either."

Funny observation. Were the ears of people from the Balkans really lower-set than others?

Rose leaned forward. "Dark, curly hair, almost like a Latino, and not very old. What's his age do you reckon, Carl?"

"Fourteen or fifteen. That's what I've heard others say, too. Could be younger, though. They mature quicker in those parts. What about his clothing?"

Assad smiled. "His shirt looks like something my uncle would wear."

Carl nodded. "Exactly. Just the sort of thing a junior office slave would have worn fifteen years ago. Where the hell did he get a thing like that?"

"A secondhand shop?" Assad ventured.

"He'd have chosen something else, surely?"

"Perhaps he swiped it from one of those charity drop boxes. Maybe it just happened to be at the top of the pile."

"Yeah, maybe." Carl put his finger to the screen. "Why do you think he's covering his face like that? And while we're at it, why would he need to steal someone else's ID?"

"Very simple," said Assad. "He hasn't got one of his own."

Carl nodded. Assad definitely had a point there; the thought had crossed his mind as well. "Either that or he hasn't kept his nose clean."

Assad frowned. "What does his nose have to do with it? You can't even see it here."

Carl sighed. "It's an idiom, Assad. Forget I ever said it. What I meant was, he might be involved in something unlawful."

Rose took her notepad and began scribbling. "Listen, if he hasn't got a national identity card of his own it means either he's not registered in Denmark or else his parents keep the card for him. My feeling is he's too self-dependent for the second explanation, so I'd go with the first."

"Could he be a Gypsy?" Carl asked. "You've mentioned it before, Rose, so maybe that's a possibility."

They peered again at the screen. Judging by his clothes and general appearance, the boy was an indeterminate miscellany of everything. Gypsy, French, central European—practically any origin was possible.

Rose scanned forward. "This is where he starts backing out, and this is where you appear at the front counter, Carl. You can see he recognizes you, right there."

Assad's face creased into a smile. "He sure didn't like the look of you, Carl. See how he runs!"

"Yeah, we recognized each other from Stark's place."

"So now we know from the missing persons notice, the necklace, *and* the fact that you saw him outside Stark's house that he has an interest in Stark's disappearance and probably knows something about it as well. Do you reckon he's a rent boy?"

They stared at Rose in astonishment.

"I mean it wouldn't be the first time a man's double life ended up being his downfall, would it? Like I said before, maybe Stark liked children. Maybe that's what this Africa thing is all about. You have to admit it's a bit weird for a boy to be so involved in this case."

"You see something weird in everything, Rose," said Assad.

"Howdy, campers," came a mutter from the doorway, and there he was again. Gordon himself, his effeminate haircut falling down over his eyes and his head rotating like a periscope in enemy waters, surveilling them.

"We're a bit busy at the moment, Gordon," said Rose, to Carl's surprise.

"In that case, I'd like very much just to watch."

Watch? Hadn't the man the slightest sense of occasion?

"Any reason in particular you're here?" Carl asked.

"As a matter of fact, yes. I've just read up on the Anweiler case. It seems to me that the deceased's husband ought to have been kept on a shorter leash. Among other things, the report states—"

"Do you mind leaving now, Gordon?" Rose said, cutting him off. "We're in the middle of another case at the moment."

Gordon smiled and raised an index finger. "The way I see it, Rose dearest, is that one is best served by bringing one thing to a satisfactory conclusion before starting on—"

"Gordon, take a look around you. Can't you see we're busy on another case? The Anweiler case is history, all right? *Solved*, get it? S-O-L-V-E-D means solved. Hasn't it sunk into that thick skull of yours yet?"

"Have you any idea how lovely you are when you're angry, Rose? It's like all the elements come together in that beautiful face of yours all at once," he replied with empathy. Was there a song coming on?

If Assad hadn't begun to snigger, Carl would have chucked something heavy at the man. Instead, he looked at Rose, anticipating the thunderstorm that was about to break, but she seemed almost ill at ease with the situation.

Carl drew himself to his full height. Not quite as tall as this puppy, but on the other hand in a different weight class altogether.

"Farewell, Gordon," he said, torpedoing the poor devil's hip with his twelve-pack, as Mona liked to call his stomach region.

They managed to hear the crash as Bjørn's hapless patsy collided with the corridor wall before Carl slammed the door so hard that even the workmen at the far end stopped drilling for a moment.

"He's wild about you, Rose," Assad commented, rolling his eyes. "But maybe you feel the same way about him, too?"

Rose glanced away. It was her only reaction and open to interpretation. Carl, in any case, had his own explanation.

"Should we carry on?" she said, trying to sound normal. "This is what I've noted down so far. Stark's got no family left, his mother having died and left him all her money. But before that, he'd already spent a lot more than he actually had. At the time of his disappearance he seems to have had no debts, and he hasn't made any withdrawals from his accounts since he went missing. There's no tax arrears, no life insurance besides the usual, and the mortgage on the house is all paid up. First-class degree from the university and never been in trouble with the police. The neighbors in Brønshøj all speak highly of him."

She looked up from her notes. "But again: Why did the man disappear? Was it some kind of sexual obsession? Did he have enemies? Gambling debts?"

"No, not gambling debts," Assad interrupted. "Why would anyone get rid of him because of money he could easily pay? A person does not throw a kite up into the air when there is no wind."

Carl shook his head. Sometimes it would help if Assad came with subtitles.

"Listen," Carl said. "My feeling is that the answer to all this lies somewhere in his trip to Africa. Rose, I want copies of all his bank statements by tomorrow, plus whatever else the two of you have already compiled. In the meantime, Assad and I are going over to the ministry to have a word with Stark's boss and colleagues. So we might not get back here today. And as for Gordon, Rose, I'd say you were best served keeping work and play separate."

He felt the stab of her kohl-rimmed eyes, but it was no use. She could do as she was told, simple as that.

The man seated in front of them wasn't exactly heartthrob material. Pasty complexion, thin white hair, and a set of worn-out dentures. If charm could be measured in terms of temperature he would be hovering around zero. He wore a wedding ring, which only proved he had found a woman who wasn't fussy.

"Yes, William Stark's disappearance was a terrible business," he said, oddly dispassionate. "I think all of us here are still rather puzzled by it. 'Distressed' is probably a better word. Stark was a highly capable man, well-liked and exceptionally reliable, so his disappearing is probably the last thing I would have expected."

"You were his boss, but were you friends, too?" Assad asked.

Daft question. How could anyone be friends with a boss like René E. Eriksen? It was hard to imagine.

"Not friends exactly, but there was a great fellow-feeling between us. Of all the people on my staff, I think William was the one I felt most attached to."

"What exactly was his mission in Africa?" Carl asked. "We understand he was down there in connection with an aid program for the benefit of a rural pygmy community, but we don't know why."

"He supervised the work. When you hire local Africans as middlemen you need to make sure things are going according to plan."

"Was his trip routine or was it because there was something in particular that needed looking into?"

"Purely routine."

"We can see he changed his return ticket and came home a day early. Is that normal?"

The department head smiled. "Actually, no. I can't say for sure, but I *think* the heat got to be too much for him. And Stark was very efficient, so he probably saw no reason to hang around once the job was done. But like I said, I've no way of knowing for certain. He never got round to writing his report, as you know."

"Talking of reports, we'd like access to Stark's files and whatever else might be relevant. Is there a computer of his here?"

"No, unfortunately. We use a server, and all Stark's tasks and portfolios have long since been handed on to other staff."

"And his laptop and other luggage from his final trip have never turned up?"

"If they had, I'd probably have been the first to know."

"What we're trying to establish is not only what happened to William Stark but also *why* it happened. Did he ever indicate to you that he might have been in trouble in some way? Was he susceptible to depression?"

Eriksen fiddled with the fountain pen on his desk. It looked like the sort of thing he'd been given for twenty-five years of loyal service. "Depression? He certainly had his ups and downs. Since it happened I've been inclined to think he may have been depressed, yes."

"What makes you think that? Was he off sick a lot?"

He smiled again. "Stark? No, he was probably the most conscientious man I've ever met. If I'm not mistaken, he never missed a single day in all the years we worked together. But yes, sometimes there was a look of sadness about him. I think his stepdaughter's illness hit him hard, and somehow I have an inkling things perhaps weren't running that smoothly with his girlfriend. He came to work one day sporting a black eye. Not that I read anything into it, but women these days can be quite determined, don't you agree?"

Carl nodded. René E. Eriksen, in any case, definitely looked like the type whose wife knocked him about a bit from time to time.

"Actually, the last couple of months he seemed to be having a harder and harder time keeping his spirits up," Eriksen continued. "So, yes, depression did spring to mind."

"And therefore you wouldn't be surprised if it turned out he committed suicide?" Carl asked.

He gave a shrug. "How well do we really know each other when it all boils down?"

René E. Eriksen's mind was in turmoil. In front of him sat two police investigators who had turned up precisely a mail delivery too early for him to assess what information to feed them. It had been damned silly of him to suggest Stark's partner had hit him, and what he'd said about that black eye. It was the kind of thing that could be checked up on. He needed to keep himself on a tighter leash. Making things up on the spur of the moment was pure folly.

The less he gave them to go on, the less chance there was of their scam being uncovered. On the other hand, if he now began working on his cover story he could draw Stark in as the brains of the department and orchestrator of the fraud, thereby removing himself from the spotlight. So skilfully had he manipulated Stark's documents that he was now able to prove it.

The only drawback then was that his associates at Karrebæk Bank would be caught up in his net, in which case they would without a doubt point the finger at him. Moreover, he would have difficulty explaining why he had not presented the documents to the police before now. Damn it. Why hadn't he prepared himself more carefully so as to provide a plausible explanation as to the appearance of these so-called new documents? Could he claim to have only just discovered them? And why hadn't he then informed the police? Why hadn't he?

He looked at the two men in front of him. Had either of them come alone he might not have been that concerned. It was the two of them together that worried him.

He knew the feeling from his time in Danida, the government's development aid agency, and from his travels through the world's most desolate wildernesses. The sense of eyes all around you, watching for signs of weakness, even in the most abject places. And right now he felt exactly like someone sitting cross-legged on a straw mat in the sand before a crackling campfire, surrounded by armed Somalis. The one commanded his attention while the other awaited his turn. All the time negotiating under changing conditions, facing new demands. He had never been good at it.

At the moment, it was the Danish investigator who was taking the lead. Obviously, he was the higher ranking officer, with the power to conclude the interview at will. As such, he was the one who needed persuading. The little Arab-looking man was the one who growled and snapped. Despite his friendly eyes and a smile which in any other situation would put a person at ease, behind this facade lurked an oddly inscrutable ruthlessness. René had seen quietly grazing gazelles suddenly torn to pieces from behind by attacking lions that seemed to come from nowhere. It was the same feeling he had now about this man.

"Yes, how well do we really know each other?" he repeated.

"Did Stark ever mention places or people to which he had some special attachment, besides his home and family?" the investigator asked. "Somewhere he might have chosen as a place to hide away, or even take his own life?"

Eriksen wondered what to say. Should he make something up? Something that would safely ease them out of here?

He looked at the Arab assistant. The penetrating stare that met his eye made him drop the notion of trying to be creative.

"I can't say that he did, I'm afraid. He was rather introverted when it came to talking about his private life."

"You weren't friends, but did you ever visit Stark at home?" the Arab asked.

René E. Eriksen shook his head. "No, I don't believe in mixing work and private affairs like that."

"So you cannot tell us anything about his peculiarities either?"

"Peculiarities?" He allowed himself a chuckle. "Aren't we all a bit peculiar when it comes down to it? Working for the Danish civil service, I'd say you need to be."

His jocular diversion maneuver had no effect on either of them.

"I am thinking mostly about his sexuality," the Arab went on.

Eriksen held his breath as the adrenaline coursed through every cell of his body. It was a question he had not been expecting. Was this a way out? Was this odd little man handing him the keys to freedom?

Could they tell how strongly he reacted to the question? It was imperative they did not.

He elected to remain silent for a moment before stroking his mustache and pushing his half-rims up onto the bridge of his nose. He drew a deep breath, folding his hands on the table and preparing to reply. The same routine as during difficult budget negotiations.

"I don't know anything for certain," he replied eventually, glancing at the Arab with an apologetic smile before turning his eyes to the detective inspector. "So you'll have to forgive me if I lead you up a blind alley that does Stark a disservice. As I said, there really wasn't any private confidentiality between us."

The two investigators nodded at him like pigeons grateful for the crumbs put out for them. Clearly, the sustenance they had come for was now finally within reach.

"I think basically he had a weakness in that respect. What I mean is . . ." He cleared his throat. "On the face of it he seemed to lead a very normal life with his girlfriend. However, on the few occasions we traveled together I found his eyes wandered in a manner that disturbed my impression of him."

Mørck tipped his head inquiringly. "In what way?"

"Well, looking at young boys in an inappropriate manner. I noticed it especially in Bangladesh."

The two men exchanged glances. Did their solemn expressions mean they were buying it? Had he succeeded in turning their focus in another direction?

Yes, by God, it seemed he had.

"Did you ever see him make advances to any of these boys?"

Be careful now, René, don't appear too certain here, he told himself.

"I may have done. I'm not sure," he replied.

"What does that mean?"

"We weren't together all the time, of course. Sometimes I'd go into a shop and he'd be outside in the street. I may by chance have caught a glimpse of his need for contact."

The Arab scratched his cheek at the near invisible transition between sideburn and stubble. "But you never saw him take any of them up to his room?" he asked, amid audible rasping.

"No. But he also traveled on his own sometimes."

"So what you're suggesting here is that William Stark was a pedophile with a preference for boys. Are there any members of your staff who traveled with Stark and could corroborate your assumption, do you think?" Mørck asked.

Eriksen threw up his hands. Sometimes, this gesture was a kind of confirmation in itself and saved him from being more explicit.

Sensing his advantage, he went on anyway. "I shouldn't think so. If Stark wasn't traveling with me, he would do so alone. But feel free to ask around the department. Far be it from me to hamper your investigation."

"It was a good idea going over to the ministry, Assad, but you've hardly said a word since. What's up?" said Carl, as they went down the stairs of the rotunda to the basement.

"I'm doing some luminating, Carl. That interview with Eriksen was very strange indeed."

"I think that'd be *ruminating*, Assad. Mulling things over."

"Mulling?"

"Never mind. You're right about Eriksen. A lot of strange things came out of his mouth."

Assad smiled. "A good thing his dentures didn't come out, too. Did you notice one of his front teeth was loose?"

Carl nodded.

Abruptly Assad held up his hand. Sounds emanating from Rose's office farther down the corridor stopped them both in their tracks. Sounds not normally associated with a mundane afternoon in a state institution milling with police officers.

"I think Rose has finished her report now," said Assad, and rolled his eyes.

It was amazing, but true. Christ!

They crept closer to her door and now could hear rhythmic thuds against the wall mixed with deep, throaty groans and Rose's utterly unbridled whining gasps.

"This is not a video, Carl. They are really shagging in there," Assad whispered.

Carl looked toward the stairs at the other end of the corridor. How beautiful it would be if someone appeared now. The initial scandal would be followed by a month of dirty looks. The tales of Rose's escapades at Station City's Christmas parties would experience a renaissance. The prestige they had worked so hard for would be down the drain and Rose would have something to answer for.

He shook his head, noting with annoyance that perspiration had appeared on his brow and that the grunting and groaning behind the door was also prompting the first unmistakable signs of arousal in his underwear.

"They can't just do that during working hours," he protested in a whisper.

"But they are, Carl. You can hear it yourself."

Carl looked at Assad and let out a deep sigh. It was at times like these that one knew who'd been through the police academy and who hadn't.

"ROSE!" he bellowed, hammering his fist so hard against the door that he gave himself and everyone else a fright.

Silence descended in a nanosecond, followed after an equally brief span of time by the sound of frenzied activity. It wasn't too hard to figure out what was going on.

"You can come out now, Gordon. We're not going to harm you," he growled, expecting a man displaying a certain amount of contrition to emerge. He was mistaken.

Disheveled and with a smirk all over his face, he appeared in the doorway, not at all remorseful, but triumphant. He had snared his prey after only a couple of days and was plainly confident he was going to get away with it, too, which unfortunately he was right about. Carl would be the last to complain to Bjørn about that kind of behavior among his staff. If he did, the boomerang would hit him square in the neck.

Just you wait, he tried to signal, as Gordon trotted past him and down the corridor. The way the spindly idiot nonchalantly did up his fly as he left was a sight Carl would not soon forget.

They waited another minute before entering the scene of the love crime.

"Oh, it's you," Rose noted with astonishing composure from behind her desk. "I thought you said you were going straight home after."

Carl glanced around the room. Documents swept onto the floor, shoes abandoned in a hurry, an empty bottle of red wine and two glasses.

"Have you been drinking during working hours, Rose?" he asked.

She gave a shrug, still surprisingly relaxed. "I suppose we had a little sip, yes."

"What about Gordon? Is he going to be a regular fixture down here? Because if that's what you're thinking, you've got another thing coming."

"Regular fixture? God, no! He's just helping me out a bit, that's all."

She giggled, and Assad cracked up behind Carl's back.

The world was going mad.

"All right, listen. We came back to pick up the car. I'm running Assad over to the hospital for his checkup. What I want to tell you is that early tomorrow you're going over to the ministry to ask William Stark's colleagues if they ever noticed anything odd about his behavior. You know what I mean."

"OK," she replied. No defiance this time.

Funny how sex could sometimes work wonders.

"Good news, indeed, Assad. Congratulations."

Carl patted his assistant's shoulder vigorously.

"It was a very brief examination," Assad responded.

"Yeah, and now you're all clear. Full recovery, Assad. Absolutely brilliant."

Carl looked around. Every white-coated nurse, doctor, porter, and auxiliary in the busy corridors of the Rigshospital deserved a hug. Only a couple of months before, the fluid on Assad's brain had threatened his life, and now it was gone.

The doctor had said it was only a matter of time until the last accumulations of blood disappeared and the nerve paths to his facial muscles, speech center, and legs would be functioning as before. Of course a program of rehabilitation would be beneficial, but Assad's line of work combined with brisk walking every day would be sufficient stimulation in itself. The bottom line was he needn't come back there anymore.

Spirits were therefore high as Carl escorted Assad down to the hospital cafeteria and placed a tray of pastries and coffee on the table in front of him.

"How did it go with the librarians on Dag Hammarskjölds Allé?" Assad asked, pastry cream all over his dusky stubble.

"They're going to call us as soon as the lad turns up again."

"Then we shall have to be quick, Carl . . ."

Assad stopped and placed a hand on Carl's arm as he nodded discreetly toward a corner of the room.

Seated behind a trolley of dirty dishes was none other than Marcus Jacobsen, staring blankly into space, hands around his coffee cup.

Before the weekend, he had been their superior, bidding farewell to his old life.

The way he looked now, it didn't seem he was able to visualize his new one.

All in all, a more perfect shitty day than most shitty days, Carl decided as he opened his front door and went inside.

"Nice work," was the first thing he said to Morten as he looked around the house. Amazing what a few hours of scrubbing and vacuuming could do to wipe away the traces of even the booziest of shindigs. Magnolievangen number 73 was pristine as never before.

"How's our old charmer today?" he asked Mika, who stood in the middle of the living room, hands glistening as he rubbed something into Hardy's naked back that smelled more effective than pleasant.

"Hardy's doing great. He's given us the go-ahead to get started using some forms of assistance. We've had a meeting with his case workers today and agreed we want him up in a wheelchair. What do you say, Hardy?" he said, slapping his patient's milk-white buttock for emphasis.

"I say it'd be nicer with a slap on the ass if I could feel it," came the hollow reply.

Carl bent down and looked Hardy straight in the eyes. They were moist, so it must have been an emotional day for him.

"Congratulations, mate," he said, feeling moved, and patted Hardy's brow.

"Yeah, bit momentous, it is." Hardy paused to collect himself. "Mika's really been working hard for this," he added, with a quiver in his voice.

Carl straightened up and turned to the brawny caregiver pummeling away at Hardy's muscle fibers, not knowing quite what to say. His feelings of guilt had been eating away at him for such a long time. Were they now about to ease? Was that what they were trying to get him to believe?

He gave a sigh and put his arms around Mika's sweaty torso as it worked Hardy over.

"Thanks, Mika," he said. "I don't quite know how to put it, but thanks a million."

"Whoa, Carlo!" came a jeering voice from the stairs. "Gone over to the enemy, have you? I knew it! I must be the only one in this house who's straight, ha, ha!"

Jesper, ever the joker. Like a germ always waiting to strike.

"Mum says to tell you to phone," he went on. "She says if you don't go and visit Gran, you owe her hundreds of thousands of kroner. What kind of deal have you got yourself into, Carlo? Sounds like you've lost your mind."

Then he laughed, so no one was in doubt.

"And you better do what she says. She's a bit off her head at the moment because of Gurkamal."

"You don't say! What's with him?"

"All she's been on about is that wedding, that it has to be in India and everything, only now it's all been put off again. If you ask me, it's never going to happen."

"Why not?"

"Damned if I know. Mum says it's because there's been problems after Gurkamal was attacked in the shop, but she's not exactly the sharpest tool in the shed, either. Do you think he's going to share his shitty little mini-mart with her? 'Course he's not!"

Carl took a deep breath. Just as long as this didn't mean she was going to turn up all of a sudden with her suitcases and fifteen cardboard boxes.

"Have you heard the news about Hardy?" Carl asked, eager to change the subject.

"Too right I have. I was here when all those cows from the local authority, or wherever they were from, came piling in. They were here more than three hours, they were. Anyway, don't forget about Gran."

"How about you go and visit her instead, Jesper?"

"You must be joking. She's gone totally cuckoo. She hardly knows who I am anymore."

"I'm sure she does. I'm asking you to do it."

"No way."

"If you won't do it as a favor, then I'm going to have to *tell* you to do it."

"Threatening me now, are we? In that case I reckon you should alert the media and tell them the very important news that Gran's too bonkers for me to waste my time. Great story. All yours, Carlo."

He turned on his heel and homed in on the fridge. "Oh, and by the way, Carlo," he hollered, his head among the dairy products, "I was up in the attic getting my old Action Men out today. What the hell's that huge chest up there? And why's it locked?"

Carl shook his head. What on earth was this psycho-infantile lout on about *now*?

"I haven't a clue what you're talking about," he hollered back. "I don't know anything about any chest. It must be something of your mother's."

20

This was another of those calls he could do without. Teis Snap had been sitting in the twilight, enjoying a lemon vodka with the palm trees in front of him and his wife indoors in her negligee. A quick shag after a hectic day did them both a world of good, and this evening was no exception. Heads and glands emptied, muscles soft and relaxed. Which was why the voice on the phone had exactly the same effect on him as a cold shower on the nether regions.

Teis put his drink down on the table. "How dare you phone me after what you've done, René?" he growled. "The agreement was that you were to inform us if you needed to sell your A shares and, more important, that we were never to sell to anyone outside our own circle."

"Agreement? To my mind we've made so many agreements, it's impossible to administrate them. For instance, I hear from the bank that you and Lisa happen to be in Curaçao. In which case I have to ask myself what you might be doing there. You wouldn't be trying to impress upon the bank that the power of attorney you've undoubtedly secured by forging my signature is genuine, would you? Or perhaps you've already done so? I'm also wondering if it might be a good idea to call the bank as soon as they open and ask what you're up to. My guess is that the authorities in Willemstad might be interested, too. As far as I know, the jail there is hardly a first-class establishment, but perhaps you won't mind?"

Teis took his bare feet off the table. "You're not calling anyone, do you hear me, René? I'm your only friend in this matter, and if I were you I wouldn't want it any other way."

"Very well, Teis. That's all I wanted to know. Now, since you're still

my friend, I suggest you put my share certificates in a plain brown envelope and send them to me by UPS courier as soon as the sun comes up. I
expect you to e-mail me a scan of the receipt for the dispatch no later
than ten minutes after you've handed over the envelope. If I haven't
heard from you by ten fifteen, local time, I shall alert the MCB immediately, do you understand?" And with that he hung up.

Teis was stunned. Of course he knew René was not only unused to
bossing people about but that he also possessed the courage necessary
to rebel, which was exactly what he had just done.

He sat for a while, staring at his phone as the shrill song of the cicadas
pierced the descending darkness, trying to ignore his wife's contented
humming from within. Then he downed his drink in one. It was night in
Denmark now, but he didn't care. He may have been an old man, but
Brage-Schmidt was going to have do without his beauty sleep.

The voice that answered the phone wasn't as wizened as usual but
younger and considerably more dynamic. Teis swallowed. Had it gotten
to the point where Brage-Schmidt passed on even his private calls to that
damned assistant of his? An African whom Brage-Schmidt, following
good old imperialistic colonial tradition, insisted on referring to as *boy*,
just like all his previous servants. Was even their most nefarious business
now being channeled through him as well?

"OK, so this is where Eriksen is pulling out," Brage-Schmidt's assistant said. "We expected it, though perhaps not as quickly and openly. So
it's a good thing we've already planned his retirement, as it were. And
with this latest development, I think we should have it all sorted within
a couple of days."

Teis's surroundings seemed at once to merge. The branches of the
palm trees sank into the darkness, the ocean fell silent, and the pale
Dutchmen who sat underneath his balcony counting bats was no longer
there. "Have you found the boy?" he asked with bated breath.

"No, but he's been seen."

"That doesn't mean you're going to catch him. Who saw him, and
where?"

"Zola's people. They spotted him last Saturday and came close to pulling him in. Now they know he's still operating in the area."

"Hmm. What makes them think that?"

"They know him. He's a stubborn little guy, so now the clan's extra prepared."

"And what if they don't find him?"

"Relax. I'm putting my men on the job, too, and they're professionals."

"Professional what?"

"Let's just say soldiers. Trained since they barely could walk to track down and finalize."

"Finalize"? Such a neutral word. Was that how one came to terms with killing? By calling it something else?

"Eastern Europeans?"

The voice at the other end laughed. "Nope. Rather more conspicuous, I'd say. Or perhaps not."

"How do you mean? I want to know."

"Former child soldiers, of course. Tried-and-true professionals from Liberia and Congo who are used to slipping in anywhere and killing with no regrets. Cold, muscular machines that a person would do well to have on his side."

"Are they in Denmark now?"

"No, but they're on their way with their so-called chaperone, a lovely black lady we call Mammy." He laughed. "Sounds so nice and peaceful, Mammy, doesn't it? But I can assure you the name couldn't be more deceiving. Just like the others, she learned to do her thing during the civil war and her motto is quite unambiguous: *No Mercy*. So she's not the kind of mother to give you a cuddle."

Teis felt a chill run down his spine. Child soldiers. It was practically the worst he could imagine. Was this what he had got himself mixed up in? Were the people he dealt with really capable of everything? And was he?

"OK" was all he could say. There seemed to be no other words that suited the moment. "What about René?"

"We've got something else planned for him. Fortunately we know where he is, more or less. But the boy is our first priority. The order in which one proceeds is not always without consequence. Especially when it has to do with killing someone."

"Yes, I understand," said Teis, even though he didn't want to understand. "May I speak to Brage-Schmidt? I've got an urgent situation concerning the Curaçao shares that needs to be dealt with within the next few hours."

"He's asleep."

"That's quite possible, but I wouldn't be phoning from the other side of the world at this time of night if it wasn't of the utmost importance, would I? I need to know what to do."

"One moment."

A few minutes passed before he heard Brage-Schmidt's rasping voice at the other end. More irritable than usual, though his message was clear: "René E. Eriksen will not be sent his Curaçao shares," he said curtly. If the fool really did call Curaçao with intimations of fraud, Brage-Schmidt would personally make sure the authorities were satisfied that Eriksen's signature and the date were genuine, as well as the rest of the document. He would say he couldn't help it if Eriksen had regretted giving the power of attorney.

"Call Eriksen at nine fifty local time, and tell him you're sending him the receipt for UPS's dispatching of the shares. Put something in the package for customs to intercept, if you like. Little plastic bags with flour in them, for example. And explain to him that if he's thinking of making trouble it'll be at his own peril. You can probably get hold of him at work before he goes home."

It was a sleepless night for René. Since his conversation with Snap his mind had begun spinning like a centrifuge. Now he had confirmation that he was drifting away from the decision-making process, and this tormented him. If true, he risked losing control of his own fate, and this was the last thing he wanted. If they ripped him off and took his shares in Curaçao anything could happen. If they could murder Louis Fon, Mbomo

Ziem, William Stark, and now a boy, they could murder him, too. But if they left his shares alone he would take it to be a concession and a consolidation of his own status within the group.

For that reason, what happened when the banks opened in Willemstad was crucial, which was why he was unable to sleep.

To begin with he paced the living room floor, glancing at the clock every five minutes. And when he'd had enough of that he went down the steep staircase into the basement and retrieved Stark's laptop from the crawl space under the floor.

Since then he'd been sitting there in the gloom, staring at William Stark's computer screen.

There were the two user names: one without a password, which he had long since trawled his way through, and the other with a code he'd found simply impossible to break.

He looked down at his notes once more. Here was a wide variety of data on Stark, his girlfriend and stepdaughter that might possibly comprise elements of a password. And with these he had tried out endless combinations and abbreviations both with and without numerals, and now he was at a loss.

William Stark had been the most systematic man in the department, and René could simply not imagine him having used a password without some logical relation to Stark himself. But which?

He switched back to the first interface and went through the list of Stark's e-mail correspondence. Here, too, there was a clear system, everything filed according to logical subject categories, then by name and then again in chronological order.

Stark was a diligent man and had copied all his work-related mail from the ministry's server onto this laptop. Presumably so as to be able to delve into his ministerial tasks at home, as seemed to be evident from the times at which he had sent e-mails out, often past midnight or very early in the morning. The man obviously didn't need much sleep.

René stretched his muscles. His own fatigue was getting the better of him, but he needed to stay awake. He didn't have much time. In three hours he had to be in his office at the ministry, and later in the day he would have to decide whether he needed to phone Curaçao. He hoped it wouldn't be necessary because he didn't want the war against Snap and his associates to commence before he himself elected to initiate it.

He scribbled some more notes down on his pad, prompted by his scrutiny of Stark's files and documents. There was a snippet about Stark's mother, scraps concerning his stepdaughter's hospital treatments and some chess tournaments Stark had taken part in years before.

After that he felt like he'd pretty much been through everything. But who was to say whether the answer lay here? Some people made up passwords on the basis of previous exploits, like a mountain they had climbed. Others used incidents that had left a lasting mark on their life. In the movie *Citizen Kane*, the newspaper magnate's dying word was "Rosebud," and the whole film revolved around the mystery of who bore the name and whether it would reside in Kane's thoughts until the very last. René shook his head as he pictured the deceased magnate's belongings going up in smoke with no one noticing that among them was a sled embellished with the name *Rosebud*, surely a relic of Kane's happiest moments in childhood. Thus the answer to the mystery remained forever undiscovered.

But what about Stark? How many incidents, brief impressions, people, animals, and things might have made a lasting impression on the man? The possibilities were boundless.

He stared at the empty field as though hypnotized, as if it might reveal the password of its own accord.

Come on, come on, he urged himself. If he didn't work it out now, he would have to give up. He certainly wasn't going to involve anyone else in figuring out the log-in details of a computer that in theory did not even exist.

But what might he find in that virtual landscape if he *did* get inside? Would there be anything he needed to know? Had Stark stored incriminating information, or was René merely going to find pictures of naked women and e-mails that concerned no one but Stark himself?

He stretched the muscles of his neck to loosen them and took another crack. First he typed in the name of Stark's mother, then her civil registration number, then her initials *and* her civil registration number, followed by her name spelled backward and in all sorts of combinations. Eventually, he crossed her off his list.

After that, he tried the names of various grandmasters of chess: Ruy Lopez, Emanuel Lasker, Bobby Fischer, Efim Bogoljubov, Bent Larsen, Anatoly Karpov and all kinds of other hits he found on the net relating to the game. Tournaments, concepts, and terminology in both Danish and English, the names of the pieces, one by one, followed by different combinations of famous moves.

No solution. A needle in a haystack.

Again, he shook his head, looked at the time, listened to hear if his wife was getting out of bed. Then he cocked his head to check the weather outside, before returning to the empty log-in field.

What could have meant something to William Stark besides his work? As far as he was aware there was nothing but chess, his lady friend, and her daughter. But they were parameters he'd already been through from every angle.

But what about the less obvious?

Nicknames? Special dates? Their first encounter? Their first kiss? What could have meant something to him?

He looked at Malene and Tilde Kristoffersen's names, trying for the umpteenth time to rearrange them, but there were far too many possibilities.

What had been most important to them? The most important of all? Most likely the daughter's illness and their efforts to make her better. Yes, it could well be that. Nothing had occupied Stark's mind up to the time of his disappearance like Tilde's health. René knew as much from the few occasions on which he had listened with rather reserved admiration to Stark's description of how much they strove to help the poor girl.

He looked again at his notes, nodded to himself and typed "Crohn's disease," expecting yet another rejection.

And then it happened. He was in, and like the phoenix from the ashes a virtual desktop appeared with a background photo of Tilde, taken in a carefree moment. No intricate combinations, no hyphens, no numerals, nothing. Just "Crohn's disease"—and voilà, he'd entered the promised land.

As his eyes widened, he heard the slap of bedroom slippers on the tiles of the bathroom floor, the door closing hard as though his wife had got out of bed on the wrong side again. He had ten, maybe fifteen minutes until he had to close the laptop and pretend he'd just gotten up himself. Otherwise, Her Majesty's prying questions would know no bounds and his fatigue would be compounded beyond endurance.

He skated across the folders on the desktop. They were neatly ordered, labeled according to the period in which the files they contained had been created, from 2003 to 2008. He clicked on a couple, finding their contents rather uninteresting at first blush, mainly large numbers of scientific studies, correspondence with doctors and the families of patients all over the world, Tilde's test results, copies of medical records, letters of protest, and respectful acknowledgments. All with the sole aim of getting to grips with Tilde's illness and trying to do something about it. Nothing new or surprising as far as René could make out.

He proceeded into the Documents library to see if there could be folders containing information that might compromise the group or reveal whether Stark had been cognizant of the Baka project fraud. For while Stark's disappearance had given rise to general consternation, René himself was more interested in finding out why Stark hadn't already gone missing in Cameroon as planned. Why had he come back early? Something must have happened in Cameroon, and knowing Stark as he did, René could only presume that some kind of prior knowledge had prompted him to react so unexpectedly.

But this was still mere conjecture.

Upon hearing his wife open the bathroom door rather less demonstratively than she had closed it and that the sound of slippers had now been superseded by the padding of bare feet, he knew it was time to stop.

He clicked on a couple of icons and took a quick look at the rest of the folders under Documents. And so it was his eyes came to rest on one without a name.

Five minutes, surely he could allow himself five minutes. So he clicked on the folder, whereupon at least twenty subfolders appeared, each specifying a geographical location and particular subject.

Some bore the names of African states, like Tanzania, Mozambique, Kenya, or Ghana. Others were more cryptically labeled: CNTCTNME, BESTKS., CNTRCT, POLI, POL2, POL3, and so on.

René found it odd. His ministry no longer provided aid to several of the countries in question, and some of them belonged to a category of states with whom they'd had considerable problems in recent years when it came to getting them to report back properly.

He clicked on a random folder. CNTCTNME, it read, clearly a file containing the names of Stark's most important contacts. He quickly ran through the list. Many of them had been crossed out in red and replaced by others a fair amount of time before Stark's disappearance, but René recognized them all.

He shook his head and opened the next folder: CNTRCT. In many ways this one seemed more complex.

René frowned as his wife slammed the doors of her wardrobe upstairs. So this was going to be another day on which nothing would please her.

He saw now that several of the contracts in the folder were the kind of confidential material not normally removed from the ministry. But upon opening the first of them to investigate further, he discovered to his surprise that it contained not the contract in its entirety, but merely an appendix.

What would he want with an appendix to a contract? he mused, moving on to the next. Here, too, the contents were an appendix rather than the contract itself. As he proceeded through the entire list of subfolders he realized that Stark had added appendices to at least twenty-five ministerial contracts. Each specified an atypical transfer of money, and only in connection with a development project of considerable magnitude whose budget Stark was responsible for.

He began to add the sums together and when he reached two million kroner René knew for certain that his had not been the only criminal activity taking place in the ministry.

He could hardly believe it. His most trusted and honest coworker, William Stark, had systematically siphoned off funds from their development projects and defrauded the state of two million good Danish kroner!

René smiled to himself, ignoring the sudden appearance and automatic nagging of his wife. Things were beginning to shape up.

Earlier this very same day he had managed to imply to the police that Stark had been a pedophile as well as pressured Teis Snap into abandoning the theft of his stock in Curaçao. And now this, the most important of all: he had found the man who, with complete plausibility, could be set up as being the brains behind the Baka swindle if it proved necessary to deflect the blame. The perfect scapegoat. A man who had previously embezzled a considerable sum of money from his ministry. In short, he had discovered an individual of extremely dubious morals, who precisely for that reason had rationale enough for disappearing from the face of the earth.

So, Lady Luck, it seemed, was still smiling upon him.

21

"**What's Rose going to** say when we go to see Malene Kristoffersen without her?"

Carl cast a glance up at the imposing gates of Vestre prison as they drove past. How many fools had he gotten dispatched behind those dreadful walls in his time? Not so few. It was just a damned shame that they came out again.

"Rose? She's otherwise occupied at the ministry. I reckon she'll get over it," Carl replied curtly. After yesterday's shenanigans with Gordon, preferential treatment wasn't the first thing that sprang to mind at the mention of her name. Besides, he didn't give a toss what she'd say. He had other things to think about.

Ever since their visit to Danida's office for evaluating development assistance he'd had a strong feeling in his bones that they had proceeded too quickly. That he should have waited to interview department head René E. Eriksen until the case had been considered from more angles.

"Tell me again why you think our visit cheered Eriksen up, Assad. I noticed a reaction when you asked him about Stark's sexuality, but I wouldn't exactly say it cheered him up."

"Don't you know what happens when you give a camel a slap on the backside, Carl? It begins to run and stretch its neck toward where it thinks its goal is. Almost as if having a long neck in itself could make it arrive faster."

"Sounds reasonable. But what exactly are you trying to say?"

"It was like we gave Eriksen a slap on the backside when I mentioned

Stark's sexual preferences. All of a sudden he seemed to set his sights on a goal and stretched his neck out toward it faster than his legs could keep up."

"You mean he'd been keeping a secret he wanted to get off his chest?"

"No, you do not understand, Carl. It seemed like he suddenly saw a goal that had not been there before."

"What sort of goal?"

"That's what I can't work out."

"You're saying he was lying?"

"I don't know. But all of a sudden there were stories that could easily have come out earlier. Stories about young boys and glances and what else the devil knows."

"*Other way around*, Assad. It's 'and the devil knows what else.'"

"Anyway, I think Eriksen had that look in his eye like when a person is given the chance to tell a good story."

"And?"

"It's just that suspecting a man you work with of being a pedophile is not a good story."

Carl turned down Sjælør Boulevard. They would soon be there. "I got the same feeling myself, now you mention it. There was a lack of . . . shame in his voice."

The house on Strindbergsvej was typical of the era in which it was built. A sloping, French-style roof and a bit of ornamentation to make it look more imposing than building costs justified. Homes like this were often divided into two, with a dwelling on each floor so Copenhagen's exorbitant property taxes could be spread between incomes. A small green oasis in the suburb of Valby that satisfied both the desire to live close to the city center and the dream of living farther away.

Malene Kristoffersen received them looking like she hadn't quite come home from her package tour. The suitcases in the hall were still to be un-packed and equal parts of self-tanner and intense sunbathing on the beaches of Turkey had left her skin discolored in the peculiar way that always made people at work envious. Despite the somewhat lower tem-peratures at home her flowing dress was colorful and light as a feather, almost certainly purchased on her vacation. She was an attractive woman who didn't need to advertise the fact, even though the look on Assad's face said he was quite impressed.

"We stayed home today. We need to sometimes when Tilde's been for her checkup. It takes quite a bit out of her," she said. "She's sleeping at the moment, so you'll have to make do with me, I'm afraid."

Assad nodded very accommodatingly. "We'd be glad to come back again if necessary," he said with a sheepish grin.

Carl wouldn't put it past him.

"I'm very grateful for what you're doing," she went on.

An unusually promising opener, so seldom heard in Carl's line of work.

He smiled slightly. "It's always a sad thing when people disappear. But unfortunately, finding an explanation so long after the event is often quite a hopeless task."

"Yes, I realize that, but I still hope. William is such a lovely man."

Assad and Carl exchanged glances. This wasn't going to be easy.

"We've been to his place of work and spoken to his boss and a couple of his colleagues," Carl said. "Mostly to gain more of an idea of what he was doing in Cameroon. Did he tell you anything about that trip before he went?"

"Yes, he did, and he wasn't keen on having to go. Tilde was doing poorly in the hospital, and William wanted to stay home and be here for the two of us. That's the way he is," she explained, adding a rather sad smile by way of emphasis.

"So he was ordered to go?"

"Yes, and at short notice, too. He was told only the day before, as I remember it."

"And what was the point of the trip?"

"They suspected one of the local helpers of running off with some of the funding."

"A local, you say?"

"Yes. A guy named Louis. Louis Fon. William had met him on several occasions and thought he was doing a good job. I don't think he really believed what they were saying. There was also something about Fon having sent William an odd text message, too, that had William puzzled. He sat by Tilde's bed all evening the night before he left, trying to work out what it meant, but it just seemed like a lot of gibberish."

"He showed it to you, then?"

"Yes. Tilde's into texting, but she didn't understand it either."

"Did you speak to William after he arrived in Yaoundé?"

"No, but he did phone just after he landed in Douala. He always did that. He complained about the heat and was sorry he wasn't home."

"But nothing about coming back the next day?"

"No."

There was a rasping sound as Assad drew his palm back and forth against the stubble of his chin. Carl could almost hear his colleague's gray matter creaking and groaning.

"I'm sorry to have to ask you so directly, but what about the possibility of suicide? Does that sound plausible to you?"

She smiled without reservation. "William's not like that at all. He was happy with his life and his work. The only thing that weighed on him was Tilde's condition. He would never leave anyone in the lurch like that, least of all us."

"And the two of you got along well together?"

She nodded. First quickly, then again, more slowly. As though the question triggered forces inside her that had accumulated over a long time. She wasn't upset, but mentally she seemed to have reached a point where feelings of grief were no longer welcome.

"We were soul mates. Do you know what I mean?" She looked up at Carl abruptly, in a manner that felt uncomfortable considering the way he and love were doing at the moment.

Assad slid menacingly close to the edge of his chair, his introduction to a round of potential shock treatment already formulated "We heard it suggested at William's workplace that he may have certain interests you possibly know nothing about. Have you any idea as to what they might be?"

She shook her head. "Nope, William was always very open about everything. There were only three things he really cared about. Tilde first, then me, then his job." She smiled, as if everything about the man were unassailable. "But what were you thinking about, exactly?"

"Open about everything, you say?" Carl knew of no one but Assad who could toss a sentence into the air so vivid that it remained suspended long after a conversation had come to an end. "Would that include the most intimate of matters? Sex fantasies and such?"

She stifled a laugh, presumably because in terms of the world she lived in, she knew William Stark's sexual desires to be as normal and predictable as could be. "How do you mean, fantasies? What's wrong with fantasies? Don't you have any of your own?"

Assad's smile was perhaps a mite too overbearing in light of the sentence that followed. "Indeed I do, but not about young boys and girls."

Malene Kristoffersen was shocked. She sucked her lower lip in and her face drained of color quicker than Carl had ever seen. She grasped the hem of her skirt, wringing the material so hard they could hear the stitching split. Though momentarily stunned, she shook her head like a metronome. The words she was looking for were on their way.

They came slowly and deliberately, like small, measured punches. "Are you telling me that William is suspected of being a pedophile? Is that what you're saying, you little shit? Is it? Answer me! I want to hear the word from your own filthy mouth, do you hear me?"

The way Assad tipped his head and turned the other cheek was almost biblical. But things could develop fast.

"Let me say it, then," said Carl. "Have you ever had the slightest suspicion that William might have pedophile tendencies? Have you ever seen him staring at children or spending too much time at the computer late at night?"

The tears in her eyes could have come from anger, but they did not. Everything about her body language suggested otherwise. She shook her head slowly. "William was a completely normal man." She swallowed a couple of times to stifle her urge to cry. "And yes, he did sit up late at the computer, but it was his work. Don't you think a woman like me knows how to uncover the inner workings of her husband—or of a computer, for that matter?"

"External hard drives are quite small these days, easy to hide away in a pocket. Did he use them?"

She shook her head. "Why did you come here, anyway? Don't you think it's bad enough not knowing what's happened to William?" She was about to say more but turned her head away with a pained expression. Swallowing was no longer sufficient to stave off her crying. It was the kind of situation that revealed a person's true age. Her skin seemed almost to become transparent. Then she took a deep breath and turned to face them again. "No, he didn't have any external hard drives, he wasn't good when it came to technology or electronics. In fact, William was as analog you could imagine. Real world, with both feet on the ground. That's how he was. Understand?"

Carl nodded to Assad, who pulled a photo out of his pocket.

"Do you know this boy? I realize it's hard to see his face, but perhaps you can recognize his clothes or something else about him?" he asked, showing her the still from the CCTV footage of Marco.

She frowned but said nothing while Assad described him in more detail, adding that the boy had been seen outside Stark's house. "Don't you think it strange for a boy of that age to be so interested in William, especially after such a long time?"

"Yes, of course I find it strange. But there could be any number of reasons, not just . . ."

Assad turned the screws. "The boy can't have been very old when William went missing."

She understood what he was getting at, and her claws were already extended. Carl gave Assad a prudent nudge with his elbow before taking over.

"The question is what relationship this boy, who must have been no more than twelve or thirteen at the time, could have to William. Can you suggest anything?"

"My suggestion is that you keep your mouths shut with such disgusting allegations, do you hear me? William was *not* a pedophile, he . . ."

She stopped, as if someone had switched her off, at the sound of padded feet in the hall.

All three of them looked toward the door as a sleepy, blonde-haired girl with angular eyebrows came into the room.

Carl tried to smile as Malene raised her hand in a motherly greeting, hoping her daughter hadn't heard what had been said, but the expression on Tilde's face was unambiguous.

"Are you OK now, darling?" Malene asked.

The girl ignored her. "Who are you?" she asked, her voice acidic.

Assad got up first. "We are from the police, Tilde. My name is—"

"Have you found William?"

They shook their heads.

"In that case I think you should go."

Her mother tried to explain, but Tilde had already passed judgment.

"You two are a couple of idiots. William wasn't like that at all. Or perhaps you knew him better than us?"

Neither of them answered. What could they say to a child like her, who had screamed out her loss on every billboard in the city?

The girl clutched her abdomen and her hands trembled. Malene made to get up, but Tilde gave her a look that clearly demonstrated just what kind of person they were dealing with. Here was a girl who knew all about pain. The body's internal knife stab, the torments of the soul, and the realization that the future had not much else to offer. And yet she did not flee from the room and leave the grown-ups with all the accusations. She stood her ground, though everything inside her clamored for her to give up. She stood her ground and looked them each in the eye. "William was my father. I loved him, he was always there for me, even when I was really ill. Ask anyone I know and they'll tell you he never did me or any of my friends any harm whatsoever." She looked down at the floor. "And I miss him so very much. Now just tell me why you're here; I'm not angry anymore. Have you found him?"

"I'm afraid not, Tilde. But we think there's someone who knows what happened to him." Carl showed her the photo of the boy. "He was at Bellahøj police station yesterday with your poster. And he had this with him."

He nodded to Assad, who produced a clear bag containing the African necklace from his pocket, placing it carefully on the coffee table in front of her.

Tilde blinked, as though the repeated opening and shutting of her eyelids could keep the world at bay and reveal to her some new path forward. She remained so long in this apparent state of paralysis that Malene got to her feet and put her arms round her without the girl noticing. All she saw was the necklace.

Carl looked at Assad, who avoided his gaze. They all knew what Tilde was going through now. A person who had never felt what it was like to suddenly be overwhelmed by the realization of having lost a loved one had either never known loss or had never truly lived. Here at this particular moment were four people, each with his or her own way of dealing with that feeling, and Assad's was definitely not the easiest.

"Where did he get it from, do you know?" she eventually whispered.

"We don't know the answer to that, Tilde. We don't know who this boy is, or where we can find him. We were hoping that you might be able to help us."

She leaned toward the photo and shook her head.

"Is he the one you think William did those things with?"

"We don't think anything at all, Tilde. We're policemen. Our job is to solve mysteries, and right now we're working on what happened to William. It was this that set us off. Have a look."

Carl unrolled the poster in front of her. Her lips trembled as her eyes darted from the necklace on the table to its image on the poster.

"I'm afraid we have to take the necklace back with us, Tilde. It needs to be analyzed by our forensics officers. There may be something on it that can tell us where it's been all this time."

Her hands wafted before her face as the tears began to roll, and she nodded. "I skived off school to put the posters up. I didn't have any left when I was finished, not even one for myself." Her head dropped. All the hopes that had been pinned to her appeal now returned unfulfilled. She twisted free of her mother's embrace and left the room. Her footsteps on the stairs were almost silent.

"The two of them were like . . ." Malene crossed her fingers. "William came into her life before she started school. She was lonely in those days. None of the other children could understand why she kept having pains, and no one would play with her. William saw to it that all of that changed." She gave a sigh. "Tilde was the reason we moved in together a couple of years before William went missing, because she really did love

him like a father and because he was always there for her when she was
feeling poorly. And it was Tilde who insisted that she and I move out of
William's house. She couldn't live there without him."

"Was it her idea for you to leave clothes and other items behind?"

She nodded. "Yes, that was Tilde as well. 'Just imagine,' she said. 'When
William comes home one day he'll be able to see we're still in his life.'"

"*When* he comes home?"

Malene looked at Carl with moist eyes. "That's what she said. She has
never said 'if.' But of course William has never been officially declared
dead, and the house is still there. The interest from his bank assets takes
care of the payments, so it hasn't been so difficult for Tilde to keep thinking 'when.'"

Carl didn't feel like asking any more questions, but Assad persevered.
"Did William do any gambling?" he asked.

Malene frowned. "What do you mean?"

"We know he paid much more for Tilde's treatment at the beginning
than he had at his disposal. Can you explain that?"

"He received an advance on his inheritance, I think."

Assad's dark eyebrows plunged. It was obvious that he, too, was becoming increasingly uncomfortable with the situation. "No, I'm afraid we
can confirm that he did not. His inheritance was first paid out when his
mother died."

"I don't understand." She shook her head, clearly at a loss.

"We are talking about two million kroner. That's why I asked if he
was into gambling."

Again, Malene shook her head. "Tilde once gave him a scratch card
for his birthday and he didn't even know what it was. He was totally
useless when it came to things like that. I can't imagine him gambling at
all. He was much too cautious to take chances."

"What about the two million, then?"

She looked at Assad pleadingly.

Carl took a deep breath. "Can one rule out his having been involved
in some kind of financial crime? Would you say he wasn't capable of that
either?"

Malene didn't reply. She was visibly shattered.

———

Driving back to headquarters, the scene out the windows of the car were like a film flickering by as each of them grappled with his own problem. Carl's was the fact that somewhere out there was a boy who represented a riddle inside an enigma. Assad's was obviously that René E. Eriksen had stuck out his neck to tell a story that didn't hold water, thereby raising a kind of suspicion that was hard to articulate.

"We're going to have to talk to him again, Assad," Carl suggested eventually, but Assad was silent.

A rather annoying habit he'd gotten into of late.

22

When Marco climbed over the fence of the construction site the night before, he first located a direct access route into the building that enabled him to move quickly and inconspicuously between the upper floors and street level. A crucial strategy for any good thief wherever there was a risk of running into guards or guard dogs.

Next, he made note of where equipment, tools, and building materials were concentrated in the various sections of the site so that he knew what places to avoid at the change of shift.

On the fourth floor he found a recess that was sheltered from the wind, gathered layers of cardboard, and made a bed from where he could keep watch through the empty window openings in the concrete walls. Here in this niche, where the lifts would be running in a couple of months, he could remain undiscovered until the morning shift arrived, then make off when they went for their break in the hut below.

Apparently there weren't many workers on the job outside normal working hours, which gave Marco the considerable advantage of being able to move around relatively freely in the evenings, at night, and on weekends, as long as he made sure not to be discovered by passers-by when he squeezed behind the fencing and climbed up into the building by the Hereford Beefstouw restaurant. In any case the night watchmen and the dogs never ventured all the way up into the concrete landscape to the place in which he had installed himself.

The building was enormous. The facade had been stripped away and the entire interior demolished, so only the staircases, supports, and floors remained. Cold, gray concrete all over, as well as an abundance of temporary elevators, tools, and equipment, bordered by portable offices stacked like Lego blocks.

From here he could look out on the Tivoli Gardens as they awakened to yet another season, Rådhuspladsen and H. C. Andersen's Boulevard, down the pedestrian street, Strøget, and a good stretch up Vesterbrogade on the other side. It was a perfect spot as long as the weather was reasonably warm, and the best possible surveillance point for keeping an eye on the Zola clan's thieving and hustling in the city center.

This Tuesday morning the van came at nine as usual, dropping off Zola's troops. This time it was Miryam, Romeo, Samuel, and six others. For a moment they conferred on the pavement before fanning out into the side streets of Vestergade, Lavendelstræde, and Farvergade, from where they could home in on the various sections of Strøget.

In the hours ahead, numerous unfortunate individuals would be relieved of possessions they failed to look after with due care. Watching his old friends spread out into the city streets like bacteria, Marco felt a growing sense of intense shame at having been a part of such beastliness.

Here, from above, he would consider how best to strike back. Perhaps he should try to win some of the other clan members over so that not all of them went down when he denounced Zola and his father. From this vantage point he could see how he might select a few and try to talk them into leaving. If it worked, they would be able to tell him who Zola had recruited to help track him down, and when they thought the hunt would be called off. Once he felt more secure he would venture out to Eivind and Kaj's apartment to retrieve his money and get out of Copenhagen. He knew there were other cities, like Århus and Aalborg in Jutland, far enough away and yet big enough and with enough facilities for him to be able to pursue his education and absorption into Danish society.

But all that was a long way off. Now that the police had seen him and the items he'd left behind at the police station in Bellahøj, would they not be looking for him, too? And if they were, what would happen if they found him? Without any ID would he end up in a refugee center? Did he have anything with which to bargain in order to avoid it?

Seemingly not.

The more he thought about it, the more convinced he was that he had nothing to offer the police. There was a strong likelihood that William Stark's body was no longer where he had found it and that Zola's people had removed all traces of the crime.

He scanned the scene from his concrete hideout, his stomach rumbling, feeling both isolated and abandoned.

She was sitting up against the grating outside the Church of the Holy Spirit, typically underplaying her role in such a way that people were neither repelled nor annoyed by the cautiously outstretched hand and exposed, crooked leg extended in front of her. Miryam had the unusual ability to catch people's eye with a smile and with a single look make them feel like she was their friend. A look that told of suffering but also the will to endure it. That was how she operated. Even the police passed her by without intervening. If she'd had the chance of another profession she would most certainly have made something of herself.

But the warmth in her eyes drained away with her smile when Marco appeared in front of her, his arms spread wide in the hope of detecting some small sign of happiness at seeing him again.

"Just leave, Marco," she urged. "Everyone's out looking for you, and they'll do you harm if they catch you, believe me. I don't want to talk to you. Just go away, and don't show up in town again."

Marco's arms dropped to his sides. "Won't you help me, Miryam? I'll make sure they don't see us together. If I keep a low profile, all you have to do is give me a signal once you know they've called off the search."

"Jesus, you idiot, what's got into you? They'll keep on until they've got you. Of course they will, Marco, so get lost now! And if you come near me again I'll get hold of the others. I might just do that anyway."

She got to her feet, straightening her bad leg with difficulty, then offered him a handful of coins before she went. But Marco backed away, holding up his hands in front of him. He had anticipated her being reluctant and having her reservations, but not that she would threaten to denounce him or try to stick him thirty pieces of silver. Anyone else, certainly, but not Miryam.

He stood for a moment trying to recall the gentleness in her eyes, the caresses she'd given him when his mother did not.

And then he took off without a word.

Five streets farther down he leaned against a drainpipe and wept. He hadn't cried since the first time Zola hit him. An unpleasant sensation began surging through his system, as though he had eaten food that had gone bad. His abdomen convulsed as if he was about to vomit. His nose ran faster than his tears. His arms and legs trembled.

Not just the others, but Miryam, too. He would never have believed it.

Most of all he wanted to close his eyes and let the world disappear. Just let himself go and scream out his despair, but he didn't dare. He wouldn't let himself be such easy prey. He was no little, simpleminded animal, oblivious to the predator. He knew how things worked.

A woman who was passing by stopped and put a hand on his shoulder, bending down to look him in the eye. "What's the matter, dear?" she asked. But instead of embracing her and drawing solace from her kindness, he drew back, dried his eyes, and said: "Oh, nothing."

Later he would wish he had thanked her, but it didn't occur to him at the time, there being but a single thought in his mind: From now on, any member of the clan is fair game.

He would survive by his animosity toward them. He would no longer steal from ordinary people, but the clan were not ordinary people, so from them he would snatch anything he wanted. And when he had harassed them long enough and filled his pockets and stomach, he would move on in life.

He found Romeo and Samuel down in Nyhavn, working over throngs of boisterous, ruddy-cheeked Swedes. So Samuel had been promoted from beggar despite his being a poor earner.

He kept his distance for a while, watching them in their work. The seemingly accidental bumping into people, the swift dips into pockets and bags, the spoils then deftly passed into the other's hand. They were skillful, and seldom needed to apologize for their clumsiness.

Marco knew their behavior patterns, knew when they would glance to the side or over their shoulders and the exact moment they would home in.

Samuel was the receiver, ambling along behind until Romeo struck. And then he would quickly step forward, sticking his hand through his pocket lining to receive the goods. His large inside pocket was already bulging visibly, so it had been a good day. Before long Samuel would signal to Romeo that it was time for a break so he could stash the spoils. And then Marco would strike.

He followed Samuel to one of the last remaining places in the city besides the central station where a person could leave a bag without being suspected of terrorism. By the revolving entrance doors on the ground floor of the Black Diamond, the modern extension to the Royal Danish Library, were locker areas adjacent to the restrooms, allowing people like Samuel to transfer the contents of their secret pockets into a shopping bag and hide them away in a locker without fear of being discovered.

Marco kept watch from the bookshop in the foyer until Samuel emerged from the restroom, shopping bag in hand. He would wait to see which locker Samuel used, then duck back out of sight. Once Samuel had gone, he would go back and work the lock.

Samuel fumbled in his jacket pocket before finding the key. Most probably he kept it on him at all times, ensuring there would always be a locker at his disposal.

He walked into the locker area, went over to the right-hand wall, bent down to one of the lower boxes, and put his key in the lock.

"Got it," Marco said to himself, withdrawing into a corner.

A minute later, Samuel was on his way back to Nyhavn.

Romeo and new victims awaited.

For students it was study time leading up to exams and the library café was packed with young people hunched over laptops. Outside, beyond the glass walls, people lounged about, enjoying the sun and the harbor. No one here would worry themselves about a boy like Marco in a setting like this.

For a moment he stared at the wall of lockers. As far as he could work out, Samuel's was number 163. The lock was simple, but he knew from experience that if he tried to force it with an incorrect key, the key would almost certainly snap in two. He had no tools with him by which he could break the lock either, nor did he possess the courage to ask for assistance at the information desk and spin them a tale about having lost his key.

He tapped his knuckles against the locker door. It wasn't solid, but a kick would merely result in a dent and make a hell of a racket to boot.

So he needed the key.

He caught up with Samuel at Kongens Nytorv and figured that if he was to steal the key without the boy noticing, he would have to create a diversion. He chose an extravagantly tattooed hulk of a man walking a couple of steps behind and to the side of Samuel who was heading purposely for the tourist traps and wilting dives of Nyhavn. He was undoubtedly planning on staying there until the day was done and the well-larded wallet protruding tantalizingly from his back pocket was empty. Provided, of course, that he hadn't the misfortune to run into Romeo first.

Marco slipped silently behind his unsuspecting mark like a heat-seeking missile, flexing the fingers of his left hand to make certain he had full control over them. Then with the ease of a cat he struck, lifting the wallet from the man's pocket, using his body to shield the move from the pedestrians behind. It was elementary.

He stopped and waited until the man was a few steps ahead before bending down and pretending to pick the wallet up off the pavement, then catching up with him and giving his sleeve a tug.

"Here," he said, pressing the wallet into the man's hand. "It was that guy over there who took it off you. He was about to hand it to someone else behind you, but I got it first."

The big man frowned, then his eyes followed the direction in which Marco was pointing, and within a second he had knocked Samuel to his knees.

Marco didn't hear what his old friend screamed, but it clearly had little effect because his punishment was meted out so promptly and emphatically that Samuel was forced to crouch down and protect his face with his hands.

It would not be the first time Marco stole from someone lying prone on the ground, often the last dregs of the night's drunks. This was easy enough, but here he was forced to wait until members of the hooting crowd that had gathered pulled the flailing mastodon away from his hapless victim. It gave Samuel a few seconds to get to his feet and stagger toward safety.

The tattooed roughneck bellowed that the little thief ought to be arrested and thrown in jail, but the onlookers showed mercy and Marco moved in and slipped his hand into Samuel's jacket pocket as the kid pushed through the throng to get away. Even if he noticed anything, his instinct to flee would overrule all else.

All he wanted was to get away.

The big man was still ranting and raving, and Marco didn't hang around to be thanked or accept a reward.

The contents of the locker at the Black Diamond were reward enough.

Back in his hideout at the House of Industry he emptied the shopping bags onto the concrete floor. For a moment he sat staring at the many items. They seemed so alive in the bleak surroundings, shades of color against the cold, gray concrete. He triumphantly removed the banknotes from the wallets without so much as glancing at credit cards or IDs. A quick count came to more than nine thousand kroner in five different currencies.

The sudden rush he felt sparked a brief outburst of laughter, an expression of relief that echoed gaily against the bare walls until his eyes once again settled on the pile of wallets, mobile phones, and watches in front of him.

Then all at once he became still inside. The dark concrete contours around him towered accusingly above his head. The many lit-up windows of the Palace Hotel and the countless diodes streaming Politiken's news headlines on the facade across the square felt like reproachful eyes, like stabbing searchlights. Here lay the property of all these people. Leather wallets and purses, mobile phones with greasy finger marks that weren't his, and no matter who in the first instance had stolen them, he knew at that moment he would be unable to capitalize on Romeo's and Samuel's thieving without becoming an accomplice.

It was an ugly feeling, as repulsive as dog mess on the sole of his shoe. At that moment he was a nobody. Just a simple lowdown thief like the rest of them, and though nine thousand kroner was a lot of money and would get him by for a long time, the day would inevitably come when it all ran out and he would have to become a thief again.

Who was he kidding?

Only then did he realize how impossible his life had become.

The hatred that had been latent within him from the first day Zola forced him to steal on the streets now flared up inside, kindling a thirst for vengeance that felt stronger than ever before.

He was a thief and would always be as long as the clan existed. Zola would still have his hooks in him wherever he went.

Marco clenched his fists and stared up at the concrete above his head as he imagined Stark's corpse with its empty eye sockets, Tilde and her gentle voice, and the policeman called Carl who no doubt wanted to get in touch with him. All these shadows lingering above him and all the nasty ones lurking behind his back could vanish at once if he now did the right thing.

There was no longer any doubt. Zola and his clan had to be eliminated.

23

"I suppose the two of you were expecting to be received with a fanfare," said Rose, skewering Assad in the gut with a rolled-up sheet of paper. "With Carl you never know what he'll do, but I'd never have thought it of you, Assad. You knew perfectly well Malene was mine, and now here she is phoning me up while I'm at the ministry, telling me how you came barging in and put the screws on the two of them. What do you think you're playing at?"

"That's not quite how it happened, Rose," Assad ventured, clearly poised to get the hell out with his prayer mat before her next sentence detonated.

Carl caught himself smirking, regardless of how unfair it was. "I'm the one you should be giving a tongue-lashing," he pointed out. "Assad said we ought to have taken you with us, but it just didn't turn out."

Rose snorted. "What good's a tongue-lashing ever done you, Carl Mørck? You've got skin thick as a rhinoceros." She took hold of his hand and slapped her sheet of paper into his palm. "But if you can do without me there, you can do without me here, too, because that's me, off. Then you can sit and have a think about what I've dug up in the meantime."

"Ha, ha, that's it, Rosie, you give 'em what for," came a voice from the other end of the corridor.

Rose's hands dropped to her sides as Gordon appeared. It was clear as day she didn't need his assistance just now, but he carried on anyway.

"I'd say it borders on harassment when your superior doesn't allow you to interview your own contact."

A crease appeared on Rose's brow. Not the kind that expressed perplexity, rather a line of demarcation, and woe betide any man who over-stepped it.

"Stop, Gordon," she snapped authoritatively, but the idiot was seemingly only capable of grasping a message in extremely small portions.

"But I suppose it's typical of the older generation of criminal investigators," he went on, undaunted. "A bit pubescently chauvinistic, the two of them, wouldn't you agree?"

"Ooh, you're a bunch of imbeciles, the lot of you!" Rose burst out, not waiting for their protests before disappearing into her office and slamming the door behind her. A bomb-proof postlude to her symphony of self-righteousness.

Carl turned to the culprit. "I've got broad shoulders, so this time I'm going to ignore that you're audacious enough to call me pubescent and a male chauvinist, not to mention lumping me in with the older generation, but you don't want to be talking to me like that again, do you hear me?"

The moron stared blankly at Carl. Was he brain-dead or just looking for trouble?

"I think perhaps you ought nod at this point, Gordon," Assad suggested drily.

So he nodded, though barely perceptibly.

"Next, let me ask you to think back to yesterday. Didn't you understand you were not only way out of line in someone else's domain but also that we'd rather have a pack of ravenous hyenas on the loose than have you running around down here?"

Gordon didn't answer. He probably had his own recollections of what had occurred, and they were undoubtedly rather more pleasant.

"OK, in that case I suggest that after Assad and I have knocked you about a bit, you get your ass upstairs to Lars Bjørn and tell him how unreasonable we are down here."

Carl tapped a cigarette from his pack and lit up in one seamless movement. Seeing the kid abruptly shy away, his gormless mug momentarily obliterated by smoke, was almost enough to save the day.

Gordon was about to protest, until he saw Assad begin to roll up his shirtsleeves. Though he seemed to get the message and immediately retreated out the door like a cowed dog, he didn't abstain from turning around at a safe distance farther up the corridor to hurl back a string of six-syllable words of Latin origin.

If that boy didn't start toeing the line soon, it wouldn't be long before he got hurt.

Carl unrolled the sheet of paper Rose had shoved at him. THE BAKA PROJECT it read at the top in ultra-bold thirty-point Times New Roman. In case anyone should fail to notice.

"Sit down and listen to what she's written here, Assad, and put another expression on your face while you're at it. Rose'll come round, just you wait and see. She knows perfectly well we can't all charge in like the Light Brigade every time we're out interviewing people."

"What is this Light Brigade, Carl?"

Carl jabbed a finger at the sheet in front of him. "Never you mind. It says here that Rose was encouraged to phone this civil servant in Yaoundé. That's the capital of Cameroon, for your information." He hadn't known himself until two minutes ago.

"The gentleman in question is one Mbomo Ziem, and according to our people down there he was in charge of liaising with the Danish international development office in connection with this Baka project and a couple of other aid initiatives in the area. However, he seems to have left the project, so Rose got hold of one Fabrice Pouka instead, who was able to tell her that the Baka project is still running, though it's now in its final year. According to him it had all proceeded according to plan, apart from someone called Louis Fon coming close to sabotaging the whole effort at one point. Rose writes that the project was set up to help an endangered tribe of pygmies in the Dja jungle in southern Cameroon to sow banana plantations and cultivate the soil with the aim of growing new kinds of crops. Apparently all this had become necessary because poaching and things generally going to pot over the years had ruined their traditional ways of supporting themselves."

Carl put the paper down on the desk in front of him.

"Is that all, then?" Assad asked. Carl knew what he meant. It sure wasn't much she'd dug up during all that time she'd been away.

"Oh, hang on a minute. There's something on the back here that she's written by hand. *LFon9876*. I wonder what that means?"

"It looks like a Skype address."

"Go in and ask her, will you?"

"Who? Me?"

Carl didn't answer, which was reply enough in itself.

Five minutes later Assad stood before him once more, sweating.

"Ouch, Carl. She dipped me right in the acid bath again. But yes, she said it was a Skype address. Finding it out is what took her most of that time, but I won't bother you with telling you how. She says she assumes the call will be answered at Louis Fon's home address in the north of Cameroon. She has tried, but there was no one who answered."

"So maybe it's not in use anymore."

"One can hear then that this is not your strong point, Carl. You can only call up a Skype number if the person you are calling has switched on their computer. And not only that, they have to be on hand to answer the call."

"Yes, yes, I knew that. What I meant was . . ."

Assad beamed. "That's a good one, Carl, but you can't fool me. Let me show you. Come into my office and we'll call from my computer. It's all set up."

In the cubbyhole, on top of the desk amid tea urns, glazed green incense stick holders, stacks of files, and a whole lot of other rubbish stood police HQ's biggest computer screen, showing an image of the kind of gray-brown mud-built abode of which there were millions in the Middle East. Definitely not a place Carl would like spending his retirement. Nothing colorful, no plants, no veranda where a man could throw his feet up on the rail. Just a window and a door, and everything the color of shit.

"That your place, Assad?" he asked, pointing.

Assad smiled, shook his head and pressed a key. The image was gone.

"First we turn on the speakers, Carl. You sit down in front of the screen, then we open our Skype account. I'll show you how. If they have a camera at the other end like we have, we should also be able to see each other."

Half a minute passed and then they heard the blooping ringtone, an infuriating sound if ever there was one, Carl thought.

Assad just managed to say, "Give it a little time," before sounds indicated something was happening at the other end.

Carl adjusted his headset, Assad gesticulating frantically to make sure he was ready. How ready did you have to be, for Chrissake?

And then the image of a young African woman's face appeared in front of him, far too close, issuing a stream of words, none of which he understood. He said hello with the kind of British accent only an English teacher like the one he had up in his native north-Jutland peat bog near Brønderslev thirty years ago could imagine was grand.

"Allo?" the woman said in reply. Hardly much progress.

"Do they speak French in Cameroon?" he whispered to Assad.

Assad nodded.

"Do you?"

Assad shook his head.

Carl hung up.

It took half an hour before they managed to coax Rose into admitting that she actually spoke the language quite well. Moreover, she accepted their apologies in return for a certain amount of as yet unspecified favors.

In less than twenty seconds she had introduced herself. The woman at the other end drew back from the screen, revealing a room into which the sun poured from every angle.

"I'll translate as we go along," Rose explained, both to the woman and the two standing behind her.

It was clear that Louis Fon's wife bore grief. She explained how difficult her situation had become during the five months since her husband disappeared, how she broke down in tears at the slightest thing.

"Everything was going so well for us. Louis had plenty of work, we wanted for nothing, and he was happy in his job. Beside me and our children, there was nothing he wanted more dearly than for the Baka to thrive and be prosperous."

"What do you think happened?" Rose asked.

"I don't know." She shrugged all the way up to her ears as a pair of near-hairless dogs stuck their pointed snouts through the doorway behind her. "I thought at first the poachers had killed him, but now I think maybe it was someone else."

"What makes you think he was killed, and who exactly do you suspect?"

"It is not something I think. Our Nganga says so. The birds' claws have spoken. Louis is no longer with us."

"I'm sorry to hear that. Who is Nganga? A medicine man? A witch doctor?"

"He is the guardian of our bodies and souls."

The three of them exchanged glances. It was something that was unlikely to stand up in court.

"But then Louis's parents gave me some money so I could travel to Dja and Somolomo and look for whatever might be left of him. It made Nganga very angry."

"So you never found out what happened?"

She shook her head, at once indignant and distressed, yet still able to deliver a swift kick to one of the dogs as it ventured too close.

"A lot of strange things were going on down there. That was all I discovered. The pygmies were dissatisfied because the Baka project had come to a standstill. First they were promised crops and new plantations, then they were given money to wait, and then finally they ended up getting almost nothing at all. That was what they all told me. They were so angry at Louis and the Danes, and I guess I was, too. But after a while I received a little money from Denmark, which helped a bit."

She leaned back, looking pensive.

"Ask her what she's thinking now, Rose," said Assad.

Rose nodded. She'd noticed it, too.

"You look like something's on your mind. Did something occur to you that we should know?"

"*Je ne sais pas.* Maybe it is nothing, but it was strange, all the same." She sat silent for a moment while Carl and the others marveled at how small the world had become. It was almost as if one could smell her cooking on the stove beside her, or reach out and touch her hair and lips. Carl half expected the floor of Assad's cubbyhole to begin sprouting grass mats.

"I was thinking about how strange it was that the man who signed the papers saying I was entitled to compensation, now that Louis was gone, was in Somolomo the same day Louis disappeared. Some of the locals in Somolomo told me this."

"The exact same day? A Dane?"

"*Oui, oui*. He must have been a Dane."

"Can you remember his name?"

Another long pause during which the soul of Africa attempted to take possession of Assad's ersatz Middle Eastern den. A pause where the woman seemed almost to have fallen into a trance from which she was unable to return.

"William Stark?" Carl suggested.

She looked up and shook her head.

"No, that wasn't it. I don't recall the name. The only thing I remember is there were a lot of e's in it."

Carl caught Assad's more-than-alert glance. Then Carl's mobile thrummed in his pocket.

Great fucking timing.

"Yeah?" he answered with annoyance without first glancing at the display. "Listen, it's not a good time right now. Call back in half an hour."

"Hi, Carl. Sorry. It's Lisbeth. You know, the one you spoke with at the library in Brønshøj."

"Oops," he groaned lamely. What was it about a woman's voice that could knock him sideways?

"This might not be the best time for you at the moment, but the boy's here again, at the branch on Dag Hammarskjölds Allé."

24

Marco checked the time on the computer. It was 6:10, so it would be a while before the library closed. But then why did the librarians behind the counter keep looking at him and their watches as if they were closing in five minutes?

Could there be others they were looking at?

He turned his screen slightly so he could see their reflections. Were they conferring now?

It was the one with the short brown hair, the one they called Lisbeth, he was most wary of. It was like she was everywhere. First here, then Brønshøj, and now here again, and no matter where it was, he'd felt her eyes upon him. Maybe this was the last time he'd be able to come here. The looks they kept sending in his direction seemed to tell him so.

He turned his screen back again and typed in another search. There were all too many policemen in Copenhagen by that name, and to make matters worse he'd just discovered it could be spelled with a "C" as well as a "K." Back to square one. Since he knew neither the officer's surname nor his rank, he reckoned his best bet was to search Google Images, typing in "Carl" and "police," which returned photos galore of the Swedish king and a single image of a policeman in uniform by the name of Carl Åge, nothing like the man he had seen. Thousands of irrelevant hits, thousands of irrelevant individuals. He expanded his search, adding "Copenhagen" and "criminal." This turned up new results, fewer in number, but still far too many.

Then he read about a few current cases in the online tabloids, noting words like "inspector," "superintendent," and "investigation," and after a few minutes of renewed googling the face of the man suddenly appeared on the screen in connection with a case he and his assistant had solved concerning a well-known doctor, Curt Wad, and a number of illegal abortions. Marco smiled with relief. There he was, jacket buttoned wrong with a sour smile on his face as he stared in to the camera, flanked by a rather smaller, dark-skinned man and a black-haired woman who looked like a punk rocker. Somehow Marco felt a kind of kinship with the little dark man. There was something about his eyes, the calm gaze, his curly hair, the hue of his skin.

Carl Mørck, Rose Knudsen, and Hafez el-Assad read the caption, so now he knew his policeman's full name. A proficient investigator, according to the article, and a specialist in unsolved cases.

Marco sat for a moment and stared into space with a rare feeling inside him. Had he really been this lucky? Wasn't this Carl Mørck just the kind of man he needed?

He read on, discovering new links that mentioned the policeman. Not everything he found was particularly reassuring. One article described an incident out in Amager where Mørck had been shot under mysterious circumstances, after which he had been on sick leave for some time. And it said his fiery temperament was legendary among colleagues.

Marco knew all about fiery temperaments. One had to be careful around them.

Again, he turned the screen until he saw Lisbeth's reflection as she stood whispering with the other librarians who still stood facing him. All his instincts were immediately alerted. He looked toward the glass entrance doors, noting that one of the male employees had positioned himself in front of them, his eyes glancing repeatedly in Marco's direction.

It was annoying and unpleasant and made Marco stand up and move to the next computer. If he couldn't get away by the entrance, at least he was on the ground floor. Then, if he needed to, it would be easy to climb through the window facing the parking lot round the back.

He picked up a book that had been left on the table and pretended to look something up, cross-checking with pages on the Web.

Maybe he was too jumpy, imagining things. Why should they be interested in him? He'd always behaved himself commendably at the library.

What could it be? Had he forgotten something on the shelf above the electricity meter that they had just discovered?

He shook his head. No, he'd left nothing behind there, he felt sure of it.

He looked out on the parking lot. All seemed quiet beyond the light green of the shrubbery. People coming and going, leaving or collecting their cars in the diagonal spaces, most of them wearing a smile. A mild May evening in Denmark such as this one could be so incredible with its sharp, clear light. It was one of the things he loved best about being here.

Marco turned back to his computer screen and smiled to himself. Now he had something to go on. The policeman's name was Carl Mørck and he worked on unsolved cases. Regardless of any reservations he might have about going to the police, he realized this was the man he had to approach with what he knew. He only hoped he could avoid having to let on that he was stateless and that his family had brought him up to be a criminal. Marco frowned. It would be difficult. To succeed he would have to find a way of passing on his information without having to meet him in person.

Which meant he needed more information that would bring him closer to the man.

Marco surfed the Web for a while. Apparently Carl Mørck's doings were a good subject for the press, several of his cases having received considerable attention. The articles included one about a politician who had gone missing, a series of arsons, kidnappings, a killer in Copenhagen's Søndermarken, the case of a secret brotherhood carrying out unlawful abortions, and much more besides. Department Q, his section was called.

Marco put on the headphones next to the computer and clicked into a couple of short TV clips featuring Mørck, his dark-skinned assistant and the weird female colleague.

Mørck was easy to read, but his assistant Assad was rather more difficult. In fact, the clips gave Marco a quite different impression of the man than he had gained from looking at the images on the net. On the face of it, he seemed kind and good-natured, and yet there was something indefinable about his eyes and gestures that Marco found unsettling. There was a darkness in his gaze that made him seem shifty and a little too much on his guard.

This man had secrets he did not want to share. Beneath his smile he was a sharpened knife, Marco knew. Far too wary for a pickpocket to even come close. As far as possible he would have to avoid this Assad.

After a few more minutes of searching in vain for private information about Carl Mørck, he opened Google Maps and printed out the woodland area where he had hidden from the clan the day he escaped. He collected the printout and drew a cross at the location where he believed Stark's body had lain. So far so good.

Again the librarian looked at her watch and glanced over to where he was sitting. She didn't look straight at him, but straight enough.

Why was she so interested in the time? There was still quite a while until closing, and why was the man still over by the entrance? What was he doing there?

The librarian's face twitched slightly as they all heard a car enter the parking lot, braking hard and pulling into the farthest space. Her expression didn't change much, but suddenly she appeared relieved.

And instinctively Marco knew he now had to raise his hand to the security lock on the window by which he sat.

It was a movement the staff behind the counter didn't like. They became agitated, and Lisbeth gave a strange nod to the man at the entrance. He nodded back and began strolling a bit too casually toward the area where Marco sat, pretending to check the shelves he passed on his way.

The windows rattled at the slamming of car doors and two figures came running, one with his jacket billowing behind him, the other scuttling crablike.

It was Mørck and his assistant.

Marco's eyes were everywhere now as he unhasped the lock on the window as calmly and as inconspicuously as possible. The man from the entrance was only a few strides away, yet Marco remained seated for a second more. He wanted to be absolutely certain that he didn't jump out before the two policemen had turned the corner and were heading for the entrance.

Now!

He took a deep breath, sent the lady librarian a sad look, pushed the window open, and jumped.

"You're joking? Did he really just jump out the window? Why didn't you people stop him?"

Carl sprang to the open window and looked out. Parked cars, otherwise nothing.

Lisbeth pointed at a young man who was sitting in a chair, moaning softly.

"Bent there tried to go after him, but he sprained his ankle clambering up onto the windowsill."

Carl nodded testily to the man. What the hell kind of condition were Denmark's young people in these days?

"What was the boy doing?" Assad asked.

"He was just sitting over there at the computer. He took a printout at one point. It might still be there."

Carl went over to the table. There was nothing there and nothing on the floor either.

"Check the wastepaper basket over there, Assad," he said, sitting down at the computer. He found himself wondering how much of his life he had wasted in front of Google's logo, wishing himself back to the time when the Internet was no more than an electrical impulse in some bloke's kinky brain.

"We could check and see if he had time to delete his searches," Lisbeth suggested, leaning her ripe breasts lightly against his shoulder as she began to type with prettily painted fingernails.

Sensing her perfume, Carl inhaled cautiously but deeply. It wasn't quite as pervasive as Mona's, but almost. The kind of scent that put every gland in his body on the alert.

"I'm sure you know, but then you just click on the triangle there," she said, leaning farther forward and doing it for him.

That was when Carl lost all interest in police work.

He wondered whether she was doing it on purpose, all his senses now converging on his shoulder region.

"There we are," she said, relieving the angelic pressure as he followed the movement of her body. "Now we can see what he was so interested in. Maybe you can tell us why, Inspector Mørck."

He stared listlessly at the screen, then woke up.

"Strange boy," came Assad's voice from behind him.

Carl focused his eyes and scrolled down to where the searches no longer seemed to be related. It all looked very systematic, and it was all about him.

"Now he knows who you are, Carl."

"Yeah, and you, too, Assad."

"I think you better keep an eye out for what's happening around you."

"I'm not afraid of a kid."

"He is not just a kid, Carl, You can see for yourself right here. He wants to know all about you. Perhaps he knows more than is good."

"What do you mean?"

"I just mean that sometimes the camel driver is driven by the camel."

Carl nodded. What the hell did the boy want with all this information?

"Look at his last search," said Lisbeth. "He's been on Google Maps. That's probably where his printout's from."

Carl clicked on the search word, only to find himself on another search page with another search field.

"Can I see which area he was searching for?"

Lisbeth leaned forward again. "Just do the same again. Click on the triangle there, Carl."

She might just have told him. Not that he had the slightest objection to the heavenly feeling of her soft breasts once more against his shoulder. As far as he was concerned, she could stay like that a bit longer.

He looked at the list of searches.

Kregme came up.

"Strange name," said Assad. "Just like the stuff in a layer cake."

Lisbeth's laughter was like feeling the gentlest of touches. Carl stared at her lips. What the fuck was happening?

"Do you live up in Kregme, Carl? That's a long way."

"No, I live in Allerød. I've no idea why he'd be interested in Kregme. Maybe he lives there himself. Maybe that's where he's off to now."

"Allerød, that's a coincidence."

"Why, do you live there, too?" he asked. The thought of her perhaps soon heading off home in the same direction made him oddly restless.

She smiled. "No, in Værløse. Just a stone's throw, isn't it?"

"When do you get off work?" he blurted out, and could have bitten off his tongue. What the hell was he playing at? What kind of an idiotic question was that? He'd be asking how she was getting home next.

"How are you getting home?" he heard himself say, purely reflexively.

"You could give me a lift, for example." She laughed out loud. So she probably didn't mean it.

Carl took a deep breath. With the possible exception of the infinity of the universe, a female's humor was probably the most difficult thing to get a handle on.

Carl looked at Assad. His smile seemed a bit too crooked. What was he thinking?

"Perhaps we could go out for a meal together?" Lisbeth added. "I'm rather hungry, as it happens. Then you could tell me all you know about this boy. I have to admit I'm curious. What do you say?"

He waited for them over on the other side of the street, crouching behind the cars parked outside the former Red Cross building.

From here he could see the policemen's car in the parking lot. Any moment now they would come out and drive off. He just wanted to see them, and what they were going to do.

For that reason he was surprised when they came out with the librarian, and even more so when Carl Mørck and his assistant parted company and Carl and the librarian headed up the street together toward Lille Triangel.

Reaching the Dag H café, where Marco had so often lent a hand sweeping the pavement and clearing up, they went inside and sat down at a table that was not immediately visible from the street.

The thing now was to decide whether to make his next move straightaway. If there were too many or too few customers, he risked being discovered, but as far as he could make out, conditions were just right.

He waited twenty minutes before walking in and past the bar, nodding to those at work behind it.

Luckily, it was no one he knew.

They were seated in a corner on the left, their elbows on the table and faces so close together that anyone would think they knew each other most intimately.

Carl Mørck seemed different than the other times he had seen him. His fierce countenance had evaporated and been oddly replaced by the kind of half-witted boyish pose Danish men assume when trying to get off with a woman. And the strange thing was that the women usually fell for it, and this instance was no exception. Something was obviously going on.

It couldn't have been better.

Marco scanned the café. For a thief this was perfect: a lively hum of voices, couples with fingers entwined, intimate conversation, joking between friends. A landscape free of cares, in which people like Marco worked best. Bags dumped on the floor, coats and jackets draped over chairs, mobile phones on table edges.

He straightened his shoulders and slid like a shadow into the passage between the bar and the cake display. If he could find a seat in the armchair on the raised area just behind Carl Mørck without the librarian seeing him, he'd be able to ease the wallet out of Mørck's jacket that hung from the back of his chair.

It took him a minute or two to weave his way between the columns and into position. He advanced no more than a couple of meters at a time, for this was the technique and would hopefully reach the chair while it remained unoccupied.

When eventually he found himself seated back-to-back with Mørck he was close enough to sense their intimacy. The librarian talked the most while Mørck sat immobile and listened, beguiled and wholly absent from the world around him.

Before long she would casually place her hand on the table next to his, and if he responded by laying his on hers, Marco could just as well sound a fanfare as he dipped into the inside pocket of Carl's jacket. They wouldn't notice a thing.

Two minutes later he stood at the top of the stairs leading down to the restrooms with the open wallet in his hands. He was going to put it back as soon as he was finished with it, but then a waiter appeared, asking if he'd like to order, and he hadn't the courage to stay that long. Mørck and his librarian were already ordering dessert.

He peered into the wallet. It was the flat kind preferred by men who couldn't care less what was dictated by the fashion pundits in Milan and New York. The stitching was coming apart, the leather was thin and shiny from wear and tear, and it had gradually assumed the shape of the body against which it had unceasingly been pressed for years on end. Moreover, it was utterly unsuited to modern forms of payment. Marco couldn't remember the last time he'd seen a wallet without slits for credit cards and ID, where cards, coins, and banknotes were stuffed into the same zipper compartment.

Marco folded his slip of paper several times and slipped it in between Mørck's old receipts and battered calling cards. The man apparently had none himself.

All I need to do now is wait, he told himself, then felt a prod on his shoulder. He looked up slowly to see his former employer, who had come up from his office in the basement.

"What are you doing here, Marco? Didn't I tell you on the phone to stay away? You attract the wrong people, people I don't care to see here. I want you to respect that. I thought we agreed."

Munthe was OK, though he was a guy with his own opinions who wouldn't shy from defending them promptly. This was definitely not what Marco wanted.

"I just need to use the bathroom, Munthe. I thought it would be OK."

At that moment his eyes were bluer than ever.

And then Marco turned and went down the stairs. But not before noting that Munthe had already removed his apron.

Sure enough, only ten minutes passed before Munthe left the premises as usual to pick up his wife in the shop next door, and Marco was on his way back up the stairs.

From this vantage point he could see their table. The waiter had placed the bill in front of Mørck, who was now on his feet, frantically checking all his jacket pockets.

He stood there gesticulating like a character in a silent movie. Mystified, shocked, feverish, and ashamed. The entire gamut in seconds. And then the librarian put her hand reassuringly on his. The bill wasn't a problem, even if it was a shame he'd lost his wallet.

Absorbed in discussion, they passed close by him on their way out as Marco's fingers did what they were best at.

25

The time was exactly twelve o'clock when Eriksen's secretary appeared before him with a printout of a scanned message saying a UPS shipment was on its way.

He studied the invoice. One bubble envelope, 320x455mm, 600 grams. It seemed reasonable enough.

He leaned back in his chair and mused on how it would feel to be holding 600 grams of immeasurable prosperity safely in his hands. Once the package arrived, his future would be brighter than he could ever have dreamed. Provided he handled the sale of his shares appropriately, their proceeds together with what he made from selling off his stock in Karrebæk Bank would not only provide a very satisfactory future: they would also lift him definitively out of the life-sapping social stratum to which he had hitherto belonged, to those unmentionable heights where luxury and beautiful women seemed to be almost inevitable parameters of daily existence. Farewell, wife and children, who had written him off anyway. Farewell, crappy little car and dismal little house. Farewell, cruel winters and terminally dull colleagues. Farewell to all the times he had stood in the checkout lines of low-end supermarkets with low-end people for whom, while they may have been his neighbors, he couldn't be bothered to spare even a thought.

Now eternal summer beckoned beyond the gates of the future, gates he was more than ready to throw wide-open.

He looked around his office and began laughing at the sight of shelves full of dreary cases and years of trivial toil. What joy he would feel at giving it all the finger. Simply baring his ass and pulverizing the self-importance of it all with a derisive emission of methane.

He laughed the way his wife so hated. He could hardly wait for the day he would use that laugh while he patted her on the head and said good-bye forever.

For a while he sat there, his face frozen in a mask of glee until it almost hurt. And then his secretary came in and placed a folder in front of him.

"While the folder you left on my desk is the budget for the draining project in Burkina Faso, it's the wrong year, despite what it says on the front. Dare one ask for a file with the right contents?"

René shook his head in annoyance. It wasn't often he made a mistake like that.

"I'll be more careful next time," he said curtly.

And then reality suddenly dawned on René E. Eriksen.

The right contents echoed in his mind as he stared at the receipt for the UPS shipment.

Who the hell was to say whether the contents of the package would be what he was waiting for?

Snap didn't sound particularly communicative at the other end of the line. He had been up since six o'clock Curaçao time, and not being allowed to nurse a two-day jet lag was no fun.

"You've got the receipt you asked for, what more do you want?" he barked. "Once the package arrives you'll see for yourself what's in it, OK?"

"And what if my share certificates aren't there?"

"They are, René. Now leave me in peace and let me enjoy what few days I've got here, all right?"

René pictured him. An overweight bon vivant who thought he was born with the right to stand first in line when the privileges were handed out.

But this time he was wrong, dammit, when it was going to be at René's expense.

"Listen to me, Teis. You can call Brage-Schmidt and tell him that if the two of you are pulling one over on me, I'll turn you both in. I've found a fail-safe way out so you can't drag me down with you."

"Come on, René, don't give me that. The three of us are in this up to our necks, and there are a thousand things incriminating you that you can't talk your way out of. Our liaisons over the years have been a bit too close for that."

René would have liked to have laughed but couldn't. The rage he was suppressing was just too powerful. "Yeah, but you know what, Teis? You're wrong, dangerously wrong. The authorities will be able to see you've given me financial advice on occasion, and that it was for this reason I purchased Karrebæk shares as a way of supporting the bank. And because you owed me favors from our school days, you told me when the prices were favorable. Nothing illegal there, and that's all they'll be able to find out. And as for the Curaçao shares, they're all unregistered, so you can't threaten me with that one. And what else is left? Bank transfers? Correspondence? Nothing, right? Phone calls, perhaps, but that's natural enough. As a friend, I've been trying to get you to stop being party to this fraud that I've long suspected you and William Stark of carrying out, but which I've only now become certain of, having found proof of Stark's involvement. That's right, it's all here in black and white. And that's what I'll be telling the police if it comes to that."

"You're bluffing, René. It doesn't become you. You'd do well to bear in mind that I'm the fox running free in the woods and you're the rodent in the mouse hole, where you belong. So you can forget all that nonsense and relax. We're on the same side, and it'll all blow over in a few days, mark my words."

Yeah, once you've killed that boy, René thought. "I'll only ask you this once, Teis," he said aloud. "When have I ever bluffed? Isn't that something I've always left to you?"

"Stop this now!" It wasn't the first time Teis Snap had hissed at him like that, but it had been a long time. René could picture his purple face swelling up with rage.

"Watch your step, René! If you threaten us, then I strongly suggest you begin looking over your shoulder, no matter where you happen to be."

And with that he hung up.

Teis Snap stared at his mobile for a moment before taking it with him from the bedroom and leaving his wife to pack their suitcases. The tone could become rough in a minute.

"What now?" said the voice that answered his call.

"The package has been dispatched and two minutes ago I had Eriksen on the line. He's smelled a rat."

"And? Once the fuse is lit, what can happen other than Eriksen blowing himself up?"

"That's why I'm calling. Getting rid of him can't wait until after the boy's been killed."

"Why not?"

"Because he's taking precautions, and knowing him the way I do, I'd say he's being too straightforward to be lying. Dull people aren't very good when it comes to playing the comedian. My assessment is he's serious."

"What kind of precautions?"

"He's constructed material that will cast all the blame on William Stark and us. We need to get René out of the way before he puts it to use, which he might well do once he discovers what's in that package. I don't think he's likely to find a stack of newspaper pages in the Papiamento language a reasonable substitute for what he was expecting."

"You didn't send that package express, did you?"

"No, of course not, but it'll be arriving very soon, anyway. But listen, isn't it about time your crew got its hands on that boy? He's only fifteen years old for Chrissake, and every scumbag in the city's out looking for him. It can't be that difficult, surely?"

"We'll see."

Teis didn't have that kind of patience, he knew René E. Eriksen a little too well. He was the toiler who put his head down and slogged his way through university without complaint. The man who gained top marks all round because he was brighter than the rest and knew how best to please his professors. No, Teis didn't like the idea of waiting at all.

"I am well aware that we agreed the order of things was to do away with the boy first and thereby make it plausible for Eriksen to have killed him and then committed suicide because of it. But surely we can find another way? Couldn't we kidnap Eriksen now, then hold off on getting rid of him until the boy is dead? I mean, if Eriksen is going to become an alleged child killer, no one's going to wonder about his having been missing for a couple of days before committing his crime. And the times of death will fit nicely, won't they? No reason to give the police too much to think about, is there?"

For a moment there was silence at the other end.

"Perhaps you're right." The voice came hesitantly. "But in that case we'll have to do it before that package arrives."

"We can get it over with right away as far as I'm concerned. Eriksen's home every evening, if I know him right. He's too scared of his wife not to be."

The voice laughed. A most inappropriate and malicious laughter that oddly enough left Teis feeling out of sorts. The feeling of having just now raised the ax over the neck of his old schoolmate hardly suited such merriment.

"But if Eriksen has a wife, we're obviously going to have to take her as well, aren't we?"

Teis shook his head. "That cow? For all I care, you can send her to hell where she belongs. I could never stand the sight of her."

"OK. It's sorted, then. I'll get the ball rolling and call the people who got Stark out of the way. A nice little home break-in, they've done it before. The only difference this time is it'll be the occupants themselves they steal."

And then all there was was a dial tone.

Teis snapped his phone shut and glanced toward the bedroom door. There was a sound of suitcases being closed.

He checked his watch. Things were looking good.

It wall all just a matter of timing.

Eriksen came home rather later than usual, acting as though everything was fine. His wife did not care for him to kiss her on account of his dentures, which she found repulsive despite being aware that periodontal disease had left him with no other option, though he gave her sulking face a fleeting kiss on the cheek nonetheless. Then he took a quick nap before bringing his dinner to the coffee table and switching on TV2 News. And apart from Lars von Trier's blunder about Nazism, the news was the same trivial bullshit as always. Who could be bothered to hear about Queen Elizabeth's visit to Ireland? An Irishman, perhaps, but certainly not René E. Eriksen or even his wife, who was pacing about in the utility room as usual, muttering her dissatisfaction with just about everything: the housecleaning, their daughter's arguments with her husband, the button that wasn't to be found anywhere after the last wash. And then there was the ceaseless ironing of anything that had the audacity to exhibit the tiniest wrinkle.

Thank God all this will soon be history, he thought, and sank into the cushions of the sofa.

The next moment shards of glass from the patio doors exploded across the room. The rush of adrenaline pumped him into an upright position as his dinner landed on the carpeting. The figures entering through the shattered doors wore balaclavas, only their eyes visible, and without saying a word lunged toward him, striking him hard on the side of the head. As he fell backward onto the sofa, legs quivering, he heard one of them say in English that now it was his wife's turn.

They hit him again, harder this time, but although he saw a glitter before his eyes like shooting stars, he remained conscious. His arms had lost all their strength and his legs refused to obey him, but inside he was still there.

What's happening? he thought, trying to move his body as the men spread out into the house.

From upstairs came the sound of tumult, as if all the furniture were being hurled aside and curtains and bedspreads torn asunder, but from the utility room, where René knew his wife was, all was quiet.

"Is she downstairs, Pico?" the man upstairs shouted.

René was terrified. Like everyone else, he had seen the papers and read about home invasions, they were a modern-day scourge, everyday life transformed into B-movie horror. Now these stories of ordinary people's sudden demise in their own homes were no longer just newspaper copy. There were always plenty of loudmouths with their wallets full of notes and there were always suspicious elements ready to lighten their burden. But René was no loudmouth.

What do they want from me? he wondered. I've got nothing worth stealing. The television's outdated, the wife's jewelry is trash, the Karrebæk shares are in a safe-deposit with Nordea . . .

His train of thought stopped there.

If you threaten us, I strongly suggest you begin looking over your shoulder, Teis Snap had said.

Cold shivers ran down his spine.

Had these people not come to steal? Had they come to kill them?

He managed to turn his head as the man who had shouted came bounding down the stairs and headed for the utility room.

"What the hell . . . ?" cried the man a second later.

What's happening? was all René could think, as cries and thuds merged into one. For a brief moment all seemed quiet, and then the clamor erupted again.

Just as he was thinking that despite everything this wasn't the fate he had wished upon his wife, the door of the utility room slammed hard.

Now René felt the floor beneath his feet again, the cushions of the sofa against his back. He stretched his neck and felt for blood. Then, seeing only a thin smear on his fingertips, he pushed himself upright until he stood, the room swimming around him.

All he could think of was to get away.

"Where do you think *you're* going?" came a severe, penetrating voice from behind as he staggered across the shards toward the patio doors.

He turned to see a pair of eyes flashing with rage in a face white as chalk.

"Why didn't you come and help me?" his wife snarled, her apron spattered red and still clutching her beloved steam iron, blood dripping from its point.

"But you can relax now, you coward, they won't be coming back," she said, her voice trembling as she scanned the chaos around them. "I slammed the first one right on the chin before he even saw me and the other one's not going to be a pretty sight in the morning either. And what were *you* doing while I was chasing them away?" she spat, taking a step toward him.

René shook his head instinctively. Nothing was going to help anyway.

"Nothing, that's what! But who were they, René?" she asked coldly. "I know you know, because they knew my name."

"I can assure you I've no idea. I'm as shocked as you are. All of a sudden they were just there."

"I think you do know. If the second one hadn't been such a hard case and managed to drag his friend away with him even though his face was still burning from the iron, I'd have gotten to the bottom of this, believe me."

She tiptoed over the shards of glass in her slippers and picked up the phone.

"I can describe them, I pulled their hoods off." She cackled. "Ugly little Gyppos, I'll make sure they get what's coming to them."

But René was having none of it. No way was he going to risk being brought down by his wife's big mouth and poorly supported assumptions while the police were here, so he forbade her, simple as that. He couldn't have the authorities poking their noses in, a mere twenty-four hours before his voluntary and permanent exile. If she was going to phone anyone, she could phone a glazier, and then a powerful dose of sedatives would be needed for this bitch who was already complaining again, now he'd put the phone back down, as well as heaping scorn on him for his laxity, his cowardice, his ugly dentures, and his bad breath.

After she'd finished spewing the better part of her glossary of foul-mouthed invective he went up the stairs to the spare room. Not to sleep, because he couldn't, though this would be his second night without, but in order to call Snap in private and confront him with what had happened.

He looked at his watch. As far as he could work out it was just about three in the afternoon in Willemstad. Still half an hour before Curaçao's banks closed for the day.

He accessed the phone's call log and quickly found the number of the hotel.

"I'm afraid Mr. and Mrs. Snap checked out a couple of hours ago," the front desk informed him. "They needed to catch a flight back to Denmark."

"A flight?"

"Yes, the KLM flight via Amsterdam leaves at three thirty."

He thanked the man, rubbed his face for a moment, and then phoned the bank in Willemstad to inquire about his shares.

"*Goedemiddag*, Mr. Eriksen. Yes, everything proceeded according to plan. We received your power of attorney after which the contents of your safe-deposit box were transferred to Mr. Snap."

So everything was in order, said the bank manager.

Only that wasn't how Eriksen saw it.

26

Boy had been hiding in the dug-out tree trunk for more than sixty hours before Mammy's boys found him.

They gave him a choice. It was simple. Either they chopped off his arms and split him open, or else he joined them and became one of Mammy's boys.

Some choice. The corpses of his entire family lay bloated in the underbrush. Everything he knew had been razed to the ground.

Within four weeks Boy was a child soldier like the others. Primitive and callous, afraid of nothing apart from being stabbed in the back by one of their own.

Their own! Boys like the ones who had murdered his beloved family, cut the throat of his dog, and deprived him of all his humanity.

And while Hutus and Tutsis, Mobuto, Kabila, and sundry bloodsuckers from half the continent did their utmost to wipe out national boundaries and one another, Boy learned to sleep with a Kalashnikov in his arms and dream about all the blood he had unhesitatingly drained from his so-called enemies.

Had it not been for Mammy and her personal project, the day would undoubtedly have come when the knife would have been used against him as well.

She selected her elite with great care, the boys who formed a ring around her and protected her from the outside world. No one could turn a situation to their own advantage like Mammy, and once she had the advantage, so did her bodyguards. It was how she kept them on her side.

When what was supposed to resemble peace finally came to Congo in

1999, Mammy had more than thirty full-fledged killers in her service, and with that kind of raw material, peace was not exactly what she wished for most. What on earth could she use these wanton boys for if killing were no longer part of the agenda?

But Mammy was not easily discouraged. In the wake of Africa's conflicts, interesting people always appeared who believed peace had not given them what they'd been expecting. People who'd once enjoyed considerable incomes they had now lost. It was in relations with people like these that she saw a future for herself and her boys.

So Mammy was the one to approach when someone had to be killed, and that was how Boy came to meet Brage-Schmidt.

No one had told Boy why Brage-Schmidt wanted to be rid of five French businessmen from Bois de Boqueteau, but he didn't need to know. Without asking questions he tracked the Frenchmen to the border of Namibia, where he cut off their heads one by one as they slept.

Brage-Schmidt was satisfied and paid Mammy a bonus of a hundred thousand dollars, then asked if he could take on Boy as his permanent problem solver for a further hundred thousand. Mammy hesitated, for Boy was her favorite. But when the man promised to treat him as his own son, make sure he received dental treatment to replace the teeth he'd had knocked out in combat, and furthermore provide him with an education and make sure he learned new languages, plus all kinds of other benefits, she eventually acceded after yet another round of negotiations.

For that, Boy was forever grateful to the both of them, and since then he had not taken a single life.

At least, not personally.

Boy had torn Zola apart on the phone after the failed break-in at Eriksen's home. Now he sat for a moment, considering the entire situation.

Mammy and two of her best boys were on their way. She would be phoning within minutes, provided their flight had landed on time in Copenhagen. Mammy always kept her appointments.

He'd only just looked at his watch when his mobile rang.

"Brief me, honey," she said, her voice husky and deep.

"How much time can you and your boys spend here, have you decided?" he asked.

"Around fifty-eight hours. We need to be in Brussels by Saturday morning at the latest for another job."

"OK. I know how good you and the boys are, so that ought to be time enough. I should warn you, though, that the kid we're looking for is a cunning one. Finding him won't be easy."

"I've got the description and his photo here. What makes him so special?"

"If you didn't know better, you'd think he'd been brought up in the bush. I hid in a hollow log as a last resort, but this one thinks ahead, otherwise his family would have tracked him down long ago. He is the rat in the sewer, Mammy. The bird on the roof."

She laughed. "But *you* we found, Boy. Both his clan and a lot of Eastern Europeans are out searching for him, you say?"

"Yes, and they've spotted him on a couple of occasions."

"OK. In half an hour we'll be at the Square Hotel. Come in an hour and show us what you've got."

The room was on the small side, but the view was good. Mammy was reclining on a patterned sofa, filling up most of its space. Her reserves were greater than ever before, she liked to say of herself with a certain kind of pride.

Boy nodded to the two jet-black Africans in basketball jerseys who were lounging on the bed watching the NBC news. He took them to be in their twenties, and yet their faces seemed in glimpses to be ancient and lined, their eyes filled with skepticism as to all the things normal people coveted. Boy knew what it was like. For them, happiness was a good, long night's sleep and fucking their brains out. And, of course, the hunt itself.

"We went for a little walk outside this evening," Mammy said. "You were right in what you wrote about the Danes. They don't even see us. As long as we don't walk together they won't condescend to look at us. This is good, Boy."

She patted him on the thigh. Long time no see.

"You're looking good, Boy. Almost thirty years of age now. How many of your old comrades have got that far?" She leaned back and looked across at her two bloodhounds on the bed. "Hey, you two. Take a look at this one. You can be like him too if you make Mammy happy, OK?"

"OK, Mammy," they replied in unison. And then slipped back into limbo again.

Boy smiled, handing her maps of the areas in Copenhagen where Marco had been seen, where they reckoned he'd previously been hiding out, and where they thought he could be now.

Mammy nodded. Her time-worn, shrewd eyes glided over the maps' main thoroughfares, the side streets, the S-train stations, and all the small, open green areas. It was astonishing once more to see how quickly she could absorb unfamiliar topography.

When they had finished she assured him the boy was already as good as dead, and that it had always been a pleasure working for him and Brage-Schmidt.

Boy nodded. Thanks that came seldom were the best.

"Catch the boy and everyone's happy," he said, turning to the young men on the bed. "He's a snake, but you can spear him, I know you can."

They sat up on their elbows. Like all soldiers, they took their briefing seriously. Sometimes it was their only defense against ambush and sudden death. Here in Copenhagen it was imprisonment and unfamiliar reaction patterns they were up against.

So they listened intently.

"Stay close to Zola's men and those working with him."

He tossed two sheets of paper with photos of Zola's people on the bed. The snakelike eyes of Mammy's boys began processing them immediately. There was no doubt these boys had been carefully selected.

"Once Zola or some of the others have encircled the boy, be ready to take over. Don't take it for granted that they will inform you, so stay close and keep your eyes open."

They nodded.

A net too widely meshed never caught a bird.

27

An unfamiliar feeling of sun wakened Carl to the sweet smell of perfume and sex.

His nostrils flared as he inhaled recollections of wantonness and no-nonsense shagging. Good Lord, he thought, eyes tight shut as he stuck his hand under the duvet and sensed how incredibly naked he felt with his half-erect member and his rump pressed close against soft female skin.

Opening his eyes tentatively to the world, he found himself staring up at a ceiling with two-tone stucco and a lamp that glowed faintly through a silk scarf.

My God, he mused, immediately aware of the sticky situation he'd got himself into.

"Are you awake, Carl?" Lisbeth purred, beneath the covers.

Did he dare say yes?

She turned over, snuggling her downy face up close as featherlight fingers drew circles around his belly button and twirled the hairs of his chest.

"It's not going to be a one-night stand, is it, Carl?" she whispered, moving the inside of her thigh against his nether regions.

Oh, wow, was all he could think, trying not to let out a sigh.

The fact of the matter was that he was confused as hell. She'd been absolutely amazing to make love to. Utterly uninhibited despite being out of training, as she'd called it. He thought himself lucky she hadn't been completely match-fit, otherwise he'd have been down for the count.

"I thought we were great last night. How about you?" she asked, rubbing her nose against his. It felt nice. Not the kind of tenderness he was used to.

"You were gorgeous, Lisbeth, and still are," he said, and meant it.

He avoided her searching gaze and closed his eyes again, racked by feelings of guilt. What the hell was he playing at?

"Do you know what time it is?" he asked, as though he was ready to sleep a couple of hours more.

"It's eight, but you don't really need to go to work this early, do you?"

She giggled as her hand crept downward. Her breathing grew heavy almost immediately.

"Did you say *eight*?" he cried, extracting himself from her arms. "I've got a meeting in twenty minutes at headquarters. Shit! Today of all days! I'm really sorry, Lisbeth, but I've got to go."

He jumped out of bed without looking at her, pulled on his trousers, and wriggled his bare feet into his shoes.

"Forgive me, forgive me," he said, pecking her quickly on the cheek and then dashing off before she had a chance to ask the obligatory question of when they'd see each other again.

Who could answer that one?

"What a predicament," he muttered as he tried to work out where he'd left the car the evening before. As far as he remembered, they'd stood and had a grope by a blossoming cherry tree that was fairly close to the scene of a murder he'd investigated some years back in the vicinity of the Syvstjernehusene housing development. It was there they had been making out like a pair of teenagers, hands all over each other. Arousing as hell, but which cherry tree, and where, for Chrissake?

"Let's park at a distance from my house," she'd said. "The neighbors are still friends with my ex."

Now, feeling like a fool as he trawled the Højlundshusene neighborhood, the thought of Mona kept coming back to him, seriously weighing on his conscience. Why did he still have these feelings for her, anyway, after she'd kicked him to the curb like that? And how come he felt so sullied, so ridden by guilt? Lisbeth wasn't just some casual one-nighter. She was so sweet and bright and warm.

Maybe that was precisely why.

He crossed another couple of streets, noting as he went that blossoming cherry trees were damn popular in these parts. What would Mona say if she saw him now, wandering about in search of his car like a confused adolescent? How would she feel if she sniffed his body?

And how would *he* feel if *she* had done the same thing?

He flinched at the thought. Of course, goddammit. It was an act of preemptive rationalization on his part.

For who was to say she hadn't?

Carl looked up and glanced around him as he realized he was basically back where he started. There they were, the green bedroom curtains behind which only a few hours ago he had cast to the wind all thought of what Mona might think about him and what he was doing with another woman.

And there was his car. Less than fifty meters from Lisbeth's house. How the hell did it take them so long to walk such a short distance?

He fumbled in his pockets for the keys and felt a lump that wasn't supposed to be there.

His wallet.

Carl frowned. Had he really been in such a state yesterday that he hadn't checked all his pockets properly when he'd discovered it was gone?

But he had, he knew he had. So how could it possibly be there now? Had Lisbeth played a trick on him? Did she want him to feel indebted? Did she somehow think it would aid the nocturnal cause? That it would help her believe she had him hooked?

He shook his head. If that was it, then she must be crazy.

He opened the wallet, convinced he was going to find a note containing something like: *Sorry, darling, your turn to pay next time.*

Or just: *I'm wild about you. Call me, Here's my number.*

He smiled as he found an unfamiliar piece of paper folded among his receipts. *Good coppering, mate*, he congratulated himself. *Can't fool me, ha-ha.*

But the note wasn't what he was expecting. Nowhere near.

It was a printout of a satellite photo of Kregme, marked with a cross in the middle.

HERE IS STARK'S BODY, someone had scrawled in irregular block letters.
ZOLA KILLED HIM.

And at the bottom was an address. Likewise in Kregme.

More than an hour passed before Carl had picked up Assad and they finally got to the patch of woods between the lake and the road on the one side and hedgerows and fields on the other.

"Sure doesn't smell good here, Carl," Assad mumbled, looking askance at a muck spreader trundling its way over the landscape. But Carl wasn't bothered. He was from north Jutland, where the delectable fragrance of shit was the smell of money. Any farmer with great ambitions needed shit, tons of the stuff.

"It's pretty open here," he said, scanning the terrain ahead where the road dipped out of sight.

He glanced at the map he'd found in his wallet. "How far do we have to go into these woods, do you reckon?"

Assad rasped his hand across the stubble of his chin. "Seventy-five meters, max. A hundred, maybe."

How could seventy-five meters, max, be a hundred?

"OK, let's pull in at that gap in the trees over there." Carl nodded toward farther up the road to the right, locating the same point on the satellite photo. "Seems like a logical place to go into the woods if you're dragging a body away from the road. A car could park here with the trunk facing the top of the hill and nobody would be able to see what you were doing unless they were doing thirty kilometers an hour. And *no one* drives that slowly here, believe me. This is hillbilly country."

"Hill Billy? Who's he? Does he own the land here?"

"Yeah, precisely," Carl replied, shaking his head. Hill Billy? Where did the guy think they were, anyway?

They stepped cautiously through the vegetation, noting snapped branches as well as stones trampled into the earth. There were a surprising number of the latter, as though someone had been here only recently.

"It looks like a whole herd was here," said Assad, indicating a pile of leaves pressed flat.

Carl nodded and looked up at the ominous black clouds that were gathering overhead. Was it really going to rain now? Brilliant timing, after so many days of scorching sunshine.

"I don't think we're far enough in yet, Carl. You can still see the traffic through the trees, so they would risk being seen from the road."

Carl nodded and peered over the treetops. Maybe they ought to call the dog unit in. This wasn't going to be easy without them.

He swore under his breath, vowing to put his rubber boots on next time, no matter how stupid they made him look. Right now his own shoes felt like two clods of mud.

"Hey," Assad called out from farther on. "I think I'm there. But there's no body as far as I can see."

Carl frowned as he pushed his way through the underbrush. The earth here was rather looser and drier than it was elsewhere. Here and there the branches of bushes and sapling trees were snapped and broken. Before Assad's battered old shoes lay a pile of earth heaped on a layer of withered leaves, so someone must have been digging here since the previous autumn.

Carl took the Google printout from his pocket and tried to see if there was anything in the immediate vicinity that he might be able to localize on the map: a tall tree, a clearing, whatever.

"Are we sure this is the right place?"

Assad nodded. "Unless a fox has been playing around with a wig of real human hair, I would say this seems to prove it."

He pointed down in to the hole. Sure enough. Hair. Red hair.

"You keep a low profile now, Assad. If there's anything you want to say, give me a sign first, OK?"

They went up the garden path to the house that, if the note in Carl's wallet was anything to go by, was where the person called Zola lived.

Assad nodded. "I will jump up and down and dance the samba before I say a word, Carl. Cross my hearth and hope to die."

"*Heart*, Assad. But don't bother dying just yet, eh?" Carl rang the doorbell, then scanned the neighborhood while they waited. A run-of-the-mill neighborhood of single-family dwellings in an average town, up where northern Zealand stopped being for folks with three cars in the garage.

In front of the house was a yellow van with nothing to distinguish it but its number plates. Carl assumed it meant someone was in, though the place seemed rather dead.

"The DNA test will likely tell us if the hair you found up there matches the specimens from Stark's home," Carl said, handing the evidence bag to Assad. "This could turn out to be a major breakthrough, but who the hell is that lad who knows so much about all this?"

"I think we can assume he has been here at some point, don't you think?" Assad replied, his snout halfway through the mail slot.

"Can you see anything?" Carl managed to ask, just before the door was flung open.

The burly guy glared at Carl and the kneeling Assad with eyes full of trouble and distrust.

"What do you want here?" he said, with the kind of measured coolness usually associated with receptionists in multinational concerns or tax authority staff just before closing time.

Carl produced his ID. "We'd like to speak to Zola," he said, expecting a cocky smile and a clear statement to the effect that Zola wasn't in.

"Just a minute, I'll have a look," the man answered, and two minutes later they were standing in a living room that would have reduced an interior designer to tears. An unusually gloomy color scheme made the walls look like they were about to fall in on top of them with all their shaggy tapestries, life-sized portraits and an assortment of voodoo-like trinkets. The room was at once pompous and mysterious, a stark contrast to the small, spartan bedrooms with bunk beds they had passed in the hall.

Zola appeared, accompanied by a huge, gangling wolfhound, and sporting a smile noticeably absent from his portraits on the wall.

"To what do I owe the honor?" he inquired in English, gesturing for them to be seated.

Carl briefly explained their business, assessing the man in front of him as he spoke. Powerful, piercing eyes. Long hair. Well-groomed. Clad in a colorful, hippyish jacket and baggy pants. The man looked like the reincarnation of a guru from a forgotten age.

He didn't react at all to the information that someone had presumably buried a body in a shallow grave close by, and that Zola had been named as a person the police ought to be questioning about it. But as soon as Carl mentioned the boy, and how he'd been close enough to him to lift his wallet, Zola raised his eyebrows and leaned forward.

"That explains a lot," he said. "Is he in your custody?"

"No, he isn't. And what does it explain?"

"Why do you come to me with these questions? Marco is an evil little psychopath. No man in the world should wish to cross his path."

"His name is Marco, you say?"

Zola turned slightly and commanded the hefty individual at his side to bend down so he could whisper something in his ear, after which the man left the room.

"Yes, Marco has lived with us most of his life, but he ran away some six months ago. He's not a nice kid."

"What's his full name? What's his age? We need his complete data. Civil registration number, everything," Assad demanded drily.

Carl glanced at his assistant, who sat with his notepad at the ready. It was obvious from the way his jaw muscles were working that he'd taken a dislike to the man in front of them. What had he seen that Carl hadn't?

Zola smiled slightly. "We are not Danish citizens, and none of us has a civil registration number. We live here only for short periods. It's our company that owns the properties."

"Properties?" Carl asked.

"Yes, this house here and the one next door. Marco's surname is Jameson and he's fifteen years old. A strange boy. He turned out to be unmanageable, in spite of our trying to do our best for him."

"What do you people do here in Denmark?" Assad probed.

"Oh, we buy and sell lots of things. Purchase Danish design and sell it abroad. Import rugs and figurines from Africa and Asia. Our family have been tradesmen for generations and everyone in the extended family is involved."

"What do you mean by 'extended family'?" Assad asked with a polemic undertone, his eyebrows arched. Carl only hoped he wasn't going to bite the man.

"We are a family, most of us, but over the years others have joined."

"And where are you people from?" Carl inquired.

Zola turned his head calmly toward Carl. It was as if the man was in a dilemma and didn't know which of them to be most courteous toward.

"All sorts of places," he replied. "I'm from Little Rock, some are from the Midwest. There are a couple of Italians and Frenchmen. A little bit of everything."

"And now you are their god," said Assad, nodding toward the poster-sized photos of the man on the wall.

Zola smiled. "Not at all. I'm merely the chief of our clan."

Another man entered the room together with the big guy who had let them in. Like Zola, his swarthy features looked vaguely Latin American. A handsome man with jet-black hair, dark brown eyes, and cheek-bones that perhaps in another situation would have signaled vibrant masculinity.

"This is my brother," said Zola. "We've got business to discuss afterward."

Carl nodded to the man. He was compact of build, though slightly stooping. His expression was friendly yet somehow shy. His eyes seemed to tremble, if eyes could do that.

"And, chief, what does it mean, not all of you being a family? Is it some kind of commune? A brotherhood? What is it?" Assad asked as he began scribbling words down on his notepad. From where Carl sat it looked like gibberish.

"Yes, my friend. Something like that. A bit of both."

"This Marco," Carl asked. "Has he got any relatives here? Anyone we might speak to?"

Zola shook his head slowly and looked up at the man at his side. "I'm sorry. His mother ran off with another man, and his father is dead."

Now Zola knew for certain what he had feared for so long. Marco had squealed.

Everything they had tried to avoid was now a reality. And in contrast to the impression he normally gave, he felt under pressure.

He hated the way the Arab's round eyes glanced with disdain at the many flower-festooned photos of himself that hung from the walls. Hated the way he regarded the silverware and the gilded candelabra. And besides being an annoying sleazeball, there was something else about him that made Zola uneasy, something the Dane did not possess.

OK, what are my options? he asked himself, as he nodded at the gringo's stupid questions and weary manner.

Shall we get rid of them, or get out ourselves? he wondered, as the policeman inquired about Marco's relatives and whether it would be possible to speak with them.

He'd looked only at his brother while telling the policeman that Marco's father was dead. Yes, my dear elder brother, his eyes said as he stared into his face. You've already lost the boy, so you might as well get used to the idea.

Finally he turned back to the Dane. They'd seen Stark's grave now, and they weren't dumb. They'd know they might be sitting across from a murderer. He nodded to himself. And they damn well did. If they asked any question that compromised him, they might just have to disappear like Stark and the others had. There was earth enough in which to bury both of them if necessary.

"We've got an appeal here for information about the man whose body we suspect was in that grave up on the hill. As you can see, he had thick red hair like we found in the soil. What's your response to that?" the Dane asked.

"Nothing, really. It's terrible, of course. What else can one say?"

"Take a look at the photo. Notice anything in particular?"

Zola shook his head, trying to figure out what the Arab's hands were doing under the table.

"How about this?" said Assad, producing a plastic bag and putting it down in front of him. "It's the same one as on the photo, but perhaps it's more tangible when you see it in real life."

Zola felt a darkness descend upon him. Before him lay the necklace Hector had told him Marco had been wearing. How had they got hold of it? Had the cops been lying when they said Marco wasn't in custody? Was it some kind of trick?

Zola leaned his head back and tried to think rationally. Could this in reality be a way out, a sword of Damocles that Marco had now turned upon himself?

He mustered a facial expression of sudden realization and snapped his fingers. "Yes, I remember now. This is the necklace Marco always used to wear."

The Arab jabbed at the poster. "And this is the same necklace, see?"

Zola nodded. "I know Marco hated us. We were too much of a clique, too self-righteous for his taste. He refused to adapt. He's violent and dangerous. Isn't that right?" he said, catching his brother's eye. "Remember how many times he came at us with a knife or a club?" He turned back to the policemen. "I know it's a dreadful thing to say, but with that temper of his it wouldn't surprise me if he were capable of killing a man and then find a way of using it against us."

He looked at his brother again. "What do you say? Am I right?"

The brother gave an answer, but a bit too hesitant and too late. Could his loyalty be on the wane?

"I guess so," he said. "But if a dead man's been lying up there in the woods, there could be any number of ways that he got there. Anyhow, it's strange the body's not there anymore, if it ever was."

Zola nodded and fixed his eyes on the Dane. "Surely there must be some traces left by whoever put him there. Personally, I believe Marco removed the body in order to cover up his own crime."

Again the Arab interrupted. "Inspector Mørck has seen the boy. He's not very big. I doubt he would be able to do that."

"Well, maybe. I don't know. He's stronger than he looks."

Zola looked again at the poster, a new idea taking shape in his mind.

"I remember now," he said to his brother. "Marco used to keep all kinds of things in his room. Maybe you could fetch that cardboard box he kept them in? There might be something there that could put these two gentlemen on the right track."

His brother frowned, albeit fleetingly.

Come on, you idiot, improvise! Zola's eyes signaled. As far as he was concerned, he could come back with anything or nothing at all. That wasn't the point. This was about winning time and leaving these cops thinking he was a man who would do his utmost to have the truth revealed.

Five minutes or more passed before the brother returned and tossed a sock onto the table in front of them.

"This might be something. I found it in his cupboard."

Zola nodded. Nice thinking. After the latest round of beatings, several of the boys had bled. The sock was most probably Samuel's. He could bleed like a pig at the slightest prod, but what did it matter?

Who could tell from a sock who had worn it last?

"What do you reckon, Assad? I saw you were really eyeing all the silverware in there."

"Yes, and the camphorwood table, the Persian rugs, the crystal chandelier, the Japanese bureau, and his Rolex. Not to mention that ugly gold chain around his neck."

"We'll check him out, don't worry. I'm with you completely on that one, Assad."

"And this story about the sock." He patted the pocket in which he'd put it. "Do you believe it? Do you think it might be a souvenir from Stark's murder?"

Carl looked out across the countryside as they drove. The trees had just burst into leaf. What was he going to do about Lisbeth? Should he jump in with both feet and carry on where they'd left off last night? He certainly felt like it now, but ten minutes ago she hadn't crossed his mind since morning. He frowned and looked up at the clouds that still hung over the landscape. If it was going to rain, why couldn't it just get on with it?

"Do you believe it?" Assad repeated.

"Hmm," he said in reply, suddenly feeling nauseous, as if he might throw up any minute. "I don't know. The DNA test will settle it. For the time being we need to find this Marco Jameson."

He swallowed a couple of times, leaning toward the steering wheel to ease the unpleasantness, but the colic in his stomach moved upward toward his breastbone like a tennis ball forcing its way through his esophagus.

What's happening? he wondered, trying to keep his eye on the road ahead.

"What's the matter, Carl?" Assad asked with concern. "Are you sick?"

Carl shook his head and focused on his driving. Was this another one of his anxiety attacks? Or something worse?

They passed the supermarket in Ølsted as Carl tried to pump oxygen into his system, Assad repeatedly insisting that he take over the wheel.

When eventually he pulled to the side and stretched his legs out of the car door, the air again smelled of cowshit, but Carl was conscious of one thing only.

Mona.

In half an hour they would be back at police HQ, and it was Wednesday.

The day Mona always worked in special detention.

28

It was 9:25 and an unusually chilly morning for the time of year as René E. Eriksen stood waiting at the arrivals gate in Kastrup Airport's Terminal 3.

His sole aim was to get Teis Snap to hand over his shares from Curaçao, and he was confident he would succeed. An ugly scene in public was the last thing Snap wanted, and Eriksen was prepared to kick up a fuss.

Hordes of scorched Danes filed past him in sandals and espadrilles, welcomed home by fluttering Danish flags and warm embraces of reunion. But where the hell was the dickhead? Had he gotten off the plane in Amsterdam? Did he find the whole situation so trivial that canal trips and *poffertjes* were more important than returning home and getting matters under control?

Or had he found a buyer for the shares that didn't belong to him?

Eriksen was in despair. If only he could be sure the UPS delivery was on the level. And if it wasn't, and Snap failed to show, what about his careful timing for the next few days?

He took a deep breath and spared himself the sight of more ridiculous repatriated vacationers as he fidgeted with the car keys in his terylene trousers.

What was the point of waiting if the bastard wasn't going to turn up?

Then, just as he was about to go, Snap and his wife came strolling through the gates with a pair of suitcases trundling in their wake.

His wife saw him first, her face lighting up in a smile as she pointed. But Snap wasn't smiling when he realized who she was pointing at.

"What are you doing here?" was the first thing he said.

"Gee, have you been waiting for us, René?" his wife asked. "Sorry we were such a long time, but Teis's suitcase wasn't on the conveyor." She gave her husband a nudge. "You were white as a sheet for half an hour, toots, ha-ha."

They moved aside, away from the throng, and René got straight to the point.

"The share certificates weren't in the package you sent. Where are they?"

Snap seemed surprised, shocked almost, which of course he would have been if the certificates really had been in the package as agreed. But this was a different kind of surprise altogether, caused more by the fact that René was already able to confront him with the matter. Or was it because he was able to be there in the first place? Was that it?

"I don't know what you're talking about, René." Snap took René by the arm and drew him away from his wife. "Why are you saying this? You can't possibly have received the package yet. Are you expecting other deliveries?"

There was something about the way he said it that sounded wrong. He was clutching his briefcase too tightly. Everything about him seemed out of sync.

"Don't take me for a fool, Teis. Don't you think I know who attacked me yesterday?" He turned his head, indicating the bandage and the bump on the back of his head. "C'mon, show me what you've got in that briefcase."

Snap began fumbling with the handle, then shook his head. "OK, Lisa, we're leaving. I think René must be suffering from some sort of brain concussion."

But René grabbed his well upholstered arm. "You're going nowhere until you've shown me what's inside that briefcase, you bastard."

Snap turned to his wife. "There's no reason you should witness this, Lisa. Take the luggage and grab a taxi home. I've got some appointments in town today anyway. I'll be back this evening, darling."

René let them kiss each other good-bye and attempted to send Snap's wife a reassuring smile, as the situation dictated. But as soon as she was out of sight, trailing the two Samsonites, he was ready.

"You're a fool, René," said Snap, seizing the initiative. "That package hasn't arrived yet, it's written all over your face. And what's all this talk about being attacked? Tell me what happened. Who did it, and where'd it happen?"

OK, so that was his strategy. A halo of innocence shining over the imbecile's Brylcreemed hair.

"Open your briefcase, Teis," he commanded, trying to grab it out of Snap's hand. "I want to see what you're hiding in it."

Snap held it tight. "Certainly not. That bump on the head must have knocked the sense out of you. Go home to your wife, René. Take the day off. You need it."

"Open it, or I'll make a scene."

Teis Snap's eyes narrowed as a smirk appeared on his lips. "You? Make a scene? Excuse my mirth, you silly little man. What on earth is there to make a scene about? You're losing your powers of judgment, René, can't you see?"

"Open it, or I'll kick your fat ass for you."

Snap shook his head in exasperation and handed him the briefcase.

Right there René knew intuitively that he had lost the first round. Nonetheless, he opened the case and rummaged through its contents: crossword puzzles, magazines, and a copy of the *Financial Times*.

How blessedly simple. So that was why for once he'd hung around in baggage claim until his suitcase finally turned up. The suitcase his wife was now on her way to Karrebæksminde with, and which he would have been loath to have left in the care of the baggage handling company.

Why hadn't René seen it coming?

"There are two possibilities here, Teis. Either you're telling the truth and the shares are on their way to me. Or else you're not, and those suitcases your little wife took with her have some very interesting contents. If the latter happens to be the case, I'd advise you to deliver the certificates to me immediately, otherwise I shall be going to the police with everything I know."

Snap didn't exactly look unnerved by the threat, but he was. René knew the guy too well.

He turned on his heel, glancing at his watch as he strode away. Ten past ten.

The day was still young.

29

"**Are you feeling better** now, Carl?" asked Assad, leaning in the doorway.

"A bit," he replied weakly.

"Would you like me to make you a cup of tea?"

Carl recoiled as a matter of reflex. "Er, no thanks." He shook his head as vigorously as he could. "I don't think I'll ever be *that* well again, but maybe Rose could do with one."

Rose thrust out both hands with a look of disgust that clearly signaled she'd rather swallow a bottle of cod-liver oil.

"Listen here, you two," she said, raising her eyebrows. The class was back in session. "I've heard back about those Maersk containers in Kaliningrad, the ones we identified on Anweiler's postcard. It's legit. The postmark matches up with the date the containers were unloaded onto the quayside. And the technicians say the photo hasn't been manipulated, so the man's as innocent as I reckoned he was all along. Case closed."

Something morphed in Assad's physiognomy. Sure, his face was still lopsided, but all of a sudden it looked different, like he was holding his breath as he sucked his lower lip into the corner of his mouth. Was he standing there enjoying his own private joke?

"Hey, Assad, what are you chortling about? Did you dig up any goodies on Zola and his lot in Kregme?"

"I'm afraid not, Carl. He owns an import/export company registered in Luxembourg, where they pay their taxes. All aboveboard, as far as I can see. Taxable income declared at two point one million Danish kroner for 2010."

"OK, How many's he got on his payroll? Not that many, surely?"

Assad gave a shrug. "They're criminals, if you ask me. I am not finished with them yet."

"What're you laughing about, then?" Rose wanted to know.

"Oh, that was just—how do you say?—the joke of the day. You would like it in particular, Rose. I just heard that Sverre Anweiler has been arrested in Flensburg with fifty kilos of hash in his tour bus, so now he's behind bars again. Fifty kilos of giggle weed, isn't that funny? He'll go down for ten years at least. Maybe he should have stayed in Kaliningrad, ha-ha-ha."

Carl frowned and looked at Rose. It maybe wasn't exactly the punch line she would have preferred.

"All right, but then I can't be arsed to add an appendix to your report," she said with a sigh. "Anyway, I've put a bulletin out on Marco Jameson," she went on, changing the subject in a huff. "Could have done with a more up-to-date photo than the one they gave you in Kregme, Carl. He's only seven years old in it, but then again I don't suppose anyone's ever bothered to take his picture since, not with his kind of background."

She tossed the photo down in front of him. She was right. It was probably more of a hindrance than a help.

"OK, Rose, you're right. Maybe you should take advantage of your new door-to-door experience and do some rounds where he's been spotted. I suggest you start off with the area around the library on Dag Hammarskjölds Allé. Perhaps the shopping streets, too. Classensgade, Nordre Frihavnsgade, Trianglen, and what have you. Ask the shop owners if they've seen him. We've got a name and a photo now, even if the shot isn't good. Just take your time, it's often the way to get results."

For a moment she remained seated, as if collecting herself to unleash a hail of protest. But then her face relaxed and became almost beatific.

"OK. You're lucky I love the rain, Carl. Oh, by the way," she added, "I have a bit of info for you. A funny little thing happened while you were out. I've been told to send you up to Lars Bjørn, Carl. Gordon's complained about you."

"Two ugly flies in one swat," he murmured as he watched Ms. Sørensen leave Bjørn's office and close the door behind her. The mummy had emerged from the crypt. Let the horror movie commence. He nodded to her as she approached, summoning his most ingratiating smile and not unexpectedly receiving only the most disdainful of looks in return.

So much for that famous personal development course of hers.

"Bit of a racket they're kicking up in there, isn't it?" he said, jerking a thumb toward Bjørn's door without expecting a reply from the old bag's colorless lips.

She tilted one eyebrow and lowered the other. Classic attitude.

"Yes, the changing of the guard here certainly doesn't make me look less forward to retirement day," she answered.

It was undeniably an astonishing statement. Had he and the she-wolf of Department A really got to the point where there was something they agreed on?

"If that apprentice in there had kept wearing his old school tie, then we could at least have called him well dressed. But we can't even say that about him, can we?"

That apprentice? Was it Lars Bjørn she meant?

She rolled her eyes with an expression of scorn that normally only teenage girls could master. The only difference was, it managed to make her look even more miserable than usual.

"You've heard about Marcus Jacobsen, I take it?" she asked.

He nodded, albeit tentatively. "Assad and I saw him at the Rigshospital the day before yesterday. Is he ill, do you know?"

"No, thank goodness." Then she fell silent, perhaps thinking the better of her rather emotional outburst. "No, it's not that. It's Martha, his wife," she continued after a moment, her voice lowered. "She's undergoing radiotherapy. No doubt he was there to support her."

Was Marcus's wife called Martha? Mar and Mar. It sounded like a pair of tightrope artists, or comedians in a silent movie.

"I'm sorry to hear it. Is it serious?" he asked.

She nodded.

Carl pictured Marcus's wife. Petite and attractive, a bundle of energy. The sort of person you'd have thought could cope with anything.

"Do you know her?" Carl asked.

"No, I don't, but I know Marcus, and I'm missing him like hell at the moment." And with that she strode off, her folders pressed tight against her already flat chest.

Carl's jaw hit his Adam's apple. Ms. Sørensen had just sworn! And Ms. Sørensen had expressed feelings for a living creature that wasn't a cat. These were revelations of biblical dimensions.

And then the door of Bjørn's domain opened and out stepped Gordon's lanky frame, limbs dangling like reeds in a stiff breeze.

"What the hell did you say to him, you gormless idiot?"

Gordon merely smiled. Apparently it was a kind of instinctive reaction of his, applicable in any circumstance.

Carl shoved past him and sat down heavily opposite Bjørn.

"Yes," he began, dictating the pace before Bjørn had a chance to. "I admit shouting at the idiot. Not so strange considering he and Rose were engaged in the horizontal tango on my turf. And yes, I gladly admit that I can't stand the sight of the lanky jerk, on top of which I won't have him running around in my basement anymore."

Annoyingly enough, his bombast seemed not to faze the acting head of Department A in the slightest, in which case he reckoned he might just as well fire off the rest of his gripe. The man facing him was by definition the type who sat around waiting for the next insult anyway.

"And another thing, Lars. I won't have you poking your nose around in Department Q. It's functioning fantastically the way it is, and seeing as the creation of the department, paradoxically enough, was one of your rare inspired moments, maybe you could force yourself into acknowledging that better men than you are now in charge. So all in all, I have to say no thanks to your changes, Mr. Chief Superintendent. And by the way, have a nice day."

He pushed himself into a standing position, drew a finger across Bjørn's desk, nodded approvingly as he noted the missing layer of dust that had characterized the happy days with Marcus, and headed for the door.

The reaction came as he grabbed the door handle. It was calm and painfully precise.

"Gordon's on his way down to Department Q. From now on he'll be my liaison, reporting back to me on a daily basis and keeping me posted on your activities and whatever progress you're expecting to make on the respective cases. He is to be informed about all your expenditures, and last of all I want him to assist you in interviewing this René E. Eriksen character. Do I make myself clear?"

At that moment Carl's torpor returned with a vengeance. His body seemed to be sucking up everything negative out of the room and storing it somewhere hard to reach. Even his legs had received a dose. They felt heavy as lead.

He took a deep breath as he tried to think of a smart comeback, a scathing remark. He racked his brains for something to say that would remain uncontested and for once make an impression. But all he came up with was emptiness and bad karma, so he decided to keep his mouth shut.

He was simply feeling too rotten at the moment.

Christ, did he miss Marcus!

"First of all, Assad, I want you to see if you can find some kind of connection between Zola and William Stark. We know both Zola and William Stark traveled a lot, so maybe there's a link there. Did Stark have business dealings with him at any point? Was anything found in Stark's house that might indicate some kind contact between them? Receipts, for instance? Perhaps Stark had some kind of bond with Kregme. You know what to look for. I'll get a unit out to do a thorough investigation of the grave site, OK? And while you're at it, follow up on those accusations Zola made about Marco being the culprit. Find out where the lad went to school and if they ever had problems with him there. And whether he's ever been involved in violent episodes or other kinds of criminal activity in or around Kregme."

"May I then take the car, Carl? Kregme is quite a long way."

"The car? I wasn't thinking of anyone driving up there again, Assad. A few phone calls to the local cops and schools ought to do it."

Assad nodded. "You fell for it, Carl. You are just like the camel who discovered it was to be married off to a dromedary . . ."

He slapped his thigh and cracked up laughing.

Carl was at a loss.

He was miles away as he went up the stairs of the rotunda.

The way things stood, the DNA analysis of the hair and the forensics report from the shallow grave would at most indicate whether it was Stark's body that had been lying there. More tangible evidence—like incriminating notes, laundry labels with dates on them, cigarette ends covered in DNA material, footprints, and things like that—were mostly the stuff of dodgy crime novels. And if providence had perchance left such evidence lying around at the scene, time and the elements would have made a mess of it by now. So what good was a crime scene investigation?

Besides, all his instincts told him that Stark's body had indeed been in that hole. And if it had, then where did they go from here?

They had to find the boy. That was the first priority. A bulletin had been issued, admittedly with an inadequate description and a poor photo, but still. A boy wandering the streets on his own at all hours wasn't exactly a common sight. Flocks of immigrant kids were another matter, but Carl felt sure that a lad who sat about reading in libraries, a lad who turned up at a police station of his own accord to report a crime on behalf of a friend he didn't have, and who'd done a bunk from a house where a man like Zola made the rules, was a lad who had learned to trust only himself.

I wouldn't have minded discussing that profile with Mona, he thought sadly, imagining he heard her dusky voice calling out to him from somewhere on the third floor.

He paused with a frown. All of a sudden it felt like his heart had missed a couple of beats. It wasn't exactly painful, but it made him dizzy and caused him to clutch at the wall to steady himself.

For Christ's sake, don't let anyone see me like this, he prayed. Why did it have to be here, the busiest place in the building? he wondered, sliding down the wall until his backside hit the stairs.

Keep calm, concentrate on your breathing, he told himself as thoughts of Mona swirled about in his mind like a nightmare where nothing would stop and nothing would start either.

What had happened with her of late anyway? From one day to the next she'd moved her practice into shared premises, which meant he had to make do with a secretary. Was being with clients more important than his needing to talk to her for a brief moment? And what had the secretary meant when she suggested Mona's client wasn't really a client? If he wasn't a client, what the hell was he? Was she cheating on him during working hours? Was it just like with Gordon and Rose, where her desk was her new altar of passion? Did it turn her on more than when he . . . ?

Carl drew his hand across his sweaty brow and detected a growing odor of death and decay. It was all coming to a head. Hardy, paralyzed in his bed in the front room. Hardy, crying. Gunshots echoing through a shack out in Amager.

"Dammit," he said out loud, trying to pull himself upright.

He had been trembling all over just before the meeting with Mona where he'd intended to propose to her. But why hadn't he trembled all over *afterward*? Was there something wrong with him, or had he just come to some kind of realization in the meantime?

His chest was really hurting now. He closed his eyes and tried to concentrate. Was the pain moving to his upper left arm? No, thank God, so he probably wasn't having a heart attack.

"Pull yourself together, you idiot," he admonished himself. "You don't have heart attacks, dammit." But the feeling of uncertainty wouldn't go away.

Was Mona right? Had they just been sex partners? In practice perhaps, statistically even, too, but that's not how it felt to him. If that was how it was for her, why didn't she feel like having sex at least, instead of nothing? What made her say they perhaps hadn't really chosen each other at all, when it wasn't true? Hadn't he waited for her all those months when she'd been away in Africa with Médecins Sans Frontières?

Why the hell hadn't he taken that ring out of his pocket when he'd had the chance?

He breathed in deeply and managed to get halfway to his feet, dizzy, his hands resting on his knees. Now the coat of mail encasing his chest seemed to be easing. The pain felt almost pleasant, like a swollen thumb you couldn't stop fidgeting with. Gentle pain that was simply telling him he was alive and should now be able to stand up and carry on.

And then all thoughts of physiology came to a halt.

Suddenly he saw everything as it really was.

These feelings he was having emanated from his body, not his mind, where they belonged. That was the issue.

It was like he'd become insensitive, callous. Hardy's struggle had turned into just another routine at home. Marcus Jacobsen's sudden departure hadn't caused any real reaction in him. Why hadn't he been thrown into a rage? Or despair? Why hadn't he flipped out when Mona destroyed everything they had together in the blink of an eye? Destroyed the moment of a lifetime when he was going to propose to her and offer her all the things he thought everyone strove to attain. And why was he unable to put his foot down about Rose shagging in her office? What had happened to his focus and determination when he was conducting his interrogations? Had he stopped giving a shit about everything, or was there something inside him he couldn't control?

Or had he simply always been like that?

There was the rub. He didn't know who he was.

God, he had heard so many people blabber on about this classic existential issue over the years. Herein lay the psychoanalysts' little gold mine, the office despots' best ammunition, the self-development courses' cornerstone: self-doubt.

Carl stretched his muscles and clutched at the small of his back, trying to muster the energy to move his body normally.

He looked upward at the seemingly endless winding stairway and decided to leave Laursen in peace. Why burden himself with another flight? William Stark *had* been in that shallow grave. All they needed to do was send that hair sample to forensics and let them do the rest. He would put Rose on to it straightaway, because all he was fit for right now was shuffling back downstairs and throwing his legs up on his desk. One anxiety attack a day he could manage OK. Two required coffee and a smoke.

He descended the three steps back down to the second-floor landing and almost crashed into Mona.

Unfortunately his mouth fell open and he stood there gawping like a teenager. Had he really heard her voice just before, as he was on his way up? In that case she might well have seen him sliding pathetically up and down against the staircase wall.

Dammit.

"Hey, Mona," he said, as indifferently as his hanging jaw would allow. "On your way over to detention?"

"Hello, Carl. You're looking a bit pasty, are you all right?"

He nodded. "In a bit of a rush, that's all. Not much sunlight down there in the basement, you know, ha-ha. Just stocked up on some self-tanner, though."

He was prattling away like an effing idiot.

"No, I've just come from there," she eventually said, in reply to his question. "I had to get the department head to back me up with a couple of prison guards before I could talk to the hoodlum. An incorrigible psychopath if ever there was one. I wasn't going to have him groping me like last time."

Carl nodded. As gorgeous as she was looking, it was not unthinkable he'd try it on with her himself.

Then she frowned. A lattice of tiny lines appeared on her face that he hadn't noticed before. She turned her head toward the light and all of a sudden he saw how loose the skin had become around her throat and how indefinable her features seemed for just a brief second. Not that she looked old, just suddenly aged somehow.

"Are you OK, Mona?" he asked tentatively.

She gave him an odd, fleeting smile and before he knew it she stroked his cheek, apologized for being so busy, and strode off, the clack of her high heels fading in the labyrinth of police HQ.

Carl remained standing, oblivious to colleagues sidestepping him with acerbic comments and ill-concealed glee.

Ignored questions burned inside him, and now they were bubbling to the surface like poison gas.

It was obvious she preferred to avoid him. It was as if she stood more firmly on her own two feet with him at a distance. Was it because his presence made her feel uncomfortable, or was it because she was already uncomfortable with herself and didn't want to be reminded of it in his company?

Was the problem that she suddenly felt she was getting older and he was holding her back at a stage in her life when she needed to fulfil herself before it was too late? Was that it? Could it be because she just didn't find him attractive enough? Or was it more concrete, the fact that his divorce from Vigga was now a reality? Had he come too close all of a sudden? Had she sussed he was going to propose to her and wanted to pre-empt him?

He shook his head. Thinking about it was a risky business.

The future prospects for him and Mona were definitely not bright.

Then his mobile rang.

"The two of you have a meeting with René E. Eriksen in his office in an hour and a half," said Rose.

"OK. But I don't think Assad's got time at the moment, and I'm—"

"No, you've got it wrong. I mean you and Gordon. Haven't you spoken to Lars Bjørn?"

Oh, Christ. Would this day's woes never end?

"And another thing. Your ex-wife asked me to remind you about your agreement to visit her mother once a week and tell you you're five weeks behind. If you don't get up there this afternoon you'll owe her five grand and she'll be coming by to collect it tonight. She's already phoned her mum and told her you were on your way. If you get your skates on, I'm sure you can get over to Bagsværd and back to the ministry in time for the interview. In the meantime I'll make sure Gordon's there when you arrive."

Carl swallowed twice.

"Why are you standing there like a zombie, Carl? You're as white as a sheet," came a voice from farther up the stairs. It was Laursen in his white kitchen garb.

But there was no time to explain when his ex-mother-in-law, Karla Margrethe Alsing, was already counting the seconds at the nursing home.

"Thank goodness you're here," said the care assistant, as he led Carl through the dementia ward. "We've had to move her out of her old room and into another because she kept smoking indoors and set fire to her duvet. Everything in that room is black with soot, and I mean everything. You should just see the wallpaper."

He opened the door of her old room. There certainly wasn't much worth salvaging.

"She was flirting with the firemen, getting in the way. Wearing nothing but her panties, I should add."

Carl gave a sigh. He had exactly twenty-five minutes before he had to be getting back. Much too much time.

"I hope you've put some more clothes on her in the meantime," he said, attempting a smile.

The caregiver nodded. Maybe that was why he looked so knackered and withdrew so hastily as soon as the guest was delivered.

"You're not to smoke indoors, Karla," the man admonished feebly. "You know you're not, we've told you before. Otherwise the whole place might go up again. You're only allowed to smoke in the garden, so please put it out now or else we'll have to take all your cigarettes away from you," was his parting shot. Probably for the twentieth time that day.

"Hello, love," she said, as though Carl had only been away five minutes. The way she sat there in her once-so-expensive, now-so-threadbare kimono, she was the queen of the Copenhagen nightlife. Elbow on the armrest, cigarette held casually between extended fingers. Nonchalant, in the way elderly women with an overinflated sense of social importance were fond of performing their smoking ritual. Rather than the cigarette being raised to the mouth, it was the mouth that was brought to the cigarette. She took a long, lazy drag through blood-red lips before slowly turning back in his direction, head shrouded in blue-gray clouds of nicotine-filled smoke.

"Only a short visit today I'm afraid, Karla. I have to head back to town in twenty-five minutes. How are you doing, anyway?" he asked, expecting a tidal wave of complaints about her new surroundings and all the furniture she herself had never considered providing.

"Oh, all right, I suppose," she replied, through heavy eyelids. "The slot's just a bit dry, that's all."

Carl looked at his watch. Fourteen hundred very long seconds to go.

30

Marco was doing pretty well in the circumstances. He had spent most of the day sitting in his little hideout amid all the construction work, wearing a yellow hard hat he'd managed to liberate, just waiting.

He had finally passed on what he knew. Carl Mørck had got his wallet back and he would already have found Marco's note, provided all had gone according to plan. He would know that it was Zola who had killed William Stark and he would know where the body had been buried.

If it hadn't been for all the construction workers and the risk of being discovered, and if the entire city's criminal lowlife hadn't been hunting him, he would have kept sitting there, enjoying the view.

Behind him the air was filled with shrieks from the children in Tivoli Gardens. Despite the heavy clouds, people were happy and full of exuberance. He saw legs sticking out from the Star Flyer eighty meters aboveground and children in free fall from the Golden Tower. Kids like himself having a fantastic time, testing their limits and courage. It was something Marco didn't need to do.

He had enough challenges as it was.

The clan was one thing. He knew them. But what about those he didn't? The ones who might suddenly catch sight of him from a window and with a quick call could summon assistance to bring him in?

He knew now that if they caught him, they would kill him. Having so many people on the streets would be costing Zola a bundle. And the only reason he would accept that kind of expenditure was because he needed to make sure by any means necessary that Marco would no longer pose a threat. Now it was serious, and if the police had been to

Kregme it was too late to call a ceasefire. He had thrown the dice. All he could do was hope and pray the police had picked them up.

For the umpteenth time that day, concrete elements and steel girders were hoisted in through the side of the site facing Rådhuspladsen. The two steel structures opening out on to H. C. Andersen's Blvd and Tivoli were taking shape, and the next level was already being built on top of the naked stories that comprised the previous House of Industry. So Marco kept to the rear corner toward Vesterbrogade since it was the least busy area of the site at the moment.

When the majority of the workmen knocked off for the day he emerged like a badger from its lair, moving to the front of the building to keep a watchful eye on the square below. From here he had a perfect view of the spot where Zola's van stopped to pick up the others.

He didn't notice the foreman in the fluorescent yellow vest until he was almost upon him, the noise from the crane hoisting iron mesh into the building having drowned out his footsteps.

"Hey, you! How'd you get in here?" The man's voice rang out through the concrete landscape. "That book and the other stuff stashed away over by the lift shaft, is it yours?"

Marco shook his head. "I'm sorry. I came with my dad. I know I'm not supposed to be up here. I'll go down now. It was just so exciting to see, that's all."

The man eyed Marco's hard hat, frowned, and then nodded. Maybe he couldn't imagine a lad like him owning a book. "You tell your dad it's grounds for dismissal if he brings you with him again, get it?"

"I will. I'm sorry, really," Marco replied, feeling the man's eyes on the back of his neck until he reached the stairway. He mustn't see me here again, he told himself, nodding to the workmen who were watching him on his way down.

I won't get past the guard, it occurred to him, so he cut diagonally across the ground floor toward the corner by the oddly named restaurant A Hereford Beefstouw. There he stashed his hard hat away as usual behind a stack of pallets before clambering over the fence like a squirrel.

Now he was out on the street in the rain and it was just past three in the afternoon. He wouldn't see the van from above today, but luckily the foreman had discovered him early enough for him not to risk running into the clan members who in two hours would be waiting close by to be picked up.

But Marco was wrong. He hadn't even made it across Jernbanegade before a cry pierced the air above the streams of cyclists in rainwear and sodden pedestrians on their way home.

"Murderer!" The word had been shouted unequivocally, and in English. He knew the voice immediately.

He stopped in his tracks halfway across the street and glanced around to see where Miryam was.

"Now we know why they're all looking for you. Chris told us, you murderer!" she yelled at him.

Marco registered the reaction from passers-by. Half of them gave him caustic, disapproving looks while the other half looked the other way, eyes fixed on the ranks of bicycles parked in front of the Dagmar cinema.

He caught sight of her in the midst of the throng, huddled beneath a poster advertising the premiere of *The Tree of Life*. Her hair was plastered to her cheeks and her clothes black from the rain. Her eyes shone with disappointment, hateful and full of sorrow at the same time.

Marco stepped out onto the street and glanced around. Was she alone?

"Yeah, you can look for the others, you coward, but there's only me. They're going to get you anyway. Murderer!" Then she turned toward the oncoming pedestrians, folding her arms and pressing her elbows tight against her body. She was clearly exhausted, had been on the street for hours, and Marco knew the pain in her leg was almost unbearable.

"Someone grab him! He's killed a man, come and help me!" she shouted, but no one seemed to think it was worth the trouble, once they saw where the cries were coming from.

Marco was in shock. He crossed the pavement in three strides, gripping her shoulders hard. "I've done nothing. You know me, Miryam. It was Zola who did it."

But his words glanced off her. Still she refused to let herself believe him. "LISTEN TO ME!" he yelled, shaking her by the shoulders. "It was me who got the police to pay Zola a visit, don't you understand? You've got to believe me."

Miryam twisted free. The expression on her face told him he was hurting her. "Murderer," she said again, almost in a whisper this time. "The police said you're trying to give Zola the blame. You're a defector and a rat of the worst kind, stabbing your own benefactor and all the rest of us in the back."

Marco shook his head and felt tears beginning to appear. Was this really what she believed? Was this what Zola had got them all to believe? The bastard.

"Miryam, Zola's to blame for what happened to your leg. The accident you had, it was something he set up. Don't you realize—"

He didn't see the hand she struck him with, but he instantly felt a deep sense of hopelessness and betrayal much stronger than the stinging physical pain.

He dried his eyes and reached out to stroke her cheek in a gesture of farewell, only to be distracted by the fleeting glance she made over his shoulder.

Instinctively, he turned to see Pico, his jaw bandaged, weaving through the crowd, forcefully shoving people aside as he went, his gaze locked on Marco.

Marco reacted promptly, leaping toward a girl who was parking her bicycle and sending her headlong to the pavement. He cried out an apology as he grabbed her bike.

He was up on the bike, cutting through the swarm of incensed pedestrians and out on to the street before the girl could react, but Pico had anticipated him, sprinting into the lane of traffic with arms waving.

Marco heard him panting behind him, but not his silent Adidas sneakers against the asphalt. He was fast, his strides long, as people stopped on the pavement to stare silently at the pursuit without the will to intervene.

Marco jerked the handlebars, wrenching the front wheel over the curb and hurtling on past the poster columns in front of the garish Palads cinema, where the hotdog stands and forest of café parasols on the open square provided a snarl of obstacles.

Now he could hear Pico calling out behind him: "Stop, Marco, we're not going to hurt you. We just want to make a deal."

Sure. A deal where he swapped the bike for a leg lock and a ten-minute wait before they threw him into the van. Fuck them!

Marco leaned forward and pedaled as hard as he could as Pico charged through the crowds in his wake. Behind him he heard a woman fall to the ground with a yelp of pain. This wasn't good.

"Hey, are you crazy or something?" someone shouted at him as a man tried to jab the point of his umbrella into the spokes of his front wheel.

And then all of a sudden Romeo was there in front of him, a flaming red burn across his cheek. Standing on the edge of the open area between the bike stands with his arms spread out, ready to risk leaping straight into the bicycle and knock him flying.

Time becomes most essential in a person's life when none is left. Only then are seconds registered one by one, and right now Marco could feel them running out.

The city traffic was flowing just behind Romeo's back, and the rapidly approaching Pico was catching up to Marco from behind. What now? He could ride directly into Romeo and bring him down with him, or else let the bike crash straight into the parking stands, in which case he would be thrown over the handlebars and into the path of an oncoming bus. But why not? At least it would all be over, he thought in this measured fraction of time, his face contorted with anguish and tears streaming down his cheeks.

"Help me!" he screamed, his voice resonating from the surrounding buildings. Rain-drenched faces turned toward him as his ankles grated agonizingly against the pedals and chains of parked bicycles before the full impact sent him somersaulting out into the street.

He heard horrified screams behind him and the squeal of brakes in front. Then he felt something hit him hard and blacked out.

"Can you hear me?" asked a voice he didn't know. He nodded cautiously, but hadn't the strength to completely open his eyes. Only when a hand stroked his cheek and the voice asked his name did he surface into reality.

"My name's Marco," he heard himself say from a distance. "Marco Jameson."

"You understand Danish, then?"

He felt himself smile as he nodded. Then he opened his eyes fully and found himself looking into a face that was mild yet concerned. Had he just said his name?

"Can you feel your toes, Marco?"

He nodded. Yes, he had said his name. He shouldn't have.

"Can you tell me where it hurts?"

He couldn't give an answer. Over the shoulder of the paramedic, Romeo was staring straight at him.

"He's my brother," Romeo said. "We'll take care of him. Our father's a doctor. He'll be here soon to pick him up."

Marco looked pleadingly at the paramedic, shaking his head. "It's not true," he whispered.

The man nodded. "I think we need to get him checked properly at the hospital. He needs to be X-rayed, just to be sure."

"Thank you," Marco whispered again. "It was his fault it happened. His name's Romeo. You have to phone the police right away, he wants to kill me."

"The police will be here in no time, Marco. Just relax. I'm sure it's not as bad as all that. Witnesses are saying it was an accident. You weren't looking where you were going," the paramedic said as the circle of onlookers nodded their agreement.

And then Romeo was gone.

"I think I'm OK," Marco said after a minute or two, drawing himself up onto his elbows. He need to see if Pico was still there lurking in the crowd, but he seemed to have disappeared, too, no doubt disinclined to be at the scene when the police got there. Marco felt the same way. He was an illegal immigrant, and the last thing he needed was to be nailed for stealing a bike, or anything else for that matter.

He saw now that they had laid his stretcher by the entrance to the Palads cinema.

"Did the bus hit me?" he asked the paramedic.

The peering faces smiled. Clearly it hadn't.

"You can thank the bus driver for his quick reactions. Otherwise it would have been a different story," said one of the onlookers.

Marco nodded. "I'm all right now. I'd like to sit up if I may."

The paramedic hesitated, then nodded, extending him a hand as someone in the crowd applauded.

"I want to go to the toilet, is that OK? I can use the ones in the cinema here."

Again his request was met with hesitation, but when Marco managed a broad smile and the paramedic checked to make sure the size of his pupils were normal, he received a nod and was allowed to get up.

"I'll give you a hand," said a second paramedic. "There's a chance you might have concussion, or something even worse."

Marco smiled again, as broadly as he possibly could.

"No, I'm completely OK. I'll be only a minute, it's just in there," he said, pointing.

"All right, but listen," said the paramedic in a serious voice. "We'll be waiting for you here, so you come back out as soon as you're done, OK, Marco?"

Marco nodded and gingerly got to his feet. Apart from his right knee, shoulder, and lower leg aching, there seemed to be nothing else the matter.

"Two minutes," he said, proceeding slowly up the steps into the foyer with all eyes following him.

He scanned the area. To his left was a café and what looked like the entrance to the smaller cinemas. Diagonally to the left was the kiosk and the toilets, in the middle stood the ticket booth, and to the right lay the way to the larger cinemas. The question was, which way to go in order to get through to the far side of the building? Going through one of the cinemas would involve having to sneak past a ticket collector, then through the darkened theatre to an emergency exit. But could he be sure of coming out on the opposite side of the building?

He had no idea. He looked around the foyer again, sensing all too clearly that time was running out.

And then he noticed a faint shaft of light at the rear of the section beyond the toilets. He hobbled toward it. It was a glass door.

No doubt a fire door, he thought, in which case it would be permanently secured, its electronic lock releasing only if the fire alarm activated.

Still he drew the handle down and pulled hard. And suddenly there he was, outside the far end of the building, with Vesterport station straight in front of him. How lucky could he be? Without hesitation he limped on, across the street and down to the S-train platforms, waiting only a moment before the next train arrived, then riding the minute or two it took to the city's central station, Hovedbanegården. He left by the exit to Tietgensgade, continuing on in the direction of Copenhagen police headquarters, trying to get a handle on what had happened and why.

Something must have gone wrong when the police had been to Kregme, for he knew now that they had been there. Zola must have turned the accusations away from himself and against Marco. Of course he had. So now, on top of everything else, Marco was also wanted for murder.

He felt himself tremble at the thought. Moreover, his knee, side, arm, and lower leg were aching badly. He was in a dilemma: he had to speak to the police, yet he didn't dare.

Standing before police HQ, he was overwhelmed. The building was at once monumental and compact, with Roman colonnades that reminded him of some ancient fortress. No way was he going inside. The building would swallow him up.

He would have to wait until someone he dared approach came out.

After an hour of seeing no one but men in light blue uniform shirts with guns and a gait like militiamen, he was on the verge of giving up.

What now? he wondered, turning to leave the parking lot where he had been standing, when a woman emerged from the middle arch together with a tall, thin man who looked anything but dangerous.

Marco thought he looked like an office worker, watching them as they walked toward the place where he stood.

"You have to go the other way, Gordon," the woman said to the skinny guy, pointing in the opposite direction. "The Ministry of Foreign Affairs is down by Asiatisk Plads, remember?"

Now Marco recognized her. It was the woman Carl Mørck and the Arab worked with.

Marco withdrew behind a parked car.

"Listen, Rose, I just wanted to—"

"I haven't got time, Gordon. A boy named Marco's been located at the Palads cinema. The police arrived just after he'd gone inside, so they're searching the place now. I'm heading over there and you've got an appointment, so you'd better hurry up."

Marco held his breath. They were all out looking for him.

He allowed the woman to pass, plucked a parking ticket from the wipers of one of the cars and wrote along its edge.

Then he ran after her, slowing down when he was ten meters behind and then keeping his distance.

When she got to the side entrance of Tivoli Gardens, opposite the station, he saw his chance.

Pedestrians from the station and the adjacent bus terminal mingled with a queue outside Tivoli's ticket booth and people leaving the amusement park. Inevitably she was forced to slow down by the throng, clutching her bag tight to her hip, and in the meantime Marco's hand darted out and delivered his note.

If they read it, they would know where the lockers were that Samuel and the others used as a temporary stash for their stolen goods. And they would know that every afternoon at five o'clock, all the clan members and their booty were picked up by a van just outside the big construction site opposite the town hall. They would know who Zola and his troops were, and what kind of activities they were involved in.

But what if she doesn't find the note? he wondered, feeling like the child he no longer wished to be. He wanted to be an adult and leave behind a period of his life he wanted only to forget. He didn't want to be vulnerable and defenseless any more, he wanted to avenge himself, to stand on his own two feet and break free.

But right now he *was* vulnerable, no doubt about it. Everyone was after him, and he had no one, absolutely no one, to turn to.

If he took a circuitous route along the city lakes, away from the center, the risk of running into Zola's bloodhounds was probably small and at some point he would reach the marina at Nordhavn, a place he knew like the back of his hand. There he might be able to find a boat where he could lick his wounds and try to figure out who might help him.

On the path running along the lakes the rain felt mild and soothing. There were unusually few people about. Only a young couple and a woman walking her dog had ventured out into the drizzle.

Marco heard something rustle in the reeds by the edge of Sankt Jørgens Sø. He stopped as a flock of cygnets glided into open water in the wake of their mother. Seven of them, he counted with a smile, then looked out across the lake and the planetarium on Sankt Jørgens Sø's southern shore. He found himself thinking that he wouldn't mind living in this midtown paradise one day.

He chuckled at the sight of the newly hatched, chirping creatures, then turned as a woman and her dachshund approached. Suddenly the dog darted between her legs and leaped into the water to attack a little straggler that had yet to emerge from the reeds.

Marco let out a cry. The woman did as well, and the mother swan turned in the water but was unable to comprehend what was about to happen, so Marco jumped in.

The water was cold, but it came up to only his thighs as he smacked his hand on the surface and the pen rose up hissing, wings outspread. The next smack struck the dog's hindquarters before its jaws reached its prey, and the little cygnet glided away like quicksilver.

Despite the woman's vociferous anger at his brutality, Marco was rather pleased with himself until he caught sight of the two police officers in black jackets galloping along the path toward him from the direction of the planetarium. They must have seen what had happened and had recognized him.

"Out of the way," he exclaimed, pushing the woman aside as she continued to harangue him.

Two minutes later he was running along streets he didn't know, his shoes squelching. The neighborhood was more closed than Østerbro. The apartment buildings all had entry phones and there were few shops. Where could he hide?

Before long, patrol cars would be out looking for him. The main thoroughfares in this part of the Frederiksberg district would doubtless be under observation, so he cut through the small side streets until he felt sure it was OK to stop and catch his breath.

He leaned up against a tree, chest heaving, and looked up at the street sign. Steenstrups Allé. At the other end he recognized the former radio broadcasting house, so the big building that loomed up on the right had to be the Forum, and behind it he knew there was a metro station. If he could get that far without being seen he could quickly slip away. But where to?

The only person he could think of that might help him was Tilde. If he could get in touch with her, she might believe him and pass everything on to the police.

Turning the corner by the Forum, he met the rush of traffic along Rosenørns Allé. The bus stops on either side of the road were teeming. Another working day had come to an end and everyone was determined to get home. Marco saw no immediate cause for alarm.

He looked ahead at the pyramids of glass that sent daylight down into the metro system and saw the gray granite stairway leading down to the station. No faces he knew, and none he didn't know that looked suspicious so he walked directly toward the entrance.

That was when he sensed a shadow move out from behind the luminous information post and realized too late that the man was about to pounce.

What to do now?

The way down to the trains was a jumble of plateaus. First there were the stairs, down which he was now bounding, then an intermediate level built around the glass column encasing the elevator. After that, some more steps down to the level where the ticket machines were located along with a set of escalators that descended in two stages to the metro trains.

Perhaps he could fool his pursuer, wait at the level where the ticket machines were, then leg it back up the stairs as the guy came down. If he could get back up to the street again, he'd have a good chance of shaking him off.

But the man was waiting on the first level. He had pulled his mobile from his pocket and was trying to anticipate Marco's next move.

He's calling for backup, Marco realized. His only option now was to carry on down to the trains.

Apart from the two of them, the place was strangely deserted. In front of him was only the sterile gray shaft that ended deep down at the platforms with automatic glass doors that screened off the tracks.

"Stop, Marco!" the man shouted, his Slavic accent echoing through the concrete silo as Marco veered toward the right-hand escalator that led down to the next level.

Maybe he could make it all the way down to the platform and up again at the other end before he has a chance to react. But no sooner had the plan materialized in his mind than his pursuer almost hurled himself down the escalator to his left. Marco picked up speed, vaulting his way down the moving staircase to the intermediate landing and on down the second escalator that led to the platforms. Here the escalators ran closely side by side, only a low glass partition separating them. Again he heard rapid footsteps behind him and turned just as his pursuer caught up and lunged over the partition to grab him.

Marco lashed out at the man's arm with his fist. He was close enough now for Marco to smell his bad breath. Then his hand locked Marco's neck in a viselike grip.

He knew the waiting passengers would barely notice what was happening, and if they did, they wouldn't intervene. They would look the other way and focus on the driverless train that was now gliding toward the platform behind the glass screens. In a few seconds, the glass screens and the train doors would open simultaneously, and then the commuters would be gone. Therefore Marco's repeated cries for help were in vain as the man dragged him over the partition on to his own escalator. Marco flailed his arms and legs to no avail. But then his foot found leverage on the moving handrail, allowing him to push off so forcefully that both he and his assailant were sent flying over the side of the escalator and out into the void.

Marco let out a scream as they tumbled through the air for the remaining three meters.

There was an audible crack as they hit the floor, like the sound of ribs breaking. In any case, the man now lay groaning beneath him, the air slammed out of his lungs.

Marco leaped to his feet and plunged through the open train doors as his assailant clutched at his chest and tried to raise himself up onto his elbows. The last thing Marco saw was the look of rage and agony on his face as he put his mobile to his ear.

The people in the train carriage stared at him without comment. No one tried to console him, even though tears ran from his eyes, but no one abused him either.

He sat down on one of the fold-down seats, angling himself so he could see forward through the illuminated tunnel. He had no idea which direction he was traveling in or where he would end up. All he knew was that the longer he stayed on the train, the more time they would have to rally the troops.

The troops? Who were they at this point anyway? Where had his assailant come from? Had he been standing there all day behind the information post, waiting in case Marco should appear? And who was he phoning right now?

Marco wrung his hands in despair as everything around him seemed to merge. The sound of the train's electric motors propelling him toward the unknown; the ding-dong from the PA system and the voice announcing the next station, Frederiksberg; the passengers sitting impassively in the cold light as the reflected glare of Frederiksberg station's glass screens warned him he better make a decision as to what to do next.

Should he get off or try continuing on to Vanløse, then leg it to Strindbergsvej, where Tilde lived? What were his chances?

He fixed his eyes on the platform as the train glided to a halt. All seemed peaceful enough. Patient eyes focused on the glass screens, waiting for them to open. Students on their way home. Posters advertising eyeglasses, information posts, ticket machines, and otherwise nothing.

Marco positioned himself at the doors and glanced over his shoulder. Still nothing.

He got off the train. He'd made his decision. He needed to get out of the open, back to his hideout. The workmen would be packing their gear away now, and soon the site would be quiet. All he had to do was get up to street level and head along Falkoner Allé and Frederiksberg Allé, then calmly make his way back to the center from the safest side of the city. This would probably work, as long as no one was up there waiting for him.

He looked in both directions before opting to take the stairway farthest from the Frederiksberg Centre shopping mall. If they were already at the station they would expect him to take the route where there was the best chance of the crowds being biggest.

Forty steps up and he would be out.

He got less than halfway before two faces with watchful eyes appeared at the top of the stairs. Instinctively Marco turned back and ran.

Now there was a train waiting at the opposite platform. The doors were open. Unfortunately it was heading back to the Forum, but what else could he do? The last passenger had stepped inside. Marco vaulted over the final five steps, hearing the sound of running behind him as he squeezed through the closing glass screens. For a moment the train remained standing as its own doors slid shut, leaving two men with Slavic features and frustrated expressions hammering their fists against the glass outside.

A month ago the men had almost certainly been walking the streets of towns like Liepaja and Palanga, dreaming of striking it rich in the West, and now it was plain to see they'd just missed out. That's when Marco realized the price on his head was a big one, and Copenhagen's entire assortment of lowlife was now hunting him.

He stretched out low across a pair of fold-down seats as they passed Forum station, raising his head cautiously to see if his former pursuer was still there.

He was, but sitting on the floor against a wall, his hands pressed to his chest. He was on his guard, but injured and in pain. Still holding the mobile in his hand.

At Nørreport station, Marco took the escalator at the far end, knowing that if they were waiting for him at street level he needed to be ready to make a dash for the botanical gardens and the Østre Anlæg park to find a place to hide.

He picked out a woman and stood so close to her as they neared the top that it annoyed her. As well it might, because if they spotted him and got too close, he would shove her into them.

Up on the street all seemed peaceful and normal. The rain had stopped and people were spilling out of the side streets on their way home.

Here in the crowd I'm as good as invisible, he told himself, as he made his way along Frederiksborggade toward Nørre Farimagsgade. From there he would catch a bus the last stretch of the way just to be on the safe side.

Now that he knew what he was up against.

31

He saw shadows everywhere as the bus passed the Palads cinema where not long before he'd come close to losing his life. Men loitering at pedestrian crossings. Men standing inactive in the milling crowds. Men who *were just there.*

You're getting paranoid, Marco, he told himself, trying to straighten his shoulders on the seat farthest back. Not everyone was after him, surely?

As the bus slowed and eased past Tivoli's side entrance opposite the central station, he noticed a group of men in fierce discussion. Though he recognized none of them, it made him feel anxious. Cut it out, he urged himself. Just one more stop, then we're down behind Tivoli and I'll be safe.

He ducked down slightly in his seat all the same, keeping an eye on the flock of men as the bus pulled in to the stop. Apart from two who were black, they looked like Eastern Europeans. Bony men who appeared used to living the hard life.

Marco kept an eye on the front of the bus to see who got on. They all seemed peaceful enough.

He heaved a sigh of relief, feeling the battering his body had taken earlier in the day. He ached, and yet he was thankful. He was still alive, wasn't he?

The bus had just started up again when he sensed a shadow moving fast on the pavement. Someone just missed the bus, was his first thought, as he looked out and saw a young black guy in a green basketball jersey staring up straight into his face as the bus pulled away.

Marco turned in his seat and saw him give chase like a hunting dog with an easy, loping stride, too fast by half.

Immediately Marco got to his feet, all his senses on alert as he moved to the exit. Fortunately the light was green as the bus turned down Tietgensgade, putting distance between him and the jackal behind.

He jumped off at the Glyptotek art museum and crossed the street behind the bus, weaving between the honking cars. The black guy had already rounded the corner farther back and was halfway toward him. Marco fumbled in his pocket and produced a couple of banknotes, then hobbled as fast as he could in the direction of the amusement park's rear entrance.

And then he froze as he read the sign: THIS ENTRANCE CLOSED FOR REPAIRS.

He looked up and saw his pursuer closing in at the same time as he sensed a sudden turmoil of flashing blue lights on the opposite corner of H. C. Andersens Boulevard. Apparently a patrol car had been waiting over by the Great China restaurant and had just launched itself across six lanes of traffic, straight toward him.

Now Marco was boxed in. If he tried to make a run for it toward Rådhuspladsen or the Langebro bridge in the opposite direction, his pursuer would catch up with him. If he tried to cross H. C. Andersens Boulevard he would run straight into the arms of the police. There was only one alternative left, and that was to clamber over the fence into Tivoli Gardens.

He leaped onto the fence just to the right of the closed gate where there was a post he could grab, and managed to wriggle over the top. Behind him he heard the patrol car screech to a halt on the bike path and saw his pursuer stop in his tracks. For once a police car with flashing blue lights was having a positive effect on his life.

Inside the amusement park, he glanced around to get his bearings, then opted for the steps that led past a carousel ride with animals in all shapes and sizes. He had seen one just like it in Italy but had never been on it. In fact, he had never seen a place like this, he thought, as he crisscrossed the system of pathways amid children on the roller coaster and the pirate ship, and the shrieks of delight when parents arrived with ice-cream. Marco felt a lump rise in his throat. Never had he felt so abandoned as in this pandemonium of happy faces and gaiety.

He saw more police cars appearing in the surrounding streets, but was sure they'd never catch him here because he knew the way behind the Pantomime Theatre and the restaurants to his building-site hideaway, which lay next to that corner of Tivoli. From there, climbing the lattice of steel girders and concrete was no problem, when your name was Marco.

The site was almost deserted. A few workmen were pottering about below, but up here where he sat his only company was the wind and his view across the city.

He felt like a hawk hovering unnoticed above the fields, eyes latching on to the slightest movement.

Now he knew how close they were. Just below, sniffing around for the smallest clue that might tell them how he had given them the slip and where he'd disappeared to. The police cars had gone now, but it wasn't the police he feared the most.

It was the black guy. Not because of his inscrutable eyes or his athletic body and sure movements. What frightened him was that he couldn't understand what a man like him was doing here.

He recalled having seen two young Africans by the steps of the central station. But when he closed his eyes and concentrated, he saw a black woman, too, standing behind them, keeping an eye on everything. It was like these were the ones in charge, while the other men seemed less resolute.

What were they all doing here in Copenhagen? That was the question. Who had put them on to him?

As far as he could see, it could hardly be Zola. He remembered clearly the time two Afro-American men had wanted to join the clan, back when they lived in Italy, and how nasty the verbal exchanges had become. No, black folks were not welcome in Zola's world.

But who, then?

Marco picked up his book. He had read it many times by now, the one he had stolen from the family on the very first morning of his life as a fugitive. The words soothed him and even the name of the main character, Nicky, made him feel better. She was a strong-willed woman who held her own against superior force, despite her lack of physical strength. A woman who didn't really belong to the society in which she lived, and yet . . .

He put the book down again and frowned.

The sounds from below were almost inaudible, which was precisely what sent a rush of adrenaline through his body. Construction sites, normally such a cacophony of sounds, were meant to fall silent when the day was done. No one was supposed to be there.

But someone was.

He went over to the elevator shaft, where he stood and listened intently. The sounds were still there, a bit louder now. Not regular footsteps, more like the squeak of moist fingers drawn across plastic.

They were here. He was certain of it.

If it was the Africans, he knew they were unlike any people he had previously been up against.

The sounds grew more distinct and were coming from two directions. One directly underneath the elevator shaft, the other by the stairwell. So now his exits were blocked.

He heard them speak. Was it French?

Glancing around he saw no immediate escape route, just a couple of obvious hiding places where they were bound to look straight away.

Why had he come all the way up here to the fourth floor? He was too high up to jump.

They can kill me here as easy as anything, but I'll put up a good fight, he told himself, his body heating up and his breathing growing deeper.

The iron bar he picked up from the floor was heavy enough that no one could survive a well-aimed blow. He gripped it tightly in both hands, pointing it at the stairs like a Jedi's light saber

He simply refused to cry now. The last thing he wanted was for these men with their ruthless faces to see him break down as they closed in on him. He wouldn't allow them to see the effect Zola had on people when they turned against him. At least that was one thing these guys wouldn't be able report back about when they were finished with him.

The first man to appear at the top of the stairs was not the one who had been running after the bus. Though Marco could see only his silhouette, the yellow T-shirt was unmistakable: *Lakers 24*, it read.

"Hello, kiddie," the man said in a husky voice, in English. "Come here to me!"

He remained at a distance, waving Marco toward him. But Marco backed away toward the side of the building facing Vesterbrogade. The closer they were to the edge, the greater the chance of taking the guy with him in the fall. It was a maneuver he had already tried once that day.

Marco looked up. Behind the black man, Tivoli's Ferris wheel with its candy-striped gondolas was rotating to the delighted cries of children and grown-ups alike. Before the wheel came to a halt he would probably die, and no one in the world would know who he was or what he might have become.

For all his resolve, the sorrow of this sudden realization prompted tears to well in his eyes.

"Poor boy!" said the young African. He had yet to produce a weapon, but Marco knew it was only a matter of time.

If he was lucky, he might be able to surprise him by making a dash for the elevator shaft and leaping into the void. Marco knew the second man was on the floor below, but if he let himself plunge to the next level down, then maybe somehow he might be able to save his skin. Maybe, somehow.

He took a step to the side, but his adversary read his thoughts and blocked his path.

There was nothing Marco could do now but watch and wait.

Not until only a few paces separated them did Marco see his face clearly. Despite the lines etched in it, he wasn't much more than five or six years older than Marco. There was a scar across his nose, white and sharply defined, and his left eye was half shut. He looked like a warrior, and yet there was nothing aggressive or angry about his countenance. In fact, he seemed more like a carpenter needing only to hammer in the last nail of the day. Placid and unwavering, cold as ice.

And then he produced the knife.

Marco took two swipes at him with the bar, though he knew any moment now the African would raise his weapon above his head and send it hurtling into his chest. It was that kind of knife: short-handled, with a finger grip and razor-sharp double-edged blade.

If the iron rod hadn't been so heavy, he would have launched it at him or tried to bat the knife aside in midair with a baseball swing. But Marco hadn't the strength, and so he stepped up close to the edge and waited.

In what he believed would be his final seconds, he heard a car sound its horn emphatically at the junction below. But the sound didn't come directly from the street, it was more like a distorted fanfare coming from right next to the spot where he was standing.

He turned his head and saw the top of the rubble chute assembled from sections of heavy-duty plastic tubing through which the builders dumped their debris into ground-level Dumpsters. Marco clenched his jaw and lunged to the side as he flung the iron bar at his enemy. It ricocheted against the concrete floor and struck the African on the shin. Then he grabbed the sides of the chute and vaulted in, feetfirst.

He heard the man's curses as he slid away.

The sections of the chute telescoped into each other and every join slowed his descent a little. The son of a bitch wouldn't catch him now, Marco decided, he was too big and would get stuck.

And then he heard the rumble above.

Oh, God, he managed to think, as falling chunks of rubble began pummeling his body. He's going to get me. How'd he ever fit into this chute?

He caught a glimpse of light from the mouth of the chute below before landing in a corner of the Dumpster among discarded fiberglass and piles of plastic packaging materials.

He stared up at the rumbling chute as his skin began to itch from the fiberglass.

Thinking quickly, he lunged to the side of the Dumpster and grabbed a short plank with sharp nails protruding from the end. The moment the African emerged he would aim a blow at his head.

But his pursuer never made it through. Somewhere higher up he must have realized the chute was too narrow and a string of curses sounded through the duct like false notes from some arcane wind instrument.

Marco brushed the glassy slivers from his clothes and could hear someone running on the level above.

He vaulted out of the Dumpster, clambered over the fence and legged it across Rådhuspladsen, half blinded by the dust of fiberglass that stuck to his eyelashes, his throat and skin tormented by the stinging, itchy fiber.

Only when he reached the mouth of the pedestrianized Strøget did he dare glance back over his shoulder. And there on the pavement in front of the huge construction site stood a woman as wide as a door and as black as the night, following him with her eyes.

He forgot all about his bad leg and ran like hell.

By the time he reached Frederiksholm's Canal and the Marble Bridge leading over to the equestrian grounds of the Danish parliament he was almost out of his mind from all the itching. His clothes felt fleecy from the insulation material, and the more he scratched the worse it got. He peered into the dark water of the canal and wondered if it might wash the glass splinters out of his clothes. Then he jumped down the steps to the jetty where small motorboats lay anchored and plunged in.

He took a couple of strokes with one arm, brushing at his clothes with the other. The water was cold but had a soothing effect.

A woman stopped on the bridge and asked if he was OK. He nodded and dived under the surface, removing a layer of millions of fibers. When he came up for air, a couple of young guys in suits stood laughing at him by the edge of the canal as one of them jabbed an index finger at his temple to indicate how totally mental they thought he was.

At the same moment Marco registered the man a couple of hundred meters away who was running in his direction.

Disappear, you two, Marco commanded silently, as his mirthful audience began pointing. But it was too late.

By now he could see the man running toward him was the one in the green basketball jersey. He had picked up Marco's scent and was clearly considering his next move.

Now Marco was trapped, but as they climbed into their car the chuckleheads in the suits were oblivious of the fact that they had just hammered a nail into his coffin.

What could he do now? Nothing.

No matter which way he swam, the African would have no difficulty following him alongside the canal, and the moment he tried to get out of the water, this cheetah would sink its teeth into him. The way Marco saw it, his only chance was to conceal himself behind one of the moored boats and hope that darkness soon would fall.

He dived again, underneath the boats this time, drawing himself through the water to where the guy had just been standing. Most likely he would take the same stairs down to the boats as Marco had used, so he had to get out of sight quickly, swimming under as many boats and as far away as possible.

And if, against all odds, the guy took to the water himself, he would swim silently and cautiously under one boat at a time until he reached the bridge called Stormbroen, where he would try to clamber back onto dry land without being seen.

If he could emerge at a spot where there were a lot of people, he might still have a chance.

But the African did not take to the water. Instead, he jumped down on to the jetty, where he calmly proceeded from one mooring post to the next.

Marco heard how he took his time, pausing at every vessel, making sure Marco hadn't climbed into one of them or was clinging to its side, or sending up bubbles of air from below the surface.

Slowly he approached, as the canal and its surroundings descended into darkness.

Finally he was but one boat away and once more Marco dove down, only to hear a splash behind him.

He swam a few frenzied strokes before surfacing to see the almost invisible face of a black man so close in the water that he turned immediately and swam as fast as he could.

For a moment, the distance between them increased, but then his strength ebbed away while his pursuer's strokes remained strong and steady.

They heard the sightseeing boat at the same time as it returned to base from the open waters of the harbor. They both stopped swimming for a moment to assess the situation and see what they were up against.

The vessel was moving quickly, and its pointed bow was coming straight toward them. Summoning all his energy, Marco swam toward the bridge. Of its three stone arches, the one on the left was blocked by a speedboat, the two others were free.

If I try the right-hand arch, he'll just follow me, Marco reasoned. He was exhausted now, his sodden clothes weighing him down. And if I go for the middle one, the sightseeing boat will run me down.

Instinctively he opted for the arch on the right, thinking he just might get through to the other side ahead of the boat and then alert the crew that he was in danger.

Even now, he knew intuitively that he was unlikely to get that far. Behind him he heard a forceful lunge that brought his pursuer close enough to pull Marco down under the surface before he had a chance to take in air. In spite of the darkness and the murky water, he could clearly see the whites of the man's eyes. The man who was now drowning him in a violent embrace. He gasped, then his mouth closed and his legs started thrashing to bring him back to the surface as the sound of the boat's motor and propeller churned louder and louder in his ears.

Then he managed to get an arm free. He twisted and turned, extricating himself from the African's grasp just enough to thrust two rigid fingers into his eyes.

The man opened his mouth in a scream, releasing a mist of bubbles to the surface as Marco's fingers gouged into his irises.

The combatants rose to the surface simultaneously like a pair of corks, the darker one momentarily blinded, Marco swimming with desperate strokes toward the middle arch of the bridge.

The boat was so close now that he could hear what its boozed-filled party of passengers were singing.

And then he heard a roar behind him and saw his pursuer thrashing through the water toward him, blood streaming from one of his eyes.

So Marco submerged again.

Underneath the surface he felt the blue hull of the boat plowing over him, and with a burst of strength propelled himself out to the boat's other side, where his fingers grabbed hold of a thick braided rope that ran along the length of the vessel at the waterline.

He was jerked violently to the surface and heard himself scream involuntarily, though no one on board noticed.

Maybe it was for the best. Maybe the predator in the water on the other side of the boat thought he had been hit. Marco could only hope.

He allowed himself to be pulled through the water in the knowledge that he had got away.

For a brief moment he smiled as he saw the dark head bobbing far behind in the wake of the boat.

The question was, had he seen Marco as well?

32

Carl joined up with Gordon in Eriksen's receptionist's office. Desert boots, gray scarf, corduroys. Was he really expecting to be taken seriously in a getup like that?

"Well, you made it on time," the beanpole said, with the kind of arrogance best rectified by some boxing about the ears.

Some interview this was going to be.

Eriksen looked peculiarly tired. Not the way you did after a hard day's slog, more like he'd been at it all night long and had also been in an accident.

"What happened?" Carl inquired, with a nod in the direction of the bandage stuck to Eriksen's neck.

"Oh, that," he replied, lifting his hand to the spot. "Silly, really. It's what you get for taking the steps in front of your house too quickly."

Gordon nodded. "Yeah, one little slip and all of a sudden you're on your back."

"Exactly," said Eriksen, sending the idiot a rather too intimate smile.

The corners of Carl's mouth turned downward. If the idiot was going put words in the mouth of their interviewee, things weren't going to be easy.

"I can inform you that we've spoken to William Stark's partner, Malene Kristoffersen, and her daughter," Carl said. "Both of them have forcefully dismissed your suspicion of pedophile activity. That's only to be expected, of course, but we've found nothing at all to substantiate it. Do you have anything more to say that might further support what you told us?"

"I don't know, really," Eriksen replied, pursing his lips in thought. "Sometimes you can observe things and overinterpret them. You brought the issue up in our discussion, not me, and it triggered some associations, I suppose." He shook his head. "I can't say I've anything more substantial, so I can only apologize if I put you on the wrong track."

Carl inhaled sharply through the corner of his mouth. He wasn't feeling that good and was also confused by Eriksen's change of tack. It was almost as if something had happened to the man since last time they spoke. As though the camel were stretching its neck toward another goal altogether.

"Quite an office you've got here," said Gordon, for no obvious reason. "I thought the Ministry of Foreign Affairs was in some ancient building."

Christ on a bike, who did he think he was working for? *Ideal Home* magazine?

Carl forced an apologetic laugh. "Gordon's in law school and thinking of joining the civil service. So he's checking out the territory while he's here."

The beanstalk looked surprised. "Actually, no, I—"

The lightning in Carl's eyes could have slain an ox. Gordon shut up abruptly. Despite possessing truckloads of megalomania and a stranger to self-criticism, he must suddenly have understood who was in charge. About fucking time.

"We'd like to know more about the project Stark went to Cameroon to sort out," Carl went on. "What was it about, exactly? We have a rough idea, but we'd also like to hear your own rundown."

Eriksen frowned. Was it a prickly question or was he just thinking?

"Actually, it was a rather simple project, basically motivated by the fact that a large part of the world's primitive cultures are suffering on account of civilization encroaching upon their domains. In this instance we're talking about a pygmy tribe known as the Baka people, an ethnic group inhabiting the Congolese jungle in a geographical area known as Dja, which is located in the southernmost region of Cameroon. It was a straightforward aid project whose purpose was to compensate for intensive poaching and the timber extraction their forests have been subjected to. The Baka still live in grass-roofed huts, under quite primitive conditions. The fact of the matter is they can no longer sustain themselves unless major efforts are made to provide them with crops and reasonable living conditions. So all in all it was a pretty basic development project."

"*Was*, you say. Isn't it still running?"

"Yes, but it's winding down."

"Hmm. And how have these people been helped, exactly?"

"Mainly by setting up banana plantations and making sure the land surrounding their villages was cultivated."

Carl eyed him for some time before posing his next question. He sensed Gordon fidgeting impatiently at his side, so he clamped his hand just above the lad's knee and squeezed. There was a squeak of astonishment, but luckily nothing Eriksen seemed to notice. He was far too focused on Carl's scrutinizing gaze.

"I can tell you we've received information that the project went idle quite some time ago," said Carl. "As far as we've been informed, not much ever transpired in the way of banana plantations or cultivated fields. Could you explain that to me?"

Eriksen put his hand to his neck and scratched beneath his collar. The idea was probably to look relaxed, but something had definitely thrown the man. Carl thought he knew what.

"I don't understand. It's news to me, I must say," he replied. "I'm shocked. We're still making payments until the end of the year."

In his mind, Carl ran through the six signs that indicated a person was lying under interrogation. Several of them were as clear as day. Eriksen's hands were placed flat on the desk in front of him, as if he didn't dare move them. Suddenly he stared into Carl's eyes without blinking, then swallowed hard a couple of times, his mouth obviously dry. So basically, all that was left were stupefaction and rage, and he'd have the entire set. But Carl didn't want to push him that far because then he would stop talking altogether.

"I'm sorry to have to divulge this information to you like this," Carl said. "But it's important for us that we understand how a project for which your department is responsible can go off the rails like that."

He protested now, more offended than angry. Yet another sign. "I can only say it like it is. The Baka project was Stark's and he was extremely proficient at delegating the work to the recipient countries, which is basically the purpose of our providing aid in the first place. This was a straightforward project of the kind that runs itself as long as the groundwork has been done well enough."

"So you're telling me no one was keeping tabs, is that it?"

"Of course there were periodic checks, but in this case they were more at the local level. Like I said, it wasn't a very big project."

Carl glanced at Gordon. It didn't matter what Lars Bjørn saw in the big dope as long as he kept his damn mouth shut until they were done. He looked hurt, but if a dead leg was enough to silence him, Carl was ready to give him a couple more.

He turned back to his prey, who now sat moistening his lips with the tip of his tongue. Clearly he was more than ready to defend himself. But why?

"How big was the project, then? How much money was earmarked?"

Eriksen raised his eyebrows and shook his head. "I can't remember offhand, but certainly no more than fifty million a year."

Carl recoiled. Fifty million a year! For that sort of money he'd personally plant bananas from here to Novosibirsk. How much police work could get done for an amount like that? How many street cops could get their overtime paid, and more besides? The number of time-off hours in lieu of wages that they'd save was mind-boggling.

"But I can get you the exact figures after the weekend," Eriksen added. "The person now in charge is on vacation."

Carl nodded. "Thanks, we'll get back to that. We've been told as well that the project's coordinator on-site, a certain Louis Fon, disappeared only a few days before Stark. Any thoughts on that?"

He'd better have, thought Carl. Otherwise, something was very wrong indeed.

"Yes," Eriksen said with a nod. "That was quite a strange story we never really got an explanation for. But Africa's like that, I'm afraid. People vanish, and sometimes they turn up again. There are plenty of temptations and dangers, not to mention chance occurrences. Sometimes things go inexplicably awry. We're talking about the world's second largest continent, you realize, and in many ways it's one big shambles."

Carl wasn't buying. If Eriksen had been more specific and tried to elaborate, or even denied ever having heard of the man, he might have come across more believably. But this sort of all-purpose waffle could mean only one of two things. Either the man was hiding something or else he was utterly incompetent at his job, and the latter option Carl refused to believe.

"I see," he said. "Another odd story, and there are apparently plenty more where it came from, I realize that. Nevertheless, I can't help but think of a related coincidence that I find at least as odd, which is that you happened to be in Somolomo the very same day Fon disappeared just across the river. What were you doing there?"

This time Eriksen kept himself together. If he was shocked, he certainly wasn't showing it.

"Yes, that's true, but there's a perfectly simple explanation. I was there to make sure things were running smoothly. The opportunity arose because I was going to southern Cameroon anyway to discuss a couple of other projects, which for various reasons never amounted to anything after they got turned over to the EU. Purification of drinking water, checks on timber extraction, that sort of thing."

"And was everything going according to plan in Dja in your opinion?" Carl asked.

Eriksen shook his head. "No, I did notice the project was proceeding rather slowly and I also tried to get hold of Louis Fon to get an explanation."

Gordon could keep quiet no longer. "So could that be why Stark went down there?"

Carl could have murdered him on the spot, but opted for another dead leg. What the hell was he playing at?

Eriksen nodded, of course. The answer had already been handed to him on a plate. "Yes, Stark flew down there a couple of days later to go through everything in more detail. Unfortunately I didn't have enough time on that trip to do it myself."

Carl took stock. Was René E. Eriksen really the kind of senior civil servant who never did a damn thing and left everything to his subordinates? Who took all the credit when projects succeeded and blamed others when they failed? If he was, then any number of scenarios were open, including ones where William Stark had exploited the situation. Because what it all came down to was that Stark had disappeared immediately following his last visit to the place, and as far as Carl could tell, a hell of a lot of government foreign development aid had disappeared as well, and into the wrong pockets. There was something to suggest that Stark's pockets had been in there somewhere, but that others had also been involved in the circus. People who might have had an interest in making off with the whole bundle themselves.

Carl thrust out his lower lip. Sometimes one was allowed to take a shot in the dark. "I reckon Stark was on the make, siphoning off funds for his own purposes," he said.

Eriksen did not appear to be particularly surprised. His reaction seemed solemn and pensive. "Our books are under constant scrutiny, so I can't imagine anyone not having noticed if that were the case."

"But accountants don't go to Africa and count the number of banana trees, do they?"

"No, of course not. Very rarely, anyway." He allowed himself to smile. In Carl's opinion, however, he didn't have much to smile about.

Fifty million a year. Hell's bells.

"So what it comes down to is that only you and Stark could tell if there were any irregularities down there. Don't you think that gave the two of you a bit too much clout?"

Eriksen fell silent for a long time, staring into thin air, lips pressed thin. His expression was neutral rather than empty, like when a person knows there's absolutely nothing he can do about a situation.

"But that's terrible, if what you're thinking is correct," he answered after a while. "In which case, the responsibility is mine."

"Anyway, we're going to have to ask you to look more deeply into it."

He nodded, his brow knitted in a frown. "Yes, yes, of course. I'll give it my full scrutiny together with the administrative officer I mentioned who's on vacation. I'll call him as soon as he returns on Monday and report back to you that afternoon."

They left Eriksen almost paralyzed on his chair in the midst of his governmental clutter and Carl didn't mind a bit.

Finding the motive behind a person's disappearance was the surest way of uncovering what had actually happened, and at the moment he felt they were getting close.

He walked along immersed in his own thoughts until Gordon interrupted.

"I think I'm rather too old to be pinched on the knee," he said, his mouth puckered with indignation. "Next time we're out on a job together I suggest we act like substantially more mature individuals. I take it you agree." He extended a hand. "Shall we say it's a deal?"

Carl studied the stairs they were approaching. A discreet nudge and a couple of somersaults on the way down could easily cause a small rupture of his neck vertebrae. He was sorely tempted.

He considered the outstretched hand and came to a halt. "Listen, Gordon. Once you've dried yourself behind the ears and taken your exams, get yourself a nice little job as managing clerk somewhere in the sticks where you have to take care of the local housing associations' squabbles about the maintenance of basement storage rooms. By that time you'll probably be able to look back with joy and gratitude on the day Carl Mørck took you out on a job and prevented you from making an utter idiot of yourself, don't you think?"

Gordon let his hand fall to his side. "You're saying I'm childish?" he said. "That's what people say about you, too."

Carl's safety valve was almost ready to blow. One more wrong word and he would explode right in the middle of a government institution.

"Anyway, I've left my scarf in his office," Gordon added. "I'll catch up with you later."

He turned and started walking away. That was precisely the angle Carl preferred to see him from.

Eriksen felt like he'd been slammed against the wall. Mørck had given him a hell of a grilling. How come they knew so much? About Fon's disappearance. About plantations that had never been planted. If they knew that, chances were they knew a lot more besides. At least that was the feeling he'd got when they'd been questioning him.

If it hadn't been for the buffoon Carl Mørck brought with him instead of the Arab, Mørck might suddenly have slipped in a question that caught him napping.

Maybe he'd given himself away already. He couldn't be sure. Even though he'd been careful to control his body language, sometimes this Mørck had looked at him as if he could see right through him. As if he knew the whole story and was only waiting to tell it.

Christ, what a terrible twenty-four hours it had been, but now it was over. A couple of minor matters to sort out and he'd be off. The proceeds from the sale of his shares in Karrebæk Bank had been transferred to his account, so now all he needed was new identity papers. There were people out in Vesterbro who specialized in that sort of thing, people Snap had boasted about. René reckoned this would take a day more, after which he'd go to Teis Snap and demand his rightful share of the Curaçao stocks.

He shoved his glasses onto his forehead and rubbed his eyes. Once he'd seen Snap he needed to make himself scarce. Amsterdam or Berlin, he didn't care, just somewhere a person could change his appearance with a minimum of bother. He could pull it off, as long as they left him alone for a day or two.

There was a knock on the door. The handle turned.

Eriksen's breathing stopped. His subordinates wouldn't just come barging in, so were the investigators back already?

It was the young assistant who stuck his head round the door, so Carl Mørck was most probably right behind him. What had they found out? Had they been talking to his staff? No, now he was being silly. They had nothing on him, nothing at all.

"Sorry, just two more questions," the novice said. "Have you a got a minute?"

Eriksen put his glasses back on. Why had he come on his own? Was it some kind of trick?

"I was wondering about something you said. My father is a highly placed civil servant, too, and he's always said that if there's one place they keep an extra close eye on travel expenditures, it's in public administration. Obviously one is out traveling more in the foreign office than other departments, but I still find it odd that both you and Stark made a trip all the way to Africa, to the same region, independently of each other, and within the space of a few days. That must have been dreadfully expensive. I know the Baka project was Stark's, and that you had other items on your agenda, but why didn't you investigate matters yourself instead of sending Stark? That was my first question. The second is this: What were those other important projects, exactly, the ones you failed to get sorted out down there? Wouldn't Stark have been able to deal with them since he was on his way there anyway? Please don't take it wrong, but weren't those two trips pretty much simultaneous? And finally, are your traveling activities in this department really that uncoordinated? Haven't you got a separate budget ledger for travel expenditures that we could have a look at? If so, we'd like to see it on Monday together with the other things we talked about."

Eriksen had sat quite still during the long bombastic monologue. The lad was a fool, no doubt about it, but his questions were relevant. The two trips he was referring to had indeed taken a lot of explaining to the accountants. It had cost him a reprimand, and even though it had happened long ago, it certainly wouldn't speak in his favor if anyone decided to take a closer look.

Therefore he ignored the fledgling's smug self-satisfaction and smiled back at him. "Naturally we have strict guidelines when it comes to trips abroad, and of course we require detailed résumés of each trip, as well as detailed reports as to their purpose, and in addition we ask which account the trip's expenditure is to be drawn from and why. So yes, of course, you can see it all on Monday."

The guy looked like he'd just made a scoop, which indeed he might have were it not for the fact that the documentation he required would never be forthcoming. And the bird would have flown in the meantime.

He extended a hand to Eriksen and was about to turn and leave when suddenly he raised a finger in the air. "Oops, I'd better not forget it this time," he said, and stooped down to pick a gray scarf off the floor before finally saying good-bye.

Eriksen stared a long time at the closed door before he was convinced there would be no more surprises from that quarter.

There was no doubt whatsoever in his mind.

After this, today was definitively his last day at work.

From the moment he clapped eyes on Gordon as the spindly spire came lolloping along the basement corridor, Carl could tell by his gormlessly gleeful expression that something was seriously amiss.

"See, I got it, Carl," he said with a grin, holding up his scarf. "You do realize it was a trick, yeah?" he added, flopping down on the chair opposite. "You wouldn't let me get a word in, so I needed an excuse to go back."

"Run that by me again." Carl felt his nostrils begin to flare. "You mean to say you went back to question him without me being present?"

"Yeah, I'm sorry if you don't approve, but I shook him up, Carl. I pointed out to him that it was illogical for two people from the same ministry to travel to the same part of the world independently of each other at almost the same time. He may have smiled when I mentioned it, but I'm pretty darn sure I gave the man something to think about. I really believe I made some headway."

At that moment something inside Carl snapped. It wasn't just this twerp and his outrageous meddling, it was downright desperation. A searing sensation in his soul that manifested itself in a snarl as his heart skipped a beat and sweat trickled from his pores.

"Fuck off out of here, you idiot," he yelled, upending his desk and everything on it in the man's direction.

Gordon fell backward against the wall but got to his feet immediately, looking at Carl as if he'd gone insane, before giving him a wide berth and retreating through the door.

"And this time, you dickhead, you keep your fucking mouth shut!" Carl bellowed, as the man vanished.

Carl stared down at his desk that now lay on its side, a deluge of folders and documents strewn across the floor.

Then he felt a jab of pain in the region of his heart that made him gasp for air but in vain. The feeling of suffocation was profound and impossible to suppress. His fingers cramped up, his arms clasped themselves tight around his diaphragm, and his legs trembled as though his body had suddenly been exposed to extreme cold.

"What's going on?" he heard Rose's voice cry out, as he slid off his chair onto the floor, legs splayed.

He sensed her presence, and that she immediately asked him where it hurt. But he couldn't feel a thing as she pulled him over to the wall and sat him up against it.

She put her hand on his shoulder and suddenly he heard himself sobbing profoundly as he felt an increasing undulation in his midriff.

"What's happened, Carl?" she asked him calmly, as she cradled his head.

At first he couldn't reply. Her skin and scent and breathing made him hold his breath. Her nearness, his angst, and all that seemed so inexplicable overwhelmed everything else.

"Do you want me to call for help, Carl?"

He shook his head as his sobs subsided into abrupt, soundless intakes of breath.

"Has this happened to you before?" she asked.

He tried to shake his head, but couldn't.

"Sort of, maybe," he stuttered after a moment, not knowing if it was true.

Then she asked him to listen to his own breathing and close his eyes. "You don't need the world at the moment, Carl," she said gently, drawing him close and holding him tight. "We'll just sit here until you're feeling better. I'm not going anywhere, OK? We're family, whether we like it or not."

He nodded and closed his eyes.

Apart from lingering on the thought of it actually being a woman and not just Rose who was soothing him, he listened to his breathing and shut out the world.

33

For Boy, this was a day filled with considerations about leaving.

The years he had spent in the service of Brage-Schmidt had been rewarding. He had no cause for complaint, but times had changed.

His suitcase lay packed on the bed in his room back at the consulate. Suits had been selected from his walk-in closet, and watches and jewelry neatly placed in his little strongbox. His plane ticket for the flight tomorrow evening was already bought.

He hadn't discussed his decision with Brage-Schmidt for good reason, but this was the way things had to be. It was best to stop while the going was good.

It had been a creative period in his life. While his employer often presented him merely as his private secretary and personal assistant, the reality of the matter was that behind the scenes he had been given free rein to deal with any problems or situations that might arise. This had led to blackmail of overzealous business contacts, false accusations leveled against and among competitors and deals to smuggle gems with a supplier of airline lifejackets. There was also the time five years ago when he recruited Mammy and a couple of her boys to feign a robbery of Karrebæk Bank in order to cover up a fatal liquidity crisis. Not to mention the numerous threats to public officials and insurance providers in nearly a dozen different countries. Yes, during his association with Brage-Schmidt he'd been able to deliver the goods, including murders and kidnappings farmed out to local or global subcontractors.

And now he had to perform one of these tasks himself, for his own sake as well as his employer's. Just this one last time and then he would be gone. That was the plan.

He had followed Mammy's movements all day. She had already deployed decoys—ostensibly disabled individuals in wheelchairs—at strategic locations in the city, ready to pounce on Marco if he should happen by. In Østerbro her crew had beaten up a handful of Ukrainians for refusing to take orders from them, and at every S-train station and some of the busiest bus stops men had been posted, with the promise of a ten-thousand-euro reward if they apprehended the boy.

Earlier in the day they had almost succeeded in bringing him in. It had cost one of Mammy's boy soldiers a twenty-centimeter gash in his hip before they managed to extract him from a rubble chute, and another one now sported an eye so bloodshot that he had to wear sunglasses in order not to attract attention. They had almost caught him, which was good, but insufficient.

This Marco was the fluttering butterfly in South America that could trigger a storm in Japan. The one that could start a domino effect. And Boy no longer wished to be a part of it. He took his precautions out of principle, for Brage-Schmidt had taught him that principles were more important than anything else.

If they captured this boy, everything would be all right. If they didn't, or if he managed to get the police involved, there was no telling what might happen. Zola had assured him that Marco couldn't possibly know anything of significance, but then why had there been police speaking with Eriksen at the ministry today? They had come too close by half, so from now on Boy had his own agenda.

Needless to say, Brage-Schmidt would be no hindrance, but a rebellious Eriksen, or an obstinate Teis Snap in particular, was another matter. Snap was the only one with a hotline directly to Boy, and if it wasn't disconnected it could end up like the cannula delivering a lethal drug into the veins of a condemned man.

The fact of the matter was that the attempt on Eriksen's life had been a spectacular failure, so consequently the man was now doubtless clutching his Danish share certificates tightly to his chest, not letting them out of his sight for an instant. A while ago Boy had called Eriksen's home number pretending to be a colleague and had learned from the man's wife that the little worm had not come home from work and she had no idea where he was.

He assumed, therefore, that Eriksen was already on the run. It was just as well.

Zola wasn't much of a problem either. He didn't have Boy's number because the SIM card was changed after every call between them. They had never met in person, and it was Boy who phoned him, never the other way round. Zola was a conceited, arrogant fool, hurtling toward the abyss like a lemming. It was only a question of when and where he would finally go over the edge.

Teis Snap, on the other hand, was another matter entirely. An amorphous type who could break down at any time, which was unfortunate given that the man had to complete an overview of the facets of their operation and would be able to point a finger in any number of directions if things went wrong, which for him they already had. He had gambled with his bank's assets. He had miscalculated when they selected their stooge in the ministry. Snap was the man Eriksen threatened because he was the easiest. Moreover, at this moment he was in possession of the gold Boy had been digging for, namely the unregistered stocks even a half-wit could hardly fail to turn into double-digit millions. Euros, at that.

And Boy was determined to take all of it with him.

The long gravel track leading up to Teis Snap's house near Karrebæksminde was lined by an avenue of trees. This remote location was ideal for those who craved space, horses, and affordable land, allowing the leeway for personal extravagance in the form of lavish buildings and a fleet of cars.

Boy had never been there before yet quickly realized that in order not to draw attention to himself he would need to park behind the outbuildings, where his car couldn't be seen from the main house.

He got out of the car and listened. If there were dogs, he would deal with them first. He hated the erratic nature that dogs in the countryside often displayed. In fact, he hated all dogs, apart from the one he himself had owned.

There were four buildings in all. White, well-renovated stables and a main house that reeked of a man who let his wife make the decisions. He had expected the property to be grandiose and sterile, but instead he found himself looking at black wagon wheels decorating the end wall and trellises resplendent with purple clematis.

Boy scanned the courtyard in front of the house. Besides a black 4x4 and the ubiquitous white Mini Cooper convertible, there wasn't much to meet the eye, but it was enough.

He frowned, pausing for a moment with his finger poised at the brass doorbell, considering what he would do if it turned out there were guests in the house.

Then he pressed the bell and waited.

Incredibly enough, Snap was still married to his first wife, Lisa. Brage-Schmidt's theory was that the age difference was what kept them together, but judging by her photos, looks might have had something to do with it, too.

Boy heard her inside the house, but the door remained closed. Most probably she was peering at his CCTV image on a screen in the hall. The camera was pointed straight at him.

"I am Brage-Schmidt's private secretary," he announced, looking into the lens.

The possibilities were several, providing she heard what he said. Most likely she wouldn't let him in, in which case he would have to go round the back of the house and smash a window. He would gain entry one way or another.

"I see. Is my husband expecting you?" came a voice from a speaker he couldn't locate.

"Yes. Hasn't he come home yet?" Her silence told him she was alone. "I can come back," he went on. "Although we'd agreed a time. Actually, I'm ten minutes late, so perhaps he's on his way as we speak. I can wait out here, the weather's nice, and I've all these lovely flowers to admire."

He stood quite still for a moment, smiling benignly, his gloved hands folded in front of the bottom button of his jacket, like an undertaker who stands in the background as the bereaved pay their final respects. It signaled humility and unobtrusiveness, the kind of strategy one learned only from the best of teachers.

Twenty seconds passed before she opened the door and barely had time to introduce herself before he grabbed her head, jerked it to the side, and broke her neck. Soundlessly and without pain, so swiftly that she could hardly have registered what was happening.

He carried her body upstairs to the bedroom, propping her up at an angle with pillows on the bed, then turned her face to the side and switched on the television.

He took his time checking the house. Rifling discreetly through people's things was a skill long since acquired. Items could be opened or inspected in many ways using the proper fingertip touch. It took half an hour to go through the place without finding what he was looking for. The scenario was more complicated now, though not unexpected.

After deleting all footage from the security camera at the front door, he discovered the wife's turned-on laptop stationed on a high-gloss black dining table in the spacious room that covered more than half of the house's ground level. The online auction on the screen revealed her interest in flowers was not limited to those found in nature. It also included paintings, a fact amply confirmed by the still lifes with flowers that decorated many of the walls.

It took him about five minutes to compose Snap's account of why he had murdered his wife and subsequently committed suicide. It was easy: his criminal activities had gotten to the point where he could no longer cope. Now René E. Eriksen, head of office at the Ministry of Foreign Affairs, would have to shoulder the full responsibility for the fraud, the killing of William Stark, everything.

Boy printed out the document, considering whether to sign it but opting instead to wait, folding the paper over the middle.

Then he went upstairs to the bedroom; sat himself in a floral patterned high-back wing armchair at the dresser with all its little bottles of perfume, scented notepaper, and envelopes that lay ready to accommodate the lady of the house's effusions; opened the sash windows wide; and gazed far out across the rain-drenched fields, waiting.

———

The halogen beam of the Mercedes's headlights cut through the darkness, announcing Snap's arrival almost a full minute before the car rolled up in front of the house.

Boy listened to the rummaging downstairs: shoes flipped off in the hall, briefcase dumped on the floor, a bit of food prepared in the kitchen, and then finally the ascent up the stairs.

Snap entered the bedroom with a plate in one hand and a glass in the other, closing the door behind him with his knee.

"How's your day been, darling?" he said, placing his supper on the bedside table, then turned to the chair next to the bed and began to undress. "Mine wasn't exactly sublime. I told Brage-Schmidt on the phone about René's crazy behavior this morning, so now he's in for it." He laughed as he turned to look at her in his underpants, halfway into his pajama top. "What are you watching? Have you fallen into a trance?"

He smiled and gazed at her, head tilted slightly to the side in puzzlement over her lack of interest in his arrival.

"Are you angry? I said I wouldn't be back until late. And why have you got the windows wide-open, it's freezing in here," he said, going round to the other side of the bed. He had just buttoned his pajamas when his eyes met Boy's.

The shock sent him recoiling backward. Boy had never seen anyone so frightened.

"Mind you don't fall," Boy said. Snap sat down heavily at the foot of the bed, his mouth agape, lips quivering as his breathing went haywire.

"Who are you?" he stammered, then turned to look at his wife.

Another jolt shook his entire body.

A minute or two later, when the human wreck finally backed away from his wife's corpse, he tried to look the black man in the eyes.

"Are you one of Brage-Schmidt's boy soldiers? How come you speak Danish?" And when Boy didn't answer, Snap began to tremble. "Who sent you? Not Brage-Schmidt, he'd never do a thing like that, why should he? He knows I can keep my mouth shut."

Boy's lips curled in a faint smile. Snap apparently found it provoking.

"What the hell are you smiling for? You can just tell me what you want. A million? Ten million? I can give you ten."

Boy shook his head. "I only want your signature, then I'll leave."

Snap was bewildered. His entire being protested against that utterance. His arms fluttered and his head bobbed up and down.

A signature? His astonishment shone like a neon sign. The man had just killed his wife, and now all he wanted was a signature?

Boy produced his folded sheet of paper and placed it on the dresser in front of Teis Snap, the blank half facing up.

"Just sign here." He pointed to the empty white of the paper.

"What's on the other side? I won't sign until I've seen it."

Boy stood up calmly and adjusted his jacket. "Sign here or else you end up like your wife. I'll count to ten. One, two, three, four"—he produced a ballpoint pen from his inside pocket and handed it to Snap— "five, six, seven . . ."

Snap took the pen.

"What did you do to her?" he stuttered, on the verge of breaking down in tears.

"Sign," Boy replied, indicating the empty sheet of paper. And Snap signed. His hand trembled as he drew the pen unsteadily across the page, exactly as if he were signing his own suicide note.

"Thank you," said Boy. "And now I want you to give me the Curaçao stocks. Then I'll leave."

"You said—"

"Give me the stocks. I know Lisa brought the certificates home with her in her suitcase. And now the suitcase is empty."

"How do you know that? Brage-Schmidt is the only person who knew. Did he tell you? Is he behind this, the bastard?"

"Give me the shares and continue to live. Your wife broke her neck. She fell down the stairs. If that's what you tell the police, they'll believe you."

Snap began to weep uncontrollably. It was not a good sign. People breaking down in situations like this meant you never knew if they were capable of making a rational decision. Right now, acting rationally meant fighting for one's life.

"Give me the certificates. Where are they? I've been through the whole house. Is there a hidden safe somewhere?"

Snap shook his head. "What makes you think I can tell you where Lisa put them? How am I supposed to know?"

"Because if you don't tell me right now, you will suffer. And believe me, I know how."

He took a deep breath. "And my guarantee? How do I know you won't . . ." And then he began to sob again.

"Because you know the power of money better than most. That's how."

Snap lifted his head and quickly wiped the tears away with the back of his hand. His professional persona had been challenged. Of course he knew the power of money. And just now the two of them were in the midst of negotiating.

"I want to speak to Brage-Schmidt," he said.

Boy pulled his mobile from his pocket and pressed the number. "I'll put the call through as soon as you tell me where the shares are. A little give and take, yes? He's waiting for me to phone."

Snap was livid now. The thought of having been stabbed in the back by his associate made him clench his fists until his knuckles showed white. For a moment it looked like he was about to lunge at the intruder, but that was fine with Boy. Ten broken fingers would probably make the man more cooperative.

"Where are the shares?" he asked again.

Snap jabbed a finger toward the dresser. "They've been right next to you the whole time, you son of a bitch."

Boy drew the dresser's floral curtain aside and exposed a drawer. He pulled it open, and there lay the share certificates, neatly bound together with a piece of wool.

At the same moment, Snap threw himself at Boy with a scream, fists pummeling.

It was the last thing he did.

When Boy pulled in to his usual parking space he sat for a while in the car, staring at the raindrops that shimmered as they dispersed on the windshield. These strangely gentle Danish spring showers were some-thing he would think back on with sadness when the black rain clouds opened up in a downpour on the edge of the Rwenzori Mountains where he intended to settle.

Now there were but hours until he was on his way. The thought filled him with satisfaction. He'd got what he had come to Karrebæksminde for. The suicide note lay on the dresser and the shares were in the briefcase at his side. It was a perfect allocation.

He smiled as he picked up the briefcase and climbed out of the car, slamming the door behind him, then entered Brage-Schmidt's residence by the back door as usual.

Making sure as always not to be seen.

34

The first thing Rose did when she eventually turned up around mid-morning was to slap a parking ticket down on Carl's desk.

"Ha-ha," Assad laughed. "How can a person get a parking ticket when they don't have a car, then? This is something only you could do, Rose."

She gave a shrug.

"I found it in my bag about an hour ago when I was looking for my bus pass. I've no idea how it got there or how long I've had it."

Carl hesitated before speaking. There was no getting around the fact that yesterday's meltdown had done something to their relationship that was hard to just ignore.

"About yesterday, Rose . . . I'd like to say thanks."

Total silence filled the room. It wasn't that she appeared moved, more like she found that sort of comment wholly out of place at work.

"OK," she said, and ran her hand through her hair a couple of times. It was disheveled enough already for Carl's taste. "So you're feeling better now, are you?"

"Yes, much better, thanks."

And that was that. Rose was hardly the sentimental type. If she were ever to succumb to heartfelt emotion, it certainly wouldn't be other people's.

Carl nodded. Right, then. The intimacy was over, the workday had begun.

"Two things," she said. "I've been round the shops in the streets surrounding Trianglen and showed people the photo of Marco. No luck. A couple of slight reactions, maybe, but nothing for me to go on. That's all

I can say, really. I got some fresh air and a pair of sore feet, though, so thanks a bundle."

"What's the parking ticket got to do with it?" Carl asked.

"Nothing. That was the next thing. Have a good look," she said, pointing her finger at it. "Block letters. See?"

Both Carl and Assad focused on the slip of paper. Sure enough, someone had written in block letters around the edge.

"I'll be damned," exclaimed Carl when he read the message: ZOLA IS A THIEF. HIS PEOPLE STASH STOLEN GOODS IN LOCKERS AT BLACK DIAMOND. THEY COME OFTEN AND EMPTY THEM ABOUT 4. THE CLAN MEET UP EVERY DAY AT TIVOLI CASTLE AT 5. MARCO

Assad rolled his eyes. "It would be very nice to have this boy's fingers when one has to scratch one's back," he said. "They can reach everywhere."

It was true. The boy was like a shadow in the shade.

"Do we still believe Zola's story about the lad having killed a man?" asked Carl.

Assad lowered his head and peered at him from beneath his bushy eyebrows. What more was there to say?

"I don't either, really," said Rose. "But we can't ignore the fact that a couple of years ago he was at the age just before puberty when the majority of pedophiles are most interested. The boy might have been forced into it, you never know. It might even have been a relationship Zola got him into."

"I'll ask again, Rose. Do you think this boy, who's putting himself at great risk to get in touch with us, could have killed a full-grown man, buried him, dug him up again, and then tried to put the blame on his own extended family?"

Rose shook her head. "Of course not, but one has to consider all the possibilities, right?"

"Why doesn't he just come and see us? I think you already hinted at a possible answer, Assad. You said it was most likely because he had no firm affiliation with Denmark and didn't have a national identity card."

The pair of bushy eyebrows dropped and two dark brown eyes darted a couple of times to the side. Carl didn't get it.

"It was Rose," Assad mimed, out of the corner of his mouth.

Carl turned his head. "OK, my prompter here tells me it was you who said it, Rose."

"Carl," said Assad. "Look at that writing. Does it look like the writing of someone who is fifteen?"

"No, it doesn't," Rose intervened. "It's as childish as yours, Assad."

"Indeed, my point exactly! Very childish handwriting, just like mine."

What kind of a thing was that to be so delighted about?

"So now we know nearly all of it, do we not?" Assad concluded.

Carl wrinkled his nose. "Nearly all of what?"

"Well, he had no identity card, so we believe he never had one at all. Therefore we also believe he is perhaps not a Dane, nor does he look like one. Unlike myself."

A grunt emanated from deep inside Assad's abdominal region. "Ha-ha. A nice nut-brown color, and curly black hair, as opposed to me, yes? The writing shows he is not very old, and yet his Danish is almost perfect. How can this be, then? It is because he has been in the country for quite some time, I think. But he is not a Danish citizen, and neither is anybody else in Zola's household, as far as I've been informed. So the boy is here illegally. He and the others from Zola's clan are not just here now and then to do business. They are here permanently and must therefore be considered to be illegal immigrants. This is why I think the boy will not speak to us."

Rose nodded. "He's afraid of us, Carl. And now we've got the entire police force looking for him."

They didn't have to wait long in the cafeteria of the new Royal Library, dubbed the Black Diamond, and Assad had to leave his sandwich half-eaten, his eyes doleful with disappointment.

The guy came ambling in with a shopping bag in his hand, oblivious to the literary merits of the location as he steered directly toward the far bank of lockers by the restrooms. Unlike Marco, there was an unhealthy look about him. He was older and rather more pallid, oddly well-dressed in a black suit and white shirt. Not exactly the kind of getup you'd expect from a person who made his living from street crime.

"Do you mind if we have a look in your bag?" asked Carl, holding out his badge.

It took the guy a fraction of a second to realize his predicament and make a dash for the exit where Assad stood, so his astonishment was indescribable when his escape was suddenly blocked by a flat hand against his chest that sent him backward, straight on his ass.

"Where's all this from?" Carl inquired a couple of minutes later, turning round in the front seat of the car and emptying the shopping bag's contents of mobile phones, watches, and wallets into the lap of their thief, who sat in the back with Assad.

The guy shrugged. "Don't understand," he said in English.

"OK, Carl, he doesn't speak Danish, so this might be too difficult," Assad said. "Let's drive him out to the marshes and kill him like the two from yesterday. What are you doing tonight, anyway, Carl? Any good parties on so we can then let our hair down?"

Carl gawped at him, but it was nothing compared to the look in the eyes of the man in the backseat.

"Hey, you know what?" Assad added. "I actually think two thousand kroner is OK for offing this idiot. I hear the Anatomical Institute is short of bodies at the moment."

With an imagination like that, he ought to have been a crime writer.

"I want to talk to lawyer," came the response in fractured Danish.

Assad smiled. "I suggest you start talking instead. Don't worry, we'll get you into a prison without too many skinheads."

His despair was hard to conceal, and his demeanor had hardly improved by the time the police van turned up half an hour later to take him away.

An hour later they were in luck again.

This time the guy who came in through the revolving doors was rather more exotic looking and seemed in better physical shape. He, too, was clad in a black suit, but his eyes were so alert that they quickly caught Carl and Assad's attention.

"If he goes over to the lockers, we close in from both sides," Carl whispered.

———

The guy refused to talk, and if it weren't for the pair of ladies' watches in his pocket, they'd have had to let him go.

Now he sat glowering at them in the interview room on the second floor of police HQ.

"We've got your mate Samuel sitting next door," Carl said. "Plus we've got officers posted at the Black Diamond so we can nab you one by one. If no one else shows, we'll pick up the rest of you at Rådhuspladsen later this afternoon."

The guy shifted slightly in his chair and kept silent. It looked like nothing bothered him: not the sterile environment or the police who were questioning him, or the handcuffs on his wrists. He was the kind of lad who wouldn't need much more on-the-job training before he was truly a menace to society. The prisons were full of them, but unfortunately there were lots more on the loose than behind bars.

Carl drew Assad aside. "We'll have to wait and see what the magistrates' court says in the morning, but I reckon we'll have a few more in by the end of the day who might be more cooperative."

"I will stay behind here for a little while, Carl," said Assad. "Maybe I can soften him up."

Carl squinted at him. He didn't doubt Assad's abilities in that area. Unfortunately.

"Listen, Assad. You know the drill. Easy does it, all right?"

"OK, Carl, but I don't have a drill."

"Never mind, Assad. It's a figure of speech."

There was a knock on the door. Carl opened it.

It was Gordon, for Chrissake.

"Have you finished yet?" he inquired. "We've got another one waiting."

Did he say "we"?

Responsiveness to the opinions of others was not a concept often applied in the office of Lars Bjørn, as Carl had long since noted.

"Even if you consider this Marco to be a key witness in the case of William Stark's disappearance," Bjørn said, "you can't just set the entire manhunt apparatus in motion, Carl. I'll be docking Department Q's budget three hundred thousand kroner in man-hours for this if you do. Maybe it'll teach you to run your dispositions by your superiors in future. So the search for the boy is off, as of now."

Carl bit his upper lip. "OK, but considering how close we are to tying up the case, I regard that as a totally imbecilic decision. Moreover, if you really want your hands on my budget, maybe you could start by instantly giving Gordon his marching orders. I don't know if three hundred grand's enough, but if it isn't you can take the rest out of the coffee tin."

Bjørn was completely unfazed and just smiled at him.

"Sorry, Carl. I'm not taking Gordon off your hands. He may have been a bit clumsy interviewing that official over at the foreign office, but he's been forgiven."

"Forgiven?"

"Yes. You hadn't briefed him properly beforehand, he told me."

Carl felt an extra surge of blood in his arteries, and his cheeks began to glow. "What the fuck are you on about, man? You're sitting across from an experienced investigator and telling him a skinny infant like Gordon has to be briefed in a case he's got nothing at all to do with? You do realize we're close to getting a really good handle on what happened to William Stark, and that it may well turn out to be a murder, or something just as bad? And now Gordon, the fucking idiot, goes off on his own, questioning one of our prime suspects and letting the bloke know we're onto him and that we're ready to start digging in his doings until we reach the bottom. For Christ's sake, Bjørn!"

"You already have."

"Have what?"

"Reached the bottom. If you can't manage a trainee on the job, I'd say you're not as fantastic as you think you are."

Carl got to his feet. In the old days this office was the place where he could summon energy to go on with his work. Now the only thing he got out of being there was a compelling urge to see how long it would take an acting homicide chief to fall from a third-floor window to the pavement below. The fucking idiot!

He heard Bjørn shout at him to stop as he slammed the door behind him and, seething with anger, strode past Ms. Sørensen, who was applauding languidly behind the counter. He even forgot to flirt with Lis.

Not surprisingly he found Gordon drooling in Rose's doorway.

"My office. Now!" he barked at the lad, underlining the order with a rotating index finger pointing the way.

The cheeky sod had the audacity to ask what he wanted, but Carl let him roast a while, tidying the folders on his desk into a pile in the corner, throwing his feet up, and lighting a cigarette whose smoke he slowly inhaled deep into his lungs.

"From now on you've got two options, son," he said eventually. "Either you pack your bags and fuck off back to Legoland, or else you start making yourself useful. What'll it be?"

"I'd say I already *have* made myself—"

Carl pounded his desk. "What'll it be?"

"The latter, I think."

"You think?"

"Yes, I do."

The pose that Mussolini struck when he wanted to impress the crowds—chin thrust up, chest and lower lip thrust out, clenched fist at his side—was the same one Carl used now. "Say you're sorry!" he commanded.

"Dumbfounded" was about the best word to describe the expression that appeared on Gordon's face. But he apologized nevertheless.

"Right, now you've officially begun your apprenticeship at Department Q. But before we get started, here's your Cub Scouts' test. And if you don't answer properly, I'll kick you out anyway. I want you to tell me the nature of your relationship with Lars Bjørn."

Gordon shook his head and shrugged. "It's nothing. He's my dad's best friend, that's all."

"I see. That would explain a lot. Public school chums, I shouldn't wonder. And let me guess, you went to the same school as well, yeah?"

He nodded.

"Right. So Bjørn wants to do your dad a favor and takes you on as his private spy so he can keep tabs on me. He's a bit of a control freak, in case you didn't know. Typical of beanpoles and second-raters."

Here the kid's defiance bubbled to the surface in spite of himself. "You don't know what you're talking about, apparently. Bjørn's tougher than anyone here."

Carl thrust his head back. What the hell was that?

"Are we talking about the same man? The teacher's pet with the perfect creases in his slacks? What could possibly be 'tough' about him? Go on, enlighten me."

"Ask him to roll up his sleeves. You've never seen scars like that in your life. Could you withstand a month of constant torture, I wonder? Well, Lars Bjørn could, and I could tell you a lot more besides."

"I'm all ears."

Gordon hesitated, but in his youthful arrogance he was unable to resist temptation.

"You won't know what BCCF stands for, obviously."

"Can't say I do," Carl replied, hands held up in submission. "But let me hazard a guess. Bjørn's Comical Ca-ca Face, perhaps?"

"You haven't a clue. What it stands for is Baghdad Central Confinement Facility, or what Saddam Hussein called Abu Ghraib prison."

"OK, and now you're going to say Bjørn worked there, right?"

"Worked? No."

What did he think this was, Trivial Pursuit? "Go on, then," Carl said, sharpening the tone. "What's Bjørn got to do with Abu Ghraib?"

"What do you think? Why do you suppose I told you to get him to roll up his sleeves?"

Carl stared at the floor, drumming his fingers on the desk. He didn't like what he was hearing now. He didn't like it one bit.

"What else, Gordon?"

He looked up at the lad and saw to his surprise that his face had turned red.

"I can see you've already told me more than Bjørn would approve of, am I right?"

He nodded.

"And you're not even supposed to know that much about him, are you? It's something you heard the folks talking about at home, isn't it?"

He nodded again.

"OK, Gordon. I think we're back on track. I've got enough on you now to bounce you out of HQ on your ass. Bjørn's been protecting you so far, but my guess is he won't be much longer if I go upstairs and ask him to roll up his sleeves at your request. Am I right?"

"Yes," he squeaked.

"So from now on, you only tell Bjørn things about Department Q that I want you to tell him. Are you with me?"

"Yes."

"Right, it's a deal."

Carl got up, thrust out his hand and gave Gordon's a squeeze that made his eyelashes do a river dance.

"Now, get yourself upstairs to Bjørn and tell him you've discovered we're dead close to clearing up a very interesting case, and that this Carl Mørck bloke is simply the most brilliant thing since sliced bread."

Gordon's mouth twisted with uncertainty. "Do you really mean it?"

"Yes, I do. Be sure to remember the word, 'brilliant.' And after that, you phone René E. Eriksen at the foreign office and ask him to stay behind after work. We want another word with him."

"Why? We're seeing him on Monday anyway."

"Because I get the clear impression the man knows a hell of a lot more than he's telling us, and that right now he's probably putting a story together about why those official trips he and Stark made within days of each other couldn't just as well have been combined into one."

"Do you know if forensics are turning anything up in that grave outside Kregme?" he asked Tomas Laursen.

Laursen wiped his hands in his chef's apron an extra time for good measure. It was a sad sight to see the man who was once the force's best forensic technician with remoulade remains all down his front.

"Yes, they're finding a bit. Hair, skin, clothing fibers. A couple of fingernails."

"Loads of DNA, then?"

Laursen nodded. "In a couple of days you should know if it matches what they've collected from William Stark's home address."

"It will. I don't need their results. Just knowing there was a human corpse in that grave is enough for me. I'm absolutely certain it's our man."

Laursen nodded. "Pity the body isn't there anymore. Any idea where it might be?"

"No, and my feeling is we're not going to find out either. You don't bury a body and dig it up again just to put it somewhere else where it can be found. It's been chopped into bits and chucked into very deep water, if you ask me."

"You're probably right. It's been seen before, anyway."

He wiped his hands again and began kneading the lump of dough lying in front of him. New success story: fresh-baked bread first thing in the morning had become all the rage at police HQ. The man was doing his utmost for the cafeteria's survival.

"One more thing, Tomas. I've learned a few things about Bjørn's time in Iraq, and I've a feeling you can pitch in with more. Am I right?"

Laursen paused with a frown. "I think you'd better ask him yourself, Carl. It's none of my business."

"So you do know something."

"You can interpret it as you wish."

"He was put in prison. Do you know what for, and when?"

"I'm not the one to ask about it, Carl."

"Can't you just tell me when it was? Was it right before Saddam Hussein was brought down?"

He tipped his head from side to side.

"A bit before, then?"

No reply.

"A year?"

Laursen smacked his clump of dough onto the counter. "Lay off, will you, Carl? It's not worth our falling out over."

Carl nodded and left the man in peace, but inside him there was anything but.

Assad was in the process of questioning a man downstairs.

Department Q's little charmer, Assad, an untrained policeman whose employment at police headquarters seemed more and more to be thanks to the good graces of Lars Bjørn. A man who was now Carl's acting superior and who had previously been imprisoned in a notorious Iraqi jail under the rule of Saddam.

Carl stopped halfway down the stairs.

For God's sake, Assad, he thought. Who are you, anyway?

He found him standing outside the interview room with a big smile on his face.

"What are you doing here, Assad?" he asked.

"I'm taking a break. They should not have to look at one all the time, should they? They must have the chance to think things over. It helps get them talking, you know? In the end they blurt it out, log, stick, and barrel."

"Lock, stock, and barrel, Assad. Who have you got in there?"

"Romeo. The one with the burn on his face who then would not say his name."

"But you got it out of him?"

"Yes, I was a bit persistent."

Carl tipped his head to the side. "How so?"

"Come inside and I will show you."

The guy was sitting on his chair. Without handcuffs, with no trace of anger, and without the protective loathing of officialdom one otherwise always encountered. What remained was a nice young man in a suit.

"Say hello to Carl Mørck, Romeo," Assad instructed.

He lifted his head. "Hello."

Carl nodded.

"Tell Inspector Mørck what you told me before, Romeo."

"What part of it?" came the reply, in a heavy accent.

"The part about Zola and Marco."

"I don't know why, but Zola wants Marco killed. We're all looking for him, and not just us. He's got other people helping him, too. Estonians, Lithuanians, Belarusians, Ukrainians, Africans. We're all looking."

"And why do you tell me this, Romeo?"

The man who looked up at Assad was exhausted. Why wasn't Assad?

"Because you promised me that then I can stay in Denmark."

Assad looked at Carl with a gleam of triumph in his eyes. Simple as that, his expression seemed to say.

"You can't just promise him that, Assad," said Carl, once they were back outside. "Tomorrow he's going to be remanded in custody, maybe even put into isolation, if he really knows as much as he was just jabbering on about. And what happens when he's no longer in isolation? How are you going to protect him and keep your promise then?"

Assad shrugged. It wasn't his problem, Carl could see. A pretty hard-boiled attitude for his taste.

"I asked him if he knew William Stark, and he did not. Then I asked him if Marco was abused sexually in Zola's house, which he denied most adamantly. This, at least, they were not subjected to."

Carl nodded. It was all useful info.

The means justified the ends, as people usually said while washing their hands.

35

Never had Marco felt the cold as much as he did that night.

He had clung to the side of the sightseeing boat when it put in at Holmen's Church and Nyhavn, but hadn't dared let go as long as he was still within the city center where Zola's people were stationed. For that reason he had allowed himself to be drawn through the icy water across the city's inner harbor, on through the canal past the Opera House, and didn't release his grip until when the boat passed the Little Mermaid. There he clambered ashore, so wet and exhausted that a couple of the day's final tourists tried to grab him, yelling that someone should call an ambulance, while the rest blitzed him with rapid-fire digital cameras as if he were some mythical marine creature. The Little Mermaid herself paled in comparison.

"Go away!" Marco cried, shoving them aside and limping off along the concourse, then on through the Frihavn harbor toward the Svanemølle marina.

This time, finding shelter among the moored boats wasn't so easy. Another warm May weekend had brought out the sailing fans in force, and a great many watching eyes followed the pathetic, shivering boy as he made his way along the jetties in the twilight. Welcome, he certainly was not.

He was still wet when he woke up inside the little covered motorboat, but a warm breeze coupled with bright sunshine was sufficient to coax him forth.

He squinted up at the sun and figured it was still early enough for him to get to Kaj and Eivind's apartment before they went off to work.

The last twenty-four hours had shaken him up. The two African boys had been so close. If he shut his eyes he could still clearly see the one with the knife in front of him, the other with his yellow-white eyes staring at him under the water.

Now all he wanted was to get away. Away from Copenhagen, away from Denmark. He dare not stay here any longer. He'd take the train to Sweden and try to begin afresh. A country so sparsely populated and so expansive that from north to south was the same distance as from Copenhagen to Rome had to be a place in which it was possible to disappear. He'd often heard the Swedish language on the streets and realized it wasn't so different from Danish. That, too, he would learn.

The way things had developed the last twenty-four hours, taking revenge on Zola meant less to him now. All he wanted was to survive.

By the time he got to Kaj and Eivind's flat, he was dry and utterly determined not to leave the place until his money was in his hand. This time, he wasn't about to let them stop him.

He knocked on the door a couple of times before Eivind came and opened it. He was a changed man, a pale, unshaven shadow of himself, though fortunately not hostile like last time. In fact, his face seemed to light up when he saw who it was.

"Marco, my goodness," he exclaimed. "Where have you been, my boy? Kaj and I have been worried sick. Look at the state of you, you look dreadful. Come in, I'll find you some clean clothes."

Marco felt his body relax a bit. His lips began to quiver. Being here felt so nice, and what a relief it was to hear kind words and to see Eivind smile.

"Guess what, Kaj?" Eivind shouted. "Marco's come back, can you believe our luck?"

Then he heard the sound of a key being turned in the lock behind him.

Instinctively he wheeled round to see Eivind with the key in his hand and a quite different, threatening look in his eye, his body bent forward as though he were about to charge at him.

Marco turned immediately to make a dash for the kitchen, but was stopped in his tracks by a blow to the head that sent him to the floor in a heap.

"Hold him down, Eivind," Kaj commanded, getting down on his knees, pulling Marco's arms toward him and winding something tightly around his wrists.

Marco tried to focus, but inside his head a blitzkrieg of light all but filtered out his surroundings, making them appear blurred and distorted.

Reflexively he tried in vain to draw his arms in toward his body and twist round, only to hear a rush in his ear as a flurry of blows rained down on him.

"Ow!" he cried, and then began sobbing. "Why are you doing this? I haven't done anything. I'll go again, don't worry, I just wanted to fetch . . ." But the pummeling continued.

Now he felt Eivind's bony knee digging into his rib cage, making it almost impossible to breathe.

"OK, we've got him," came the sound of Eivind's voice above him. "Come straightaway, and hurry."

Marco saw the two men clearly now. Eivind with the mobile in his hand, straddling his midriff, and Kaj crouching in front of his head with a tight grip on his lower arms. Kaj didn't look well. His face was swollen and battered, with dark bruises fanning out over the delicate skin of his neck.

Marco lay still and felt the tears running down his cheeks as he looked into Eivind's desperate eyes. Eivind, of whom he had been so fond.

He, too, had abandoned him.

Perhaps it was the tears, or perhaps the fact that Marco seemed so small and helpless, lying beneath the two men. All of a sudden it was as if Eivind saw him for who he was: their boy, whom they had taught to write and speak better Danish and play cards, and to believe that he had a future ahead of him like everyone else.

As this dawned on him, Eivind's tired features transformed from furrows of anger and frustration to searching eyes and quivering lips. Then, finally, tears burst forth to follow their path through the lines of his aging face.

"I don't know what you've done to them, Marco," he stammered between sobs. "But if you don't vanish from our lives for good, they'll come back again, and we'll never be able to cope with it. That's why we have to hand you over to them. I hope to heaven they do you no harm."

Kaj showed less compassion. "I hope they do to you what they did to me. Do you understand, Marco? They've destroyed our lives. We're too frightened to even go to work anymore and it's all your fault."

Marco shook his head. They were mistaken. That wasn't how it was. It wasn't like that at all.

He squeezed his eyes shut and wriggled his body slightly so Eivind could tell he would remain still if only he wouldn't press his knee so hard against his chest.

He knew that in five minutes they would be here because they were all over the neighborhood. Slavs, Balts, Africans, Zola's people, it didn't matter which of the gangs came, the result would be the same. Zola had demonstrated with the utmost clarity to what lengths he was prepared to go, and the people working for him certainly had as well.

He turned his head to the side as slowly as he could, his eyes scanning the room for possibilities. They were few.

On the wall above him was a little shelf with a lamp on it, a pair of leather gloves and an oval-shaped bowl containing a few coins and the keys to the storage room in the basement. He knew this shelf well. The cord of the lamp ran up the wall adjacent to his knee, and by his feet were galoshes and the slippers Marco had always worn indoors. Nothing of use to him here.

Now he could tell how Eivind's position above his body was growing uncomfortable for him because he kept shifting his weight, turning his knees outward until his lower legs were almost resting flat on the floor.

Marco lay quiet as a mouse. Any moment now, Eivind would try to adjust his position once more and then he needed to be ready, for he would have no other chances.

He breathed deeper, and deeper still, tensing his buttocks and abdomen slowly so Eivind wouldn't notice, and at the same time he cautiously drew his arms inward, prompting Kaj to tighten his grip. Everything depended on Kaj not letting go.

At the same moment the toes of Eivind's shoes made contact with the floor, Marco thrust his hips upward with all his might and wrenched his arms to his sides. The result was enormous, as was the sound of the two men's heads colliding above him.

Eivind slumped to the side, toward the shelf, dislodging its contents onto the floor, while Kaj sank backward, his legs buckled beneath him. Both howled with pain, but their wailing did nothing to stop Marco as he kicked Eivind hard in the shoulder, sending him sliding against the baseboard.

Now he was free and leaped to his feet.

Kaj reached out to grab his leg, but Marco kicked his arm back against the wall.

Then he heard a car screech to a halt outside. By the time its door slammed shut he was already in the kitchen. Here, with his heart pounding in his chest, he realized the door to the back stairs was locked and the key wasn't sitting in the keyhole. So he grabbed a kitchen knife, climbed onto the counter, opened the window onto the backyard, and jumped.

He heard the sound of fists hammering against the front door and Kaj and Eivind's pitiful attempts to get to their feet and open up.

It was difficult to climb onto the roof of the bike shed with his hands tied and also hold on to the knife. Only when he had crossed through two more backyards and had slipped into the labyrinth of side streets did he dare to stop and sever the bond around his wrists.

He made it precisely twenty meters down the street before he saw the Balts at the other end. They hadn't seen him yet, but it was only a matter of seconds.

So he ducked into the nearest stairwell where he stood with his back pressed up against the blue-painted door of a massage parlor and kicked at it with his heel.

"Open up, open up, open up," he repeated silently, in time with each kick.

Now he could sense someone running toward the place where he stood as cries erupted at the other end of the street.

"Open up, please, open up."

Then he heard a sound behind the door.

"Who is it?" a voice asked, in heavily accented Danish.

"Help me. I'm only a boy and there are people after me," he whispered.

A moment passed as the thudding feet against pavement flagstones grew ever louder. And then the door opened, so suddenly that he fell backward into the room.

"Close the door, close the door," he pleaded, lying on his back and looking straight into the sleepy face of an Asian girl without makeup.

She did as he asked, and five seconds later the man outside dashed past.

She called herself Marlene, though her name was doubtless something else. She drew him over to a blue-striped sofa beneath a framed price list on the wall itemizing massage services in a variety of languages. She sat him down so he could catch his breath and have a good cry.

A moment later two more girls appeared. Like the first, they were in nightclothes and anything but ready to meet the challenges of a new day.

"What are you running from?" one of them asked, stroking his cheek. She was gentle and engulfed in a heavy scent of perfume, but her face was pockmarked and her body oddly proportioned, with tremendous breasts that defied gravity.

Marco dried his eyes and tried to explain his predicament, but it was obvious they understood little more than that some Eastern Europeans were running around outside and shouting. The information made them visibly uneasy, prompting them to withdraw into a corner, where they huddled together, whispering.

"You listen," the one who had comforted him eventually said. "You cannot stay here with us. In two hours a man comes for money. He must not find you here, otherwise trouble, not just for you, for us, too."

"We give you some food," the third girl added. "You wash, and then you go. You can only go out back door, but we try to get you across the yard and through a apartment to Willemoesgade. Then you on your own."

He asked them to please call a taxi, but their hospitality would not extend that far. Calls from their mobiles were checked every day by their pimp, to make sure they weren't freelancing outside opening hours. And who but a john would want a taxi?

Marco felt sorry for them. These were full-grown women living alone here, and yet they were being tormented in the same way as Zola tormented his own. He didn't understand. Why didn't they run away as well?

The women did as they promised and led him through the yard and up the back stairs, then on to the second floor of the building across the street, where the man lived who had allowed his flat to be used as an escape route. He was just an old customer, the girls explained, who would do anything to help them out.

"Next time, extra loving treatment for you, Benny," one of the girls promised. So that was probably why. He certainly looked satisfied with the deal.

Marco knew Willemoesgade. Here he had gone from shop to shop without securing work, so at least the proprietors here weren't hostile, if they even recognized him. The only problem was the Irma supermarket on the corner, where there was a high turnover of young lads managing the bottle return and you never knew where they were from. So Marco crossed the street and continued toward the junction of Østerbrogade.

He was entering dangerous territory indeed. But maybe he could quickly flag down a taxi to take him to the airport train station where he could jump on a train to Sweden and then he'd be free.

He leaned up against a wall and stuck his hand in his pocket. There was just under five thousand kroner left of what he'd taken from Samuel's shopping bag. A tidy sum that was sure to get him far. Soon it would be summer, and the weather was mild. What more could he ask? Sleeping under the stars was free, and once he'd got farther north, around Dalarna or Jämtland, he knew he would have little trouble finding an abandoned house or an empty summer cottage rarely in use. He'd be all right, though it pained him to think of all the money behind the baseboard in Kaj and Eivind's apartment. Now he had to start again from the beginning, and who could tell how things would go next time around?

The cabs that passed by were taken, so Marco decided he would walk along Sortedamssøen and then up to Trianglen, where he knew there would be ranks of taxis waiting for customers.

But he never got that far.

Suddenly he saw Chris's van parked sideways on the pavement some distance farther up the street. Presumably the Balts had alerted Zola's right-hand man after Eivind had called them, and now the van was there, waiting to pick up its cargo, dead or alive.

That cargo was Marco.

He felt cold inside. If only he had the courage, he would sneak up to the vehicle and slash its tires with Kaj and Eivind's kitchen knife that he still had concealed under his jersey.

He looked along Sortedam Dossering. Maybe he should run that way, though it could be dangerous if someone blocked his path, with the lake on one side and hardly a single side street on the other. It was not an optimal route. Either he had to go back the way he'd come, or else he would have to stay put and wait for a vacant taxi.

Marco did not let the van out of his sight. Everything evil was symbolized by its presence. How often had they sat on the floor in the back, being led like lambs to slaughter into a life they'd been unable to refuse? How often had he lain there exhausted, dreaming that the drive would never end? But it always did. Every single day they ended up in their prison in Kregme. Eat, sleep, then off again early the next morning, such was their life. How he hated that van.

His chain of thought was broken abruptly. Was that his father coming out of the shop behind the van? And wasn't that Zola himself right behind him? Were they so keen on finding him that they were now out in person, going from door-to-door? They were insane, there was no other word.

He ducked behind the trees and watched them spitefully as they went into the next shop. People like Zola and his father should never be allowed anywhere near children.

He saw the cyclist coming from the direction of Trianglen. An ordinary-looking type, though obviously unfamiliar with the bike he was riding.

Marco smiled to himself. That's not yours, you just stole it, he thought, comparing the bike's size, age, and color with its rider. Whatever made him think nobody would notice?

Then, all of a sudden, the guy wrenched his front wheel over the curb and headed straight for Marco, who managed to run only a couple of steps before the cyclist sailed right into him.

There were other cyclists on the cycle path who shouted to the man that he should watch where he was going, but Marco knew better, so instinctively he rolled to the side on the ground as the guy tried to grab him. He drew the knife from his jersey by reflex and stabbed his assailant in the ankle. There was a roar of pain as the man recoiled and fell backward. Marco leaped to his feet and legged it as fast as he could.

"Not that way, Marco," cried a voice from the other side of the street. Marco looked up and saw that almost everyone was staring at him. In the same instant he also saw a man come running around the corner of Ryesgade at full speed and he was now only a hundred and fifty meters away.

Marco glanced around. A taxi from Østerport station with its green for-hire light on was heading toward him. He darted across the road to flag it down as the cyclist got to his feet and his second pursuer closed in.

"There's one more, Marco!" the voice shouted.

He looked over his shoulder and saw his father standing with his hands cupped to his mouth. He was about to cry out again, but at the same moment Zola came from behind and shoved him so hard that his father lost his footing, stumbled over the cycle path and out into the street.

Marco saw the bus slam on its brakes and swerve. He heard people scream as his father disappeared beneath it, but was immediately compelled to turn and face the new threat bearing down on him. It was a dreadful moment. His father had just been run over, and Marco himself was surrounded on three sides as he stood at the curb, his arms flailing at the oncoming taxi.

An immigrant sat behind the wheel, the kind of taxi driver who didn't own his own vehicle and wanted to demonstrate how content he was to drive someone else's, as long as it had a leather interior and a motor powerful enough to leave everything else in its wake.

"Drive!" Marco commanded shrilly, his whole body feeling like it was about to collapse.

Two of his pursuers appeared alongside the taxi, hammering their fists against the window as the driver gave them the finger and floored the accelerator.

They took off so fast that Marco didn't manage to see his father under the bus, only the blood spreading over the asphalt and the horrified crowd that had gathered on the pavement within seconds.

The last thing he saw before the Skoda Superb shot across Trianglen was the bus driver behind the steering wheel, face buried in his hands. Then his eyes locked on to Zola's. The man was standing with his head held high, cold as ice amid the tumult of onlookers, none of whom seemed to have noticed what he had done.

That's what's in store for you, Zola's look told him.

"Terrible accident. Happens all too often, if you ask me. People drive like shit." The taxi driver looked at Marco in the rearview mirror. "Where to?"

Marco sat with his head back, gasping for air. If he leaned forward he knew he would be sick. His father had tried to warn him, and for that Zola had killed him.

His father had tried to save him. His father.

Marco pictured his eyes. They were green-brown and full of warmth. This loving gaze was from a distant time, he realized that. But his father had just tried to warn him, so who cared about the time in between?

Now his father was dead and Zola had got away. And the taxi driver was asking him where he wanted to go.

Only five minutes ago he would have said the airport. Yesterday, he would have said Tilde's house.

Now, he no longer knew . . .

Zola had murdered in cold blood, and Marco had seen with his own eyes how he'd done it. The man was completely without feeling, as he must also have been the time he turned Miryam into an invalid. William Stark had been killed just as cynically, and most likely others besides. And it was with that same callousness that Zola would have killed him. Feeling nothing.

"Have you gone deaf, mate, or what? Where do you want to go? You've got money, yeah?"

Marco nodded and passed two hundred kroner to the driver.

"OK, two hundred. Think about it for a bit."

Marco shook his head. He didn't need to think. Zola's eyes had decided for him. Marco was staying to complete his mission. Zola was going to pay, no matter what.

"They weren't half after you, those guys out there. Something to do with drugs, was it? Yeah, I know all about it. As soon as you start doing a bit of business for yourself, they flip totally out, don't they? It's a downer. Well, whaddaya say? Found out where you want to go?"

"Do you know the Hereford Beefstouw next to Tivoli Gardens?" Marco asked.

"Sure, I'm a taxi driver, aren't I? Ask me something I don't know and you can have your two hundred back."

36

"**Eriksen has left the** ministry, Carl."

Carl looked at his watch. "He's off early, then. When's he——" He broke off, realizing from the look on Gordon's face that for once he seemed to have something important to say, so he shut up.

"Eriksen has handed in his resignation with immediate effect. He went straight to his boss after we'd been over there, announced he was ill, and said he wouldn't be coming back."

Carl frowned. "Dammit, Gordon. I don't know what you've done, but you've certainly set something in motion."

He called for Rose and Assad and filled them in on the situation.

"Assad, you call Eriksen's home and see if he's there. And Rose, you call the ministry and get hold of the department head. We need to know what's going on here. And when you're done with that, call the Frederiksværk police and ask them to keep an eye on this Zola bloke and see if he's about to do a runner. And to make sure they grab him if he tries."

"On what grounds?" she asked.

"You'll think of something, Rose."

"And what about me?" asked Gordon.

"You check Eriksen's background. We want to know if he owns a summer cottage or some other place where he can lie low. Call the tax authorities, people like that."

It warmed Carl's heart to see how disappointed the boy looked.

———

Assad nodded and snapped his mobile shut.

"It was Department Q's very own Rose," he said, putting his feet back up on the dashboard.

"That's nice. Now let's try and sum up," said Carl, changing lanes. How come the traffic was already like being inside an anthill?

Assad nodded again.

"First thing is, do we agree that your methods of interrogation go a bit too far, Assad?"

"Too far? How do you mean, Carl? Aren't they just creative?"

He shook his head. Creative? One day Assad's creativity might just be their undoing.

"Secondly, I now know that Lars Bjørn spent time in Abu Ghraib prison while Saddam was in power. Don't tell me you didn't know, Assad, because I won't believe you. Just tell me if you and Bjørn knowing each other has anything to do with that."

Assad raised his head and stared out pensively along Ballerup Boulevard. Not exactly an uplifting sight.

Then he turned to Carl and nodded calmly. "Yes, it has. And now you must ask me no more about this. OK, Carl?"

Carl glanced at the GPS. Two more junctions and they'd be there.

"OK," he replied. So far, so good. It was a step in the right direction. The question was, when would he take the next one? He certainly wasn't going to let Assad off the hook that easily.

"All right, back to business. What did Rose have to say? Did she get hold of that department head?"

"Yes, and she got a rather more nuanced story than the one Gordon gave us." He skimmed through his notepad. "I have it here. I wrote it all down." He tapped his finger against the page. "It is true this René E. Eriksen has resigned his position with immediate effect. The reason he gave was that after having spoken with us he realized Stark had committed fraud and that it was his fault it was never detected. With this weighing down his shoulders he could no longer remain with the department.

The permanent secretary said that by rights he ought to have been suspended, but Eriksen was looking so poorly that they agreed he should go on sick leave as of that same day. Most likely there will be an internal investigation at some point, but for the moment he was unable to tell us any more."

"OK." Carl peered at the house numbers. A couple more and they could pull in. "Now it's up to us whether we believe this or not. Is it really plausible that Stark's actions shocked Eriksen as much as he claims? And not least of all, are we prepared to believe Stark was doing something illegal?"

Assad nodded. A bit absently.

For someone living in Rønneholtparken, the single-story dwelling in Ballerup maybe wasn't that bad, but the location at the end of a dreary residential avenue was awfully bleak. Though the street was lined with trees, their closest neighbor was the Ringvej 4 motorway. Not that one actually heard the traffic that much, one simply smelled it. All in all, he'd rather stay put in the concrete boxes of his own estate, lined up in rows in the open landscape, with lots of friends around.

They rang the doorbell and were received by Eriksen's wife, who clearly let them know they could come in for a minute, but she had other things to do besides answering their questions. Therefore she declined to offer them a seat, or ask if she might fetch them some refreshment.

"Looks like quite an accident," Carl commented, pointing to the tarpaulin the emergency glaziers had rigged up where the window was supposed to be in the living room.

"I wouldn't call it an accident. It was a planned assault, the day before yesterday. They smashed the window and set about attacking us, but I fended them off with my iron."

Carl frowned. "I'm sorry, I'm not with you. As far as I know, nothing's been reported to the police at this address."

"No, I wanted to call the police, but my husband wouldn't."

"Hmm, strange. So what happened? Did they make off with anything?"

"As I said, I sorted them out with my iron before they had a chance."

"So you do not actually know if this was intended to be a burglary?" Assad inquired.

"I don't know what it was. Ask my husband." She laughed, for no apparent reason.

"Would you happen to know where he is at the moment?" Carl asked, as he scanned the interior. Was there any sign of Eriksen being at home, but not making himself known?

"Nope. I assume he's stuck his tail between his legs, seeing as how he packed his job in all of a sudden."

Assad cut in: "Excuse me, madam. But do you not care?"

She smiled. "He's my husband, and the father of my children."

"So you don't, then?"

She seemed astonished by his reasoning but smiled again, nevertheless. She'd probably been good-looking once, Carl thought, but it was a lot of gold teeth and upper-lip hair growth ago.

"Do you know if your husband might have had problems, something weighing him down?" he asked.

"I suppose he must have, otherwise he wouldn't have been hanging around the airport at the crack of dawn, frothing at the mouth and waiting for Teis Snap."

"Uhh, Teis Snap?"

She put her hands on her hips. "Yes, Teis Snap. Haven't you read about him in the gossip magazines?" She laughed. "Never mind. He and my husband are old schoolmates. Though 'mates' might be pushing it a bit, considering the nonsense he's been putting in René's head."

"What nonsense?"

"Stock trading. René had a lot of shares in Teis Snap's bank, Karrebæk Bank. Tell me, haven't you checked up on him? What kind of policemen are you?"

Carl looked at Assad, who shrugged.

"What kind of money are we talking about?" Assad asked.

"I've no idea. He was discreet about it, I'll give him that. He was on the bank's board of directors as well."

"Might he have gone to see his friend, this . . . what was his name, now?" Assad flicked back through his notepad. "This Schnapps guy."

"Snap. Teis Snap. I really wouldn't know. He's more likely gone to a hotel, the louse. And as far as I'm concerned, the creep can stay there."

Creep? Was this her take on "to love and to honor, for better or worse"?

Carl's mobile thrummed in his pocket. If it was Mona, everything else was on hold.

He glanced at the display but didn't recognize the number. Was she calling from work, maybe?

"Helloski, Monsignor!" said the voice.

Who the hell was that?

"Gordon T. Taylor here. I've checked up on René E. Eriksen like you asked me to. There's a lot of stuff about his education and career, but what struck me as interesting was that he recently sold off his shares in Karrebæk Bank for ten million kroner and that he's a member of the board, besides. Kind of strange, wouldn't you say?"

Christ on a bike. Ten million.

"Tell me something I don't know, Gordon," Carl teased, and hung up. That'd give him something to think about.

He turned to Eriksen's wife, but then his phone rang again.

"For fuck's sake, Gordon," he snarled. "It can't be that hard to grasp, surely? When I hang up the phone, it means we're finished talking."

"Carl?" came the sound of a woman's voice. "Is that you? It's Lisbeth."

The furrows in his brow relocated immediately to his hairline. Lisbeth! He hadn't given her a thought.

"Oh, sorry, Lisbeth. Thought you were someone else. Listen, I'm in the middle of an interview. Can we talk a little later on today?"

"Of course. Sorry if I've caught you at the wrong time." She sounded disappointed. Maybe she had reason to be.

He said good-bye and promised to call back as soon as he had time. Somehow, it seemed neither true nor false. Just odd.

"Sorry about that," he said, turning back to René E. Eriksen's wife. "What I was about to say before was that your husband recently sold shares to the tune of ten million kroner in the bank whose board he happened to be on. Did you know about that?"

She asked him to repeat the sum.

And there she stood, wide-eyed, looking like her entire life was up for revision.

"Karrebæk Bank, Bente Mønsted. How can I help you?"

Carl nodded to Assad, who sat listening in. The GPS they'd had put in the service vehicle along with a wireless phone and all manner of electronics was nothing if not practical. He felt like a millionaire.

"I'd like to speak to your boss, Manager Snap. Could you put me through, please?"

"I'm sorry, whom am I speaking with?"

"Detective Inspector Carl Mørck, Department Q, Copenhagen police."

"I see." There was a pause. "I'm afraid I have to say Mr. Snap hasn't been in today."

"Is he off sick?"

"To be honest, I'm not quite sure. He's just come back from a vacation in the Caribbean, but nobody's seen him at the office yet. I know he met with our brokers in Copenhagen yesterday, but we haven't been informed as to his schedule for today, and he hasn't answered our calls. He's still jet-lagged, I imagine."

"I see. Maybe it'll help his jet lag if I call him instead. I seem to have a magic touch when it comes to getting folks to answer their phone. Can you give me his home number?"

"I don't think I'm authorized to give it out over the phone."

"In that case, I'll call the Næstved police and ask them to stop by in five minutes. It'll look great, a couple of burly lads in full uniform turning up at the manager's secretary's office, don't you think? But if that's the way you want to do it, it's fine by me. They can give me the number over the phone. But thanks for your help."

"Well, if it's really necessary, and it sounds like it is, then I suppose I can."

Assad gave him a thumbs-up. It worked almost every time.

Twenty seconds later it was Assad's turn to call, but this time Carl's magic touch didn't work. No reply.

"Check his address, Assad," Carl instructed. "We'll drive down there. There's something fishy about this, if you ask me."

"Fishy?"

"Yeah, something that doesn't add up. We've got Eriksen vanishing all of a sudden. We've got him and Snap on the board of directors together. Eriksen's just sold off a whole barrowload of stock, and now we've got Snap, who might or might not be off sick. Some funny coincidences, I'd say. It wouldn't surprise me if the two of them were planning on meeting up somewhere."

"Karrebæksminde is all the way down around Næstved, Carl."

"Yeah, but we don't care, do we? The day's still young."

"This is like half a sheikhdom," Assad commented, staring out over the fields around the tree-lined gravel driveway leading up to Snap's country home.

"I probably should have been a bank manager," he added a minute later, before pressing the doorbell.

They stood and twiddled their thumbs for a minute or two at the heavy main door, until eventually Assad tried the handle. Naturally, the door was locked.

"Check the outbuildings and the garage over there, Assad, and I'll take a walk around the house."

Carl noted down the registration numbers of the three cars parked in front of the house, then went back to his vehicle and ran a check. All three belonged to Karrebæk Bank. Did anyone say perks?

He walked through a small apple orchard, the trees all stunningly in blossom, before coming out on the rear side of the house where there were neatly staggered terraces leading up to the house and wide-open windows upstairs.

He looked around the neatly cultivated surroundings, puzzled by all the sheets of paper that littered the garden. Probably they'd been left on a windowsill and had blown out of one of the open windows. Whatever the reason, they were now scattered all over the place and also hung in the many fruit trees and the tall poplars further back in the windbreak facing northwest.

He picked up a sheet off the terrace. The paper was rather coarse, probably handmade. He sniffed at it. Notepaper belonging to a woman, definitely. Now she'd need to stock up anew.

"Hello, anyone home?" he shouted up at the windows, at least expecting some half-deaf maid to pop her head out, but there was no reaction.

"I'm wondering about those windows," he said to Assad a few minutes later. "Are you any good at climbing?"

Assad hitched up his trousers. "The only difference between me and a monkey is the banana," he replied, followed by a hearty laugh.

Carl wasn't sure he got it.

As it turned out, the job was not without difficulty. "I don't think it can take my weight," Assad said, testing the trellis halfway up the wall. It looked like he was having a vertigo attack, the way he was clinging to the ivy.

"Come on, Assad. You've only got another meter to go. You don't want me to climb up there, do you?"

There was a splutter of complaints that might have been interpreted as a "yes," but then his voice became serious.

"It's a good thing we googled Teis Snap, Carl, so we know what he looks like," he called down, clinging to the window frame.

"Why's that?"

"Because then I can say with certainty that he is the one lying here, stone dead. I suppose one can assume the lady on the bed is his wife."

37

He stood in between the trees of the windbreak, from where he had a view of most of the estate without being seen himself. The sight that met his eyes was disconcerting indeed.

He had prepared himself for a confrontation with Snap over the Curaçao stocks and had expected it might become violent, which was why he carried a medium-duty hammer in the near-bottomless depths of his coat pocket. It was poorly suited to knocking in nails, but eminently effective against the skimpy armor of a man such as Snap.

"If they can attack me physically, then I can strike back," René had reasoned, before noticing the sweep of flashing blue lights against the whitewashed wings of the house.

The courtyard in front of the house was a bustle of activity. There were maybe ten vehicles in all, among them two ambulances. It was the ambulances he watched with particular attention, and twice the paramedics carried shrouded bodies from the house. He almost dared not consider whether it was Teis and Lisa on those stretchers, but who else could it be? No one else lived there.

There were also a lot of men milling about, most of them presumably local police, but also some who were not. Police technicians in white smocks, their superiors in plain clothes, and worst of all, Carl Mørck and his Arab assistant. So they were that close to them now. How fortunate that the fool Mørck had brought with him the day before had come back and unwittingly let him know how interested they were. Otherwise, he probably would not have got away in time.

René looked out over the lawn with sheets of paper everywhere. It was a disheartening sight. One sheet with writing on it was caught in the poplar a couple of meters above his head. Typewritten, with a signature at the bottom. How terrible to think that Lisa might have been writing those very words when it happened.

When it happened. He tried to comprehend the true weight of those three words.

Rather, when *what* happened? Who had done it, and why? Was it the same people who had attacked him and his wife?

He had more or less decided the incident was Snap's doing, but now he no longer felt so sure.

But who, then?

He had never met Brage-Schmidt, but according to rumor, it was no coincidence the man had amassed a fortune, that he was incredibly dynamic and efficient in all he did. *Dynamic and efficient.* Again, attributes that could be interpreted in so many different ways.

René closed his eyes and ran the situation through in his mind. Brage-Schmidt was a young man no longer, so obviously he had hired someone to do this, if indeed he was behind it. But what was his motive? Was it the same as what had brought René himself to Karrebæksminde?

He gazed across at the array of people and ambulances that were silently departing toward town. Two minutes ago he had been prepared to stay put until everyone had gone, but now, where he had begun to think more rationally, he realized there was no need.

It was about money. Lots of money. And this was almost definitely no exception.

The figures still milling in the front of the house now spread out in all directions. A couple of officers were slowly coming his way, apparently combing the lawn and surrounding areas. They're probably looking for footprints, he thought, as he looked back over his shoulder to see his own deep imprints in the earth.

He knew it was lucky he hadn't got there first, for otherwise he would have left traces all round the house. He retreated warily back along the line of trees and down to the main road, where his car was discreetly parked.

When finally he opened the door and got inside, he felt certain. The bodies on the stretchers had been those of Teis and Lisa, and they had been murdered. Brage-Schmidt had played a crucial role throughout their scam, and René was convinced he still did. Greed knew no bounds. Not in his own case either. If Brage-Schmidt had had these people killed in order to grab the Curaçao stocks, then they almost certainly were in his possession now.

In any case, he was willing to drive the hundred kilometers north to find out.

Wrought-iron lanterns, a fountain with no water, rustic latticework in front of all windows. This was how the former consulate for a number of Central African states looked. Grandiloquent and ugly.

René locked the car and buttoned his coat. Of course he could put an old man like Brage-Schmidt in his place, and if not, the hammer lay ready in his pocket. Now it was his turn to demonstrate that he was dynamic and efficient.

The door knocker was stiff on its hinges. He probably doesn't get that many visitors, he mused, knocking once more and noting that with lights on in so many windows somebody had to be home.

His eyes found a gate in the wooden fence that surrounded the garden with its tall fir trees. Perhaps he could go through there and catch a glimpse into some of the rooms. Then he'd know better whether Brage-Schmidt was home alone.

As a boy he would on rare occasion pluck up the courage to sneak into his neighbors' gardens on Twelfth Night and blacken their windows with a sooted cork, but that was many years ago. And qualified jurists who had made a career in the civil service did not count the furtive sneaking about in which he now engaged as being among their greatest skills. For that reason, he felt awkward and clumsy as he sprang from shrub to shrub, eyes fixed on the light from the windows that flooded out into the garden.

That must be the living room, he thought, as he tiptoed forward.

It was a room that more than anything reminded him of the myth of Ernest Hemingway, or perhaps just a poor B-movie. Never had he seen as many hunting trophies in one place. Buffalo and antelope, beasts of prey and animals he had rarely even seen pictures of, all mounted in neat rows, glass eyes and glossy pelts side by side with the weapons to which they had succumbed.

He felt disgust as he crept closer. Now he could hear a man's voice. It had to be Brage-Schmidt's, with his characteristic compressed rasping voice brusquely barking out sentences that lacked either warmth or patience.

"If you saw him in Østerbro today, heading out of town in a taxi," the hoarse voice said, "then I suggest you think hard about where he might be now. And when you've found out, let me know. If you can't get hold of me, make sure the Africans are fully informed."

There was a pause in the conversation. René moved forward. He had not seen Brage-Schmidt before, so his plans might have to change if it turned out the man's physique still fit the chauvinistic image he'd striven to cultivate with his hideous display of slaughtered animals.

"No, I don't know where your people are, that's your job, not mine," the voice continued. "That's the way it is, Zola. Do your job, or else get the fuck out."

It was clear to René now that this was a one-way conversation. The man was probably on the phone.

He listened closer and followed the sound to a patio door that stood ajar a few meters away. Here was a way into the house. What luck.

A few more steps and he was there. What a brilliant surprise it would be. Finally the two of them would meet. Finally they could settle the account that had been years in the making.

He gripped the hammer, stepped up to the door, and found himself staring into the eyes of a black man with a mobile phone to his ear. He was quite young and possessed a voice that was one hundred percent Brage-Schmidt's.

A second passed before the man hung up and put the phone in his pocket. He seemed calm, far less surprised than René.

"Come inside," he said in a completely other voice. "You must be René Eriksen. Welcome."

René frowned and accepted the invitation, his grip tightening around the shaft of the hammer in his pocket.

"Yes, and you? Who are you? And why were you impersonating Brage-Schmidt?"

The man smiled and sat down. Perhaps he was trying to instill in him the same kind of confidence as an executive offering a cup of coffee to an underling before giving him the sack. It wasn't reassuring.

"It's a long story. Won't you sit down?"

"I prefer to stand. Where is Brage-Schmidt?"

"In the drawing room next door. He's taking a nap at the moment, so you'll have to wait a bit until I wake him."

"And while he's asleep, you look after the business, I suppose."

The man spread out his hands. That's how it appeared.

"So you're who we've been holding conference calls with on the phone the past couple of years?"

Again, the extended black hands with their white palms.

"Every time?"

"Conceivably. Mr. Brage-Schmidt has had a lot of business to attend to lately."

René looked around the room. Behind the African, double-barreled shotguns and slender rifles hung from the wall, and above them, hunting bows and quivers of arrows. Mounted vertically next to them were two needle-sharp spears with broad, double-edged heads. On the floor beside a low elephant-foot table stood a crock made from the hollowed-out foot of a rhinoceros, full of what looked like an assortment of cudgels. To the other side was a vitrine containing knives for almost every conceivable purpose.

It wasn't exactly the place he would choose for an armed confrontation. In that case, it would be wise to withdraw immediately. The odds were against him in an arena like this, hammer or not.

"So I can't speak to Brage-Schmidt now?" he asked.

The African shook his head. "I think it best we make an appointment for tomorrow. How about ten A.M.? I know he'll be able to receive you then."

René nodded. By ten o'clock tomorrow he'd be far, far away. So he would just have to make do with what he'd earned from selling off his shares in Karrebæk Bank. He'd get by, all the same.

"OK, that'll be fine. Tell him I'm looking forward to meeting him."

The African stood up. "And what may I tell him it's about?"

"It's nothing special. We'll deal with it tomorrow."

Then the man put out his hand, but René was wary and held back, turning instead toward the patio door with a brief word of thanks. He'd be back at ten in the morning.

He reached for the doorknob, but the African lunged forward and delivered a swift, brutal karate chop to René's throat.

"You're going nowhere. I don't trust you," he spat, as René sank to his knees, gasping for air.

"Tell me why you're here."

René tried but couldn't. Every muscle in his throat was paralyzed, and his right arm as well.

It was obvious that the African was about to strike him again, so René raised his left hand and waved it in submission.

He felt a warmth spreading from his right shoulder as blood trickled down his arm. Which was when he produced the hammer and smashed it into the African's knee.

He'd expected a roar of pain, but not a sound passed the man's lips, even though his leg buckled sideways and his eyes were wide with agony.

"You devil," he snarled, toppling forward and clamping René's head in what felt like a potentially fatal grip. René raised his hammer again and struck, forcing the African to let go. When the man got to his feet, blood from his hand was dripping onto the floor, but still he bore the pain.

Two pairs of eyes immediately sought the spears that were mounted on the wall, but the African had the advantage of already being upright and began limping toward them as René struggled to get to his feet and stop him.

The man was alarmingly agile, despite his injuries. The resoluteness of his reactions and the lack of hesitation filled René with mortal dread. Now he knew who he was dealing with. It was one of the people Teis Snap had told him about. One of the boy soldiers.

And he realized this was a fight he couldn't win.

It made him let go of the straw to which most people would cling when looking death in the face and instead watch the man's movements as he pulled the spear from the wall.

"Why *did* you come here and what is your business?" the African asked calmly, as he aimed the weapon directly at René from a distance of only two meters.

"I've been to Karrebæksminde and seen what you did to Teis Snap and his wife. It was I who called the police and told they should come out here. But I had no way of knowing for sure if I was right, so I came to warn Brage-Schmidt ahead of time in case it turned out I was wrong."

The man's lips curled in an oddly false smile. "What you're telling me is not true, is it?"

René shook his head. "No. I came here to kill him myself. Are you one of the boy soldiers Snap told me about?"

"No. I am Boy."

"Then farewell, Boy." René swung the hammer above his head and straight into the man's body, leaping aside at the same moment.

Nevertheless, Boy's spear plunged through the palm of his left hand and came out the back.

Strangely enough he felt no pain until he grasped the shaft and pulled.

As his whole arm exploded in pain from the severed nerves and ruptured muscles, he staggered toward the glass showcase with its display of knives, gasping for air and keeping his eyes fixed on the African, who was already bending down to pick up the hammer.

Slowly and deliberately he limped toward René with his eyes fixed on his throat and the hammer raised.

He could throw it, but that wasn't what he wanted. It was clear he wished to be as close to his victim as possible when he killed him.

Facing Boy, René jerked his elbow backward and broke the glass of the showcase. He pulled out a knife, whose length and weight more than matched the hammer.

Now he had the knife in his hand, yet he kept backing up toward the wall. At that precise moment he simply lacked the will to use it.

He felt a door handle behind him, turning it at the same instant the African lunged with the hammer aimed at his throat.

At that precise moment René felt as if he were not present. His body had separated from his brain, his limbs from his torso, his bleeding hand from his arm. Only the hand holding the knife retained a life of its own, protecting his.

By the time the blow came, René had drawn the knife to his throat, and instead of the hammer striking him, the knife warded off the blow and sliced into the hand of his attacker, so deeply that blood spurted from the artery in the African's wrist.

Boy was stunned and tried to draw back, but somehow René held on to him, blood soaking his skin, and the hammer fell to the floor.

Only now did he see the unfettered rage boiling in the African's eyes. Boy tried to head-butt him as the blood drained from his body. As René jerked his head back, his body pushed open the door behind him, causing both men to tumble into the adjoining room.

The African lay gasping on top of him, teeth snapping at René's throat. Then his movements became slower and slower, until eventually there were none.

René tried to catch his breath. He was no longer a young man, and right now it felt like the shock and the adrenaline threatened to make his heart stop. Then suddenly, in a single deep intake of breath, the reaction came, and with it the sense of disgust. He pushed the dead man away and lay staring up at the ceiling for a long time before being able to turn over on the floor and actually see where he'd landed.

He found himself looking directly at a pair of feet. Two pole-like legs and the sort of sturdy lace-up shoes that usually only a backpacker might wear. Slowly his eyes moved up the legs, well aware that it was Brage-Schmidt standing above him. He also realized that right now the man had the advantage, and that all he had managed to survive until now had been in vain.

Then he closed his eyes and gave himself up to his fate.

Our Father, who art in heaven . . . , he prayed silently. It had been so many years since the last time he had recited the words. And now they returned to him on this final day.

With a strange feeling of calm he raised his eyes toward his executioner, only to discover that the man sat in a wheelchair and that his eyes were completely empty.

René got to his feet so abruptly that he almost slipped in the blood on the floor.

The man in front of him was totally paralyzed. The shelves that surrounded him were filled with pill bottles. In the windowsill were unopened packets of incontinence pads. On the table were bottles of spirits, cotton swabs, disposable bedpans, and foam-rubber wipes like the kind used in hospitals.

René bent forward toward the man and looked directly into his eyes. There was no reaction. None whatsoever.

He stepped over the African's body, picked up one of the wipes and wrapped it around his hand, from which two of his fingers hung by tendons. He could do no more about it until he was far away from there.

Then his eyes fell upon a green cardboard folder on which Brage-Schmidt's full name and civil registration number were printed.

He opened it, and his eyes grew wide as he scanned the first page.

Brage-Schmidt's hospital records described in objective detail the circumstances of his brain hemorrhage and the date it occurred: July 4, 2006. Way before their fraud began. So that was why he never showed up in person at board meetings. And why the African who called himself Boy had been impersonating him.

René shook his head. "I wonder what would have happened if you hadn't ended up like this," he said out loud, and patted the man's cheek.

What a miserable life he'd had. He would be better off dead than go on living like the vegetable he'd become.

He went through the house until he found Boy's room with a suitcase packed and ready to go. And there were the shares. Neatly gathered in a bundle bound with yarn.

He picked them up and held them to his chest for a moment. Then he realized he had left a trail of bloody footprints all over the house, not to mention his own blood that had been spilled.

So he returned to Brage-Schmidt's room, finding a box of matches on his way. He paused briefly and regarded the motionless figure in the wheelchair before placing his good hand around the man's mouth and nose and pressing hard until the breathing ceased. It was peaceful and quite without drama.

Oh, Lord, you poor man, he thought. No need for you to suffer what's to come.

Then he picked up a bottle of surgical spirits from the table and emptied it over the two bodies.

As he stepped back to light the match, he noticed the dead African lay with his head tipped back enough to reveal an upper set of dentures. He stood for a moment and considered this baroque coincidence. Then he made an impulsive decision. He removed the false teeth from the corpse and put them in his pocket, after which he replaced them with his own.

Then he picked up another bottle of spirits and doused the African once more before backing up and striking the match.

There was a deep, muffled sound as the fumes ignited, and a blue flash of light illuminated the musty room like a sudden burst of sparkling midday sunshine.

38

Zola snapped his mobile shut and sat back heavily in his chair.

His contact had just uttered the cathartic yet definitive ultimatum: "Do your job, or else get the fuck out!"

It was on the basis of this unambiguous message that he was now attempting to work out a couple of plausible scenarios.

Clearly something had to happen now. The risk of Marco evading their pincer movement was growing. Because even at a distance Marco could be dangerous, especially now that he'd witnessed Zola sending his father to his death. On that point, however, Zola was quite satisfied. If he couldn't count on a person one hundred percent, then he would have to go. On top of which there was no longer anyone he had to share with when the spoils were counted up.

Do your job, or else get the fuck out. That meant either they found out where Marco was hiding so Zola's hyenas could tear him apart, or else Zola would have to pull out. Thus nothing had really changed. The same question remained.

Where was Marco?

The boy had headed off north in a taxi, but what could they conclude from that? Nothing. The next minute he could have asked the driver to go east, west, south, or anywhere at all. The network of streets was unending, but the Africans needed something to go on. The fucking Africans.

He nodded to Chris, who sat at his side. "Get hold of Pico. I have an order for him."

Chris dialed a number, waited half a minute, then handed Zola the mobile.

"Give me Pico," was all he said.

A moment passed before the man on the other end answered stutter-ingly. Zola was sick and tired of how bad Eastern Europeans spoke English.

"I don't know where," Pico stammered. "Before on the corner, now gone. Talked to man from you. It was Hector, man here tells me. Other-wise, nothing."

Zola hung up, handed the phone back to Chris and sat staring down Bredgade with veiled eyes.

His years in the business had taught him at all times to stick to the simple guiding principle that the harder it was for the authorities to trace the crimes of his people back to him, the longer and safer his career would be. It was why he had developed this system of phoning, why the years had been so lucrative, and why to this day he had a clean record.

The system was simple: no one in the clan besides himself and Chris owned a mobile phone. That way people could get in touch with him, but if they were apprehended there was not a single communication from them to Zola for the police to find and use against him.

In addition, over the past few years he had established the network of Eastern European auxiliary troops who had now joined the hunt and who could pass on messages to his own clan members in their various territo-ries. Usually this setup worked well, but there was nothing usual about the present situation.

As things stood now, the phoning system was too problematic and the weakest link in his empire, a ball and chain around his feet.

"Let's wait a while. He'll call back," said Chris.

But Zola didn't feel he could wait. For every minute that passed, there was the risk that Marco would strike. The police had already been at their door in Kregme, and it had been Marco's doing. Nothing was sacred anymore and nothing was safe as long as that boy was at large. So how long could he wait?

Then the phone rang. Chris handed him the mobile.

"It's Pico," said the voice at the other end. "I have Hector right here."

"Where are you people now? I couldn't get hold of you. And why are you calling?"

"I'm in the street they call Pisserenden," Pico answered. "Hector just come and tell me Romeo and Samuel both gone. They not been at Nyhavn for long time. First, Samuel does not come back, then same with Romeo. This not so good, Zola."

"What do you mean? Explain!"

"Police were in Black Diamond. We know now they grab them at the lockers."

Zola leaned back and stared at the ceiling. Fuck! Was it now that everything was finally going to happen?

"How?"

"They were just there, waiting."

He nodded, as one whole side of his face grew cold.

"OK. Keep away from there! And Pico, get everyone together before we pick you up. We need to know where everyone is and what's going on. If any of you know where the Africans are, make sure they know Marco headed north. Give them Stark's address."

"Why? He could be gone anywhere."

"Just do it, Pico. Or maybe you have a better idea?"

He hung up, took a deep breath, then typed in the number of the house in Kregme. It was Thursday, and Lajla would be making ready for his return. The house would smell of fresh-baked rolls and tempting willingness, but today he had other things for her to do. She would gather together everything of value. Everything of precious metal, and of course the jewelry. Just to be on the safe side.

"I was just about to call you, Zola," Lajla said when he got through. "There's a car parked at the end of the road, and it's been there for quite some time. I took the dog for a walk and went past it on my way out to the main road. I wanted to see who it was, and if there were other cars just parked for no apparent reason. And there were. Up on the hill were two vans and men in white clothes. I think it was the police."

"Which hill?"

"You know the one. The place where Marco disappeared. What do you think they've found?"

"How should I know? What about the car parked at the end of the road?"

"It's still there. They're just sitting there."

Zola gripped the armrest of his chair. The police, with his people in custody. Police, watching his house. Police, snooping around where William Stark's body had been buried. Dammit!

"Just stay calm, Lajla, it's got nothing to do with us. But you better collect all our valuables and hide them good, in case anyone comes to search the house."

She hesitated but seemed composed. That would change once she heard the clan was breaking up and that he had shoved his brother, her off-and-on boyfriend, to his death.

He handed the mobile to Chris and rolled down the side window so the warm air could chase the chill out of his body.

For more than twenty years he had been a part of this flock, the people he called his clan. He had seen them bow in the dust at his behest and seen them perform countless acts from which only he had benefited. They had been faithful to him. The question now was whether their time, and that of the clan, had come to an end.

He looked momentarily at Chris, his right-hand man, his ultimate shield against anything bad that might befall him. Chris was the one he would miss the most.

"Give me a cigarillo," he demanded. Chris did as he was told, along with a lighter.

Then and there he decided that moments where tobacco smoke floated lazily over his head in the dry air and mingled with the scent of the tropics would soon be a central feature of his new life. He could no longer trust Samuel, that meathead, to keep his mouth shut, and once Lajla found out what he had done to her lover, he would no longer be able to trust her not to thrust a knife into his heart.

Objectively, it was quite simple. He would have to abandon the valuables he had amassed in Kregme. It would give the police something to chew on in kroner and øre. It didn't bother him that much.

The rest of his fortune was waiting for him in Zurich. A bulging bank account, nourished over many years by the incomes of companies that appeared to be legal, although they were anything but. Once he had collected all his assets, he had to decide in which of two ways to use them.

Either he took the money and lived peacefully for the rest of his life with an abundance of women in Venezuela or Paraguay, or else he would put together a new clan. There were markets enough to exploit, but harsh winters and months of darkness like those in Denmark were definitively a thing of the past. He had time enough to decide, and the world was a big place.

Looking at it like that, his situation was perhaps not so bad that something positive couldn't come of it anyway. He only hoped that Marco, who had forced him into this situation, got what he deserved. That the Africans would succeed in tracking him down, and the sooner the better.

Zola looked at his watch.

Another half hour to wait and he would drive in to Rådhuspladsen and harvest the spoils of the day. He would need some cash to tide him over on the journey. Credit cards could be traced just like mobile phones, so if he was going to make a safe and orderly exit he would have to exhibit the greatest of caution.

As Chris gazed absently out of his side window, he opened the glove compartment and took out his false passport and the couple of thousand kroner that always lay there, ready and waiting, and slipped it all surreptitiously into his pocket. He didn't need questions from Chris. Who could tell what he might do if he caught wind of what was going on?

"Let me do the driving, Chris," he said, indicating that they swap places.

His helper looked at him with surprise, but he had learned not to question the validity of his master's commands.

Zola slapped him on the back.

"Listen to me now, Chris. There's something we have to do." And then he explained to him what it was.

As soon as they reached Rådhuspladsen, Chris was to tell the waiting clan members to take the train home from Vesterport station instead. That he and Chris had important business to attend to so they could get Romeo and Samuel out of custody fast. And as an extra safety measure, they would ask the group to turn over the day's haul to Chris in case the police were waiting for them at home. Afterward Chris was to tell them that he and Chris were going to pay a visit to the best solicitor in the entire kingdom of Denmark. Zola happened to know precisely which one. He was never unprepared, not even in a rotten situation such as this.

It was plain that Chris was moved by this display of concern for the members of the clan. Had it not been for the black bag on the seat between them, he would have grabbed Zola's hand and kissed it.

They reached the square two minutes before five, and nothing turned out as Zola had planned.

Chris managed to get out of the van and begin collecting their haul as the clan members stood about uneasily, listening to him tell about what had happened during the day.

But as he was about to lift the satchel of booty onto the driver's seat, a cry went up and at once Zola's people scattered. Only Miryam and another girl remained when the police charged in from all sides.

Zola didn't have time to think before he floored the accelerator, causing the entire square to reverberate with the screech of the van's spinning wheels.

He did, however, have time to assure himself that the money he'd taken from the glove compartment was enough for a plane ticket, and that it was odd the police hadn't stationed patrol cars to thwart an escape attempt such as this.

And he even managed a brief laugh before the windshield suddenly shattered in a thousand pieces and something heavy struck his knee.

What he didn't manage, however, was to see the truck heading straight at him from the opposite direction.

Marco's taxi driver turned out to be more than worth his two hundred kroner. He swerved into the cycle lane and deposited Marco right outside the Hereford Beefstouw where he could jump out unobserved and scale the construction site fence in seconds, ending up at the rear of the site as the building workers were leaving by the main entrance.

He knew he had to be doubly on his guard this time, and he knew that if the Africans or someone like them came back, he would not be unarmed.

He found a claw hammer on the first floor and weighed it in his hand. One side of the head was heavy and blunt, the other, used to extract nails, curved down into two prongs as sharp as awls. Not quite as good as a gun, but at least as good as a knife.

Marco was no longer afraid. Rational emotions such as fear and anxiety occur primarily in those who love life, who believe in the future and the people they hold dear, and don't want to lose any of these things. But when hatred takes over, love is forced aside, and with it, fear.

The way he felt at the moment, only the hate remained.

Zola had murdered his father before his very eyes, and if Marco hadn't been there it would never have happened, he knew that. Indirectly it was his fault his father had been killed, because his actions and presence had prompted his father to abandon his loyalty to Zola and warn his son instead.

Marco stared vacantly into the distance. "His father"! If only he could caress those words, he would. They gave rise to such deep emotion, and now, like the word "son," they were no longer a part of his world. A cold-blooded push from the man Marco hated most in all the world had deleted these words from his vocabulary, and this was something he was ready to avenge at any price—along with the murder of William Stark, Tilde's stepfather. Not until he had had his revenge would he again be able to look forward.

He crept on all fours across the concrete floor to check the rubble chute through which he had escaped the day before.

It was empty now, of course, so the African must have extricated himself. Marco couldn't help smile at the thought of how he had managed it.

Only when he reached the fourth floor did he begin to feel safe. All was quiet except for one or two workmen lingering around the huts below.

If he laid low until darkness came he could spend another night here in his den. There was always the risk that someone, against all common sense, might figure out he'd come back here, but in that case he felt ready for them. And if no one came, he would try to get close as possible to the house in Kregme and do away with Zola for good.

He frowned at the thought. It would not be easy, and he wasn't sure he could do it. He wasn't sure at all.

He found a slab of concrete, dragged it across the floor to the very edge of building's low wall facing Rådhuspladsen, and used it for a chair. Resting his forearms on the wall, he gazed out over his entire kingdom.

It was almost five o'clock. Soon Chris would arrive in the yellow van to pick them all up.

He couldn't see the vehicle yet, but what he saw instead were men with alert eyes on two of the adjacent street corners.

He didn't like these guys. Not only because they all seemed to be looking his way, but also because he couldn't recall having seen men like them standing like that, and in such numbers.

Were *they* after him, too?

He strained his eyes to see, waiting for one of them to make a move, but none of them did. If they were plainclothes police, then some telltale signs were lacking. The intense gaze, the posture, the hands in pockets, the bulge of the holster. But he was just too far away to tell.

And then he caught sight of Miryam limping toward the square from Farvergade, and a couple of other clan members appearing from the Strøget. As they crossed Rådhuspladsen, the men stationed on the corners turned slightly in their direction. Marco nodded. They were police, no doubt about it.

He shook his head. So now it was the clan's turn. He had seen to it himself with the note he had written on the parking ticket and dropped into that policewoman's bag, but now it felt very wrong. Did he seriously believe he could get at Zola by making life hard on his slaves? It wouldn't work. Zola would go free, and all the others would bear the brunt.

He wanted to call out to Miryam and the others and warn them, but all at once the yellow van turned the corner of Vesterbrogade and steered directly toward the waiting flock.

He had expected them to slide the side door open as usual and climb

in, but instead Chris jumped out from the passenger seat with a black
satchel in his hand and began discussing something with them. But why?
Why didn't they just drive off? And who was behind the wheel?

Then he saw his old friends depositing the day's haul in Chris's bag,
and then abruptly scattering like frightened birds as men rushed them
from all sides.

In the split second where Chris turned toward the open passenger
door, obviously in doubt as to what to do, Marco realized that the man
behind the wheel was Zola.

Instinctively and driven by hatred, he picked up the slab of concrete
on which he had been seated and raised it aloft as the van revved up and
the screech of its spinning wheels echoed between the buildings.

And then he hurled it with all his might, without a thought for the
danger in which he had suddenly put the innocent people below.

An eternity passed as the slab descended, and the smoking rubber of
the van's wheel spin seemed to propel the vehicle forward. Marco held
his breath. So bound together were this plummeting chunk of masonry
and Marco's bated breath, that if it had gone on falling forever, he would
have forgotten to breathe.

And when finally it smashed through the windshield and was gone,
the world came to a standstill. Only the van remained in motion, veering
diagonally across the street and colliding head-on with an oncoming
truck in a sickening crunch of metal against metal. The outcome was
inevitable, and a wave of shock stunned onlookers as the van overturned
in the collision and was squashed beneath the enormous truck. This time
Goliath had proven stronger than David.

Marco drew back, then darted ten meters to another spot by the wall
from which he could observe events undetected.

Most eyes were directed on the scene of the accident, and were
horror-struck.

A few looked up.

And Marco realized he was on the run again.

39

"**This is no easy** case, Carl," grumbled Assad. "I would not like to be in the shoes of those South Zealand and Lolland-Falster police right now."

"You said it, Assad. Snap's killing was a nasty business indeed," Carl replied. "His wife's neck was broken, and Snap had his larynx crushed before being strangled to death. What kind of person's capable of that? Do we know if Eriksen has any kind of background in the Danish commando forces or anything like that?" he asked, overtaking a car that was hogging the middle lane at eighty kilometers an hour.

Assad shook his head. "No, he doesn't. The army rejected him. It was something to do with his back."

"Well, now we've got a warrant out on him. We'll have to see what happens."

An alert came over the police GPS. There was only twenty minutes until the pickup at Rådhuspladsen. They'd have a job making it on time.

"Has Rose gathered the troops?" he asked.

Assad gave him a thumbs-up. Of course she had.

He stomped on the accelerator and turned on the blue light and siren.

They skidded to a halt in front of Tivoli Gardens' main entrance, leaving the car halfway on the pavement so it couldn't be seen from Rådhuspladsen. They hurried toward the square, arriving at the same instant as a van careered across the road and smashed into a truck that was headed for the building site, heavily laden with construction iron.

All was chaos. On their side of the road a pair of plainclothes officers took off in pursuit of fleeing men in dark suits while others surrounded a couple of young women who had remained behind. Out on the street cars slammed into the back of one another in a pileup as the van was crushed flat against the asphalt, sparks flying in all directions. Onlookers screamed or stood paralyzed by shock. Some yelled at the police that it was their fault.

Lars Bjørn was hardly going to pat them on the back for this.

"What's your name?"

"Miryam Delaporte."

"Profession?"

"I don't have one. I beg on the streets."

Carl nodded. She was the first to say it like it was. Respect.

"You're one of Zola's clan?"

She nodded. Some of the other women trembled at the mention of Zola's name, but not this one.

"Where do you come from, Miryam?" asked Rose.

"From Kregme, up in north Zealand."

"I see. Is that where you were born?"

She shrugged. "I've never seen my birth certificate."

OK, so it was like that.

"What do your parents say?"

"I don't know for certain who they are. That's how it is with many of us. We're one big family."

Rose and Carl exchanged glances. Surprising, how dispassionate she was.

"And that's all I'm saying," she added.

Carl drew his chair closer. She had good eyes, not just beautiful, but alive and alert. She had noted how Assad sat impatiently behind her, constantly shifting things around on his desk, and she had sussed that behind Rose's friendly facade was a determination to keep at it as long as necessary.

She was also well aware that the room she was in was not the path to freedom.

"I can tell you that Zola was killed in that accident," Rose continued. "You saw for yourself how bad it was. Might that not loosen your tongue?"

She turned her head away. There wasn't a trace of reaction in her face.

"Earlier today, another man was killed out in Østerbro. He died under a heavy vehicle, too. All of a sudden he just flew out in front of a bus. We don't know who he is, but we think he may be one of your people. We've got a photo here of the man's face. May I show it to you?"

Miryam remained silent, so Rose shoved it across the table toward her.

It took thirty seconds or so before curiosity got the better of her and she turned to look at it.

Both Carl and Rose saw her reaction. She didn't give a start, nor were there any facial contortions. It was something more profound, something deeper, like a sudden, sickening pain in her diaphragm. She drew in her stomach a bit, leaned slightly forward and adjusted the position of her legs.

"Who is he?" Carl asked. "Someone you cared for?"

She said nothing.

"OK, we'll find out soon enough. You're not the only one here at police headquarters. There are others from your group we can ask," said Rose. "The guys are the ones who talk the most, in case you'd like to know. But why is that so, Miryam? Is it because you women are afraid of being beaten if you talk too much? Is that how you got that bad leg of yours, Miryam? I can tell it didn't happen by itself."

Still no answer.

Now Assad stepped forward and pulled a chair up to her side, almost as though he were her solicitor, a kindly disposed person who would answer on her behalf.

"As you can see, she is saying nothing, so ask me instead," he said calmly, looking at Rose.

She frowned, but Carl nodded. Why not?

"Is it because she's afraid of getting beaten, Assad?"

"No. She is afraid of not belonging anywhere, that's why."

The girl turned her head toward him. Perhaps she wondered what he was getting at, or maybe she just didn't understand.

"And then she is afraid of herself," Assad went on. "Afraid she cannot be anything else than what she is. A simple thief and a beggar no one wants anything to do with besides her so-called family. And she is afraid they will think she has a looser tongue than they do, and that in a moment I will beat her until she bleeds."

Carl was about to protest, but noticed how the skin around her eyes tightened and her gaze grew more intense.

"That's enough, Assad," Rose cut in, but Carl put his hand on her shoulder.

"Assad's right. That's exactly what she's afraid of. Not to mention the risk of our booting her into the asylum center where she'd be together with those who'd know she'd been talking. I understand her better now, Assad."

He turned to the girl, who sat with her fists clenched in her lap.

"You know who Marco is, don't you?"

"I told you, I'm not saying more," she replied, almost in a whisper.

So she was softening up.

"Rose, can you tell me what we can do for Miryam if she helps us find out what Marco's got himself into?" asked Carl.

Rose's eyes narrowed. "As long as she's not cooperating, I'm not saying," she answered. "But I will say to Assad that if she doesn't help us, I think Marco's going to be hunted to death."

"How do you mean, Rose?" Carl asked.

"I think Miryam knows very well who Marco is and that she feels attached to him. Which I understand, because Marco's a good boy."

Carl weighed the situation for a moment. Interviews were an art form mastered only by a select few, and right now they'd obviously run into problems. But apart from that, he found Rose and Assad's interaction quite interesting. He didn't know quite where Assad was heading, but somewhere inside her Miryam certainly realized by now that she wasn't going to get away with keeping her mouth shut.

"You lived with Marco, we know that already," Rose went on. "Zola told us the boy grew up with the rest of you. Why not just say it's true? Or could it be you hated him?"

"She did not hate him," replied Assad.

"Why won't she answer, then?" Rose rejoined.

"Because she . . ." Assad leaned quickly forward and clasped his hands around her face. "Because she is ashamed. That is why."

Time to step in before he really gets started, Carl told himself.

But then Assad surprised him again. "You do not need to be ashamed, Miryam. Leave that to the others," he said, and let his hands fall to her shoulders.

Before she could wriggle free, he drew her toward him and held her tight. "There, there," he said, laying one hand gently behind her neck. "You are free now. There is no need for you to answer to anyone anymore. You are really free, Miryam. No more begging, no more stealing. If you help us, everything will be all right, do you understand?"

Some sort of reaction was to be expected, but not that she would be sitting there, fighting back the tears as her body relaxed.

Then she extricated herself from his embrace and looked him straight in the eye.

"The other day, I saw Marco outside a cinema, and I hit him in the face." She swallowed a couple of times, stemming her tears. "I didn't want to believe him. I didn't want to. But then I saw the despair in his eyes."

"Believe what, Miryam?" Rose took her hand and held it tight. "What was it you didn't want to believe?"

"I didn't want to believe something that could take my home away from me, just like that other man said before."

"Explain what you mean."

She raised her head. "I only knew for sure it would happen anyway when you showed me the photo of Marco's father." She pointed at the police photo of the dead man's face. "Oh, God, I knew it then, but only then."

"So the man there is Marco's father?"

She nodded. "One of the others told me Zola had pushed someone under a bus. I didn't know who it was. I thought it was Marco and that he deserved it."

"No one deserves that."

She nodded and lowered her head. "I know."

Carl indicated it was time for Rose to let go of her hand. He drew his chair up close.

"Tell us then, Miryam. What is it you now know?"

"I know it was all true what Marco said. I know it was Zola who pushed me into the road the time my leg was crushed, and that he was the one who killed his brother. I know that if Marco says Zola has killed others, too, then it must be true. I know that now. But I just don't understand."

He laid a hand on her shoulder. "Go on, Miryam. Let's hear it all."

She nodded again. "Two of the boys called Pico and Romeo came back one day and gave Zola a photo they'd taken from a house. They talked about the African necklace and about the man who was wearing it in the picture. I saw the photo later that day and recognized it."

"You recognized the necklace?"

"Yes. I remember I thought it was pretty. I'd seen it on a man they brought in with them one night. He was unconscious, so I thought he'd been drinking. But that was all I saw, because they sent me next door to the other house. I thought maybe he'd had an accident up on the main road and that they were helping him."

"And what did they do with this man?"

"I don't know. But I don't think it was anything good."

"Why do you think that?"

"Because I heard Zola's car drive away later the same night, and Zola never did that if he didn't really have to. At night he liked to be in bed with one of his women."

"Does that prove anything?"

"No, but the next day there was a muddy spade leaned up against the bins, and Chris's and Zola's brother's boots were covered in mud, too."

"So you think they killed the man?"

"I don't know, but I think he died." She stared pensively into space. "That has to be what Marco found out, too."

"What makes you think so?"

"The spade, I guess."

"How quickly did they come back?"

"After about half an hour."

"So if they'd buried the body, it could have been in the woods at the top of the hill?"

She nodded.

"We can confirm all this, Miryam. The man's name was William Stark and his body is no longer in the grave up there. Have you any idea where they might have moved it?"

She wiped her runny nose with the back of her hand. "There was a gravel pit close by. They went there sometimes for target practice."

Carl nodded. "OK, Miryam, thanks. We're in possession of some of the man's belongings and we also have a dog with a good sense of smell, so there's a good chance we'll find him."

"What's going to happen to me now?" she asked.

Assad got to his feet and quickly left the room while Rose remained seated.

Resolving situations was mostly her field.

"The motive, Assad, what is it? If you see the connection, then speak up," said Carl. "In any case we've got a fair amount to go on now, like Miryam's and Romeo's statements, and what Marco's been going around saying. We've got two missing persons, Stark and René E. Eriksen. We've got a link between Eriksen and Teis Snap, now deceased, as well as between Snap's bank and once again, strangely enough, our Eriksen. We've got a person who disappeared in Africa and a development project in the middle of nowhere that never materialized. Basically, a long chain of individuals and circumstances all connected in some way to René E. Eriksen."

Assad rasped a hand across the stubble of his chin. "The question is how this chain is then joined together, is it not? What came to the desert first, the camel or the dromedary? Do you understand, Carl?"

"Here we say the chicken or the egg, Assad. But I think we've got to assume that since Eriksen is at the center of all the links, the whole story begins in his ministry, and therefore he's still the one we need to concentrate on getting hold of."

"And Marco?"

Carl nodded. Yeah, where was Marco?

There was a sound of footsteps in the corridor. Unmistakably Gordon's big flat feet.

"Rose isn't here," said Carl, without looking up.

"Oh, really? Actually, it's you I wanted to see, Carl."

What now? Was the dork about to sound off again with more of his dubious bright ideas, or was it just some excuse for not having got his ass into gear with the job Carl had given him?

"I did as you told me. I checked up on Eriksen's financial affairs and discovered he recently sold off shares in Karrebæk Bank to the tune of ten million kroner."

"So you said two hours ago."

"I know, but we were interrupted. I really would have preferred to discuss it some more with you, but then I decided to pursue the matter myself."

"And what matter would that be?"

"Well, I ran a check on Karrebæk Bank and found out the name of the chairman of the board is Brage-Schmidt."

"Chairmen are always called something like that. A little hyphen now and again. Anything less would never do. So where are you going with this, Gordon?"

"Here comes the odd bit."

"Well, come on, man, before we turn to dust."

"Brage-Schmidt happens to be honorary consul for several central African states."

"Not including Cameroon, by any chance?"

Gordon nodded, making the fringe of hair dance above his eyes like a line of washing in a stiff westerly.

"Well, I'll be . . . damned. Cameroon's honorary consul on the same board as Eriksen, who's disappeared, and Teis Snap, who's stone-dead?"

"Yes."

"And he's loaded, yeah?"

"Major shareholder in Karrebæk Bank, yes."

"Have you spoken to him?"

"No, I didn't dare, thanks to you."

Carl smiled. Good boy. He was beginning to learn. A little respect was a good thing.

"Assad, check and see if this Brage-Schmidt's at home, will you?"

A couple of minutes passed before his curly head reappeared in the doorway. "There's a message from someone called Lisbeth on my voice mail. Has your mobile conked out, or is it because you can't be bothered to talk to her, Carl? This is what she asks."

Lisbeth! Shit.

He pulled his mobile out of his back pocket. Blank screen, dead as a doornail. That explained it.

"And what about Brage-Schmidt?"

"I think we should drive up there, Carl. He lives in Rungsted."

"Drive up there? Why?"

"Because his house is on fire."

They saw the coil of black smoke a mile off, spiraling into the sky above the Øresund strait. The flashing blue lights of ten fire engines and the feverish activity surrounding them assailed their senses as they turned into the road. The asphalt was already awash with sooty water.

The blaze was enormous, and it seemed clear that nothing would be left of the grandness of the residence but its foundations and its memories. The heat had melted the paint jobs on the Audis and Mercedes parked opposite, and the leaves of the surrounding trees were smoldering. Pandemonium reigned.

Carl shielded his face and tapped the fire brigade chief on the shoulder.

"Are there any fatalities?"

"Yes, we've pulled two bodies out."

"Can they be identified?"

The man broke into a wide smile, the way only a hardened firefighter could when asked such a question. "You'll have quite a job on your hands. I think you'd better start by finding yourself a couple of heavy-duty body bags and some good blokes with microscopes."

Carl looked over at the two heaps he was pointing at. Leaning against one of them were a pair of wheels and a crumpled metal frame.

"Was one of them in a wheelchair?"

"Looks like it. Most probably the owner of the house. A couple of the neighbors say they haven't seen him for ages. Maybe he couldn't get about."

"Brage-Schmidt?"

The fire chief checked his notes. "That's it. Jens Linus Brage-Schmidt, Honorary Consul, it says here."

Carl surveyed the hardworking firefighters, the boiling steam and the blaze. How the hell could anything burn like this?

"Any theories about what caused it?"

"That'll have to come later. But inflammable liquids are in there somewhere, no doubt about that. The neighbors say something smelled like spirits just before they raised the alarm."

"What about the other fatality?"

"No idea. The only person registered at the address was this Brage-Schmidt."

Carl walked over to an elderly couple standing just inside their wrought-iron gate, as if it could protect them in some way.

"Oh, how awful, how awful," the wife kept saying. "All our houses could have gone up in flames. Just look at our Mercedes."

Carl stood scratching his neck. Brage-Schmidt could hardly have been their best friend.

"Were you the people who called for help?" he asked.

They shook their heads emphatically. Obviously they were steering clear of the entire affair.

"OK, then, thanks. Let's just cross our fingers the hand-grenade depot explodes in the other direction, shall we?" He raised a finger to his imaginary hat in parting and they were back inside their house before he knew it.

"Over here, Carl," shouted Assad.

He nodded toward a youngish couple who, like their elderly neighbors, seemed to slot in nicely in these opulent surroundings. What it cost for all the makeup in which the woman had encased herself would have fed a fair-sized Bangladeshi family for at least a couple of decades.

"Well," she said. "Ernst had a feeling there was something amiss, so of course we advised the fire brigade."

She forgot to say "forthwith," Carl thought, then the sentence would be complete.

"We've already spoken to the police," said the man, when Carl showed him his ID. "Nothing more to say, really," he added. "We neither saw nor heard anything. People up here aren't very nosy."

"That's a shame. Did you have any contact with Mr. Brage-Schmidt?"

"Oh, you know. A bit of Rotary when he was younger. Not much of late, though. The delivery boy came with groceries every day and left them in the garage, but to tell you the truth, we never saw him come out to take them in. He was a bit peculiar."

Carl nodded as he and Assad walked back toward the smoldering ruin.

"Have you spoken to the fire investigators?" he asked.

"Yes, but they're no further than us, Carl, because the fire's still burning, sort of."

"Have you been over there?"

Carl pointed to a path that cut through the meter-tall beech-tree hedge surrounding the majority of houses along the road.

"It's too hot, I think. Why?"

"We could have a word with the neighbors from round the back."

"In that case, you can just as well talk to him over there."

Carl saw a boy standing at the curb with his bike. He seemed oddly intense, his eyes aflame and a reddish-yellow glow reflecting in his face.

"Assad says you live in the house behind here. Did you notice anything strange going on today?" he asked, as he approached.

The lad shook his head.

"No one who happened to be walking along the path or who squeezed through a hole in the hedge?"

"There isn't a hole. There's a gate."

"How do you mean?"

"You can get from our road into the consul's garden through a gate. That's what the Negro always does."

"The Negro?"

"Yeah, the one who lives in the house."

"We didn't know anyone was living there apart from Brage-Schmidt. But you're saying someone does?"

"He's lived there for years. He always leaves his car on one of the other roads and walks to the house from there."

It was from the mouths of babes and drunks that the truth emerged.

Carl gave the lad a friendly punch on the shoulder. Thanks for the tip.

"Let's have a look at those barbecued bodies, shall we? I think I know who the other one is now," he said, drawing Assad over toward the two charred mounds lying on the tarps by the hedge.

The flesh was as good as burned away. There were still remnants of leather on the exposed bones of one the body's fingers, probably from the armrest of the wheelchair. From the permanent S-shaped position of the corpse, it looked like he'd been sitting in it when the place went up.

The other body was little but a heap of scorched bones held together by fused tendons and charred muscle. The eye sockets were burned empty and the facial skin melted off. It was impossible to tell whether the person had been white or black, let alone male or female.

"What's that?" said Assad, indicating the corpse's mouth. He glanced around. There were no forensic technicians in sight.

He stuck his finger in between what had once been lips and pushed the slop of remains aside.

"I've seen these dentures before," he said.

Carl gave a nod of surprise as Assad wiggled one of the front teeth with his finger.

There was no doubt about it, Carl had to admit. The body was René

E. Eriksen's. A set of choppers like that wasn't something you forgot in a hurry.

Assad wiped his hands on his trousers. "What do you say, Carl?"

"The same as you, probably, that now they've all bumped each other off, and the case is drawing to a close. I reckon Laursen will agree, once he sees the technicians' reports and the DNA analyses."

40

For a long time Marco thought about how much space emptiness can actually take up inside a person. Only hours ago everything had been so chaotic, yet so, so straightforward. He'd been on the run, his father and Zola were still alive, and the clan had been working the streets. But now both his father and Zola were dead, and a whole lot of clan members had been arrested.

And here he was, wondering what was next. Was he free? With Zola gone, who would call off the hunt? And how was he supposed to get along with no money at the same time as he was wanted by the police?

It was all so difficult. No matter how hard he tried to think, his mind was awash with sorrow, relief and fear, rendering futile all attempts to make any kind of decision.

Perhaps it would all pass if he just waited a day or two. Why should they all be after him when Zola was no more? And why should the police continue their search as well? After all, he'd done nothing wrong. No, a couple of days lying low, considering his next move—that's what he needed. And who could tell? Maybe now he could even get his money out of Kaj and Eivind's apartment.

He hailed a taxi outside the Søpavillion nightclub and a quarter of an hour later he was standing in front of Stark's house. Inside there was a bed and some food, he knew that. A good place to pass the time and wait.

He looked up the drive as the taxi pulled away, immediately seeing an old Mazda parked at the end of the house, tailgate raised and back doors wide-open. Bulging black trash bags had been deposited along the wall of the house. And now came two more, in the hands of a woman he recognized as Tilde's mother.

Marco ducked behind a tree with his back to the lake.

His head popped in and out from his hiding place as Tilde's mother began to load the car, like an inquisitive animal, registering every movement. What if the girl was there, too? What new options would be open to him then? Wasn't this the moment for him to take his chance?

He took one step out from behind the tree. The car was perhaps only fifty meters away, yet his legs felt like lead. How would he ever be able to tell them the truth?

"Why are you standing there, watching my mother?" said a voice from behind.

Marco gave a start and whirled around to find himself face-to-face with Tilde, her shoes covered in mud, her trouser legs wet.

"It's lucky I was down here by the lake. What is it you want?"

She seemed ethereal in her loose blouse, with her hair hanging down her back. But her face was like stone. He hadn't seen her like this before, and it certainly wasn't the way he'd hoped they would meet for the first time.

"You're the one the police have a photo of, aren't you?" she said coldly.

Marco frowned.

"If you touch me, I'll scream. OK?"

He nodded. "I won't do anything to you," he replied. "I just want to talk with the two of you. With you, I mean," he added, correcting himself.

"Why?"

He swallowed. How to begin?

"The police say you know something. How come you know William?" she asked, getting straight to the point.

"I don't. But I know what happened to him."

She struggled to appear calm, but everything inside her was screaming that there was nothing in the world she wanted to know more, yet was afraid to hear. It was so obvious. Marco could hardly stand to see her like this.

Tilde's voice trembled. "If you don't know him, then how do you know it's him?"

"He had red hair and he was wearing an African necklace. I've seen a picture of him, and it is the same man I saw. I just know, that's all."

She put a hand to her mouth, the other fluttering at her hip.

"You say 'had' red hair."

Now was the time. "I'm very sorry, Tilde, but he's dead."

He'd expected her to collapse with a howl of anguish, that she would clench her teeth and take out her grief on him with her fists, but she didn't.

Instead, she seemed to retreat inside herself, as if something inside her had been extinguished. A spark that might otherwise have ignited the desire to look ahead, a fire to fuel the dreams these past years had taken from her. Everything went out at once as her arms fell to her sides and her head dropped.

Standing there, she resembled someone resigned to facing a firing squad. No tears, no struggle, no cries for mercy, no cries in anger. Just a person yielding to her fate.

"Are you sure?" she asked in a tiny voice.

"Yes."

And then she began ever so quietly to sob.

Marco put his arms around her as she cried, and told her everything that had tormented him for so long. And when he told her his own father had played a part in the death of her stepfather, he too began to weep. But instead of pushing him away, instead of spitting on him, she drew herself still closer to him so he felt the warmth of her breath against his cheek and the rapid pounding of her heart.

"I knew it," she said, tears pouring now. "I knew he was dead. William would never just leave us, so I knew."

"I'm off with this first carload, Tilde," a woman's voice called from the house.

She pulled away from Marco, dried her eyes on her sleeve, and told him to stay put.

"I'm staying here," she called back, stepping forward into sight. "Is that OK?"

"Yes, fine. Just stay in the house till I come back. I'll bring us something to eat. What would you like?"

From behind the trees Marco could see her whole body trembling again. But her voice was under control.

"Whatever," she replied. "I'll leave it up to you."

They waved to each other, and when the car was gone she turned to him.

"We're moving all our stuff out now. The police were here a few days ago, and after that, my mum didn't want anything left here."

"Why not?"

"They said all kinds of things about William that upset her. And something about you, too."

"About me? What did they say?"

"It doesn't matter; it wasn't true. And they said he'd spent money that might not have been his. That's something we simply can't understand. We don't believe he kept things secret from us. You wouldn't either, if you knew him and had been in the house. It's not a home with secrets."

"I *have* been in the house," he said.

Her face darkened as he told her about the times he had hidden there. About his curiosity, and the strange bond he felt he had with the place. And he told her about the time he'd hidden in the safe, and his puzzlement over the code inside.

"I don't like the idea of you just breaking in. I don't even know if I should be standing here, talking to you. It seems wrong all of a sudden."

He nodded, but said nothing. What was there to say? He understood her completely.

"Have you lost your tongue?" she asked after a moment.

"You don't have to talk to me. I just came to tell you the truth. Now you can pass it on to the police. Tell it to a detective called Carl Mørck. He was here, too."

She looked surprised. "I know who he is. He was the one who told us about you."

Marco looked up at her. So they had actually had contact. That was good news.

"What was that code in the safe you mentioned?" she asked. "Will you show me?"

She lay on her back on the floor and peered up inside the safe.

"A4C4C6F67," she repeated to herself a couple of times, until she could remember it by heart.

Then she wriggled out and looked at him pensively.

"It's a chess move," she said with a frown. "A4 to C4 to C6 to F6 and 7. But why? It makes no sense at all."

She shook her head. "William and I often played together, and those moves are useless, believe me."

"I've never played chess. What does it mean? What's C6, for instance?"

"It's a square on the board. If you think of a chessboard, there are sixty-four squares in all. Eight horizontal and eight vertical. Each square has a label, starting in the bottom left corner, then moving horizontally from left to right, A, B, C, and so on, and from bottom to top, one, two, three, four, and up to eight."

Marco tried to picture it. "So C6 is three to the side from the left and six up?"

"Yes, it is, but it's a move that doesn't make much sense."

"But it was written inside the safe as well, so I don't think they're moves in a game. Maybe it's supposed to indicate something else entirely."

"A chessboard, perhaps?"

"But I just said . . ."

"Yes, I know, but maybe something that looks like one. Something with sixty-four squares."

They looked at each other at once, the same thought dawning.

"How many flagstones are there in the patio?" Marco asked.

She took his hand and tugged him out of the house and into the garden.

The weather was still warm even though it was late in the day, but Tilde began to shiver as they counted the flags.

"You're right. Eight one way and eight the other," said Marco, trying to figure out what she was doing.

"This ought to work," she said, picking up a white stone form the flower bed.

Then she counted the flagstones, index finger extended, and every time she came to one of the squares in question she wrote its number on it: A4, C4, C6, F6 and F7. Seven flagstones in all.

"You do it," she said, and pointed at A4.

Marco glanced around.

"Over there," she said, nodding toward a spade that was leaned against the shed.

Marco stuck it between the flags and upended A4.

There was a frenzy of insects in the sand, but nothing else.

"Dig into the sand," she instructed.

He thrust the blade downward and felt an immediate resistance.

"Be careful," she said, growing excited. "Use your hands."

He got down on his knees and scraped away the sand until a small plastic container appeared in front of him. Now he, too, began to breathe more rapidly.

He opened the lid and removed the contents. Two gold rings, a coral necklace with matching bracelet and earrings, two brooches shaped like daisies, and a floppy disk labeled with small block letters: "AN INTERNATIONAL PERSPECTIVE ON PENSION FUNDS, RETIREMENT INCOME SECURITY AND CAPITAL MARKETS," it read.

Marco didn't get it. The jewelry wasn't worth much, and he couldn't make sense of the disk at all.

Tilde sat for a long while on her haunches, considering the items one by one before speaking. "Mum said she was sure he'd got rid of everything. But there was one time when I was really doing poorly and thought I was going to die, and William said that one day when I got married I was to wear the same jewelry as his mother had on when she got married." She pressed her lips together. "And then there's this." She clutched the disk tight in her hand. "I knew why he never finished his thesis. He didn't have time because of my illness. And look, he . . ."

Then her face contorted as the tears ran freely.

Marco let her cry, but put his arm around her shoulder.

She looked up at him when she calmed down again. "Look. He tried, anyway. He set his work aside for another time, and he saved the jewelry for me."

She shook her head as she collected herself. Then she dried her eyes and stood up abruptly.

"Come on, it's no use waiting. We need to dig them all up."

Ten minutes later they were sitting with four more open containers in front of them.

Under C4 they found a notebook, under C6, some bank statements, and under F6, an envelope on which was written "My Will." And under F7 lay a plastic pocket full of documents bearing the ministry's logo, on front of which was written the words, "BAKA PROJECT," in bold capital letters.

Tilde opened the notebook and recognized William's handwriting straightaway.

She scanned the first page, then raised her hands to her head and began massaging her forehead with the tips of her fingers.

Marco could see the tears welling again.

Her eyes glided repeatedly up and down the first page, and each time her face grew slightly paler.

"Aren't you going to see what's on the other pages?" he asked.

She shook her head.

"What's wrong? Are you feeling sick?"

She nodded.

They remained kneeling on the ground for a while, and then she put the notebook back in the container.

"The police were right. William took a lot of money. It's all recorded there." She pressed her lips together, then continued. "And he did it for me, I know he did. That makes me very sad. And sorry that I can't talk to him now."

Marco knew the feeling better than anyone.

"What about the other things?" he asked.

She picked up the bank statements that had been hidden under C6 and paged through them before putting them down again with a sigh. "It's the same. All the deposits and payments he made. It all fits."

"Fits?"

"Yes. He transferred money into the account and paid my hospital bills the same day. I recognize the names of all the places I was, and the dates, too, more or less."

"He really loved you, didn't he?"

"Yes."

Marco looked away for a second. He wondered if she knew how lucky she had been.

"Will you open this, Marco? I don't think I can," she said, handing him the envelope with the words "My Will" written on it.

He opened the envelope. Inside was a document written on a solicitor's letterhead and stamped with the word "copy" in red. It was headed LAST WILL AND TESTAMENT.

"He's left everything he had to you and your mother, Tilde," he told her.

She squeezed her eyes tight shut. It was simply too much for her.

Marco picked up the final collection of papers that had been buried under flagstone F7.

"Any idea what these are?" he asked her, waiting until she opened her despairing eyes.

"They're from his workplace. The Baka project was the last thing he was involved in, I think."

"Why would he bury it here? It can't be as important as the other stuff, surely?"

She shrugged. "I don't know. Maybe we should hand it in to his office."

They heard the car pull up outside.

Tilde turned toward the sound. "That'll be my mum. But why isn't she parking in the drive?"

"Are you planning to show her all this?" he asked, as she tossed the items back in their respective containers and gathered them together.

She shook her head. "Will you put them back in the ground, and the flagstones, too, while I go out to her? I'll call for you when I've told her you're here. Then you can tell her everything you've told me, because I don't think I can do it myself, OK?"

Marco nodded, though he was afraid of how her mother might react.

He hurried to do as she'd requested, and when he'd finished he leaned the spade back up against the shed. Everything had to be as it was before. He stood looking at the patio and nodded to himself. He had scuffed away Tilde's chalk marks as best he could. They weren't completely gone, but it was good enough. No one would know what they'd been up to.

Hearing the car horn sound insistently a couple of times in the road, he wondered if it meant Tilde wanted him to come out front.

He brushed the dirt from his hands and walked cautiously round the side of the house toward the drive, not wishing to give anyone a start.

He saw the rear end of the car, but didn't recognize it as Tilde's mother's. Maybe he just hadn't noticed it before. Maybe it *had* been two-toned. A lot of old cars were.

He heard Tilde's scream from the street at the same instant as he sensed a movement at the corner of the house, but before he could react, a black figure leaped at him with such force that they both stumbled backward, slamming their heads against the rough planks of the bike shed and landing in a heap on the ground. He saw something flash in the air above him, but didn't realize it was a knife until his assailant lunged at his arm and raised the weapon once more.

"Help!" he screamed, hammering his knee up into the man's groin and rolling to the side. "Help me!"

But apart from the noise of their heavy breathing, there wasn't a sound to be heard in the neighborhood. No one reacted. And now Marco recognized the man. These wild eyes, this white scar, the shiny blade. He was the one who had confronted him at the building site, the one who'd got stuck in the rubble chute. And the savagery of his expression made it plain that this time he would not fail.

"Help!" Marco yelled again, jumping toward the shed as his adversary lunged at him again, twisting his ankle in the process and almost losing his footing.

His loss of balance now proved costly as Marco grasped the handle of the spade and swung it through the air, its sharp edge leaving a deep gash in the man's left shoulder.

He dropped the knife in a roar of pain, clutching the gaping wound as blood pumped out of him.

For a split second he stared at Marco with his yellow eyes, then fled back to the car that was waiting in the road.

Marco ran after him and saw Tilde in the back of the car, being held down by a huge corpulent black woman. A woman he had seen before.

Then, as he sprinted toward the car, he was stopped abruptly in his tracks by the crack of a gun and a bullet that slammed into the house wall behind him.

There was another shot, and the sound of a second projectile whistling past his ear.

He ducked back round the side of the house and stood for a moment, hyperventilating. It was because of him they had caught Tilde, and now the situation was hopeless. If he approached the car, they would kill him. But what else could he do?

Then he shut his eyes and shouted at the top of his voice in English: "Let her go. I'll come instead."

He peeked round the corner and saw the man he'd taken out with the spade screaming inside the car. Judging by the blood on the pavement, he was in bad shape.

Then he saw the woman in the backseat slap the driver—the one who'd done the shooting—on the back of the head, and the car took off down the street.

Marco ran after it, trying to pick out the number plate, but it had been covered up. A hundred meters farther down the road the vehicle suddenly stopped and a small item was dropped out of the side window onto the asphalt.

Then the car disappeared.

Marco was stunned. Was he now to blame for more misfortune befalling this little family? Was it to be Tilde and her mother's curse that he, his father, and the tyrant, Zola, had ever existed?

He proceeded cautiously toward the object in the road, full of dread. What could it be? A hand grenade? Or worse still: a body part they had cut off her?

Then he heard it ring. It was a mobile phone.

He picked it up and answered: "Yes?"

"We'll kill her unless you give yourself up," the woman said in English.

Marco felt a shiver run down his spine. "Zola's dead. Why are you still hunting me?"

"He's not the one who's paying us."

His shoulders sagged. "I was going to surrender myself to you. Why didn't you let me?"

"We've got other things to think about now, thanks to you."

"Let me speak to Tilde."

"You'll see her when we do the exchange. We'll call and tell you where. If you go to the police, we'll kill her. If we sense something is wrong when we exchange you two, we'll kill her."

"But I—"

"We'll be in touch," the woman snapped, and hung up.

Marco rang back immediately, but the line was already dead.

When the world collapses into tiny pieces, one is able to comprehend the individual elements of the catastrophe as it unfolds. Thus it must have been for the hapless souls in the Twin Towers on 9/11, as well as for the stunned onlookers who witnessed it all from the ground. For Marco, that moment where he stood in the middle of the road, totally impotent, was but one of a chain of misfortunes leading to the definitive finale: his own demise.

He knew now that he had to make a sacrifice. There was no time to acquire a firearm, for where would he get one, and who would sell him such a thing? And even if he tried to fight back, he ran the risk of not only losing his own life, but of Tilde losing hers as well.

Then he saw a car turn the corner and head in his direction. He stepped aside reluctantly as the vehicle braked.

"What's the matter with you, kid?" the woman shouted.

It was Tilde's mother.

The last person in the world he wanted to speak to at the moment, yet in reality the most important of all.

"They've taken Tilde," were the first words he said.

The rest he told her as she stared at him, her eyes wild, and insisted they drive to police HQ.

Immediately!

41

"**Can you pop up** to the interview room, Carl?" Assad asked over the phone. "I have something exciting for you."

"I'm not sure I can cope with more excitement today," he replied, shoving aside Rose's stack of printouts on Brage-Schmidt's financial transactions and career movements. "But give me a couple of minutes, I'll be right up." He hung up and called Rose again.

Where the hell was she?

Even though she hadn't yet got hold of all the documents he'd asked for, it was becoming clearer and clearer to him what lay behind the events of the past few days. The exact whys and wherefores were unknowns, but nonetheless he felt he was beginning to see the perspectives involved in large-scale misappropriation of development funds and their subsequent siphoning off into the accounts of the individuals who had lost their lives over the past few days. The way things were shaping up, this was clearly a case for the fraud squad and other experts in economic crime. They'd have plenty to dig into.

The murders of Snap and his wife down in Karrebæksminde and the apparent arson attack in Rungsted that had cost a further two lives weren't strictly speaking a matter for Department Q, but it was hard not to suspect that in some way or another they were connected to what had happened to William Stark.

As Carl saw it, Stark had either known too much, or else he was deeply involved in what Snap and the others were up to. But Stark was dead, they knew that now, and whatever criminal activity he might or might not have been engaged in was academic at this point.

Now his role in the Stark case was closed. At some point a presumption-of-death verdict would be pronounced, and maybe one day a dog or a Boy Scout would come across the remains of some bones that Malene Kristoffersen could properly consign to the earth with a regular head-stone. Then everyone could get on with their lives. Everyone but Stark himself.

Carl stared at the two phone numbers on the slip of paper before him. One was Mona's consultancy, the other was Lisbeth's.

The way he was feeling at the moment, he hadn't a clue which to choose.

"Have you seen the time, Carl?"

He looked up at Rose, standing in the doorway, then at his watch. Almost seven.

"I'm just popping out before the shops close. Anything you need?"

"No, thanks. I'm on my way upstairs to Assad. He's got the last of Zola's boys in interview. He claims he's got something interesting for us. After that, I'm off home."

"OK, but come down here again before you go. I've got something for you guys, too."

Carl sighed as Rose's footsteps faded down the corridor. You'd better take care of this now, the phone numbers in front of him seemed to be insisting.

He looked at them again.

These were two women, each with her own qualities. No doubt about it.

"This here is Hector, Carl. Say hi to Carl, Hector," said Assad.

Carl nodded. No need to be hostile. The guy seemed softened up already.

Hector put out his hand, but shaking it would be a bit much, Carl reckoned.

"Well, now," he said, plonking himself down on a chair by the desk. "No handcuffs, I see, so you've been a good boy, haven't you, Hector?"

He nodded.

"Hector is the oldest in his generation of Zola's children," Assad explained, clapping him on the shoulder. "Everyone saw him as Zola's successor when the time came, and now he is sitting here telling me that all his life he has dreamed of getting away."

Carl looked at Assad and gave a wry smile. "So therefore you've told Hector that he could be in line for a permanent residence permit, is that right, Assad?"

He raised a thumb. "Exactly, Carl."

Christ on a bike!

"Tell Carl then what you told me, Hector." Assad turned to face his boss. "Now the interesting part is coming."

The guy looked dapper in his black suit. If Assad had been able to fulfil his promise, his appearance certainly wouldn't be a hindrance to his assimilation into Danish society. If only a tenth of Denmark's sartorially challenged citizenry—himself included—dressed like Hector, the nation would take possession of haute couture's yellow jersey from the Italians and the French.

"I said there were two things that went terribly wrong today," he said in fluent English. "One was that Zola killed his brother out in Østerbro. If he could do a thing like that, it meant none of us was safe. Until then, I thought I was, at least. The second thing was the Africans. I saw them beat a couple of guys to a pulp. I think they were from Estonia, and they were plenty nasty, too. But the blacks scared me because they were so young, and their eyes were so cold. And now they're out on the streets, looking for Marco."

Carl frowned. Here were two important pieces of information he'd need to follow up on, and then he was finished with the case.

"Why are they still hunting Marco, now that Zola's dead?"

"They're contract killers. People like them do what they've been paid for. Their reputation depends on it."

Contract killers? In Copenhagen?

"Have you any idea where Marco is now?"

Hector shrugged. "Marco's good at playing hide-and-seek," he replied.

"You heard where they were from, didn't you, Carl?" said Assad.

"Yeah." It wasn't what concerned him most at the moment.

"People like them don't talk," said Hector, taking a gulp of the water Assad had placed in front of him, the only luxury in this cramped and barren room. "So none of us knows who hired them. All I can say is it wasn't Zola. He kept well away from blacks."

Carl looked at Assad. "What are you thinking, Assad?"

"I'm thinking about a lot of things, Carl. I'm thinking about a consul for African countries, a man who is chairman of the board of the same bank that the deceased Snap was the manager of. And a second man who disappears after visiting Africa. Then a third, who goes missing in Africa. And a fourth, a mysterious African who has vanished from the consul's house. Then there's the swindle involving development funds for a project in Africa, and a man who works professionally with aid to Africa whom we find dead, together with the consul. And now these Africans, running around Copenhagen and scaring macho types like Hector here."

Carl nodded. "You're right, there's a connection with Africa in all of this. But unfortunately the man most likely able to provide us with answers to all our questions is now little more than a charred lump in a very small body bag over at the Forensic Medicine Institute. A bit of a problem, wouldn't you say?"

"Yeah, I sure would."

"Listen, Assad. That's the second time today. You can't go promising streets paved with gold to everyone you interview, you know."

Carl sat down at his desk, shaking his head as he turned on TV2's news channel. Maybe they'd be able to catch something about the arrests they'd made during the day.

"But why not, Carl? It's so much better than thumbscrews, I'd say. Carrots are always better then whips."

"So are you suggesting that if you couldn't trick them with your promises, you'd torture them?"

"Torture, Carl, what is torture, exactly? Can it not be many things?"

They stared at each other for a moment, but neither of them took the initiative to carry on the discussion. It was too volatile an issue.

"I had a word with the guys in the violent crime section," said Carl. "They've heard nothing involving Africans the last few days, apart from the usual pusher problems on Istedgade. So what are we supposed to do? We can't just go running up to Lars Bjørn with vague accusations about two Africans whose identities we don't know, saying they pose a threat to a lad whose whereabouts are unknown, can we? I don't know about you, but I reckon we're done with this case."

"Say, do you know what, Carl? You will not find the camel if the sand is lying in dunes, but . . . erm, how does it go, now?" Assad stared at him, perplexed. It must have been the first time his camels had let him down.

Carl tapped a cigarette from his pack. The two phone numbers were still sitting there in front of him, and soon he'd be heading home. What to do?

"What I mean is, if the sand is lying in large . . ."

Objectively, Mona probably wouldn't show that much interest, but if he rang Lisbeth instead, wouldn't that mean Mona was out of his life for good? Was that he wanted?"

"Now I have it, Carl. If the sand piles up into dunes, you will not find the camel. But if the wind begins blowing hard, you can easily see the humps. Ha-ha. That was a good one, don't you think?"

Carl looked up at him wearily.

"And?"

"It means we cannot know the whole truth until the wind begins to blow a little. I mean, how can we know we are done with this case if we don't poke around in it some more?"

"Well, to begin with there's no wind blowing, and besides that we haven't the manpower at our disposal to work up a gale out there, have we? So don't you think we should give those camels a break and let them have a little rest in the dunes?"

"You understand the moral of the story, Carl, that's the main thing. But then we'll just have to wait until the wind starts blowing by itself, won't we?"

Carl nodded. This was a moral he liked. If nothing else, it meant he could allow himself to throw his feet up on his desk and do sod all.

"OK. Now I'm going to have a smoke and watch the news. And if Rose isn't back in ten minutes, I'm gone."

He wedged the cigarette between his lips, already sensing the assuaging effect of the nicotine his body craved. He'd been waiting all day for it, and now . . .

"Forget about that cigarette, Carl," came a voice from the doorway.

And there stood Rose, with the heartiest smile he'd ever seen her wearing, holding up a paper bag from the bakery.

"Warm wheat buns, lads. I'll bet you forgot today's supposed to be a holiday. It's the fourth Friday after Easter."

She opened the bag and a wonderful aroma filled the room, bestowing upon their gloomy surroundings an undeserved aura of everyday coziness as well as dim recollections of candles, radio dramas, and end-of-season balls at the Hotel Phønix.

"Delicious," Carl conceded, already salivating.

And then the phone rang.

"We've got two people standing at the desk here, asking for Carl Mørck. Do you want us to send them down?"

Marco was scared. Much more than he had been out on the streets. There, at least, he'd had a chance, but now he felt like he was throwing himself directly to the lions.

His breathing grew heavier as he passed through the corridors, feeling hemmed in by the cold, unforgiving walls of Copenhagen police headquarters. From the outside, the place looked like a fortress, but inside it felt even worse, and at this moment they were leading him down into a basement from which the only way a person could get out seemed to be the same way as he got in. All of a sudden he was a cornered rat surrounded by a pack of club-wielding boys, out to kill him for the fun of it.

And Tilde's mother, who had not loosened her grip on him since parking her car, wasn't making things any better. All the way to headquarters she'd screamed and yelled at him in desperation. That she'd been able to find her way with the shock and adrenaline coursing through her body was a small miracle.

But Marco understood her, for now he had told her all about Tilde and the black men and their threats, and what had happened to William Stark. She had reacted fiercely, attacking him verbally, then crying, her entire body trembling. So much pain and anxiety all at once was too much for her to manage. And suddenly she had struck him, only to regret it immediately and apologize in a shaky voice. And now, as they hurried down the stairs to meet the police officers with whom he'd been playing cat-and-mouse for the past few days, it seemed like she was about to undergo a total meltdown.

Marco knew this was to be his final hour as a free person in a free country. If he survived what the evening had in store for him, he was sure he would be thrown out of the country, but to where?

With all that had befallen him in life, he feared the worst.

Therefore the sight that confronted him was completely unexpected.

Mørck and his two assistants were seated around an untidy desk, munching bread rolls that crunched noisily as the TV news blathered in the background. A sweet, reassuring aroma hung in the air, and the faces that turned toward them were friendly enough, but also profoundly astonished.

Once they realized who their visitors were, all three rose to their feet abruptly, as though witnessing nothing less than a miracle.

"You're Marco, aren't you?" said Mørck, stepping toward him. He towered above the boy as he reached out with his long arms.

Marco's heart was pounding. The man from whom he had fled had stopped smiling now. His lips were pressed tight, his eyes much too intense.

And then he grasped him and lifted him up, as though he were about to crush his every bone.

"Thank God," he said quietly, clutching him to his chest for a moment. "You're OK."

He set him down again and bent forward to look into his face.

"There's a lot we want to ask you about. Do you want to talk to us now?"

Marco nodded, holding his breath. The man had put his arms around him. He seemed accommodating and glad to see him. It was just too overwhelming. If he didn't watch out, he'd start to cry. This was the last thing he'd been expecting.

"Good boy," said the one called Assad, and patted him on the head. Even the girl with the black makeup smiled at him.

"Thank you for bringing him in, Malene," said Mørck.

She nodded, and then it burst out of her: "Something terrible's happened. Please help us!"

Mørck caught her gaze. Now they could all see the desperation in her eyes. "What happened, Malene?"

It was a simple question, but it triggered a burst of tears, beseeching, and rampant alarm. Marco could see how hard it was for the three police officers to follow her disjointed, staccato narrative.

But when she said two Africans who were pursuing Marco had taken Tilde, they stiffened.

The woman they called Rose asked them both to take a seat. Mørck put a hand on Marco's shoulder and squeezed it warm, just the way his father had done all too rarely, and then he turned his attention to Malene.

Marco trembled. He had never experienced anything like this. It almost pained him physically to think of how all his misgivings had been put to shame. Especially now, when it wasn't long before he would have to sacrifice himself.

Assad asked if he should make some tea, but Mørck stopped him abruptly and sat down in front of Tilde's mother, taking her hand in his.

She began to speak, slower now and more coherently, as Rose and Assad whispered to each other in the background.

On the flat screen behind Mørck a reporter was speaking outside Tivoli as a streaming text at the bottom of the screen told of police rolling up a band of thieves from north Zealand that had been ravaging Copenhagen, and that many arrests had ensued.

Then the newscast cut to one of the more dramatic arrests showing several officers subduing a fiercely resisting man.

It was Pico.

Mørck turned to the boy with a grave expression on his face. "May I see the mobile they left in the road for you, Marco?"

He handed it over and Mørck studied it. A quite ordinary Nokia, five or six years old, from the time the company had been riding high. Marco had stolen hundreds of them.

Mørck turned it over in his hands. There was a number on the back in felt-tip, probably put there by whoever had got the phone unlocked before selling it on. These things were to be found all over Copenhagen, Marco knew that better than anyone.

"Give this number a call, will you, Rose?" Mørck instructed. "It might be this one's, or another one entirely. It may even be the one we're waiting to hear from."

She entered the number. The mobile in Mørck's hand rang.

"OK, so that's sorted. But have a look at the display and check the number the kidnappers called from, Rose. It looks like an African country code."

She glanced at the display, then left with the phone in her hand.

In the minutes that followed they succeeded in getting Tilde's mother to breathe more regularly, but they couldn't make her hands stop shaking.

"How are you feeling, Marco? Not too good either?" Mørck asked.

He shook his head in confirmation.

"We'll get Tilde back, you'll see," he said. But Marco didn't like the looks he and Assad exchanged.

"The Ivory Coast. That's the country code," Rose announced as she came back in. "I don't think we're going to get too far with that number, unfortunately. It doesn't seem to be registered in an existing name."

"Oh, God," Tilde's mother gasped.

Then the African mobile in Rose's hand beeped quietly.

"It's a text message," she said in a quiet voice.

"What's it say?" Mørck asked.

"It says: *Pusher Street, Christiania. Tonight eight P.M.*—and they want Marco to come alone, otherwise . . ."

Her voice trailed off as she looked up at Tilde's mother, then handed Marco the phone.

They had exactly twenty-five minutes.

42

For Carl, Free State Christiania was familiar territory. There wasn't a nook or a cranny in this colorful, unique, and anarchic oasis into which he hadn't poked his nose back in the dawn of time, not a single house he hadn't entered, clad in full uniform and his country-boy naivety.

Fredens Ark, Loppen, Operaen, Nemoland, Pusher Street, Den Grå Hal, the Green Light District, Sunshine Bakery. Each was a name with its own story, its own incidents. And because he knew the place, Carl also knew how hopeless their task was.

Carl's viewpoint was ambivalent. From a policeman's perspective, Christiania was a den of vice, a nest of riffraff, but seen from a different angle it was a place where a person could breathe freely and live the dream of an age before Copenhagen was handed over to the yuppies and everything was drawn in straight lines. Christiania was—and remained—an umbilical cord to the capital's charm and to ideas in free flight. A bicycling, environmentally protective subcultural powerhouse where dogs and beautiful people had turned an ugly former military barracks into what was arguably Denmark's biggest tourist attraction.

But, as is so often the case, the best intentions and ideas became subverted by stupid individuals without norms, twisted and distorted until they were no longer recognizable. Thus, Christiania existed in the eternal dilemma: to give freedom free rein, or to rein freedom in?

In recent years, the people of Christiania had been given the right of self-determination, so now they alone were responsible for how the free state functioned. Not surprisingly, both good and bad had come of it.

Now the days when smiling policemen in sensible shoes could stroll unchallenged through this cultural collage were long gone. All forms of police presence were anathematized, so that only the most recently hatched or most implacable officers felt like stirring things up in a place like Pusher Street.

People on that street could smell a pig a mile off, and given the chance, they'd make sure the cops never wanted to come back again. If it hadn't been for Pusher Street, Christiania would have been a kind of paradise. Instead, if there was anywhere the police could count on resistance, it was Pusher Street in Christiania, and somehow the Africans had sussed this out.

Carl closed his eyes and tried to walk himself through this graffitied Klondike in his mind. There were guys openly stationed by the end of the street nearest Prinsessegade, keeping an eye on who came and went. At the other end, close by the colorful vegetable store, there were people sitting in the cafés or under lean-tos with equally watchful eyes. Of course a person could enter Pusher Street unseen by way of one of the side streets, though lookouts were posted there, too, amid the uninhibited commerce in hash and skunk. But coming in that way meant it would be well-nigh impossible to get an overview of what was going on along the entire length of the street, which in this case was imperative.

The question now was how the Africans were intending to deal with the situation. Doubtless they'd be expecting that once they'd got their hands on Marco and the girl had been released, the boy would start to kick up a fuss. For that reason one would have to assume they would be sticking close to the buildings along the street so as to be able to drag Marco somewhere quiet and pacify him with a hypodermic needle or a beating.

While the people of Pusher Street tended to be rather nonchalant when it looked like violence would erupt, most would surely draw the line at assault on a minor. The Africans would scarcely want a confrontation with a mob of that kind, so they would act swiftly and without drawing attention to themselves.

Carl showed Rose and Assad the police map of the area and pointed out the various options. The street itself wasn't long, but it ran like an artery through all kinds of lanes and alleyways, some of which openly housed criminal activity while others seemed quaintly and peacefully rural with their allotment gardens. Personally, Carl favored a route from the entrance on Bådmandsstræde that led past Fredens Ark and Tinghuset, and therefore he decided he would offer it to Assad, since he was unfamiliar with the area.

Rose was to follow Marco at a suitable distance from one of the side entrances on Prinsessegade, continue past Bøssehuset and proceed toward Pusher Street from the opposite side. Carl himself would run the gauntlet directly from the main gate down toward the Freetown area, where he figured it most likely the Africans would be waiting for Marco.

Malene pleaded with them to let her come along, but was firmly instructed to remain at HQ in the company of a highly irate Gordon, who had long since been looking forward to heading home to Mama's cooking.

Thank God I have a team that blends in here, thought Carl as he walked through the gate. Rose looked like so many others in Christiania, and no one was going to suspect someone of Assad's color and shabby appearance of being who he was.

Carl, on the other hand, was feeling less than inconspicuous with the hasty makeover Rose had given him. Her hair spray had fixed his combover in a vertical position, and his eyes were rimmed with a liberal daubing of mascara. Back in the eighties he'd have looked like a poet down on his luck, but now, eleven years into the new millennium, there were but two possible interpretations: either he was sick in the head or else he was a cop wearing an incredibly bad disguise.

Aware that he had to do his utmost to live up to the first interpretation, he greeted the immigrant guy at the toasted almond stand just inside the gate with a cheery howdy, his mouth a bit too slack.

There were a lot of people on Pusher Street this evening. The last police raid there had led to a number of arrests, but, as everyone knew, weeds always grew best where the soil had been turned.

Carl scanned the street and estimated that there were just as many stalls selling dope as there had always been. It was fine by him. As long as it was out here that people bought and sold, there wouldn't be as much need for hash clubs all over town.

As far as he could see, neither Rose nor Assad had reached the street yet, so everything was going according to plan.

He positioned himself on a corner next to the building they called Maskinhallen and tried to look like he'd run out of steam, slightly wilted and possibly a bit stoned. Apart from a girl with two kids on her carrier tricycle, no one looked in his direction.

To his consternation he realized there were quite a few black men on the street. A couple of slender Somalis with anoraks on and their hoods up, a couple of Gambians he recognized as pushers from in town, and then an assortment of extremely well-fed tourists—black, as well as white—from the cruise ships, wandering on the heels of the Free State's local guides, cameras sensibly tucked from sight.

Now he saw Rose and Marco appear from one of the side paths a little farther down Pusher Street, and half a minute later Assad also arrived on the other side of the street. Rose was standing a couple of meters from Marco, her attention seemingly everywhere else but on the boy.

Assad walked a way toward Carl, then positioned himself by one of the hash stalls, sniffing the goods with what looked to Carl like a surprising measure of professionalism.

They waited for ages. By now it was at least a quarter past eight, and even at a distance it was easy to see that Marco was becoming increasingly edgy and impatient. After another five minutes he moved a bit farther away from Rose, and then, counter to everything they'd agreed on, began to wander off along the street. Slowly, yet forcing Carl and Rose to follow while keeping their distance.

Marco was clearly on his guard. Merely the way he walked, treading the cobblestones so softly, revealed that he was more familiar than most with the asphalt jungle's pitfalls.

Careful, Marco, or they'll spot us tailing you, Carl managed to think, just before a black figure stepped around a corner and grabbed Marco by the arm.

At the same moment Carl's view was blocked by a huge, black, gold-festooned female cruise-ship tourist. For a couple of seconds he was unable to see what ensued, but he began to run, Assad and Rose likewise.

"Hey, take it easy!" the fat woman cried indignantly, as Assad got there first and shouldered her into the path of a Christiania transport trike that supported a large cargo crate.

He stopped and glanced around in all directions, pointed toward the corner of Mælkevejen and set off again as fast as he could. Incredible how a man of his thickset stature could accelerate so quickly, short legs and all.

Carl halted next to the immense black lady as Rose charged off in pursuit of Assad and the black man in front of him. "What's the problem?" the woman snapped, nostrils flaring.

He studied her for a moment. Why the hell did she have to stand just there?

The guy can't run from Assad when he's got Marco to drag along with him, he thought as he looked around. But maybe he didn't even have Marco any more. Maybe someone else had taken over and made off with the lad in a different direction and Assad and Rose were pursuing the wrong guy. He knew there were two of them working together.

Carl ran back and forth between Nemoland and Tinghuset, but there was no sign of them anywhere.

"Did you see a black guy run past holding a young boy?" he asked a junkie who was standing outside the bakery and seemed relatively conscious.

The guy gave a shrug and stroked his straggly beard.

"If anyone ran by here, Satan would have given them a nip in the ass," he replied sluggishly, indicating the monstrous mutt at his side that looked like it could have devoured the Hound of the Baskervilles in one mouthful. "Sixty-seven kilos, he weighs," he added proudly.

Carl nodded. Fucking dog, fucking situation, too. Dammit. If only they'd had more time to prepare the exchange, he would have made sure they had airborne back-up.

Then none of this would have happened.

He grabbed his mobile and began to enter a number to start a more widespread search, and as he did so he noticed a slender young girl coming straight toward him. She looked like Tilde and seemed confused, with movements as mechanical as a zombie someone had simply pushed in a certain direction.

"Tilde!" he cried, and ran toward her. But she didn't react. Had Marco been given the same treatment?

How in the world could they have let it happen?

"Henrik, Carl Mørck here," he said, when he got through to the duty officer at the dispatch desk. "We need patrol cars currently on the prowl in the vicinity of Christiania." He passed on as good descriptions of Marco and the African as he could, then gave a loud whistle to call their own operation off. It was the only thing he could do, given the situation.

He turned back to the girl and approached her warily.

"Tilde," he said, cautiously. "You're free now. Do you remember me? Carl Mørck, the policeman?"

It took a long time for his words to register. "Where's Marco?" she finally asked in a tiny voice, and glanced around with frightened eyes. The last couple of hours had not been good for her.

"Did they inject you with something, Tilde? Can you remember?"

She nodded listlessly. "Where's Marco? Is he all right?"

Carl drew her toward him. "We're looking for him right now."

Suddenly he heard footsteps running along the adjoining lanes. He saw Rose sprinting barefoot down the one lane, past the barracks, and from the direction of the canal came a black man at full speed with Assad right on his heels.

"Head him off, Carl!" Assad shouted breathlessly.

Carl spread out his arms and sprang into the path of the African like an enraged bull confronting a toreador. The problem, however, was that Carl was at least thirty-five kilos heavier than the lively lightweight racing toward him, whose musculature had doubtless been genetically conditioned to perform the most mind-boggling maneuvers.

For that reason he decided to hurl himself to one side, thereby giving himself exactly the same odds as a goalkeeper facing a penalty kick. And as he landed unceremoniously in a heap on the ground, the two men tore past him and up Pusher Street, where Rose was waiting for them.

Unlike Carl, she chose to throw herself straight at the man's legs with all her weight, toppling him like a tree in a forest. She heard a crack as his head hit the cobbles and suddenly he lay very still.

Carl watched as Assad, out of breath, was reaching for his handcuffs, and whistled to draw his attention to a horde of dark, unshaven faces that looked like extras in a Pirates of the Caribbean movie, watching Assad's every move.

"OK," said Assad, discreetly sticking the cuffs back into his pocket and turning to face his audience. "This bastard was trying to kidnap a young boy. Anyone here got some string?"

Not five seconds passed before a guy removed his belt. "Here, use this. Just remember I want it back, yeah?"

Carl got to his feet, realizing with a flinch how heavily he had fallen. It hurt like hell.

"Any of you lot seen a brown-skinned boy with curly black hair, about fifteen years old? He was here less than five minutes ago and disappeared over there," he gasped.

No one answered, but the disdainful look on their faces said they had more than enough to deal with already.

Behind Carl, Rose noticed the unconscious man was breathing more irregularly now, and that blood was running a little too steadily from a gash in his head, as well as from his shoulder, as though an existing wound had suddenly opened up again underneath his shirt.

"I'll call an ambulance, OK?" she shouted, as she opened her mobile, clearly put off her stride by some booing from the crowd in front of her.

"Shut your gobs!'" she yelled back, stamping her foot and flailing her arms. "Even scum like him has the right to fair treatment."

Then she glanced at the display on her phone. "See? Now you made me dial the wrong number!"

A faint ringtone could be heard somewhere behind them, and everyone turned around.

Carl looked at Rose and studied the puzzled look on her face.

"This must be the last number I called, so it has to be the mobile the boy was carrying," she said, scowling at the faces in front of her.

Then the crowd parted and someone pointed to where the ringing was coming from. The Christiania trike with its cargo crate.

The guy seated in the saddle shook his head and gave a shrug, as if he had no idea what was going on. But Carl sensed a lie.

The man was wearing gloves, and the hood of his anorak was drawn tight, so only his eyes were visible. It was a rather strange choice of apparel, considering the mild springtime weather.

Carl looked at the cargo box on the trike. It was big. Maybe just big enough.

"Hey, you," he called out, approaching the man. "Would you mind showing me what's in the—"

Before he could reach out and stop him, the guy was off, pedaling away like mad.

"Rose, you look after Tilde," Carl shouted, setting off in pursuit. "Help us, for Chrissake!" he yelled up the street, as the dealers stepped aside with a collective frown of bemusement.

Carl knew damn well that one never ran on Pusher Street, but what about cyclists?

"Stop him!" he yelled again, his chest tightening as Assad sprinted past, together with the guy who'd lent them his belt.

"Hey, almond man!" he heard Assad scream, so loud that the words echoed off the wall of the Spiseloppen restaurant.

The vendor standing with his cart by the entrance turned around.

"Shove your cart into the path and block his way!" Assad shouted. "You'll get a thousand kroner!"

The almond man burst into action, trundling his handcart in front of the gate, loath to pass up a potential source of income. After all, a thousand kroner was more than enough to repair any damage to his beloved almond cart.

The man fleeing on the trike veered off toward the large shed that housed Christiania's refuse collection depot, recycling center, and a lot more besides. He braked hard, leaped from the saddle and tried to dodge behind a pile of rusty machinery, only to find his path blocked by a group of men who had just finished work and were standing around with beer cans in hand, enjoying the weather. They weren't the sort of blokes you just shoved aside.

The only option left was to run inside the wooden building with its red-painted window frames.

By the time Carl arrived out of breath ten seconds later, Assad and the almond vendor were already inside, looking about.

"Where the fuck did he get to?" the Christianite exclaimed.

Carl quickly took stock. The large, high-ceilinged space was a festival of color. On the wall above the entrance hung a five-meter-tall mask, a caricature of a former Danish prime minister who was particularly despised in these parts. The floor and shelves were a clutter of machine parts and assorted junk, and further back was what looked like a jumble sale of everything from miniature racing cars to palm trees carved in wood with sombreros on them.

All in all, not the easiest place to apprehend a young black man with gymnastic talent.

"Try up there, one of you," Carl instructed, pointing to the ceiling where an office of gypsum boards and wood had been constructed on top of the crossbeams. Then he turned around and went back outside to the cargo trike.

The silence that came from it made him uneasy.

If they had injected Marco with the same sedative as they had used on Tilde, only a much larger dosage, then more than likely they had already carried out their mission. It was a dreadful thought.

He pushed the bolt aside and lifted the lid of the box.

And sure enough, there was Marco. Curled up and inert.

Carl lifted him up and carried him into the shed and found a blanket on which to lay him, while Assad and the other guy clattered around among all the scrap metal.

Pulling up Marco's sleeve, Carl ascertained that if there was a pulse at all, it was terribly weak.

Carl felt despair welling inside him. After all, it was his fault this had happened.

He got down on his knees beside the seemingly lifeless figure and began to attempt resuscitation. It was years since he'd done it last, and on that occasion the girl in question, the victim of a traffic accident, had died. Now the whole experience came back to him. The girl's smooth skin, the mother's anguish as she looked on. The paramedics who had gently pulled him away and taken over. It had taken Carl weeks to get over it, but if Marco died on him it would stay with him forever. He knew that now, as he knelt there, pumping the boy's fragile rib cage.

He turned his head as a movement caught his eye, and saw the giant mask vibrate slightly in the draught from the entrance so it looked like the ex–prime minister's mouth was moving. How strange to notice something so irrational and inconsequential in a situation like this, he mused.

"Come on now, Marco," he whispered, as Assad hurled rusty junk out of his way and his Christianite helper rummaged about in the office above his head.

"He's not up here," the guy called down through a window.

"And there are no other exits down here, so he must still be here somewhere," Assad shouted back from the far end of the shed.

Carl continued his efforts, now performing mouth-to-mouth. If only someone would come and help him.

Then he resumed the heart massage.

"Call an ambulance, Assad," he yelled. "I'm afraid we're losing Marco. He's very heavily sedated. He may even be dead already."

And then came the faintest of whispers from beneath him: "Owww, that hurts . . . !"

Carl looked down into Marco's open, anguished face.

"You're breaking something inside me," the boy gasped, half suffocated.

At that moment the mouth of the great mask on the wall above them opened, and the African tumbled out, falling two or three meters to the floor below.

He seemed stunned as he lay there, but only for a couple of seconds.

"He's here, hurry!" Carl barked, climbing to his feet.

"Stay lying there, Marco," he said, and turned to face the African, prepared for combat.

When the man got up, Carl saw he had a gun in his hand, and that his finger was curled much too tightly around the trigger.

I'm going to die now, he thought, and was at once filled with a singular feeling of calm. He raised his arms in the air and watched as the African came toward him, then lowered his weapon and aimed it at Marco.

A shot rang out, giving Carl a start, the sound implanting itself deep inside him. And then he saw the blood on the African's hand. The gun was gone.

He lifted his head and looked up at the office under the roof and saw the Christianite standing in the window with a pistol still smoking in his hand.

Only then did Carl recognize him. He was an undercover narc from Station City.

"I'm coming down," he shouted, disappearing from view.

"Look out!" cried Marco from the floor, as Carl spun around in time to see the African lunge at him with a knife in his unwounded hand.

The shadow that came flying from out of nowhere was just as unexpected.

It was Assad. Enraged and utterly without fear, he aimed a high, flying heel-kick at the African's chin, but his adversary was skilled in the same art and managed to spin around so the bones of their feet clashed together in kicks and parries. Assad tumbled backward, but the African remained on his feet and raised his hand to hurl the knife at Marco.

He's insane, Carl managed to think, before the guy suddenly went limp and dropped the knife on the floor. There hadn't been a sound.

Carl didn't know what was happening. The African staggered sideways, clutching at whatever was at hand to stay upright. Finally, he slid to the floor in what seemed like slow motion, down-for-the-count unconscious.

Carl turned to Assad and the undercover drug-squad officer. Assad smiled and extended his palm. In it was a heavy metal nut.

"If he gets up he can have another one. There's plenty more where it came from," Assad said, thrusting his hand into a box of rusty nuts, bolts, and assorted odds and ends.

By now Marco had raised himself onto his elbows, white as a sheet, but alive and kicking.

"Tilde?" was all he could say.

"She's OK. Rose is with her."

The smile that appeared on the boy's face was almost unnatural. "I want to go to her," he said.

If a person ever needed someone to look up to, this boy was Carl's number one candidate at the moment.

He looked out through the doors where a group of tourists were standing, seemingly enraptured. Maybe they thought they'd come just in time to catch the day's Wild West show. Whatever it was, a couple of them burst into enthusiastic applause.

Only the enormous black woman from the cruise party who stood in their midst seemed rather less exhilarated. Gripping her bag tightly, she stormed off.

"Mikkel Øst, drug squad," said the undercover officer, shaking hands with Assad and Rose with a look in his eyes that said he was less than satisfied with how the situation had developed.

He would have to turn in his weapon until the internal investigation of the shooting was concluded. Most likely he was relieved and annoyed at the same time. A four-month undercover stint in Christiania's drug underworld wasn't exactly a walk in the park, especially when you were interrupted just before results began to show.

Carl thanked him. "If we run into each other again, let me know if there's anything I can do for you, yeah?" And then both Mikkel Øst and the ambulance containing the African were gone.

By now Tilde had appeared with Rose and was standing with Marco, their arms wrapped around one another. What each of them had just been through was apparently best dealt with jointly.

"There's something we have to do," said Tilde, when eventually she seemed more or less recovered. "Will you phone my mum, Carl, and tell her we all need to meet at the house in Brønshøj? Marco and I have something to show you."

Half an hour later Tilde and her mother were hugging each other in the driveway of Stark's house.

"What did they do to you, Tilde?" her mother asked, deeply shaken.

"They stuck a needle in me, and then I was gone until they woke me up. I sat on a bench by a shawarma stall for ten minutes out there before I could walk. It felt just like when they give me an anesthetic at the hospital. You feel a bit nauseous afterward, but I'm OK again now."

"And what about you?" Malene asked Marco.

He nodded. "I'm OK, too, even though my legs still feel like they're asleep."

Be thankful it's not a lot worse, thought Carl.

"What is it you want to show us?" asked Rose.

Tilde took a deep breath before letting go of her mother and leading them up the drive to the back garden.

"You do it," she said to Marco.

"Are you sure?"

She nodded. "No more secrets. We've kept this one long enough."

So Marco lifted the flagstones one by one, placing the buried treasures in a row as he explained to them how they'd been discovered.

Five white plastic containers. Five testimonies from a dead man.

Carl shook his head and looked at Rose and Assad. How extraordinary to think it had all started with a missing persons notice, and now it was ending with a code written inside a safe and some plastic boxes buried in a garden. Sometimes police work was like a lottery. You checked your ticket stubs, hoping you have drawn at least one winning number.

I don't think we need to show them everything, Marco's eyes seemed to be saying to Tilde, but she took the containers one by one and explained what was in them.

Malene Kristoffersen needed a chair. There she sat with the jewelry and the little notebook in her lap, along with the certainty of how systematically the man she had loved had committed fraud. Even when Tilde began to speak in his defense, her hands remained clenched, her face a picture of shame and disappointment. Clearly, she felt betrayed.

"I think you should make sure all this gets into the right hands," she said finally, handing Carl the bundle of documents bearing the foreign ministry's logo.

Carl studied the uppermost sheet for a moment, then nodded. It was just as they'd thought.

If William Stark had embezzled from his ministry and the Danish state, he was but an amateur compared to his superior. Eriksen's signature was everywhere.

Carl handed the bundle to Rose. "We'll go through this later, OK?" he said, then pointed at the last box.

"What's in this one?"

"Nothing of much use to us, as far as I can see," said Tilde. "It's William's will."

"His will?" Malene whispered.

Tilde nodded. "He was leaving everything to us, Mum. All his money, the house. Everything."

That's when they saw the cracks appearing in Malene's facade. All the noble qualities she had attributed to her partner through the years came flooding back now. She was confused, embarrassed, and full of grief and anger all at once.

"You're right. His will's of no use to us now, Tilde," she said tearfully. "William's estate will be confiscated to cover the costs of his fraud."

She lowered her head and allowed her tears to fall unhindered.

Then Marco stepped forward and whispered something in Carl's ear.

The lad was definitely imaginative, he'd give him that. Carl nodded.

"OK, Malene and Tilde," he said. "I think I'd better ask you to hand over the notebook and the documents. Would you please give them to Assad?"

The girl nodded and gently picked up the notebook from her mother's lap, hugging her briefly. Then she gathered together the papers that documented Stark's deceit and handed it all to Assad.

Carl looked around, then pointed over to a pile of bricks stacked up behind the bike shed.

"Over there, Assad."

Assad stared blankly for a moment at his boss, but as Carl produced a pack of cigarettes and his lighter, the penny dropped.

"Oops," said Carl, as he set fire to the stack of papers with the notebook on top. "I'm afraid there's been a little accident. Would you happen to have some water handy, Rose?"

He gave her a penetrating look until the frown on her brow smoothed.

"Yes, as a matter of fact," she said, cottoning on. "There's the lake down there, of course. But I'm afraid it's too far because this bucket's got a hole in it."

Marco was silent most of the way back to police HQ, and Carl understood him well.

Judging by what the lad had told them, this had been the worst and the best day of his life rolled into one.

"What's on your mind, Marco?"

He shook his head.

"Why won't Marco say anything, Assad?" he asked over his shoulder.

"I think perhaps he is trying to assess his situation at the moment," came the reply.

Carl looked at Marco in the passenger seat. "Is that right, Marco? Are you wondering what's going to happen now?"

The lad seemed smaller than ever.

"Is that it?"

Marco lowered his gaze and nodded his head slowly.

"Tell me what you're thinking."

"I'm thinking that all the things I dreamed about are never going to happen. Now they'll put me in a detainment center and then I'll be thrown out of the country."

Carl frowned and looked into the rearview mirror, where Rose and Assad were exchanging glances. Marco's state of mind was clearly affecting them.

"That's not at all certain, Marco," Carl replied, trying to ease Marco's mind. With his sparse knowledge of state policy regarding illegal immigrants, he realized this wasn't much consolation.

"What would you do if you could decide for yourself?"

Marco sighed. "I just want to be completely ordinary. Go to school, study, look after myself."

It wasn't much to ask, and yet.

"You're only fifteen, Marco. You're too young to look after yourself."

The boy turned his head to look at Carl with raised eyebrows. Of course I can, his expression said.

"Where would you live, Marco?" Carl went on.

"Anywhere. As long as I can be left in peace."

"And you think things would work out? Without going back to crime?"

"I know it would."

Carl looked out at the traffic crawling along Bispeengbuen, and at the surrounding buildings. Out there among the twinkling lights were thousands of human lives that failed to make the grade when society needed them. So what better chance did this boy have?

"What makes you think you'll be able to take care of yourself when so many others can't, Marco?"

"Because I have the will."

Carl glanced into the rearview mirror again. The two of them were just sitting there, surprisingly passive. This wasn't an easy situation to deal with on his own, dammit.

He took a deep breath and let out a sigh as he thought back to the look on Malene Kristoffersen's face when they said good-bye, the way she'd stood there with William Stark's last will and testament in her hand. It was a document that would change their lives significantly. Tilde would be able to continue her treatment, and they'd be given the freedom to do as they pleased.

All because he'd happened to have a lighter and lit a little bonfire.

Carl nodded and caught Assad's eye in the mirror.

"Assad! That bloke you know, the one who's good at forging identity papers, do you still have any contact with him?"

He felt a pat on each shoulder, and now both of them were all smiles.

But then when he turned to Marco, he saw that the boy was shaking all over.

"Is something wrong, Marco?"

The boy leaned forward in his seat, trying to make his limbs obey and his body relax, but he couldn't.

"I'm not sure I understand, Carl," he said after a moment. "Do you mean . . ." And then he began to cry.

Carl reached out and stroked the boy's back.

"Rose and Assad, you tell him. He'll believe it from you."

"It's all up to you, Marco," Assad pronounced.

"Yeah," Rose added. "But we don't want to know where you are until you've found a proper place to live. We don't want to hear that you've taken root in some Dumpster in some town in Jutland, you get it?"

And now they heard the boy laugh. Apparently he was beginning to believe in it himself.

"But listen, Marco," Carl added. "Not a word about this to anyone, understand? Not even your kids or grandkids, OK? In return, we expect you to tell us everything you know about Zola and the clan in Kregme, and all the stunts you were pulling out on the streets. If you do that, our colleagues back in town will have something new and concrete to go on, and it'll be a big win-win situation all round."

Marco nodded and was silent for a moment. "What will happen with Miryam?" he asked.

"We'll have to see. She's probably not the one who will be the hardest for us to help. She's been very cooperative."

"OK, then I'll be cooperative, too." He sat still for a while and stared out over the city. "Is it really true, all this?" he asked eventually.

They nodded, all three.

"I just don't get it," Marco said, shaking his head. "But thank you so much." Then came another slight pause. "Can we make a detour to Øster-bro?" he said. "There's something I need to do first."

They pulled up in front of a doorway where a pair of teenagers stood making out. Marco asked Carl, Rose, and Assad to go in with him.

There was no answer when they rang the bell, so Carl pounded his fist against the door.

"Police!" he shouted, loud enough for everyone in the apartment building to hear.

It did the trick.

The two occupants seemed both frightened and reluctant when they saw four people standing at their front door, but at the sight of Marco their expression turned to intense anger.

"That one, we won't let in. Or you either, for that matter. Where's your ID, anyway?" one of them demanded, full of skepticism.

Carl pulled out his badge and stuck it in front of their faces. The two men exchanged glances, still shoulder to shoulder and unwilling to let them in.

Then Rose stepped forward. "We'd like a bit of consideration here, so if you gentlemen don't mind, please step aside so as not to inadvertently prevent three officers of the law from carrying out their duty. The pair of you seem a bit slow-witted if you ask me, but I'm pretty sure you can understand that excessive denseness can easily be rewarded with correspondingly large doses of rage and nice, tight handcuffs."

Carl was thunderstruck. It was almost like listening to himself.

The upshot was that the two men frowned simultaneously, then thought the better of it and stepped back to allow the frothing goth inside.

Then Marco beckoned them on to the little bedroom that could have fit into Assad's cubbyhole at HQ three times over.

He opened a drawer and rummaged about until finding what he was looking for: an old-fashioned metal comb. He raised it in the air before getting down on his knees at the wall opposite the narrow bed.

Placing the comb in the groove between the floor and the baseboard, he ran it back and forth until he located the indentation where the comb found purchase.

Then, with a sharp tug accompanied by the protests of the two men, the baseboard gave way.

The relief that passed through Marco's body was clearly visible to all.

He stuck his fingers into the hole and pulled out a clear plastic bag.

"Look," he said, holding it up in front of them. "Now I have sixty-five thousand kroner to make a start. So you needn't worry about me living in a Dumpster, Rose."

43

Summer 2011

Carl looked at the two notes on the desk in front of him. They'd been there for a month and a half now, staring at him every time he'd tried to tidy up. Wasn't it about time he chucked them out?

He tipped back on the rear legs of his chair and tried to picture the two women in his mind's eye. Strange, how quickly faces from the past were erased.

The past. Had it really come to that? Had his passivity in the wake of Lisbeth's phone call and the wreckage of his relationship to Mona, with whom he'd been together for a number of years, now been consigned to the file marked THE PAST? He wasn't sure he approved of the idea.

He picked up the two notes and for a moment considered crumpling them up and lobbing them into the waste-paper basket with a well-aimed overhand toss.

It was sure as hell no easy decision.

"It's come, Carl," said Rose, suddenly materializing in front of him.

"What's come?" He looked at her without much enthusiasm. It had been a rough week in which nothing had gone right. And now something had arrived that most probably wasn't good.

"The presumption-of-death verdict in the William Stark case. They've accepted the circumstantial evidence, so despite no body being found yet, they've decided to terminate Stark's life on the basis of DNA samples."

Carl nodded and put both slips of paper in his breast pocket. In a way, it was good news. At least the probate court could now begin to get the estate sorted.

This is great for Tilde and Malene, he thought, once he was alone again.

He took a look at TV2's news channel where the reports on the tremendous monsoon-like downpour on this second day of July described a near-catastrophic scenario. Had it not been for the unfortunate fact that sewers everywhere were so hopelessly overburdened that at this moment shit was literally erupting from drains in hundreds of basements, including their own toilets at the end of the corridor, he would have been delighted by some of the consequences.

As if by an act of divine retribution, Pusher Street was completely flooded and laid to waste. The makeshift stalls were deserted, and not a single gram of hash was to be seen. Turnover must have dropped by millions of kroner in a matter of hours. Easy come, easy go. And the water had inundated Istedgade, too, closing down basement massage parlors and leaving the whores and pimps totally idle.

Sodom and Gomorrah had got what was coming to them.

"Jesus, what a stench down here," Laursen said as he poked his head into Carl's office. "How about coming upstairs and getting the smell of fresh-baked bread in your nostrils instead? Not everyone has left yet. Hell of a cozy place for a birthday party when all you've got is a one-and-a-half-room apartment."

He chuckled and plonked his increasingly expansive backside onto the chair opposite Carl. "Anyway, listen. I haven't had time to tell you this yet, what with that pork to roast and all," he said. "Word came in today about that unidentified body from the fire up in Rungsted. You think you're ready for this?"

"Go on."

"They found out who made the dentures Assad fished out of the mouth of the corpse."

"Yeah? Who was it, then?"

"One Torben Jørgensen, a dental technician up in north Zealand. They belonged to René E. Eriksen, just as you guys assumed."

"Course they did," Carl groused. "We said we recognized them, so they could have saved themselves the bother."

"Yes, possibly. The only thing is, the DNA analysis of bone marrow from the corpse shows that the bloke wearing the dentures wasn't of Caucasian descent. Turns out he was Negroid."

Carl frowned.

"Assad and Rose! In here, please!" he hollered.

Both he and Laursen were a bit shaken at the sight of Rose as she appeared in the doorway with the pinkest hair this side of a luxury retirement home in Florida.

"Hey, Laursen, whassup?" said Assad, still with his trousers rolled up above his knees after a go on the prayer mat.

"The corpse with Eriksen's teeth in its mouth was that of a black man," Carl stated. "How about that!"

Assad's eyebrows did a little somersault. "*What?*"

"The dentures *were* Eriksen's," Carl went on. "Forensics located the mold at a dental technician's up in north Zealand."

Assad flopped down on a chair.

"But this means Eriksen ran off and got away with everything," he said dully.

Carl nodded. This conclusion had dawned on him, too. What a crock of shit.

"I reckon we can now assume we know who killed Brage-Schmidt and our unidentified black man," he said. "And if he could do that, then most likely he's also our perp in the murders of Teis Snap and his wife, wouldn't you say?"

"Yes," Assad added. "Not to mention all the others."

Rose bobbed up her new hairdo. As if they hadn't already noticed it.

"Listen to you, talking out of a certain part of your posteriors. Can't we agree that in reality we know fuck all? These are all just assumptions so that at least we can talk ourselves into believing we've got just a little bit of all this sorted. When it comes to assumptions, I couldn't care less."

Carl made a mental note to remind her of this last little statement when the time came. It would surely be only a question of days.

"One more thing," said Laursen. "You probably already know, if you've checked your emails. They found Eriksen's car. It's standing, covered in dust, in a side street in Palermo."

"*Palermo?*" Carl spluttered. "That's effing Sicily!"

Laursen nodded.

"Yeah, looks like he just took off in his old car and managed to drive all the way through Europe without getting stopped."

"Hurrah for the Schengen open-border agreement," Rose grumbled.

"Yeah, it's a bit of a trek," said Carl. "But you've got to admit Palermo sounds like the perfect place for someone needing a new ID and maybe a new appearance."

"Interpol is already on the case, so I've heard," said Laursen.

"Oh, that's nice," Carl replied with a sigh. "And Interpol covers a hundred and ninety countries, so there just might be a chance he's decided to go somewhere else, don't you think?"

Assad shook his head. "You never know, Carl. It's not for sure."

"True, but as far as I can see we're never going to find out where René E. Eriksen, or whatever he's calling himself now, has gone into hiding. And with all that money he apparently took with him, I'd say we're never going to find him. That's been my experience in these kinds of situations. End of story."

The windshield wipers were going flat out as Carl approached the motorway. He'd already seen several vehicles abandoned in the deluge.

Only a lunatic would want to chance a thirty-kilometer trip in weather like this. If only he had somewhere to crash until morning.

Then he remembered the notes in his pocket. If he turned left, it'd be to Lisbeth. If he took a right, he'd be headed for Mona.

He smiled fleetingly at the thought, then the smile was gone.

What the hell made him think that these two women, who more than likely already had a new rooster in the barnyard, would want anything to do with him?

And with that, he took the notes from his pocket, rolled down the side window and cast them to the wind. See if he cared!

After an hour and a quarter, a Venetian version of Rønneholtparken loomed in front of him.

Christ! he thought. There wouldn't be many cars able to start in the morning without the help of a hair drier, his own included.

"Is the basement OK?" was the first thing he called out, as he stepped through the front door.

No answer. So most probably it was all a mess.

He glanced into the living room, finding the place unusually dark. Had they left Hardy alone with no lights on? What the hell were they playing at?

"Hardy?" he ventured quietly, so as not to give him a fright, and at the same moment all the lights went on.

"Ta-daaah!" howled Mika and Morten, and Carl nearly jumped out of his skin.

They stepped aside to reveal Hardy sitting upright in a colossal high-tech wheelchair equipped with all manner of joysticks and whatnots in front of his face.

"This is it, Hardy. Show Carl what you can do!" cried Morten.

Carl was still giddy with joy. The sight of Hardy propelling himself forward with a broad smile had reduced them all to tears.

The hugs and the heartfelt words of congratulation seemed like they would go on forever. As of today, a new era had announced its arrival at Carl's house. Nothing less could describe it. Carl laid his head back on his pillow and tried to fall asleep, but couldn't. Every time he closed his eyes, he saw Hardy's happy face and the empty bed in the living room. He sighed at the thought of all the things they could do together now, if only he could live up to it.

After another half hour spent musing about Hardy and the future, he reached out for the stack of junk mail he'd brought upstairs and tossed on to the duvet beside him.

A bit of consumer surfing and he'd be asleep in no time.

Much better than counting sheep, at any rate, he thought, sifting through the offers.

Then suddenly, in among the supermarket ads, there was a postcard.

Who in the world would ever send them a postcard? It had to be to Mika or Morten, surely. Maybe one of their friends who'd been at the party and just wanted to say thanks.

He looked at the name and saw it was his own. Only then did he notice that, besides the name and address, there was nothing written on the card. Instead, there was a little snippet of a text stuck on with glue:

The special exhibition of African jewelry was quite remarkable. The selection of handmade rings, bracelets and necklaces . . .

That was all. The rest was snipped off.

A wry smile appeared on Carl's lips.

"Well, I'll be . . . ," he said to himself, conjuring up the image of a boy with nut-brown skin.

He turned the card over and stared at the motif for a long time.

Aalborg Tower—more than just a view, read the caption.

EPILOGUE

Autumn 2012

"**You're not leaving already,** are you, Richard?"

She turned herself over on the sheet, displaying her body from every angle as the hair under her arms quivered in the breeze stirred up by the fan on the ceiling.

"Look. Wouldn't you like to put your tongue in here?" she coaxed, drawing the tip of her finger around her navel and arching her back.

He smiled and tossed two hundred-dollar bills onto the sheet beside her. She'd been one of the better ones, but once was enough. There were other fish in the sea, as they said. Plenty of them.

"Oh, Richard, two hundred! You're so good to me!" she purred, fluttering the banknotes across her nipples. "Come again. Soon!"

The air outside was exceptionally dry, and the heat rose from the street in waves. Even the street vendors were dabbing their brows with greasy kerchiefs.

But René wasn't bothered by the heat. A year and a half spent in ten different South American countries had taught him how to cope with a climate where most people from northern latitudes were forced to give up.

It was all a matter of listening to one's body. Plenty of liquids, pauses in air-conditioned bars, elegant, airy clothing, helicopter journeys where others went by car, horseback rides where others were forced to trek. Throughout South America these amenities were there for the taking. Paraguay, Bolivia, Guyana. Wherever he traveled, there wasn't a country where status and money couldn't provide him with whatever he wanted.

René stretched and squinted up at the sun. It was still too early for his siesta; time for a quick manicure and perhaps a bit of shopping to see if anything caught his fancy. It usually did him a world of good.

A woman smiled to him from the sidewalk and waited a moment to see if he would take her up on the offer, but René was sated.

Since getting his dental implants and chestnut-brown hair transplant and having the bags removed from under his eyes, he looked like a million dollars, all set off by a deep copper tan. All those years of passionless embraces and dutiful sex were now definitively a thing of the past.

Maracay wasn't among the most beautiful towns in Venezuela to hang out in, but it was here the women gave him the most value for money.

He nodded to himself. By now he'd become so accustomed to his new status that he had to sit and concentrate for a long time to recall how it had all come about.

He knew that theoretically there could be a warrant out for his arrest, but it didn't worry him. If all traces of him had not been entirely erased by the blaze at Brage-Schmidt's place, which he felt sure they had, he could always relocate. He never spent too long in one place, anyway. His next stop would be Uruguay, where it was said the women were absolutely stunning. Once he'd been to all the South American countries whose infrastructure seemed least forbidding, he would move on to Asia.

René intended to age in style. Slowly, and for a long, long time. All he had to do was look after himself.

He certainly had the means. The Curaçao stocks were worth a lot more than he had ever envisaged, so regardless of how extravagant his lifestyle was, he had more than enough money to keep him going for the rest of his days and then some.

He turned a corner onto one of the main thoroughfares, inhaling the scent of wealth and suitable company in the comfortable certainty that it was here he belonged.

A shop with a marble facade and armored glass prompted him to stop. It wasn't the first time he'd walked past it, but this time he decided to go in. The Elephant Automatic watch by Fabien Cacheux was exactly what he was looking for. This subtle combination of simplicity and daring and the exceedingly brazen design of the strap appealed to him, as did the sign in the window that discreetly but firmly drew the attention of inquisitive souls to the fact that only eleven of this model existed in the entire world. For the modest sum of $47,300, René decided it was now time to become a member of this very exclusive club.

He smiled indulgently as he watched the reflections in the window of those less fortunate who could only stare at the timepiece. He turned around toward them and nodded to a man across the street who stood waiting for a bus, wearing an abundant overcoat that seemed completely out of place in all the heat.

There was a time when he'd been like that himself.

When he came out with the watch on his wrist and his old Tag Heuer in a little box in a plastic bag, he felt wealthier and better equipped than ever before. Tomorrow, when he drove the two hours to Choroní Beach for a loving farewell with Yosibell, a woman capable of more than most, he would allow her slender, red fingernails to stroke his watch strap.

And then it would be good-bye, Venezuela.

He noted that the man was still waiting at the bus stop as he strolled by the next shops along the street. But South America was like that. Sometimes everything functioned to excess and buses came hard on each other's heels like stampeding animals. Other times one might just as well forget about it and walk.

Which apparently was what the man finally decided to do. But it was strange that he should choose to walk off in the opposite direction from that in which the bus ran, René thought as he turned down a side street that last time he was here had smelled so delightfully of perfume mixed with hibiscus, freesia and pitahaya that he had almost swooned.

By now the afternoon siesta had descended heavily upon the narrow street. Shutters were closed, behind which folks were in the process of eating or napping.

Glancing over his shoulder, he saw that he and the man in the overcoat were the only ones left on the street, and at the moment the man was gaining on him.

Easy now, René told himself, and then recalled how the waiter at the hotel the evening before last had suddenly asked him if the accent that flavored his English was Scandinavian, possibly Danish, because he'd once had a girlfriend from over there and she spoke the same way. And when René had said no, he'd done so rather harshly. After that, the waiter had had his eye on him.

Of course he had switched hotels, but not his name. So what good had it done?

Now the man in the coat was walking a mere twenty or thirty meters behind him, so René walked faster. Ahead lay another three or four narrow streets that led up to one of the wide avenidas, so all he had to do was keep up a good pace.

Then all of a sudden he had the impression he'd seen this man before. Was he the one who'd been standing at the counter in the police station when he had given a statement about a minor traffic accident on Calle Marino? Were they starting to catch on, in spite of everything? The thought sent a shudder down his spine.

Now he began to run, and despite his age and years of total physical inactivity, a personal trainer and a routine of early-morning jogging on the beaches had given his legs new life, enabling him to dart around corners and down a narrow alley without his pursuer being able to keep up.

Feeling victorious and quite pleased with himself, he hid behind a stack of cardboard boxes and promised himself he would forget about Yosibell at Choroní Beach and grab a flight south that very evening.

He stayed there for a while, until feeling certain the man was caught up in the lattice of small streets and had lost the scent.

But as he stepped out, there the man was at the end of the lane, aiming a gun at him.

His panicked brain screamed for a solution. Police salaries were miserable and René had the means to sort things out. So he approached the man, intending to make a deal.

But as he was about to put forward his proposal, the man instructed him to take off his watch and hand it to him.

René was startled. Had he fled from a simple thief? Was that all this was about? With ill-concealed annoyance he unfastened the timepiece, thinking the son of a bitch had no idea he was now in possession of something only ten other people in the world owned. May it put a curse on him.

"The bag, too," said the man, pointing the barrel of his gun at the plastic bag containing René's old Tag Heuer.

He handed it over.

"And your wallet."

Dammit. This was getting out of hand and was going to cause him a lot of bother, cancelling credit cards and waiting around for new ones. He was going to be here longer than he'd wanted.

"C'mon," said the man impatiently, eyes following René's hand as he reached into his inside pocket and handed him his alligator skin wallet.

The man opened it, satisfying himself that it was full of credit cards and plenty of bolívars and dollars.

The fucking bastard just stood there smiling at him. Had it not been for the gun, he would have given him the same treatment he gave Brage-Schmidt's black slave.

"Now the cell phone," he said.

No, goddammit, nothing more. That was it.

"Sorry, I haven't got one," René said.

The man seemed not to believe him.

"Give it to me now," he said.

"I've already told you I haven't got one. I've given you everything else, so if I had a phone I'd give you that, too. I'm not stupid."

The man frisked him quickly, but missed the back pocket where his phone was.

"OK, so you don't have a cell phone," he said. Then he stepped back and for a moment looked like he was about to shoot. But instead he smiled toothlessly. "You've been cooperative, so I'm letting you go. Not everyone is that lucky."

He began retreating backward, and as he reached the end of the alleyway, he stuck the pistol into his pocket and disappeared around the corner.

And at that moment the phone rang.

René reached instantly into his pocket and muted the ringtone. Then he put the phone to his ear.

"Hey, Richard, it's Yosibell. The water up here is as clear as glass and my skin is moist. When will you be here?"

He was about to answer that he might be delayed, but he never got that far.

"You told me you had no cell phone!" a voice yelled from the far end of the lane, footsteps picking up speed.

René looked back over his shoulder. The man stopped a few meters away from him. Heart pounding, he turned and stared into the man's eyes. They were totally calm, tranquil almost, just like the hand pointing the gun at him.

"You know what?" he said coldly. "I hate people like you. People who lie."

He shook his head, rather like an exasperated father scolding a naughty child.

"So now you have to pay the price," he said, and fired the gun.

René heard Yosibell's voice berating him as he fell to the ground.

The last thing René E. Eriksen sensed was the pounding of heavy footsteps on the ground next to him. And then, finally, the phone being eased from his hand.

ACKNOWLEDGMENTS

I would like to thank my tireless and patient wife, Hanna, for keeping my nose to the grindstone and helping me through the long process of writing. Thanks to our marvelous assistant, Elisabeth Ahlefeldt-Laurvig, for her research and innumerable talents. Thanks to Kjeld Skærbæk for transport and all manner of help. Thanks also to Eddie Kiran, Hanne Petersen, Micha Schmalstieg, and Karlo Andersen for valuable and insightful comments, and to my inestimable editor, Anne C. Andersen, for her keen eye, boundless energy reserves, and overview. Thanks to Karsten Dybvad and Anne G. Jensen for showing me around Copenhagen's House of Industry in the early stages of its conversion. Thanks to Gitte and Peter Q. Rannes of the Danish Centre for Writers and Translators at Hald Hovedgaard for their hospitality. Thanks to Peter Garde for use of his magnificent house in Kera, Crete. Thanks to the girls of the Maeva publishing house in Barcelona for their sterling efforts in various situations, to Mathilde Sommeregger for purchase of a writing desk and rental of an swivel chair, and to Alba for recovering my lost suitcase with the book's synopsis and all my research inside it. Thanks to Gordon Alsing for use of his retreat in Liseleje. Thanks to Police Superintendent Leif Christensen for corrections relating to police matters, as well as to Police Superintendent and Press Coordinator Lars-Christian Borg. Thanks to physiotherapist Mette Andresen and to Leo Poulsen of the Royal Library in Copenhagen.

Special thanks go to Henning Kure for his fantastic editorial work, cutting and trimming and thereby giving me back my enthusiasm and clear-sightedness when it was most needed.

Thanks to Dirk Henning for his hospitality in Yaoundé. Thanks to our guide, Louis Fon, who has given name to one of the characters in this book; to my friend and traveling companion Jesper Helbo; and our nine strong and good-humored scouts, as well as to our Bantu ranger and cook for an amazing expedition into the Da jungle of Cameroon.

With the publication of this novel, adlerolsen.de has provided support to the Baka Sunrise Association in recognition of that foundation's important efforts to provide schooling to the children of the Baka people.

Turn the page for a sneak peek.

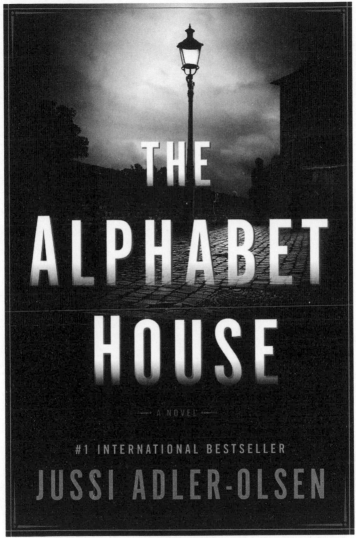

978-0-525-95489-7

Available wherever books are sold

DUTTON
— est. 1852 —

CHAPTER 6

The sensation of flies dancing on his eyelids and the gentle rocking of a pitching sea in a summer wind with cold spray settling like dust on his cheek had been competing for a long time with irrelevant sounds and an increasingly severe pain in his back. Then, in the trough of a wave, the water rose and hit him in the corner of the eye. Bryan blinked and felt the next splash more distinctly. The strange, massive pain in his back was spreading down his thigh.

Big, feathery snowflakes whirled over his face as he opened his eyes and drowsily tried to tune in to reality.

A narrow strip of snow-laden sky emerged above him, separating the station roof from the stationary train. Around him, stretchers were being removed. SS soldiers were getting off the front end of the train, one by one, their packs and rifles slung over their shoulders.

A couple of them hopped over the edge of the platform and walked farther along the tracks, chatting and joking casually with helmets and gas masks dangling from their backs.

Soldiers on their way home.

With a grating, screeching sound the rear car was detached from the rest of the train to reveal a view of hills and the town's buildings that were emerging from the mist. Another couple of snowflakes landed on Bryan's cheek, momentarily blending dream with reality. He raised his back a bit to lessen the effect of the coldness radiating from the ground and slowly looked around for James in the jumble of stretchers on the platform.

A row of vertical posts supported the station's half roof, creating a passage of less than two meters toward the wooden building. Stretchers were standing up against the wall in scattered blankets of snow. Some of the patients had already been taken away. Bryan fell back resignedly, imagining that he and James had already been split up. The dry rumble of an engine started up as yet another truck backed up to the chute at the far end of the platform.

Several men appeared and inspected the recumbent patients. Slapping their arms sharply against their bodies to shake off the loose snow in the folds of their coats, they grabbed hold of the nearest stretchers. After a while Bryan's was the only one left on the platform, apart from a stretcher that was half-hidden by a mail truck. At the end of his blanket the sharp imprint of naked feet stuck up, crowned by a dark, reddish patch. Bryan looked down his body and cautiously wiggled his toes. The piece of colored paper was pinned to the edge of his blanket, shining like a splash of blood against the white background.

Through clusters of wind-driven snowflakes another building was discernible in the distance. The majority of the railway cars had been moved there. Small black dots were calling out happily as the cars approached. Bryan recognized the mood. He, too, knew what it was like to be received by family and friends after a long period of active duty. He prayed wistfully that it would happen again.

Then a door opened in the wooden building behind him. Two elderly men in civilian clothes helped each other light cigarettes in the doorway, then ambled toward the locomotive without closing the door behind them.

A moment later, soldiers slowly began to stream out of the foremost train car. Not cheerful, expectant lads on their way home to Mom's cooking or a sweetheart's embrace, but weary, stooping men whose forward movement was propelled solely by the constant push from behind. A man on the platform received the first of them, took hold of his arm, and led him along the train past Bryan. The rest followed passively, escorted by armed soldiers in overcoats.

The men getting off the train were SS officers from all the different corps. Elite German soldiers, authentic Nazi heroes. Bryan could scarcely tell one from the other. Suddenly his distaste surfaced. Distaste for all those collar insignias, skull and crossbones, riding breeches, stiff-peaked caps, medals, and decorations. Here was the enemy he had learned to hate and fight against so savagely.

The stream of expressionless soldiers and bobbing stretchers continued toward the pallid, whitish light of the opening at the far end of the platform. Another truck was backing up to the skids.

Its arrival was drowned out by the crunching sound of boots in the frosty snow. The last man in the column shouted at the escort in front and pointed at Bryan and the other stretcher.

Some soldiers took hold of them and followed the sagging flock of men.

At the end of the train they put the stretchers down for a moment. It took time to fill the truck up. A railway worker started to walk across the rails, knocking the switch points with a long pole as he passed. A soldier shouted at him threateningly, gun raised. Dropping the pole in the snow, the man slithered back the way he came, finally disappearing behind a big sign that towered between the sets of tracks. FREIBURG IM BREISGAU it said, in proud, clear letters.

Not a single one of the officers who stood there waiting had said a word. Everything had taken place precisely according to plan, making it impossible for Bryan to look back and see whether James was lying on the stretcher a couple of meters away.

It must have been quite late in the afternoon. The sun would soon be setting. The street seemed deserted, apart from the SS officers guarding the area in front of the freight station.

So this was their destination for the time being. Freiburg, a town in the Rhine district by the French border in the southwest corner of the German Reich, was only fifty kilometers from the Swiss border and freedom.

In the semidarkness two rows of figures were seated on benches in the back of the truck. Between them, several stretchers lay slantwise across the floor, so tightly packed together that the ends stuck under the feet of the seated figures. Luckily Bryan had been placed under a soldier with short legs whose boots didn't rest so heavily on his frozen shins.

When the last stretcher had been loaded, the accompanying soldiers jumped in and rolled down the tarpaulin while the escort closed the tailgate.

The sudden darkness made it impossible for Bryan to see. The shape beside him was lying quite still. Forty men were breathing heavily and irregularly. There were a few scattered murmurs and grunts. Two guards squeezed down side by side at the end of the bench and talked quietly to each other.

Then Bryan felt the shape beside him move. A tentative hand groped the side of his body and found his chest. There it remained.

Bryan seized it and returned its quiet squeeze.

Gradually, as the silhouettes acquired faces, Bryan realized the truckload of patients had several things in common. But one was more obvious than the rest, a common denominator that now included him and James.

They were all mentally ill.

James had already tried to make him understand this with meaningful glances, pointing out one or two men in particular.

Most of them sat quite still, heads bobbing from side to side as the truck rumbled along. A few sat tensing their necks, eyes fixed on an imaginary point in the air. Others twisted their arms together awkwardly and rocked almost imperceptibly back and forth, alternately clenching and spreading their fingers.

James rolled his eyes and pointed to his open mouth. "They're pumped full of medicine," Bryan deduced in agreement. They, too, had been sedated and the poison was still in their bodies, as exhibited by their slow-motion reflexes and unusually sluggish brain activity. If they'd had a chance to stand up, they would have fallen over.

Bryan began feeling a mixture of relief and renewed anxiety. So the red tag meant they were mentally ill. This had been their objective and therefore they were relieved. But now they'd been lumped together with this group of mentally warped soldiers, and what did the Germans propose to do with them? The master race's care of the incurably ill could easily be accomplished with a syringe, or even more simply with a bullet.

Those were the rumors.

The civilians at the freight goods station had obviously not been meant to see them. And now they lay in darkness, rumbling toward unknown territory. Two soldiers had been set to watch over them. This was the source of their worries.

Bryan tried to smile at James. James showed indifference. He still didn't see any occasion to worry.

At every bend of the road the legs of one of the soldiers swung to and fro above Bryan's feet. The railroad had to bend, twist, and turn itself through the snow-covered terrain alongside fields, drainage trenches, small streams, and natural inclines and slopes in the landscape. Their journey took them around the southern edge of the Schwarzwald and the town of Freiburg. They had passed a lot of small stations and stops on their way that could have been used for unloading if they were going southward. So Bryan had to assume they were heading north or northeast into the Schwarzwald itself.

Most likely the idea was that they were meant to disappear here in some way or other.

Up until now the country had been fairly flat. James rocked forward and back on his own axis, bumping into Bryan as regularly as the tiny jumps of the second hand on a clock. The sound of the engine echoed off the walls of the houses. Graveled surfaces gave way to cobblestones and suddenly, for a matter of seconds, to caressing, lulling asphalt, then churned-up, frozen dirt roads. Not one moment resembled the last, yet time seemed an eternity. Bryan noted his impressions, convinced that the next stop would be their last.

James had dozed off, breathing heavily, leaving Bryan with an uncomfortable feeling of isolation and claustrophobia. Recalling James's promise, he tried to ignore the urge to jump up, and out. An urge that continued to grow as the effect of the medicine wore off.

One of the guards got up, treading on Bryan's thigh with his hobnailed boot. In his effort to control the pain, Bryan didn't notice the guard pushing a patient back toward the bench. But he did hear the tarpaulin rip open as the patient collided with the truck's sideboards, his elbows jutting stiffly backward.

Half the canvas wall suddenly fluttered out into the air and was slung with hollow-sounding cracks against the driver's cab. The soldier who had indirectly caused the situation threw down his weapon, striking James hard and waking him up, while the muzzle pointed straight at Bryan's face.

As the soldier thrust his upper body over the side of the truck, stretching as far into the semidarkness as he could, Bryan reached cautiously for the rifle.

But on meeting James's eyes, he stopped. James shook his head slowly.

The countryside behind the soldier's silhouette was lit up by the reflection of white-clad fields. This was more than enough light for Bryan, whose profession had been to survey landscape, no matter what time of day or night.

Farthest toward the west, in the middle of the flat countryside, there was a distinct gray hilltop that even fledgling navigators would be able to recognize. This naked peak was grooved by verdant, terraced vineyards and had the pompous name of Kaiserstuhl. An outpost of France and a connecting link between the Schwarzwald and the Vosges Mountains, it disappeared into the distance, giving him a landmark. Treetops passed in view alongside the truck. Bryan cautiously propped himself up on his elbows. Small figures were gliding around over the drainage trenches, accompanied by cheerful voices. Children playing winter games and dancing along the frozen canals on their skates. A single glimpse of this reality, and the face of war acquired another new dimension. It had been a long time since Bryan and James had been two Canterbury youngsters who stormed at full speed under the low bridges connecting the cattle paths, bending at the knees and shrieking with delight, gliding crunchily over the ice. What happy, innocent, childish pursuits.

The next swing of the truck knocked Bryan's elbows out from under him, and the treetops disappeared behind the tarpaulin and the soldier's sweaty, self-satisfied face. When the SS youth finally got a firm hold on the tarpaulin, he squeezed himself in between two of the patients and held on to the flap for the rest of the journey. Like a couple of brass weights, the short-legged patient's boots dangled over Bryan's shins at more and more of an angle, indicating that the truck was climbing again.

The heavy vehicle shook as it drove up the stony road, rattling as if they were driving over bare rock.

This was where they were headed. Up into the wilderness.

After another hour's drive the transport came to a halt.

Several men in white were ready to receive them. James's stretcher was pulled out over the edge of the truck before the two of them managed to give each other a farewell squeeze. The two porters who had taken hold of Bryan's stretcher slid on the slippery ground, almost dropping him. In front of them was a dark, pebbled clearing encircled by a narrow border of dead fir trees.

Behind them towered dense formations of snow-crowned pine trees that provided shelter from the worst gusts of wind. The landscape faded away into the valley below in a mist of snow crystals. There was not a single light to reveal any sign of life down in the Promised Land. Bryan assumed Freiburg was now directly south of them.

They had been driven a roundabout way.

The courtyard was partly hidden behind the windbreak. The badly shaken-up passengers were hustled around the stretchers and trudged apathetically behind the soldier in command. Another truck came into view, empty and with the tailgate hanging open. The flock of men who had left it had been lined up farther down the compound, where several three-story buildings came into view. The pale-yellow gleam from the windows shone softly over the yard. Bryan gave a grunt when he saw the Red Cross sign painted on the sloping flat roofs. It resembled an ordinary hospital, apart from the numerous sandbags heaped up against the walls at regular intervals, the barred windows on the second and third stories, and numerous guards with dogs. Seen from the outside, the rectangular boxes were far superior to the hastily assembled reserve hospitals the wounded Royal Air Force men were sent to in ever increasing numbers. "But don't deceive yourself," thought Bryan as he was carried toward the buildings.

Little by little the patients were grouped at one edge of the compound. All in all about sixty or seventy men stood waiting as the stretchers passed by them. Farther ahead the porter carrying James from behind tried to push back the arm he'd let flop over the edge of the swinging stretcher. Against a background of glazed yellowish frost two fingers stuck out from the others in discreet disregard of danger, waving a V-sign back toward Bryan.

Several yellow buildings, slightly staggered in relation to one another, became visible from where they were now assembled. Two of them had their foundations stuck solidly into the rock, whereas the rest were scattered over the tree-encircled plateau that constituted most of the area. The tops of several posts could be seen above a lush undergrowth of holly. They supported the fence between the walls of rock. Farthest away a steel-wire fence cut blatantly through the area, its frost sparkling in the glow of the occasional lights. Down by the gate stood a small group of officers, talking in a cone of light beside a black car with a swastika on the front door and pennants swaggering on the front fenders. An officer stepped out of the group and waved the guards from the nearest building over toward him. On receiving their orders they ran the hundred meters over to the assembly, guns erect and coats flapping, to pass on the commands.

When they began moving this time, the stretchers were at the head of the procession. A few of the silent figures kept standing about apathetically and had to be egged on by the soldiers with threats and shoves. Apart from the dry crunching of hundreds of feet on the frosty snow and the sound of trucks in the distance, the panting of the porters was all that could be heard. From where Bryan was, he could see nine or ten buildings, all in all, several of them connected in pairs by white-painted wooden corridors. It was one of these complexes they were heading for, the farthest of the twin blocks.

Apart from a single wall lamp shining faintly over the entrance, the building lay black and lifeless.

A nurse wearing a cap stepped through the door, shuddered slightly in the wind, and indicated that the procession should turn and follow her over toward two wooden barracks that lay immediately to their left. The porters protested but did as they were told.

The barracks were tall, single-story wooden buildings with golden, frost-rimmed windows under the eaves. Shutters and heavy curtains shielded the windows from the glare of the towering floodlights outside.

The door of the barracks led directly into a room in which dozens of thin, striped mattresses lay side by side in the middle of the floor. The walls were lined with support beams. Weak lightbulbs and hoisted-up parallel bars, rings, and trapezes hung from the ceiling. The far wall of the gymnasium was bare. A single door led into the adjacent building. Four buckets served as latrines. Dark, shabby-looking chairs, each encircled by a small canvas booth, stood at the end where they had entered.

The porters slid Bryan off onto a mattress halfway down the room, stuck his case file underneath it, and disappeared with the stretcher without having made sure their patient was lying properly.

The stream of shuffling, empty-eyed figures into the barracks ceased. James lay only a few mattresses away, following the last arrivals with his eyes. When all of them were either sitting down or lying flat on their backs on the hard beds a nurse clapped her hands and strode down between the rows, repeating the same sentence over and over again. Although Bryan couldn't understand her, he understood his fellow patients' confusion and clumsy attempts to get undressed and pile their clothes beside the mattress. Not all of them did as they had been told and had to be helped roughly by the porters who had been watching the scene, making subdued comments. Neither James nor Bryan reacted, but let porters haul their shirts up over their heads, making their ears smart. Bryan noted with relief that James was not wearing Jill's scarf.

One of the naked men got up, arms hanging limply by his sides, and began peeing mechanically over both the mattress and his neighbor, who made a feeble evasive attempt. The nurse rushed forward and struck him on the neck, instantly interrupting the stream, and led him over to the buckets at the far end of the room.

Bryan counted himself lucky not to have had anything to eat or drink for several days.

The door leading to the back building opened and a trolley was wheeled inside, loaded with blankets.

It remained there for some time.

The floor wasn't cold, but the draft from the entrance gave them goose-flesh. Bryan curled up in order to keep warm.

After a while someone started groaning. Several of the naked men were trembling visibly. The two nurses who had been ordered to watch over them shook their heads in irritation and pointed toward the trolley. Apparently they were supposed to fetch their own blankets. A couple of thin, gnarled men jumped over the mattresses with no sign of embarrassment and snatched a blanket, unaware as to whether it lay at the top of the heap or the bottom.

The rest of the men stayed where they were. Dazed. Their minds clouded over.

Bryan lay there for several hours. The monotonous rhythm of chattering teeth grew louder as the men grew colder. The nurses sat nodding, stealing some sleep on the stools at the far end of the room. They had left the recumbent patients to themselves long ago.

In the feeble light Bryan could scarcely tell James's huddled body from all the others. Then he saw a corner of Jill's scarf sticking out from under the mattress. "For God's sake, leave it there!" he begged silently. Suddenly James shot up in bed and rushed toward the pails. For a few seconds one of them resounded hollowly.

The act itself lasted only a moment, but the reverberations of his upset stomach and chills kept James frozen in his awkward position for some time. Then he snorted in exasperation and fumbled around the buckets without finding paper to dry himself.

Without any further hygienic considerations James rushed over to the trolley, seized a blanket, and ran nimbly back to his mattress. "Why didn't you bring me a blanket, idiot?" Bryan thought, and considered following suit as he glanced over at the dozing, uniformed women beside the end wall.

But he didn't.

Later that night the outside door opened with a crash, immediately followed by a blinding light as the ceiling lights were switched on. Bryan lay motionless. Without hesitation the SS soldiers went straight over to two men who lay huddled in their blankets. They bent over them, found their case notes, and tore off a corner of the front page.

One of the men thus branded lay beside James. The bundle of rags lying on top of him was James's blanket. Bryan doubted whether he himself could have been so cunning.

James had deliberately fished only one blanket out of the pile.

CHAPTER 7

The night inspection had woken the whole room. Even though by then most of them had been dressed in nightshirts and the blankets had at long last been distributed, the moaning increased hour by hour. The effect of the medicine was wearing off.

More and more of them tried to shut out their surroundings by way of rocking movements, awkward contortions, and blank expressions. Bryan had never seen anything like it. For his own part he lay quite still.

Some men he had never seen before switched on the lights and cursorily inspected the crowd of bodies on the floor. One of them was wearing a black, ankle-length coat, buttoned to the neck. When he stamped on the floor everyone looked up. He rapped out an order and a couple of the patients reluctantly got up and tugged at their neighbors' nightshirts until they, too, rose to their feet. Finally only six or seven men remained.

Accompanied by a couple of orderlies, the man in the coat asked one of the recumbent patients a question without receiving any reply. He signaled to his assistants to take hold of the patient under the arms and force him into a standing position. When they let go of him again, he collapsed like a rag doll and struck his neck on the floor between the mattresses with an impotent smack that made Bryan gasp. The nurses glanced up at the officer as they knelt down to help the unconscious man back onto his bed, but he was already striding straight over to Bryan.

When Bryan stared into the pale face that was inspecting him, he chose to get to his feet.

The swaying movements and slight trembling at the knees were genuine enough, since he hadn't stood up for several days. The blood rushed from his brain and made him dizzy. When they let go of him, however, he remained standing. James was the only one of the seven to follow his example.

. . .

During the smarting, painful delousing that followed, Bryan tried to move closer to James, but the women continually slapped their rubber gloves against their rubber aprons, making sure the patients were in constant movement.

James stood in a line alongside a grubby tiled wall, hugging a numbered shirt like all the others and waiting for the next row of showers to become vacant. One of the naked men stood in the bath, head bent back and staring wide-eyed straight up into the shower. He stood like this for a long time and when he began to scream with pain the howls spread from one deranged man to another like a wolves' chorus.

Blows and threats restored order almost as quickly as the commotion had erupted. The man who had started it stood moaning with bloodshot eyes as they beat him, totally unaware of what was going on around him. Then they dragged him by the hair and flung him against the wall. He didn't stop moaning until they pulled the straitjacket over him and hauled him away.

The last Bryan saw of James until they both were in the gym again was as he apathetically let himself be pushed under the ice-cold showers, smiling and humming softly, still hugging his shirt.

Inside the gymnasium they were all equipped with the same-sized shoes and arranged in three rows alongside the ribbed walls facing the middle of the room. A few of them were sorted out immediately and grouped together along the outer wall. Among them Bryan could recognize a couple of the poor fools who had fetched their own blankets during the night. They apparently didn't understand their special status.

In the meantime several tables had been placed in front of the canvas booths. The man in the long coat had discarded his flowing garment and was sitting with other security officers and white-coated representatives of the medical corps. There were no longer any women among them.

One of the men gave a start when his name was called out. A soldier hauled him in front of this court of inquiry. Several names were called without anyone reacting, whereupon a security officer looked over his list and began calling out a number that, as far as Bryan could tell, corresponded to the shirt markings. Bryan wished desperately he could understand what was being said. He listened intensely. As his confusion grew, an officer pointed at him and a soldier dragged him into the line.

James was among the last to be called. According to customary Prussian thoroughness they had apparently been called up in alphabetical order. He, too, had to be pushed into line.

The wounded soldiers were behind the curtains an average of about two or three minutes before they were led out again and placed in a new row against the back wall in the same order as before. They didn't seem to have been harmed, but stood at attention in a ridiculously exaggerated manner with expressionless gray faces.

Soft muttering and rustling sounds could be heard from behind the curtain. Nothing alarming. One of the patients shouted his replies like shrill orders, whereupon a couple of those who were waiting their turn clicked their nonexistent heels and puffed out their chests.

Behind the faded green canvas one of the officers sat behind a flimsy desk reading Bryan's case notes while a doctor looked over his shoulder. The soldier who had led him in pushed Bryan down onto a chair in front of the desk and then hastily withdrew to the other side of the curtain. As the officer ran his finger down the page, the attitude toward Bryan seemed to change slightly. They nodded to him, addressed him respectfully, and nodded again as Bryan tried to control the fear and uneasiness that was about to overcome him. Even though they smiled at him they could become his executioners at a moment's notice.

The questions they asked hung heavily in the air. The security officer drummed his fingers on the edge of the table and glanced up at the doctor, who immediately grasped Bryan's wrist in order to take his pulse. Then he shone a light into Bryan's eyes, slapped him on the side of the head and shone it again. Bryan felt paralyzed and didn't notice the doctor walking around him. The smack of hands being clapped right in front of his face made him blink and hunch his shoulders with such a start that his entire torso shook. However, the observers didn't appear to regard this as anything unusual.

The doctor walked behind the officer who, looking up from his papers, did an about-face, grabbed something from the tabletop, and flung it toward Bryan, all in one movement. He would not have been able to defend himself even if he'd tried. A pain at the bridge of his nose made him open his eyes wide.

Apart from that he kept a straight face.

From the next compartment came the sound of a blow that made the patient cry out, and then another blow that made him stop. The security officer smiled at Bryan again and conferred with the doctor, who spoke so fast that Bryan would not have been able to understand a word even if it had been his mother tongue. The officer shrugged and got up as Bryan was led out to the others.

Here he came to stand just opposite James, who was still waiting in the relatively short line. His dripping-wet shirt still clung to his body. Just under the neckline was a dark shadow. Bryan stiffened. James was wearing Jill's scarf again. Even though this crazy act could prove fatal, James appeared relaxed and calm. But Bryan knew better. Beneath the facade he radiated terror. All his senses were on red alert. Without his talisman he had nothing to cling to.

But it would also be his death if he didn't get rid of it.

"It's okay," Bryan mouthed, but James just shook his head silently and took a step forward like the others.

The chief security officer finally got up from his seat and signaled to the little group of men over in the corner who had helped themselves to blankets during the night to line up beside the curtain nearest the door.

Behind the curtain loud bursts of anger almost raised the roof and the canvas began pulsating as if a fight were going on behind it. The chief security officer's face was bright red when they tore down the curtain and hauled the man who had been questioned across the floor, his feet dragging after him and torment painted all over his face.

Two guards seized his arm. The culprit stared wildly at the apathetic assembly, searching in vain for something to cling to. Bryan looked at him with eyes out of focus. Blood was quietly trickling down the man's forehead. He, too, had been hit by something. Perhaps he'd made the mistake of trying to ward it off.

The senior officer sat down heavily on the corner of the table behind him, smiling cruelly at the guards as they dragged the patient around among the others so they could see him at close quarters. Then he stopped smiling. Breathing deeply in aggressive concentration, he roared his accusation at the rows of men who again began to fidget nervously. The words tumbled out in bursts as the furious man stood with his hands clenched behind his back, rocking back and forth on his toes. There was no mistaking one of the words.

Malingering!

The man stopped trembling when he heard the charge. He let his head fall limply forward, aware of his guilt, unmasked and prepared to suffer the consequences.

Suddenly the officer stopped short in the middle of his outburst of rage. Then, smiling jovially, he spread his arms wide as he appealed gently to his audience. Bryan grasped that he was trying to get other malingerers to own up, if there were any. Nothing would happen to them as long as they stepped forward now, while there was still time.

It was impossible to look over at James as long as this beast was inspecting them. "We're not giving ourselves up, James!" Bryan pleaded silently, mostly to himself.

The officer stood waiting, nodding smilingly at the groups of men for just as long as it took Bryan to say the Lord's Prayer. Then suddenly he stepped behind the accused, drew his pistol, and executed the culprit with a shot to the back of the head before the man could manage to scream.

The rest of the assembly scarcely reacted. Blood welled out of the man's head for a moment and flowed slowly across the floor toward James. Bryan watched imperceptibly. James stood stock-still, white in the face, but no more so than the protracted standing at attention could warrant.

The two guards took hold of the body and dragged it across the floor. One of the white-coated doctors was still shielding his face with his hands in delayed shock. When he came to his senses his protests sounded feeble and remote. The security officer turned on his heel. No report would be written about *that* incident. Protests were out of the question.

Bryan began counting the seconds while James was behind the curtain. When he reached two hundred, James was led out again, remote and paralyzed. The next man in line stood still, ignoring the shouts of the doctor who was holding the curtain open. As the soldiers tried to grab him under his arms he quietly toppled forward. The soldiers took the next one instead and pulled him around the man on the floor. He had rolled onto his side and was sobbing almost deliriously, constantly repeating a name Bryan had heard before. A sweetheart, wife, mother, or daughter?

James had begun humming again, slowly and tonelessly. His skinny, red-eyed neighbor stood ruminating in his straitjacket as urine dripped down his shirt, which grew darker and darker.

Bryan imagined he might have lapped up the shower water too eagerly while staring up into it.

He awoke with a start. Someone had shouted, "Leave me alone!" Could it have been him, since he had understood it? Bryan shuddered at the thought and glanced over at the nurse who had just been standing beside his bed. So he'd only been out for a moment. The nurse poured a glass of water and put two tablets in his neighbor's mouth. She hadn't heard anything. Maybe he'd dreamt it.

By now the whole ward lay quiet. Bryan looked cautiously around, cursing the short second when he and James had become separated on their way from the wooden barracks. Otherwise they would be lying side by side now. This would undoubtedly have felt safer. As it was, Bryan lay in bed number five to the left of the door, while James lay at the far end on the opposite side. Twelve beds on Bryan's side, ten on James's. That was six beds too many in relation to the construction of the ward. Now the beds had scarcely a half meter between them. They were sticking haphazardly out from the wall. Some were in front of a window, others in between, but most of them stood completely at random. It made an extremely disorderly impression.

This pale-green ward with its high ceiling was about twenty meters long and ten meters wide. It constituted Bryan's entire world. Besides the bed, his earthly possessions consisted of a timeworn chair that stood in the central passageway together with twenty-two other such chairs, a hospital shirt, a pair of slippers, and a thin dressing gown.

Apart from four beds already occupied by unconscious, wounded, and bandaged patients, the whole ward was filled with soldiers from the same transport who had been ordered into the bed they happened to be standing next to. A couple of them kept their shoes on in bed and messed up the bedclothes before the nurses had distributed the pills. Each man was fed two white pills followed by a gulp of water from a mug that was passed around and constantly filled up from a white enamel jug.

The nurses had almost completed their round.

The smell of the first meal was indefinable and scarcely appetizing, but extraordinarily tempting nevertheless. Bryan hadn't dared think about food for days, but now his mouth was watering, making the final waiting moments torture.

The lumps on the iron plate looked like celery but were tasteless. Perhaps it was turnip cabbage. Bryan didn't know. His family was used to quite different food.

The men's greedy scraping with their spoons and animal-like chewing spread through the room like wildfire, and Bryan realized that not all their senses were numbed.

The plate over on James's bed was already empty and tipped dangerously over the edge of his bed. His relaxed face and the regular heaving of his chest were clear proof of man's incredible ability to adapt to circumstances. Bryan envied James his peaceful slumber. The dread of revealing himself in his sleep still preoccupied him. A single word and he would end up like that poor soul in the gym who was now lying between the barracks, flung into the snow.

They had seen him when they walked past.

A sweetish smell blended with the blandness of the turnip cabbage and a growing dizziness overwhelmed Bryan's train of thought. The pills were starting to work.

So he was going to sleep, whether he dared to or not.

The man to his right lay on his side, staring at Bryan's pillow with dead eyes. From under the blanket came the sound of a series of pent-up explosions from the gases he was apparently unaware he was releasing.

That was Bryan's final impression before sleep overtook him.

Catch up on the rest of Jussi Adler-Olsen's
New York Times bestselling Department Q series

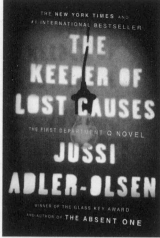
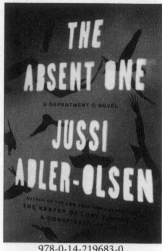
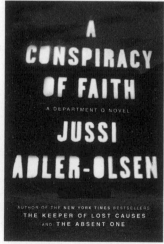
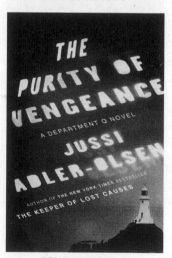
Available wherever books are sold

PLUME